CLOG!

A Novel

By Dan Smith

ISBN-13: 978-1493772186
ISBN-10: 149377218X

For Miss Kay, Joyce and Janice

A work of fiction

In the late 1940s through the early 1970s, Cranberry High School in the mountains of Western North Carolina had a string of spectacular square dance teams. I graduated from CHS in 1964 and watched one of those teams during my one year at the school. It was a joy and the experience stuck with me.

In 2012, editor Cara Modisett asked me to write a piece about those teams for Blue Ridge Country Magazine and I did. The story won an international magazine award. And it planted the seed for this book.

CLOG! is a work of fiction. That means it's made up. Like so much fiction, it is loosely based in fact, but fact has not found its way between these covers. Any resemblance between the characters, their actions and the events in *CLOG!* is coincidence. These characters are not real people.

Let me say it one more time: None of this happened. It probably could have and something like some of it may very well have, but this book doesn't tell those stories. It tells its own story and that story is a mountain tale told for fun.

Acknowledgements

In any undertaking as complex and detailed as a novel, there are many people beyond the author who make significant contributions. *CLOG!* is the result of a collaboration among people who care about this story. I want to thank everybody whose eyes landed on any part of the manuscript, including the agents who sent it back saying, "We regret that your story …" There were a lot of those and I love you all, especially the agent who said there "wasn't enough at stake." You've all served to improve what I started writing.

Joyce Watson Langson and Janice Watson Greene helped significantly with character development and dance sequences. They read the manuscript as I was writing the first draft. The list of those reading and offering solid advice at various stages of this 10-rewrite process is long: Roland Lazenby, Alison Weaver, Christina Koomen, Leah Weiss, Keith Ferrell, Cara Modisett, Dan Radmacher, Christine Ward, Paulette Jayabalan, Nancy Agee, Teresa Shadoin, and quite a few others.

Members of Blacksburg's Hurrah Cloggers (Phil Louer and Amanda Waering) helped me understand square dancing. A couple of old high school friends threatened my life if they found themselves in the book. That was helpful.

Tom Field, my former business partner at FRONT magazine and one of the best designers in the Eastern U.S., designed the cover. Liv Kiser, a wonderful young photographer who is fighting the good fight against Type 1 diabetes, shot my photo. Liv is special and inspiring.

Thank you all, even—maybe especially—those of you who didn't like *CLOG!* You helped make it better.

Part I

Monday, March 18, 1963, 11 a.m.

It was coming up on a year since Grayson McCourry died, leaving Eb and his brothers and sisters fatherless. Gray died at Asheville's St. Joseph's Hospital from a poisoned batch of moonshine he got into on one of his too frequent blackout trips out of town. Those escapes started when Gray began drinking again after nearly ten years off booze and while he was actively involved in AA. Gray's sponsor, who came by every few days to check on Gray's progress, called it a "slip," but Delia McCourry, Eb's mom, knew better.

Gray was a large, robust man, a college football player at one time, but he weighed a hundred pounds lying there in an iron lung that was breathing for him at the end. Last time Eb saw him, Gray was ashen, bald and his hands shook uncontrollably. Eb hated remembering his father that way, hated what happened to his family in the months since, and saw little future in being where he was.

He felt lost at school and if he couldn't play football his senior year—as the team doctor had ordered because of the knee that had buckled in Eb's final game the previous fall—he would have nothing. Most of his life and his identity revolved around that football team and even his future and the scholarship he'd counted on were in doubt now.

"Mom, can I go up to Aunt Nell's for the summer?" he asked as she picked up little sister Dane's clothes from the floor.

"That girl will never learn to put stuff away," muttered Delia, a small, dark, attractive, 50-year-old woman with burgundy hair stacked on top of her head. Her life had been harder than she expected or wanted. "Why do you want to go way up there in the country? There won't be anything to do and you don't even know anybody. You'll be crying to come home in a week.

"You know you're not playing football. That's final. You're minding that team doctor because you're not spending the rest of your life on crutches or in a wheelchair." She was firm with the warning.

"This is not about football. I just want something else, Mom," said Eb, avoiding a confrontation he knew he'd lose. "I don't know what yet, but at least I can take the summer to think about it. Even if I did try football, it wouldn't be at a school with thirty-five-hundred students like Sky High. What's Toe River, three-fifty, three-eighty? The players wouldn't be as good or as big, and the wear on my body wouldn't be as hard. But I'm not even thinking about that right now. Would you at least call Aunt Nell and see if it's good with her?"

Eb thought a moment. "Mom," he said, "I know you feel responsibility for me, but I'm seventeen years old and you're going to get Social Security for me and the others whether I live with Aunt Nell for the summer or stay here. Think how much more food you'll have without me here."

"Oh, Eb," said his mother, sounding weary and getting his point immediately. "You know Aunt Nell's up in years and she lives quietly. Don't be disappointed if she turns you down. It would be a major disruption for her."

"I think she'll be fine with it, Mom," said Eb, "and you know I'm not any trouble. Maybe, if it works out, I could go to the high school there. I think I'd like that."

"You are a good boy, Eb McCourry, but remember what I said about the football. Maybe you could be on the square dance team if you wind up at Toe River High." She grinned and picked up a wadded pink sweater.

"Yeah, Mom," said Eb, smiling back at her. "I'll become a dancer instead of a quarterback. When Elvis starts singing country music."

Eb paused, considering. "You're kidding about the square dance *team,* right?"

"No, Eb, I'm not. They've won national championships."

Monday, March 18, 10:22 a.m.

Bobby Lee Ledbetter rolled his eyes again at what Joss-Lynn asked. Wasn't no amount of money on earth he wouldn't spend for his darlin' girl, but a square dance team with a New York coach just to win a trophy could cost buckets of money.

Joss-Lynn was not one of these teenagers who never asked for anything. She asked for everything. Demanded it. Pitched a fit if she didn't get it. The trophy—known as Old Smoky—was the most prestigious square dancing award in the region and it was all but owned by Toe River High School, a tiny school of 350 or so students in four grades far back in the mountains. Joss-Lynn first said she wanted that trophy the previous fall when her high school team finished second to Toe River and she nearly had a breakdown, screaming, crying and creating such a fuss that the Asheville Civic Auditorium manager called the police.

Old Smoky would not likely make Bobby Lee Ledbetter's precious baby any happier than the little yellow 'Vette or the fancy dancing lessons, or all those shopping trips that took airplanes to get to.

Surely wouldn't. That didn't mean he wouldn't do everything he could to win Old Smoky. Didn't mean he'd think about it long. He had to be careful with it, though. This one involved some official people, politicians and school board types, and they wouldn't be fooled with—unless the money was right. Bobby Lee By God Ledbetter had the money. He sure did that.

Bobby Lee Ledbetter's Used Cars. Everybody in Western North Carolina knew that name, that face, that loud, insistent, barking voice, selling those used cars and travel trailers. He wore good suits that he had special made. The look was pure virgin wool, hand-crafted Biltmore Homespun class. The salesman in him was pure mountain bullshit that brought the old boys out of the hollers to buy them used cars by the dozen and gave Bobby Lee the money to buy square dance teams if he wanted them.

In 1963, that damn Old Smoky trophy would to be won by Joss-Lynn Ledbetter and her Land of the Sky High School team. That's the way it was going to be. He'd see to that.

Bobby Lee cut a striking figure: sharp, hawk-face features with high cheek bones and sunken eyes. He was six-feet-three-inches tall, wiry, long-necked and straight, with large hands and feet, and gleaming teeth that seemed constantly on display with that used car salesman's wide, dull-eyed smile. His hair was dark, swept straight back and heavy with Brylcream. He was breath-mint drenched and generous with the Old Spice.

He leaned forward and reached for the intercom button. "Lottie, git in here. I need you to make some calls to New York City. We got a coach to buy."

Monday, March 25, 9:03 a.m.

Blond, stocky, neatly-dressed Sonny Ball sat in the waiting room outside Bobby Lee Ledbetter's office, sunk down into an over-stuffed burgundy Corinthian leather chair, trying to keep from staring at Arlene Shining Feather. She perched straight-backed across from him on the outsized leather sofa. She had landed at Asheville-Hendersonville Airport at eight o'clock and saw Sonny standing there with a sign saying "Miss Shining Feather" when she stepped on the tarmac. Sonny recognized her immediately.

She was tiny, dark, straight as a lodge pole and about as Indian as god ever made anybody. Strikingly beautiful with full lips, high cheek bones, a slender nose, large brown eyes and black hair coifed in a French twist. Trim, fit, graceful, regal. A dancer from New York who knew her place near the top of the pecking order. She handed her bag to Sonny and said, "Lead."

Sonny knew when to talk and when to shut up and this was a time to do what he was told. He drove the big, silver Imperial convertible straight from the airport nineteen miles down U.S. 25 to the office, not a word between them. She sat in the back seat.

At the office Arlene was growing impatient. Bobby Lee

was late and she did not like waiting. "Y'all can go in now," said Bobby Lee's secretary, Lottie, as pleasantly as she could. Arlene Shining Feather did not make eye contact with Lottie. Lottie noticed.

Bobby Lee bolted upright from his huge, hand-crafted chair behind the mammoth walnut desk in front of his floor-to-ceiling window and almost leaped across the massive room, his hand extended full length. Arlene Shining Feather took it briefly, limply and said, "Let's get to it."

Lottie closed the door and as the three of them sat, the door bolted open again. A young blonde fireball, overdressed, over made-up, swept into the room, big teeth gleaming in a broad smile. "Hi, Daddy!" Joss-Lynn Ledbetter yelped. "That Tiffany bracelet I ordered came in at Freidman's and I need for Sonny to take me to get it."

"Honey-doll, we're in a meeting right now and I need Sonny here. You'll have to wait a bit." From Bobby Lee's tone, it was clear who was in charge and, it wasn't him. He didn't even ask why she wasn't in school because he knew it would start a row.

"Daaaaaady! I been waitin' for that thing for a week and I want it," she said in an urgent whine. Bobby Lee knew he might as well give it up. He had no chance. "Sonny, take her and get right back. You got the checkbook?"

Sonny nodded.

"Who's this?" said Joss-Lynn, nodding toward Arlene. Before her father could answer, she said to Arlene Shining Feather, "You an Indian?"

"Cherokee," said Arlene in a clipped, direct response to the rudeness.

"Everybody says that. Bet you're Italian or something."

"This is your new square dance coach," said Bobby Lee, looking at Arlene for confirmation. "She has a ballet school in New York City and is one of the most respected dancers in the country."

Joss-Lynn spun on her heel and headed toward the door

without responding to her father or to Arlene. "Come on, Sonny," she said, impatiently, ignoring the introduction. She stopped, turned back to Arlene, looked at her sternly and said, "We'd better win that trophy. I want it." Then she was gone.

"Impressive," said Arlene, who was being treated like a 19th-Century servant of British gentry by a smart-assed, spoiled rich kid.

"Oh, yeah, she's that," said Bobby Lee, missing the sarcasm. "She'll be your star dancer."

"Mr. Ledbetter, you're assuming a lot."

"Call me Bobby Lee," he said, leaning against his desk, arms folded, his smile gone. "I'm paying a lot to make those assumptions. You fit what we want for this position and we're going to pay you for it. You got the numbers. Six thousand dollar annual teacher salary, which is average in this system for your education and experience. Forty-four thousand more for working for the dealership. There's also the fifty thousand dollar contribution for your dance school in New York. That sound about right?" Bobby Lee picked up a gold case and took out an unfiltered Chesterfield and reached in his pocked for a gold Zippo engraved "BLL."

"I'd appreciate it if you wouldn't smoke," said Arlene. "I have an allergy." She was lying, but the smoke annoyed her so much that she might as well have had the allergy. He put the cigarette case back on the desk without response.

"We're going to buy you an air conditioned bus to take these kids around in, tailor-made costumes of any design you want and any other miscellaneous items you'll need. You'll be staying at the Grove Park Inn until you can find an appropriate furnished apartment and we'll have a car of your choice for you."

"We've talked about everything but dancers, Mr. Ledbetter," said Arlene. "Where do I get dancers who will perform at the level I will require?" She was sitting on the front edge of her chair, leaning forward, ankles crossed, hands folded in her lap.

"We got two dance schools here in town," said Bobby Lee. "There's the North Carolina School of Ballet and Modern Dance and there's a special program linked to the high school for kids who dance in the afternoon and read and write in the morning. My daughter's in that. I provided the seed money for the program two years ago." He didn't mention that he started the program after Joss-Lynn was turned down for admittance into the School of Ballet and Modern Dance in Raleigh.

"Some of the best young dancers in North Carolina are at those schools and you get your pick. I've already talked to the people I need to talk to and they're in. I'm paying them a thousand dollars a kid for dancers. It's a contribution to the schools, so it's easy to hide."

"How legal is this?" said Arlene, her brow wrinkling slightly.

"There's nothing illegal about it. I've talked to the principal and the athletic director at the high school and told them what they need to know, which ain't everything. You're going to be on the teaching staff, but you won't have any classes. I'm paying the bulk of your salary as an employee of mine. The money for the dancers will be disguised as a donation to the schools, which I make sometimes anyway. This'll be bigger than usual. I'll form a boosters club and run the other stuff through it."

"Sounds like you've thought of everything."

"I ain't filthy rich because I missed something," said Bobby Lee Ledbetter, an oily smile creasing his face.

"I don't much like this," said Arlene, "but if we don't get an infusion of money, our school's dead. We've worked too hard ..."

"Yes, ma'am, I know," Bobby Lee interrupted. "You need to start this week. There's a lot of work to do and a summer exhibition schedule to get ready for. In eight months, you're going to win Old Smoky for Joss-Lynn and I can tell you that Toe River High School and the other mountain schools ain't going to give it to you. Them kids grew up a-dancing like this and they ain't going to take kindly to a bunch of prissy-ass ballet dancers and a New York coach trying to take it from them. For them, it's pride. For you … well, we know what it is for you 'cause I'm paying it. And I expect value for my money."

Arlene felt like she needed a bath as she left Bobby Lee Ledbetter's office.

Tuesday, April 2, 9 a.m.

Arlene Shining Feather was spared the indignity of meeting her new dance team on April Fool's Day, but she harbored a queasy feeling about this commitment, which she was beginning to see as a necessary evil. One of the best dancers in New York City, the first Cherokee to dance at the American Ballet Theatre, a graduate of the Juilliard School of Dance, a modern jazz performer with Martha Graham and a dancer on national television was now the coach of a high school square dance team in a remote corner of North Carolina. She was doing it for the money, here to win a brass trophy for a spoiled teenager.

Tough times force uncomfortable compromises and Arlene Shining Feather knew she must flex her big jaw muscles, bear down and win that damn trophy. She could then go home with upwards of a hundred thousand dollars, enough to save her small, exclusive school, and bump the academy's status and quality up a notch, making it competitive with the prestigious dance organizations. She would take one for her school by selling out to this team.

For a while, it would be attached to her identity: Land of the Sky High School. Nickname, the Constellation. Colors, light blue and powder orange. Student body, thirty-two hundred in grades ten to twelve. Notable achievement, led the nation for the past ten years in Merit Scholars.

Sky High was set back off McDowell Street near Biltmore, a small, elegant, wealthy suburb of Asheville where in 1895 Cornelius Vanderbilt built his 250-room "summer cottage," the outlandishly ostentatious Biltmore House. The high school was a beautiful, huge Italian Renaissance building, constructed of gray stone in 1927 when Asheville was flush. It sat on twenty two wooded acres and looked like a college campus.

Arlene walked purposefully into the impressive, sloping, heavily curtained auditorium and saw, standing in a line before her on the stage, perfectly arranged by height that differed by an inch end-to-end, twenty young dancers in black leotards who looked like they were not only hand-picked for her, but hand-made. They stood perfectly erect in the first ballet position, arms down in a slight curve, palms in, feet at forty-five degree angles, backs straight, eyes ahead. Nobody twitched as she strode down the burgundy carpet.

She walked directly to the front of the auditorium, a few feet below the stage, stopped and looked over the dancers for a moment, like a general assessing her army. She took a step back, gazed directly into each set of eyes and spoke.

"I am Arlene Shining Feather. I will be your coach for the next few months and we will become the finest square dance team in the history of North Carolina high school competition. I will expect each of you to be the best dancer you can be every minute of your lives while I am here and I will not countenance any deviation from that goal." She paused for effect, keeping her eyes direct and focused.

"We all agree that square dancing, compared to what we are accustomed to, is provincial and does not require our full talent, but we will pretend it does and we will work it to perfection."

She broke the eye contact, took a few steps to the right, then turned and walked to the end of the dancer line to the left. She stopped and looked back into the dancers' faces.

"You will compete against dancers who grew up clogging, buck dancing and sliding in ways you will find surprisingly difficult to do at times. It is second nature to them. It is at the heart of a part of their culture." She paused and took a breath. A dancer coughed and the sound all but echoed in the still room.

"We are invaders here, interlopers, cultural warriors and they will fight us with everything they have. I can't emphasize enough to you that the stakes here are high for these small schools and we represent an outside threat to something they hold almost sacred.

"The only way we can possibly lose sight of our goal is to lose sight of our opponent and to underestimate the teams we will be competing against. Square dance is what these kids do. They take great pride in being the best and, frankly, they don't have much else to be proud of.

"Don't underestimate them. Don't overvalue your own talent in this kind of dance and for god's sake, work at it. This will not be given to you. I guarantee that."

She turned abruptly on her heel and walked out of the auditorium. Her three assistant coaches handed out schedules and assignments. "Sounds like we're going to war," groused a handsome, dark-haired dancer named Billy Staples.

The game was on.

Friday, August 16, 7 a.m.

Eb McCourry's knee—the bad one—hurt, and it had a lot of company. Eb thought he could likely give the Christian names of his new Toe River High School Red Tail Hawks teammates to every bruise, every pull, every ache, every abrasion, every sharp, piercing scream he wanted to yelp. Gaylen, Mickey, Harold, Perry, Terry, Barry…

He rolled to the edge of the small bed in the attic of his Aunt Nell's white shingled country house in Cranberry, N.C. The floor looked too far away to get to without more pain. Eb rose and hit his head on the steeply slanted ceiling. One more bruise wouldn't matter all that much.

He clinched his teeth and poured over the edge of the bed as slowly, gingerly as he could. His toes landed on the glossy pine floor harder than he wanted but softer than he expected. "Oh, Jesus," he mumbled. If Aunt Nell heard him taking the

Lord's name in vain, the football beat-up would become a mosquito bite.

Eb had to get to a phone. It was downstairs. So was the bathroom. So was breakfast. So was Aunt Nell, who was doubtless wondering why he was still in the bed at seven o'clock on a pretty Friday morning, not understanding how nearly dead he thought he was.

He wanted to call Smoky and see if his friend and fellow new-comer lived through practice. The two of them were brand new Red Tail Hawks and no doubt they'd lost the same number of red feathers from their asses. They didn't *wear* targets to their first practice in pads yesterday. They *were* targets of every cheap shot, every blind side, every double and triple team that could be cobbled together on short notice. Gaylen Anderson speared Eb in the face with such impact that Eb got up picking his face mask out of his mouth, which it was supposed to protect. He'd chipped a tooth.

Eb lifted the suddenly heavy, black Western Electric telephone, the one that felt like it could be a bludgeon in the right circumstance, and spun the tight rotary dial. Seven-three-three-two-one, he dialed. On the second ring, Smoky picked up. Eb didn't expect that. Smoky should at least be laid out and not able to get to the phone, especially with all those brothers and sisters in the house scrambling to answer. "H'lo," Smoky said far more cheerfully than Eb appreciated.

"You going back?" Eb asked, almost as if challenging.

"Today? Yeh. Nine o'clock. Ain't you?"

"Smoky, I been playing football about ten years, since I was seven, and I've never felt like this. I've been hit by a concrete mixer and never felt like this. I've been tarred and fea..."

"Oh, come on, man. You knowed this was a-comin'. You seen it soon as we strapped our jocks on yesterday. That dang Mickey Buchanan had blood in his eyes and all we could do was take it, 'cause that's how it's got to be. Like an initiation. We're initiated.

17

"Today, I'm getting' my licks in and I expect you ought to get yours, too, if you got 'em in you. And I think you prob-ly do."

"I'm not sure I can get even, Smoky. But if you're goin' back, I gotta go. Teammates. Brothers. Oh, shit, that hurts." Eb sat down hard in the straight back chair in the hall.

So this is how it works, Eb thought. You invite people to beat hell out of you, and believe it's not only acceptable, it's desirable.

The closest Eb ever had to a girlfriend once said, "The only explanation for boys is aliens." That'd be about right. Today's practice would be a fine opportunity to prove her theory. It was time to be a beast.

Friday, August 16, 11:33 a.m.

"You boys done alright," said Gaylen, standing over Eb and Smoky as they slumped in front of their lockers, peeling off wet, nasty football clothes. "What's you'un's names again? Smoky Swain and Elbert what?"

"Eb McCourry," Eb answered as short as he could. Gaylen and Carl Blackthorn had sandwich-tackled him twenty minutes ago and Eb's teeth still shook from it. He hadn't forgiven Gaylen yet.

"McCourry, yeh. That's it. Elbert McCourry. Glad you boys are here. We need people who hit hard and ain't afraid."

"Eb," said Eb, forcefully correcting the "Elbert" reference.

Gaylen stuck out a large, hard hand and Eb shook it without returning Gaylen's enthusiasm. Gaylen Anderson was a hard-bodied, round-shouldered, six-foot tall, one-hundred-eighty-five-pound linebacker and a team leader, though just a junior. Eb could see why others looked up to him.

"This your standard welcome to new people?" Eb asked. "Beat hell out of them, then stick out your hand to make nice? I can see why the county's got a population of twelve."

Eb looked small between Smoky and Gaylen, the only one of the three under six feet. He stood five-feet-ten, one-hundred-sixty-five sinewy pounds, with a weight-lifter's chest and arms and a distance runner's thin legs. His hair hinted at the color of old brick and freckles dotted both sides of his nose and cheeks.

Gaylen looked puzzled. "You boys knocked the shit out of some people today," he said, as if to pardon Eb's and Smoky's bruises. "Hell, it's a violent sport and we gotta know who we're dealin' with. This is a team that's a player or two away from a championship, so expectation's pretty high."

"You might want to lower it for a day or two while we visit the hospital," said Eb, finally finding a smile. He reached back with a balled fist and cold-cocked Gaylen on the right shoulder, knocking him to the floor, then extended a hand to help him up. "Teammates? Right? Knock the shit out of each other teammates."

Gaylen grabbed the extended hand and let Eb pull him up.

Eb looked younger than seventeen until he spoke, but his voice was a smooth, mature, Southern-accented baritone, like that of a radio newscaster. Gaylen heard him and felt him and would remember both.

Now Eb had a bigger problem because of Aunt Nell's refusal to have him live with her. Where was he going to stay, so he could remain a part of this team, this town, this school, this culture?

Sunday, August 18, 1:32 a.m.

The bed shook hard enough to wake Eb from a light sleep. It was a steady, almost rapid shake and Eb had drifted too far off into dreamland to have a thought about why it was shaking. Then he felt a hand move across his hip to the front of his briefs and over his penis. The big, rough hand squeezed and Eb suddenly understood why Aunt Nell warned, "Be careful, son. I'm not sure about that man."

Eb got out of the large, high bed deliberately, not suddenly, slipped on his jeans and Madras shirt, picked up his loafers and the small suitcase that lay open on the floor. He slipped quietly out the front door of the old house with the peeling white paint and the loose shutter out front. Eb walked briskly—bare feet in his shoes—a mile down the highway to Aunt Nell's front porch. He sat in her glider all night and when he heard her making coffee in the morning, he knocked lightly on the front door.

"What are you do…" she said, then caught herself. She knew. "Oh. I'm so sorry. Come on in. I'll get you some coffee."

Nell knew and Eb knew she knew. The neighbors called Aunt Nell a "good Christian woman" and that meant she didn't talk about sex, even when a loved one had nearly been molested by a suspected pedophile.

Aunt Nell announced the end of summer vacation early in the week, meaning the time had come for Eb to go back to Asheville, to his family, even though he was working out daily with the Toe River High football team in pre-season drills. Eb wanted to stay and go to school and insisted his mother had more than she could handle. Aunt Nell said she couldn't take on a teenager at her age. She was sixty-two, nearing retirement as postmistress of the tiny office half a mile down Highway 25, and she'd already raised her kids. She had a quiet life and she liked it that way.

Eddie Brown, a fifty-year-old bachelor who lived with his housekeeper up the road in a frame house with a big garden out back, had been friendly to Eb and offered that if he ever needed a place to stay, come see him. So Eb did and Eddie said he'd love the company. Eb and his suitcase moved in Saturday afternoon. That night, Eddie told Eb they needed to share a bed until the housekeeper could get the spare bedroom ready.

***

"Let me tell you about the children's home," Aunt Nell said after an uncomfortable silence. "I'll talk to the director, who is an old friend of mine, and she can make arrangements for you to stay there through the school year if she can find an opening. My guess is that she will be able to."

Nell put a steaming cup of coffee in front of Eb and he poured in thick, fresh cream and three tablespoons of sugar. Nell smiled. "Milkshake, huh?" she said. Eb nodded and took a sip. He pulled back quickly. It was hot. And very sweet. He smiled.

Nell explained that Beech Mountain Home for Children was run by the regional Presbytery, which also owned the hospital and a junior college. The Home sat in a beautiful spot outside Newland, about seven miles from Nell's house in Cranberry. As Eb listened, it became clear to him: This was an orphanage, plain and simple, and Eb wasn't an orphan, he reasoned. He already felt unsure enough about his identity without adding "orphan" to his resume.

"I don't know, Aunt Nell," Eb said. "It's nice of you to ask, but people will think I don't have anybody who cares about me."

"Let's go up there this afternoon after church and let you look around," she said. "You might be surprised." Eb nodded. What did he have to lose?

***

Eb stepped out of Nell McCourry's blue-on-blue nineteen-fifty-four DeSoto Firedome station wagon, the size of a beach cottage, and looked at a group of pretty girls standing outside a lodge about forty yards away. Eb looked at Aunt Nell. "This'll do," he said, and she laughed out loud because she saw the same thing he saw.

The campus was breathtaking, heavily wooded with huge hardwood, poplar, maple and evergreen trees, eight buildings, three dorms each for boys and girls of varying ages, an administration building and dining hall with a large multi-purpose gymnasium. A pond lay out back, stocked with smallmouth bass. Two bare hills sat just off the center of campus quad. They had become the facility's home-made ski slopes.

All this for about sixty kids who'd been figuratively left by the side of the road for one reason or another, generally having to do with poverty or parental alcohol abuse. Eb learned that almost none of the residents was a true orphan. The children's parents visited Sunday afternoons. Some of those parents were waiting in aging, rusting cars when Eb and Aunt Nell drove up.

At what he found to be the "Big Boys" dorm on the opposite end of the quad from where he'd seen those pretty girls, he spotted a football teammate he recognized, a freshman named J.W. Greene. This place was alive for Eb. He looked at Aunt Nell and repeated, "Thank you. I like this." Nell put her hand on his head and mussed his red hair. "Thought you might," she said with a warm smile.

Eb and Nell went back to Cranberry, retrieved his clothes and Eb settled into an attic room in the "Little Boys" dorm that evening, after a call to Nell's friend the administrator, who said there were no empty dorm rooms, but she'd create a place for Eb. It was the only space left at the facility and he became the only kid on campus with a private room. School started in two weeks, football looked good and now he had the promise of a stable home. He'd stepped from a pile of steaming crap at Eddie Brown's house the night before into a home he hadn't imagined.

Monday, August 19, 8:56 a.m.

Arlene Shining Feather sat in the big leather chair facing Bobby Lee Ledbetter's massive oak desk, wearing a powder orange sundress and sandals. She had a wide, white ribbon in her hair, holding it off her face. The outfit was no statement. Asheville was in the middle of a heat wave where temperatures were climbing near ninety on a daily basis, unheard of in this mountain city where Floridians sought escape from the summer heat. Bobby Lee Ledbetter recognized the reality of the heat, too. A light blue seersucker replaced the expensive, handmade wool Biltmore Homespun he generally preferred. He wore a white shirt with tie that bordered on pink. "We're certainly looking seasonal … if you're in Guatemala," he said to Arlene, that big TV grin shining. "Don't remember it being this hot."

"You wanted a report," said Arlene impatiently.

"Yeah, you're right, I got a lot of work to do today, so let's get to it. You don't waste much time, do you?" He settled behind his desk and organized several papers.

"As I am sure you know, we've won every competition we've entered since we formed," she said. "That's 14-0 this summer with an appearance at a function for the governor in July and another exhibition at the state fair, where we were treated as the headliner. We've beaten teams from every state that borders North Carolina, mostly mountain schools, small schools. Our team's technical grasp of this kind of dance is flawless. The only problem we've had is focus and motivation. These dancers are in a league that normally doesn't include square dance, so this is not much of a challenge to them on a personal basis." She turned the page in a loose-leaf notebook that was nearly full.

"We saw some teams at the state fair that we will compete against at the Mountain Youth Jamboree and, frankly, I wasn't as impressed as you apparently are. They are all similar in what they do, how they dress, how they approach this. I didn't see a lot of creativity of the kind that will be required to win on a significant scale. Toe River High School was there and its more creative costume was the biggest difference between it and the others." Arlene closed the book.

"What about Joss-Lynn?" said Bobby Lee.

"What about her?"

"Well, how's she doing?"

"She's a good dancer and she helped teach some of the other dancers early-on. They passed her quickly, though." She looked down at the book, away from Bobby Lee's apparent displeasure.

"What do you mean 'passed her'?" he said.

"Mr. Ledbetter, let's forget we're talking about your daughter for a minute. Joss-Lynn does not have the extensive training these other dancers have. You can tell she has had some ballet, some tap, some modern and a good bit of square dancing, but the other dancers' lives are built on dance. They do it eight hours a day, seven days a week and they are good." She paused, waiting for the bomb she knew was coming.

Bobby Lee pondered her speech for a second. "I want one thing to be as clear as it can possibly be, Miss Shining Feather. This whole trophy pursuit is about Joss-Lynn. It is about keeping my daughter happy. I want her to feel like she's leading this team, not that she's just a part of it, and I want to see her holding that trophy on the stage at the Asheville Civic Auditorium in November. Is that something you understand completely?"

"Yes, Mr. Ledbetter, it is," Arlene said, nodding only slightly. "I thought I would tell you the whole truth."

"The whole truth and the only truth that makes any difference to me is winning that Old Smoky trophy and seeing Joss-Lynn smile while she's holding it. Thank you for your report. Competition starts for real in three weeks and I'm getting eager to see y'all kick some ass."

For the first time in her professional career, Arlene Silver Feather felt uncertain.

Monday, September 2, 9 a.m.
Square dance coach Lilly Wilkerson stood up at her desk in the upstairs corner classroom she'd occupied for years and handed the uniform patterns to Joyce Watkins, her team co-captain. "You'll need to get these over to home ec as soon as you can and start the girls working on sewing them," said Miss Lilly in a tone that implied urgency. "Mrs. Clapsaddle has the material. We don't have much time to get these ready for the season. There's three uniforms here like last year, and they're all different."

Miss Lilly, which is what everybody called her, designed the uniforms, except when an inspired home ec student— usually a square dancer—took a shot at it. Some of the uniforms were impressive. Some, Joyce once said in a whisper, "look like space suits."

Miss Lilly was a striking woman of thirty eight, whose demeanor was more royalty than mountain school marm. She was tall and angular, five-feet-eight-inches tall, trim with a long stride and a purposeful walk. Her head was too large, her chin a shade too small and her hazel eyes huge and expressive. The straight, uninterrupted brown slash of eyebrows across her forehead, gave her a look of more severity than was real. Her soft, milky complexion was nearly perfect—reflecting her Irish ancestry—and young. She wore her hair short and curly, a light brown mop that she tolerated much more than she loved. She dressed better than a high school teacher needed to and far more elegantly than most could afford. Hers was a business look and it reflected perfectly her approach. She was stylish, simple and accented with scarves and jewelry. With all her imposing physical attributes, she was the picture of grace in everything she did. She moved like a toned athlete with the delicate touch of the dancer she was, and smiled warmly or disapproved with a subtlety that disarmed.

Toe River High School's colors were green and gold, but Miss Lilly was not restricted in color or design in her uniforms because she bought her own material—out of her pocket and sometimes with the help of the dancers' families, those that could afford it. More than seventy percent of Avery County's eight thousand residents were on some kind of government or church relief, so there wasn't much help.

Miss Lilly was not going to cut corners on style any more than she'd trim out a slice of grace. It was a package and the look was part of it. So was the idea that the team was investing itself in every level of the sport, something she stressed at every opportunity.

Miss Lilly insisted that's how champions were built.

Monday, September 2, 9 a.m.
Backstage at the Sky High auditorium, Arlene Silver

Feather ripped the tape from the big box, encasing the first of the new square dance uniforms, the ones Bobby Lee Ledbetter authorized from Hollywood. They were designed by Crupney and Company, which made costumes for movies and had outfitted everything from B-westerns, to Biblical drama, to sixteenth-century French ball gowns. Crupney had a room full of Oscars, but found this request for high school square dance uniforms from the heavily-accented, but obviously well off, man in North Carolina oddly interesting and sufficiently lucrative to pursue.

With her ballet background, Arlene was no stranger to exotic costumes and these were theatrical without being gaudy. Something about the design struck her as classic and appealing, understated in the use of school colors with enough sparkle to complement, but not so much as to distract. The costumes were like everything else having to do with this square dance team. They were first class and smelled of money well spent.

Arlene opened a box and held up the girls' western-style blouse. It had a bright, shimmering white silk body, powder orange yoke, collar with sky blue piping and a deeper orange pocket flap. A second blouse reversed the blue and white. A navy rhinestone cluster—denoting the team's nickname, Constellation—rested on the pocket. The skirts were sky blue with two tight powder blue lines of piping along the bottom, and an orange belt. Deep blue dance shoes had ties to mid-calf. A white satin scarf tied at the side of the neck completed the costume.

The boys' shirts were similar to the girls' and they wore string ties and navy blue pants. Each had a tall, white cowboy hat with side-upturned brim and small blue and orange feathers clustered on the band.

This was classic western square dance with a distinct touch of class that Arlene hadn't seen before—but could expect to see at these prices. She looked at the invoice. Five hundred dollars per costume. Ten thousand dollars for twenty complete uniforms.

Toe River's football uniforms, pads and helmet cost less than fifty dollars each. Its homemade square dance costumes may have been priceless to some, but forty dollars bought enough cloth from the weaving mill in Spruce Pine, where Miss Lilly's brother-in-law was a foreman, to outfit twenty members of the team. The design and tailoring were free, courtesy of Miss Lilly's imagination and experience, as well as that of Emily Clapsaddle's home economics students.

Tuesday, September 3, 8:46 a.m.
Toe River High School's three-hundred-eighty students went to class in four scattered buildings whose architecture would never make a case study for visionaries. The main classroom/administration building was a three-story brick structure at the front of the campus that Eb's granddad McCourry helped build in nineteen-twenty-seven. The white-shingled, two-story agriculture building looked like a thrown-together afterthought and had classrooms for social studies and history, as well as agriculture, which occupied the entire basement. The gym was a green, shake shingle barn that Eb called "The Coliseum" the first time he saw it and the name spread through the school, always followed by a guffaw. Finally, the one-story brick library, built in 1950 and was the campus' newest addition, also housed home ec, wood shop and science classes.

The Coliseum seated roughly two hundred people, none of them comfortably. Fifty of those were in two rows of balcony bench seats on one side of the gym. The balcony encroached out over the basketball floor and sometimes the it blocked shots from the side. Visiting teams didn't like it. Toe River's basketball players knew where to shoot.

All Eb's classes except biology were in the admin building, which sat thirty yards up the hill behind the football field and was fronted with two enormous sugar maple trees, which turned blaze red in mid-October. The hill ran down to the football stands on the east side of the stadium, nearest the

27

school and it was paved with heavy buffalo grass—the soft, spongy kind.

The fourteen-hundred seats in these east stands were new to the school, purchased for forty-five hundred dollars from Appalachian State Teachers College in nearby Boone, which was renovating its stadium. The money to buy the set of stands, made of steel and wood, was donated by three businessmen in Avery County who graduated from Toe River High School, played football and had kids on the team.

Monday morning, the day school started, Eb couldn't resist heading down to the stadium and taking a short nap before beginning classes in earnest. It was a pretty summer morning, warm and bright with a gentle breeze, and he'd been up since six o'clock. Eb missed all of first period, assuming that this was a relaxed and permissive atmosphere he would exploit. That was Colt Hill's English class and missing it was Eb's first serious mistake at Toe River High School.

As Eb hurried down the hall toward English class this second day of school, already a minute late for the 8:45 start, Colt Hill stood in the hall, held the classroom door open and glared at Eb. Hill was short, built like a weight lifter with a steel-hinged jaw and eyebrows that rose sharply at opposite angles over dark brown eyes, giving him the piercing glare of a prison guard. A dark-haired, crew-cut widow's peak intensified the seriousness. His dress was casual: half-sleeve madras shirt, pleated khaki canvas pants, white T-shirt and socks, large brown shoes that looked more like they belonged on a factory floor than in an English class. His brass belt buckle showed a relief of a grand piano. Hill had twenty-inch biceps that the football players called "Colt's guns." He was imposing.

"Mr. McCourry, I presume," Colt barked in a surprisingly high-pitched, almost feminine, voice as he knocked Eb off balance and into the wall. The index finger of his right hand was in Eb's chest like the point of a pool cue, holding him in place harder than Eb thought possible. "You cut my class yesterday, Mr. McCourry and you didn't grant me the dignity of trying to hide it. I saw you sleeping in the grass and I hope you enjoyed yourself and that you learned a good deal there because I want a thousand-word essay on my desk before school starts tomorrow, giving me the details of your meditations." He pulled the finger back and Eb felt like he might fall to the floor. He quickly slid into the room and found a seat at the back.

"Front row, center, Mr. McCourry," said Colt Hill, as if addressing the entire class in order to seal the new boy's humiliation. Eb quickly moved to a seat being vacated by a pretty girl in a pink sweater, filled nicely in the front. Eb gave her a faint smile.

An hour later, following a class mostly taken up with an assignment to write a brief autobiography, one that Eb relished, Colt stood at the door of classroom number two-oh-one as his students filed out. Eb wanted to leave by the window, but it was a two-story drop to concrete. He had no choice but to pass Hill, who stood in the doorway, blocking half the exit. Eb turned sideways and slid through. "Remember, Mr. McCourry, a thousand words before eight-thirty. Make them good words." Eb grunted and nodded as he squeezed by. He didn't want to take the chance of further agitating his piano-playing, weight-lifting, plow-blade tough English teacher by speaking.

Monday had been a laughably easy day. Eb registered for biology, which he was taking for the second time because he couldn't pass it, and he not only had to pass, but to make a good grade if he was to qualify for a football scholarship. Second period was geometry with an old Navy submariner named Hap Hilton who liked to listen to Paul Harvey's national radio news show ("And now, for the rest of the story …") at noon for the first fifteen minutes of lunch hour. World history, which Eb liked, followed his post-lunch study hall and something called sociology wound up the day with what Eb hoped was a marshmallow course. It was taught by a woman everybody called Miss Lilly. Her last name was Wilkerson. She coached basketball and square dancing, Eb discovered. He found it exotic that the school had a square dance team, as his mother had mentioned.

On this day, in Eb's fifth period class, Miss Lilly opened by telling the students she had four square dancers down with mono and she needed some backups right now because she had no bench at all. She was making her appeal to the student body. The square dance team was determined with tryouts in the spring and summer and changes were unprecedented. So was mono. Eb paid little attention to the announcement until after class when a tall, pretty girl with cascading dirty blonde hair stopped him in the hall outside class, just as he was preparing to bound down the steps.

"You're the new football player, right?"

"I'm one of them," he said, nodding. Her eyes were robin's egg blue, her even teeth protruded slightly and the corners of her mouth curved up in a natural smile. She was slender and her legs were long, her hips curving abruptly into a small waist. There was a warmth about her that appealed to Eb and put him at ease.

"You ever dance?"

"Sure. Some. You know, frug, swim, twist, shag, stuff like that. Not so much structured. More free-form." He danced a couple of impromptu tap steps, smiled and said, "Why?"

"I'm Joyce ..." she said, extending a large, soft hand, looking straight into his eyes and nearly transfixing him.

"Eb McCourry," he said in the middle of her sentence.

"...and I've watched you practice football for two weeks. My boyfriend is the left tackle, Harold Wiseman. You seem to have a certain grace and balance. I'll bet you could square dance." She talked fast and left little room for reply, but Eb liked the part about being watched for two weeks and about grace and balance. He didn't like that Joyce had a boyfriend.

Eb laughed. He didn't mean to, but hers was an absurd notion. He was already playing football and trying to learn a new system, had a thousand words to write, was attending a new school and just moved into a new home. He had a lot of adjustments to make. "I don't think so," said Eb. "That'd be a lot. Why don't you ask your boyfriend?"

"He's a *tackle*!" she said, pointing to what she thought was Harold's obvious shortcoming. "This is important to the school." Her brow crinkled with a serious look. "Square dancing is not simply an activity here. We've won two national championships and eight state championships at Toe River. We have won every Old Smoky trophy but one. Right now, though, we have a problem and I think you might be able to help."

"Joyce," he said, trying to gin up some courage, "I'm sure you have people in the ninth grade who would do far, far better than me and would even have a future at it. I'm not a dancer; I'm a football player. What you saw on the field was me playing football, not dancing for a national champion. Now if you want to ask me for supper or something, we can talk, otherwise, I need to get to class."

"I want you to dance," she said firmly and with no room to negotiate. "Do it for me and I'll owe you one. Do it for the school. Do it for the people of the county. I don't care why you do it, but dance with us. I told Miss Lilly about you and she said to bring you in. I gotta do that. I'm the co-captain of the team."

Eb had to think on the offer for a moment. What could she mean by "I'll owe you one"? Could be an opening.

Eb swallowed harder than he meant to. "I guess," he said. "What do I have to do and what exactly is it that you owe me?"

"Great!" said Joyce. "We'll figure out the payback later, but come to the auditorium upstairs after football practice this evening. Take a shower first." Eb grimaced at the instruction and started to protest but he couldn't break in. "I'll show you a few basics that'll get you through the tryout. Remember this: it is highly unlikely you'll ever get on the floor during a serious competition. But we need bodies, backups, people to work with in practice."

"I gotta write a thousand-word essay tonight and I don't have a way home," Eb said, thinking about the payback and those lovely long legs.

"Mr. Hill caught you doing something stupid, didn't he?" said Joyce, brightening. "Don't pay much attention to his gruff act. He's all bark."

"His finger in my chest didn't feel like much of a bark. It felt more like a bite from a bear. I don't want to experience the whole fist."

"He uses those same fingers to play some of the best Chopin you've ever heard," said Joyce. "I'll drive you home. You scratch my back, I'll scratch yours."

Eb hoped she was being literal, but knew she wasn't. She had a boyfriend and she had his attention. He didn't know which was worse.

"By the way," she said, "you have beautiful green eyes." Eb swallowed hard.

Tuesday, September 3, 6:08 p.m.
Joyce met Eb at the auditorium door and he heard voices from the stage. There was loud, rhythmic stepping in unison, echoing off the old oak floor, to the fiddle/banjo music that was playing. Eb saw seven pairs of boys and girls—more than half of them football players and cheerleaders he knew or had seen—moving together, with Miss Lilly pacing among them. "Get in step," she said sharply, putting her hand firmly on the shoulder of one of the football players.

Give her a Smoky the Bear hat and she's a drill sergeant, thought Eb. She stood straight, stared directly at the dancers, and spoke with military authority, directing with broad hand movements. "Smile, Janice," she said, aiming at a pretty dancer who was not smiling. Her voice was firm, powerful and sharp as she barked orders, her speech precise, direct and without wasted words.

Joyce took Eb's hand as he moved toward the activity and said, "No, don't go over there. You'd be in the way and Miss Lilly doesn't like distractions. We'll work over here."

Eb leaned in and whispered, "She ought to be a football

coach." Joyce smiled and pushed him toward a spot removed from the activity.

Joyce handed Eb a worn piece of paper, written on both sides and obviously something with a history. "Miss Lilly gave this to me in eighth grade when she asked if I was coming out for the square dance team in high school," Joyce said. "It tells you what you'll need to know for the tryout. Read it and learn it. I'll be back in a few minutes and we'll go over it with your feet. Smile. Don't stop smiling. That's as important as your feet." Eb smiled. "Hold that," she said, squeezing his hand and stepping away.

The paper from the corner pocket of Joyce's purse was typed and mimeographed in blue ink, some of it faded, some smeared from moisture. A corner was torn off and it looked like soft drink had been spilled on the bottom. It was folded twice and obviously kept safe in something that compressed it like an old and dear flower. Eb read the directions.

CLOG

- *Both feet on the floor, weight on the right foot.*
Sounded easy enough.
- *With the left foot, hit the floor with the toe (if you had taps on, it would make a wonderful "tap" sound. That is the "a."*
He tapped and imagined a magnified sound.
- *Now slide the left foot forward slightly and bring the heel of the left foot down. That is the "slap." (Weight goes to the left foot.) Right foot is now off the floor.*
- *Come down on the ball of the right foot (that is the "ball") and bring the weight back to the right foot, lifting the left foot off the floor.*

Without realizing it, Eb's feet began moving slowly, concisely, lifting, striking softly, following the rules that governed a form of folk dance hundreds of years old. It originated in Europe and traveled to Appalachia, where it was flavored with Cherokee dance steps and stylings. It was the first form of street dance evolving in urban environs during the Industrial Revolution, he learned. Its appeal was understandable.

Eb moved like a natural, feeling the steps and the music as he tentatively danced.

Joyce joined the dancers, taking a boy's hands at the front and sliding into the formation with grace and ease. She moved well. Eb liked to watch her, but he had to cram. She danced through three 12-minute sequences, while Eb tried to mimic what the dancers were doing, reading his paper and moving his feet. Miss Lilly cut her eyes his way and watched briefly, noting the intensity of his face. Joyce excused herself and re-joined him, as the dancers took a brief break.

"You ready to dance?" she said.

Eb wasn't so sure, but said "Yes," and she took his right hand in her left, set her feet together and said, "Weight on your right foot. Lift your left foot and bring the toe down …"

And they were off, without music. The dance took Eb immediately. It seemed natural, a kind of flow that progressed easily and built to a crescendo. His heart was beating faster and not just from the pace, or even from his closeness to this girl who had quickly captured him. Eb liked this square dancing.

Joyce stopped, went to the record player and re-started the record. "Now, the music. Let's try it again," she said and here they went, "*A-slap-ball-change* …" She let his hand go and he kept dancing, like a child learning to walk. Same steps over and over, simple and elegant. The music was high-pitched and sweet. Eb had heard this kind of music before, but he had never listened. It was hillbilly music and far from the rock 'n' roll he normally listened to without thought. Eb was smiling naturally, forcing nothing. He wasn't a boy who smiled a lot and certainly not over nothing. "Woo-hoo," he said, louder than he meant.

Miss Lilly stood at the far corner of the stage and hid her face from Eb, feigning disinterest. But he could feel her eyes on him. He caught a picture of her every time he turned. At one point, he thought he saw her smile. He mentioned it to Joyce. "Probably gas," she said, the faintest laugh leaking out. "Miss Lilly can't smile. Not possible."

Eb and Joyce went through the clog and the buck, twenty intense minutes each, half if it without music. Finally, Joyce turned face-on to Eb and said, "I thought so. Wish you'd been here two years ago. You'd be calling." Eb didn't know what she meant by that, but it sounded good. He felt like he'd thrown a touchdown pass against tall defensive backs in the waning seconds.

Eb looked more tenderly than he intended at Miss Joyce Watkins, Toe River High School champion square dance team captain and his personal coach. He couldn't be sure, but he thought maybe he was in love. He wasn't sure whether he was in love with Joyce or with square dancing. Close call.

Wednesday, September 4, 6:10 p.m.

The Toe River High square dance caller, Buster Hanford, had called since he was fifteen and was generally thought to be the best in the state at the high school level. He was a thick, strong backup fullback on the football team. Today he worked off to the side with a girl Eb had seen in sociology class, a senior named Becky Blake. She was obviously another late addition to the team.

Joyce and Eb worked on steps again. "Who's she?" Eb asked.

"Your partner, if she sticks," said Joyce.

"I thought you were my partner." Eb's brow crinkled and the corners of his mouth turned downward.

"No, I'm Buster's partner, same as the last four years," said Joyce, feeling Eb's disappointment as she spoke. "You and Becky are alternates. She's actually pretty good, the last one cut each of the past three years. She's danced with her church group all that time and she knows the moves. She could step in pretty easy. I think Becky would be a good, solid addition. She

35

doesn't make mistakes. Look at her and Buster."

"If she's so good, why wasn't she on the team?"

"That's complicated," said Joyce. "She wasn't really good enough until this year and she's a senior now. It's hard to add a senior who's not a starter."

"I'm a senior and I'm not a starter. I can't even dance." Eb's hands slipped into his pockets and his head drooped.

"You can too dance, and you're a boy. It's easier to find girl dancers than boys. I'm going to have to introduce you two and get you started dancing. Let's go on over."

Eb felt like Joyce had broken up with him. She pulled him by his left hand and he followed without enthusiasm.

Becky was a slender, high-hipped, long legged, flat-chested girl with waist-length brown hair, huge hazel eyes and cheekbones that hinted at a Cherokee ancestry. She was gracious and seemed genuinely happy to meet Eb. "I've seen you in class," she said in a high-pitched, almost falsetto voice. "Didn't know you danced. Did you dance at the school you came from?"

"No," Eb said, "and I'm not real sure I dance at this one, either." Becky laughed and Joyce punched Eb on the arm, too hard, he thought. He grabbed the arm, grimacing in fake pain, massaging it. "Elbert's a smart alec …"

"Eb," he interjected. "Name's EB!"

"… but you two will be fine. I need to get to practice. Keep dancing. Show him some steps, Becky. Elbert, shut up and dance."

Joyce stepped away and Eb's eyes followed her until she linked hands with Buster. "Dammit!" he mumbled under his breath. "Dammit, dammit, dammit."

Becky held out a hand, smiled and said, "Do-se-do, Eb."

"And do-se-do to you, Becky," he said, his eyes still on Joyce.

***

Miss Lilly called an abrupt halt to drills. "Let's go through

36

this all the way once and see how we do. Elbert, get the record."

"Eb," he said, weakly, almost under his breath.

He stood with the record player arm posed over the record while two lines of couples formed, mirroring each other. They watched Miss Lilly's hand, held high in the air. When she was ready and lowered her arm, Eb set the needle down, the music started and Buster began the call.

"Left … left … left," he snapped, bringing everyone in step to the crisp tempo. To Eb's inexperienced eye, the seasoned dancers worked as a unit, their heads bobbing and feet stomping to a mountain rhythm that transcended time and place. The dancers slid in and out of intricate formations. Eb thought of a kaleidoscope he once saw, where colors bled seamlessly from one design into another without effort. At Buster's command, simple sounds like "little apple," "twirl," "shoot the star" and "give us a kiss" took on new meaning and the dancers interpreted perfectly, fluidly.

Buster kept the pace swift, crisply speaking instructions and seeing instant response.

"Girls in the bread basket picking out dough," he said as the girls moved to the center of the formation and began clogging, their feet slamming into the hardwood boards in unison and giving Eb a swelling in his chest that he couldn't explain.

The music rose and the shoes on the hardwood floor clattered. Eb felt like he was watching a movie as the set hurtled toward a finish.

"Shoot the star!" Buster yelped in his forceful deadpan. "Girls out for the carousel."

It all came back to the "do-se-do" and the dancers assumed the position and circled once around. "Swing your partner for the big circle."

The finish was coming. Eb watched closely. "Get ready," warned Buster and then suddenly, "Hit it!"

Dancers leaned left, then right with a loud *stomp!* The move was astonishing. It was smooth, sudden, dramatic, and

Eb wanted to jump up and shout.

"Circle and do-se-do, it's time to go."

They shuffled to the front of the stage and the boys knelt, each girl sitting on her partner's knee. "Give us a kiss." And the girls planted one on the boys' cheeks. Eb watched Joyce and wished he was in Buster's place on the end of that kiss.

"Say goodbye." Girls threw a kiss to the audience and everybody shuffled off stage. Eb applauded wildly, full of emotion and admiration.

He lost himself, imagining being on stage before a cheering full house at the Asheville Civic Auditorium. It was the same dream he'd often had with football, throwing a long touchdown pass to win the game, fans going nuts.

The dancers all looked at Eb, off somewhere in his own world, and began laughing. Miss Lilly smiled, then turned her head away before Eb saw her. She knew he was hooked and Eb certainly knew it, as well.

Thursday, September 5, 3:05 p.m.

Hap Hilton got Eb's attention the first day Eb sat in the all-male geometry class and heard this come out of Hap's mouth by way of introduction to geometry: "The angle of the dangle is in direct proportion to the heat of the meat." Half the class didn't get it. The other half didn't know if it was acceptable to laugh. Eb laughed out loud.

Hap was a big, square man with a big, square head, light brown flat-top haircut, wide gray eyes, wider smile, ears that stuck straight out and hands the size of hubcaps. He wore size 17EEE cowboy boots and loud plaid shirts with half sleeves and button-down collars, tucked tightly into khaki pants. Everything about him was big. Six-feet-four, two hundred and sixty pounds. He'd been a two-way tackle at Gardner-Webb College in Hickory fifteen years before and they'd named him All-Carolinas Conference because nobody could block him when he was on defense and nobody could get by him when he was on offense.

Hap liked to laugh, liked to joke and liked those who joined him in his levity. As with everything else about him, his laugh was large, loud and came up all the way from his feet, sounding hollow, then thundering. When he coached, he was a different man: intense, demanding, sometimes profane. Eb watched him knock down Toe River's biggest lineman—hulking David Farris, who also played trombone in the marching band at halftime—like David was made of balsa wood. Carl Blackthorn, who weighed nearly a hundred pounds less than David, blew by David's feeble block and made a hard tackle. Hap's reaction scared poor David so that he peed his pants and was on the verge of tears. Hap didn't actually hit him that hard, but he knew how to make maximum impact with minimum effort. Everybody's eyes were averted.

On this day, school ended and football practice was scheduled to be short because Friday was game day—Toe River's opener against Cloudland, Tennessee, a mile over the state line at the foot of Roan Mountain. Eb stopped by Hap's classroom on the second floor of the main building, which was cooled by those two big red maples outside his massive windows, to ask him about Miss Lilly. She intrigued Eb.

"What do you know about Miss Lilly that you can tell me, Hap?" Eb said.

"Why do you want to know?" said Hap, erasing a geometry assignment from the blackboard.

"She's my coach."

"So'm I. You askin' people about me?"

Eb looked directly into Hap's eyes as Hap sat in the big red rocking chair behind his desk.

"I never had a woman coach," Eb said. "I want to know about her, maybe figure her out some. I don't know what she expects. Hap, I really like dancing up there with her team, but I ain't no dancer. What if we get in a pinch and I have to dance and I screw up? I keep hearing, 'The stakes are high' with dancing and I don't know what that means."

"I'll tell you this, Elbert McCourry, she's the best dang

coach at this school, man or woman." Hap rocked forward, put his hands and arms on his desk. "Maybe the best coach at any school in the state. She's the most demandin' coach, the most knowledgeable coach, the most carin' coach. She puts in more hours and more study than the whole football staff combined and she don't make a penny for any of it." Eb stared at Hap, absorbing the gravity of this woman.

"She's hard-core tough," Hap continued. "We've had football players show up for practice with feet so beat up they couldn't run. Miss Lilly worked 'em raw when they couldn't get a routine down. We see a real benefit from her discipline 'cause it slops over into the habits of the football players."

Hap ran his big hand through his brush-cut hair and kept talking.

"She don't get the respect she deserves in her own back yard, even though down in Raleigh and all over the state they know about her and some people are even in awe of her."

Eb was leaning forward on the desk, his elbows to the side and his fists tucked up under his chin. He was alert, hanging on every word.

"School board here won't pay women coaches, no matter what they do," said Hap, almost matter-of-factly. "Miss Lilly's base teaching salary's less than mine and I never finished my degree. I learned math in the Navy. The explanation the board gives—when it gives one at all—is that the men have to support families, but that's bull. The women work hard and deserve the pay, especially this woman. Most of 'em have families, too, and this county's so poor, people work when they can."

Hap stood up, walked around the desk and put his hands on Eb's shoulders.

"Miss Lilly's a national champion, son. Nobody else from Avery County ever won so much as a state championship before her. Don't let that get too far from you when you are tryin' to figure her out. National champions are special. You pay attention and you'll be fine."

There was a long pause as Eb absorbed the lesson.

"Where's she from? Was she a dancer?" Eb asked in rapid succession. He'd heard rumors about New York, an illicit love affair that went wrong, dancing at Radio City Music Hall.

"She was raised down in Plum tree, about four miles from here and she was a good square dancer as a girl," said Hap. "She went off to Appalachian State and got a teaching degree with a minor in dance, then went to New York at the end of the war. Ended up working' for the Rockettes, but not as a dancer. She was in the office. Lot of people will say she danced with the Rockettes, but she didn't. She wasn't that kind of dancer."

Hap took on a stern look."There's always rumors about what happened to certain teachers, but Miss Lilly came back here and got a job with the school and she's been here ever since. Got married in about 1950 to a good guy who's a gem mine engineer in Spruce Pine. He commutes the 25 miles to work every day so she can be close to the school. He really dotes on her. It's nice to watch."

Hop cleared his throat and sat back at his desk, the rocking chair creaking as he eased his bulk into its seat.

"She started the dance team her first year back and won Old Smoky the second year. String's been going pretty much since. Couple of years ago, the judges decided Toe River'd won it too much and gave it to Sky High in Asheville. Nearly broke Miss Lilly's heart 'cause it was just unfair, especially considering that her team had overcome a lot of injury and sickness and dismissal of the lead couple because of broken team rules about dating."

Eb wanted to know what happened in New York, whether there was anything to the love affair, but he guessed he'd got as much out of Hap as he would, so he didn't push it.

Hap turned the conversation around and asked about Eb. "Your name, McCourry, is common up here," he said. "You got family in the county?"

"Mama is from Squirrel Creek," Eb said, "and Aunt Nell lives in Cranberry and raised a family there. There's

McCourrys all over the place and Buchanan is a family name of ours, too. My grandma was Cora Buchanan. Mama says she was mean as the devil. We're pretty deep here."

"You know where the name 'McCourry' came from?"

"Never thought about it and mama never offered."

"It's a family name of mine, too, so I looked it up. Seems it began as Macquarie and the Macquaries were from the Isle of Mull off the coast of Scotland. John Macquarie was known as 'the George Washington of Australia' because he played a big role in founding it. They tell me all the Macquaries left Mull and came over here. Not one of them is left over there." Hap pulled a large-format book from his book and opened, turning its pages carefully.

"I picked up one of our kilts at the Scottish Festival on Grandfather Mountain last year. Ugliest thing I ever saw, a dull green and black and red. Looks like an unhappy Christmas. Here's a picture of it." Eb looked at the book, *Tartans,* and wrinkled his brow.

"Ugly," he said. "Really ugly."

Hap opened that broad face again, put his arm around Eb's shoulder and said, "Let's go to practice. We got a game to get ready for."

The more Eb learned about the dance team and his coach and this rural county the more he liked them all, the more he felt at home. The more he felt at home, the more he knew would be asked of him and the pressure to produce would grow. He wasn't quite sure if he was ready for that.

"The stakes are high here" kept ringing in his head.

Thursday, September 5, 9 a.m.

For some time Miss Lilly watched as Mickey Buchanan grew increasingly angry, bitter and mean over the past year. The pace of his anti-social—almost sociopathic—behavior seemed to be on the increase. Mickey was her best natural dancing talent, a boy who could clog with anybody in the country and whose smooth grace gave this Toe River High

School square dance team its identity and its best chance to be a champion.

He was the reluctant star, a young man so angry, because of a humiliating family situation he could not influence, that he threatened unity, chemistry and performance with every sneer, every remark, every bumped shoulder. Something had to be done and Miss Lilly wasn't sure she could do it by herself.

So, she called in Smoky Swain.

Smoky was not a dancer, didn't want to be a dancer. He was a football player who had little interest in the classroom. Everybody liked him. He'd been at the school only a few days, one of several transfers, but the weeks he spent with the football team in the summer showed him to be, without question, a leader. He seemed to know most of the students in the junior and senior classes and people gravitated toward him. Even Mickey Buchanan liked him. Or, perhaps more accurately in Mickey's case, didn't hate him.

Smoky stuck his head through the doorway of Miss Lilly's classroom and tapped gently on the door frame. "Ma'am?" he said.

"Come in, Smoky. Thank you for coming." She pulled a desk from the front row alongside her big oak desk and pointed to it. "Take a seat. I'll get right to it. I need you to be part of the square dance team."

"Can't dance a lick, Miss Lilly," Smoky said, a broad grin creasing his face. He removed a green John Deer cap and ran his fingers backwards through his long, dark, sandy hair, combing it. "Never could. Love to help you, but ..."

"I don't need a dancer," Miss Lilly said, leaning forward at her desk. "I need somebody to watch Mickey Buchanan, to keep him under control and to prevent him from destroying this team."

"Ma'am, I don't know how I could do that. Why don't you throw him off the team if he's a problem? Nobody's worth all that trouble."

"We need him and maybe more importantly, I think he

needs us," she said. "We can't leave him with nothing. His life isn't great right now, but I think there's a good kid in there somewhere and we have to help keep the unruly Mickey from taking over completely."

"What would you want me to do? I can't go beatin' him up every time he gets out of line," said Smoky, crinkling his brow. He lay his cap on the desktop, wiped a bead of sweat off his eyebrow and leaned forward. It was a hot day with no breeze and Miss Lilly's class was always a few degrees warmer than the rest of the school.

"Just be there. Mickey seems to respect you. If he starts to get out of hand, get between him and trouble. Talk to him if you can, but guide him away from those bad instincts." Smoky nodded. "We'll tell the dancers you're the new equipment manager and that will cover this. Since we don't really have much equipment to manage, you won't be spending a lot of time at anything but watching Mickey. I want you to room with him on overnight trips and to watch him closely, especially before and after practice. That's when trouble seems to happen. Would your parents approve?"

"I'll do what I can, Miss Lilly, and my parents won't mind. They like me bein' involved in as much as I can. But you have to understand that this can't interfere with football. That's my game and we have a pretty good team. That Appalachian Conference championship trophy belongs in our case and it's my job to get it."

Miss Lilly smiled. She wished Smoky Swain could dance. Lacking that, maybe he could keep Mickey Buchanan dancing.

***

Eb stopped Smoky in the hall outside Miss Lilly's room. It was a few minutes before practice and he wanted to talk to her. "What in the world are you doing at square dance practice?" Eb asked.

"She's recruiting me," Smoky said, smiling broadly and swirling in a circular dance move.

"No. It's come to that?" Eb smacked Smoky on the shoulder.

"You'll see. Gotta git."

Gaylen Anderson passed Smoky in the hall and saw Eb walking away. "Hey, man, you want to do down to Old Fort with me after practice sometime? It's about forty miles down the mountain and I'm going to see my girlfriend. We'll be back by supper."

"Sure," Eb said. "I ain't got nothing going on. Just let me know in time to tell the house parents at the home. They gotta know if I'm going to be out a while."

At that moment a short, erect and beautiful girl passed and stopped Eb in mid-thought. His eyes followed her as she started down the stairs. "Who is *that?*" he said.

"That's Lizetta McEntire and you can forget it," said Gaylen. "Best looking girl in five counties and she's smarter than most of the teachers. Sweet, good heart and damn near untouchable. Her daddy's a lawyer and politician and mother's an artist. She scares hell out of most of the boys."

Eb ran over to the top of the stairs to watch her descend, his mind seeing her in slow motion as she swayed down the steps with a lovely grace, her books cradled to her rounded chest, her dress bouncing, her auburn hair shining from above. She stopped one step from the bottom, looked straight up into Eb's eyes—as if a sixth sense had told her he was there—and smiled. He backed away from the rail quickly, embarrassed, his heart fluttering.

Eb took a moment to compose himself and tapped lightly on Miss Lilly's open door. She was writing something but looked up and waved him in. She pointed to a seat, but continued writing. When she finished she opened a desk drawer and slid the paper into it. "What can I do for you?" she said, waving him to a desk in front of hers.

He'd never been this close to her, one-on-one. They'd talked across the dance room, mostly her giving him instructions and him following them. Even sitting, she looked tall. Her eyes were penetrating, dark and focused. Her small, delicate hands made the pencil look larger than it was and her almost complete lack of a chin folded in a comic look, one that lasted briefly. When she spoke, the comedy disappeared.

Eb knew he needed to get to the point. "I think you can tell I like square dancing and I want to know something about it, some history, anything you can tell me. This isn't what I thought it would be at all. When my mother told me the school had a square dance team, I laughed. Seemed funny then. Doesn't seem that now."

"You're a writer, aren't you, Elbert?"

"Eb," he said. "Yes, ma'am, I am. How'd you know?"

"Mr. Hill told me. Said you wrote one of those thousand-word overnight essays he gives students"—she pronounced it "stood-its"—"for doing something stupid and he said it was the best he'd seen in 20 years. Mr. Hill is not often loose with praise."

Eb suppressed a smile, but couldn't help lighting up. "A thousand words is easy, ma'am," he said, more smugly than he meant.

"Square dancing, the way we do it, anyway, is fairly new," said Miss Lilly, laying down her pencil and folding her hands on her desk. "Old time square dancing is as old as the mountains and its people, but the dance we practice is an evolution that is still in process. Competition has changed the core of it. A lot of the competitive aspect dates to about nineteen-twenty-eight when a man named Bascom Lamar Lunsford started his Mountain Dance and Folk Festival in Asheville."

"Is that the Mountain Youth Jamboree?" Eb asked, leaning forward and stretching his arms over the desk, grabbing the outer edge with his hands. "The one with the Old Smoky trophy?"

"The festival predates the jamboree," she said, "but, yes, they're part of the same thing. Point being, though, that when teams were formed for competition they had to keep doing better and different steps and formations. Clogging, for example, didn't used to be part of square dancing, but it is showy and noisy and gets a lot of attention, so it gave the teams that clogged an edge.

"Amplification of music in the nineteen-forties moved it along. The records they were playing like 'Under the Double Eagle,' 'St. Anne's Reel,' 'Angelina Baker,' 'Soldier's Joy,' 'John Henry,' all of which we still use, led to taps on the shoes of some dancers so you could hear their steps over the music. Then came the uniforms, the matching outfits that were usually more western than mountain."

"Yeah," Eb said, "ours look like a B-western movie, and the colors and sequins seem loud to me."

"It's part of the show biz," Miss Lilly said, making a broad gesture with her right hand. "You have to do that. Everything amplifies everything else and it becomes a package. Sometimes the dance gets lost in the flash and that's when we have to go back to the basics and work on steps and the formations."

She picked up the pencil from her desk and put it in a cup, looking away from Eb briefly, thinking about his question.

"Square dancing used to be for everybody," Miss Lilly said. "It was a social event held at festivals and churches and other gatherings, and people just jumped in and danced, no instruction offered or given. I'm afraid that what we've done with it, through the competitions, is to take away the feeling that anybody can do it. We've professionalized it. I don't like that part, but it's where it is and it's what we have to live with."

A knock at the open door interrupted Miss Lilly. "Sorry to bother you," said Joyce Watkins, "but I'm going to be a little late for practice. Gotta run an errand for my mom. Hi, Elbert." She winked at him.

Eb nodded and smiled. "Thanks for letting me know," said Miss Lilly.

"I've picked up that there's a real rivalry with Asheville and us," Eb said, continuing the conversation without missing a beat and including himself in the "us." "I don't understand the rivalry part. Asheville's a big place and the high school is huge by the standards we know here. That's where I'd be in school if I was still living at home and I didn't want to go there. Too big. What is it, ten times the size of Toe River? Why would they be a rival?"

"First," said Miss Lilly, "they want the Old Smoky trophy in the worst way and have for some time. They won it a couple of years ago, and there was a dispute about the win, but we don't get into that." He could see something dark in her eyes at the very mention.

"Asheville, to some up here, represents an invasion into our culture. It's always been something of a writers' colony and an arts community that attracted people from all over the country, people who never took the time or put in the effort to learn or even care about the culture of this area."

Miss Lilly took on an intense look in her eyes. "The tourists and retirees come into the mountains, build these fancy houses and rarely even visit them. They're not part of our communities and most of them can't even pronounce 'Appalachia.' They call it 'Aa-pal-A-chia,'" said Miss Lilly, her mouth widening, "instead of giving it the 'attitude' sound. 'Aa-pal-aa-chia.'

"We have been dismissed as bumpkins, hillbillies, hayseeds, rednecks … you pick the derogatory and stereotypical term." Miss Lilly's voice was rising and becoming even more pointed. "Now they want our trophy and, by grannies, they can't have it, if I have anything to say about it!" Eb saw the exclamation point at the end of her rant and liked the passion.

"Thank you, Miss Lilly," Eb said. "That helps me understand and I want to understand. I'm never going to be good at this, but I can understand it."

"Get ready for practice," she said. "And thanks for asking. I don't revisit our roots enough and maybe I ought to."

He could see a fight coming and it likely wouldn't be a pretty one. But Lizetta McEntire was a pretty one. An eye-popping pretty one.

Part II

Friday, September 6, 7:15 p.m.

Coach Buster Woodson pulled Eb out of warm-ups and told him he wasn't starting the opening football game against Cloudland High. Eb wasn't surprised because he was new and Barry Bates started at quarterback—actually "tailback" in a single wing, but Eb never got used to that term—for the past two years with some success. Eb knew the data on Barry: senior team captain, solid runner, good technician and the Hawks won fifteen games in two years with him taking the ball first. Eb also knew Barry couldn't throw a lick, but passing hadn't often been necessary the last two years because the running game was substantially above average. Eb's guess was that with runners who were mostly underclassmen on this team, passing would be necessary. If Eb were at quarterback, Barry would be in position to run the ball more. But Barry got to go out first to lead the offense.

The problem was clear right away. Cloudland picked up a Barry Bates fumble on the third play of the game and scored. A series later, one of the sophomore runners, J.W. Greene, fumbled and Cloudland had the ball at Toe River's five yard line. Carl Blackthorn—by himself—ended that series all the way back at the twenty five yard line by laying out everybody who tried to block him. Eb had played the previous year with two guys who would wind up in the NFL, but he'd never seen a better defensive football player than Carl Blackthorn, who was about two thirds the size of the two future pros, but quicker than light.

Carl was a sinewy 5-feet-9, 165 pounds, dark-skinned, with a Cherokee face a sculptor would remember. He was hard as a plow blade. Carl spent summers working in various fields picking vegetables, putting up hay, hoeing, sweating, hardening his entire body. His family became migrant pickers and left him on his own when he was sixteen and he hadn't had a home since. Not that he had much of one when they were around. His father was a violent alcoholic and his mother nearly worked herself to death to keep the kids fed and clothed.

Carl stayed with various people overnight and sometimes for a week. He was invariably clean, pressed and upbeat. He had a smile like an airplane landing light and was beyond expressive when he played football. After making a tackle, he often picked up the guy he'd manhandled, dusted him off and said something like, "Don't worry, I be back. You do better next time." He had a distinct speech impediment and Hap told Eb teachers treated him like he was "slightly retarded." Carl didn't play offense because he couldn't learn the plays. Eb had seen him struggle trying to play guard and center, often going against the flow of the offense, running into the ball carrier, causing chaos. Defense simply required that he follow the ball and tackle the player who held it. He did that.

Eb took Carl home to Asheville later in the season and Eb's mother loved Carl immediately. He became one of her kids. They bantered back and forth, Eb's mom mimicking Carl's speech, Carl howling with laughter, Mrs. McCourry putting another plate of food in front of him. Carl and Eb became fast friends, but the small, muscular Cherokee on the warpath often made practices difficult for Eb.

Under normal circumstances, because of Carl Blackthorn alone, Cloudland, a small school cut out of the side of a mountain across the Tennessee line, had no chance against Toe River in football, though the school's square dance team was formidable. Still, the Hurricanes scored against the Red Tail Hawks' offense—not the defense—and the Toe River offense was not moving in the direction it had hoped. Coach Woodson called Eb over and said, "Go throw it." Woodson smiled. That was all Eb needed. He sprinted onto the field, took over the huddle and said, "Barry, move to fullback. We're going to score right now."

Eb took note that Cloudland's defensive backs were short, but they were tough guys who'd stick a helmet on your chin.

Ed noticed, too, that Terry Gervin, a six-foot-two-inch end, had been left with little to do and Terry was looking at Eb with anticipation. "Left end down, wingback across on two," Eb said. "Terry, catch the damn ball." Terry caught the damn ball and he caught it and he caught it.

By the half, Toe River was up 27-6. Coach Woodson took the starters—and Eb—out at the end of the third quarter with a 41-6 lead. Barry Bates' move to fullback was smooth and productive. He was happy to be there. Everybody was delighted with the new quarterback.

As Eb left the field for the last time that evening, Mickey Buchanan passed him running out to play defense. "Think you're hot shit, huh, EL-bert? You ain't. Wait 'till Mars Hill comes in here and kicks your skinny ass."

Eb winked at him. "It's Eb," he said. "Remember the name, remember the game." He thought Mickey would smack him.

About a minute after the game ended, as Eb walked off the field talking to one of the Cloudland lineman—a kid who hit him hard a couple of times—he felt a *whump!* from behind and almost went forward on his face. It was Joyce. She jumped on him from behind, wrapped her arms and legs around him and rode Eb for two full steps. "Good game, El-bert!" she yelped.

"Eb, dammit, Joyce!" he said, grinning. His chipped front tooth was on full display. "You better go see Harold or Mickey Buchanan won't be the only one wanting me dead. He's a bonafide shit."

She climbed down, circled behind him and smacked him on the butt. "Those eyes sure are green," she said and she ran off to find Harold.

Joyce Watkins had Eb McCourry and she knew it. He didn't mind so much, but he wondered where it could go with his left tackle standing squarely in the doorway.

As he walked toward the locker room, he saw Lizetta McEntire standing at the fence between the stands and the football field, looking straight at him and smiling. He looked behind him to see who she might be aiming the smile at, but saw nobody. He looked back toward her and she was gone.

Saturday, September 7, 6:30 a.m.

Eb wiped the sleep from his eyes as he walked into the Beech Mountain Home for Children cafeteria, the smell of bacon, eggs, biscuits, gravy and pancakes filling the air. He was not yet fully awake, having celebrated the win over Cloudland until nearly midnight, going over to Ruby's Diner in Banner Elk after the game, drinking Cokes and talking excitedly in the parking lot. Horns blew as Toe River students passed the players. The feeling was good.

Square dance class was at 9:30 this morning at the school and Eb needed to shake loose some cobwebs, rub a few sore muscles and wake up.

He slipped into the serving line which was growing by the minute as the kids awoke and made their way across campus to the dining room. Eb immediately felt a pull on his arm. It was short, blonde-haired, slightly bow-legged, big-eyed Maryellen Streit looking up at him. "Go sit down," she said. "We have a surprise for Friday's hero." Eb looked embarrassed, but he followed instructions.

In a minute, she and Judi Aldridge, a tall, ample brunette, walked out of the kitchen with the largest plate of pancakes Eb ever saw. The pancake on the bottom was the size of the plate and it was stacked with six more, each decreasing slightly in size. "Our hero," swooned Maryellen, batting her eyes and sliding a chair up close to Eb as she sat briefly.

"Smartass," Eb said, barely above a whisper. That language wouldn't play in a Christian children's home where vespers was held every Sunday at 6 p.m. and church was mandatory. They both grinned wider.

Maryellen and Judi were cheerleaders and square dancers who lived in Big Girls Cottage. They worked in the kitchen on a regular basis. Each resident had a specific job on campus. Maryellen was one of the dance team's best, a senior who had started since her freshman year, which was nearly unprecedented. Miss Lilly didn't like to start freshmen, but Maryellen was simply too good to be an alternate.

Eb didn't mind the pampering, but knew he'd better not ever expect it. He picked up a fork, cut into the pancakes and took a huge bite. "Slow down," bellowed Maryellen. "There's no contest here." Eb wondered at the veracity of that statement. There was a contest everywhere.

Saturday, September 7, 1:15 p.m.

Miss Lilly brought cold cut sandwiches with mayonnaise, lettuce and tomato and grape Kool-Aid for everybody's lunch following square dance practice at the school. She knew they'd work hard and wanted a small reward at the end of the session. She was right. It was a tired group that gathered at the table. The football players were dragging.

Eb loved cold cuts, but his family could never afford them at home, so he ate three sandwiches, subtly taking the final two when he thought no one was looking. Miss Lilly was. The sandwiches were soggy from the generous slices of tomato. Eb devoured the food, then excused himself, off to Old Fort with Gaylen to see Gaylen's pretty girlfriend. It would have to be a rushed trip because Eb was normally expected back by eight o'clock, unless he had special permission.

Gaylen's car was in the shop and he had his father's rusting bucket of bolts (his dad, an old Navy man, called it that), a nineteen-forty-six Dodge coupe with a police car spotlight at the driver's side window that you could control by twisting a handle from the driver's seat. The Dodge was powder blue on the bottom with a white top and had a charm that was undeniable. Gaylen's infatuation with the big rounded coupe was not in its color or its aerodynamic shape. He loved its sturdy dependability. He could not claim either for his much newer Simca, a tiny French car made by the Italian Fiat.

The Dodge had what Gaylen called a "police interceptor" engine and would nearly fly. There was a low roar when Gaylen turned the engine on. This had been a police car at one time and cops don't drive junk, Gaylen said.

Gaylen and Eb were about fifteen minutes out on an hour's trip down the mountain when Gaylen pulled out a cigar, long, crooked, almost black.

Eb smelled it the minute Gaylen unwrapped it from the cellophane. "Want one?" Eb looked at the cigar then at Gaylen, for a long moment.

"You mean that after what you told me about setting the woods on fire and your mama whipping your ass until it looked like a camp fire, you're going to light that ugly, smelly thing?"

"That's about it," said Gaylen.

"Sure, give me one."

Eb knew nothing about smoking except that his mom smoked and his dad had smoked before he died, coughing himself hoarse every morning and evening. They smoked Kools and Chesterfields and both had husky smokers' voices. The Chesterfields were unfiltered and the Kools smelled like cow crap. His mother said they smoked those brands because it's all they could get during World War II and "old habits die hard." She smiled and blew a puff of smoke in Eb's direction when she said that.

Eb watched Gaylen drive with his left hand and put the round end of the cigar into his mouth with his right hand. He took a small bite out of the end of the cigar and spat it out the window. "Gotta have a hole for the smoke to come through," Gaylen said. Eb followed suit. The tobacco tasted sharp and bitter-sweet.

Gaylen rolled up his window and nodded that Eb should do the same. "Gotta be careful lighting it," Gaylen said, "so we don't want no extra wind blowing in here." Gaylen put the cigar in his mouth and struck a large wooden match. He put the flame on the end of the cigar without puffing. He burned the cigar all over the tip, heating it evenly. Finally, it began to smoke. Gaylen blew out the match, took a puff and let it out slowly after holding it in his mouth for seconds.

The smoke stunk up the entire interior of the car, but Eb

didn't say a word. He got the box of matches from Gaylen and followed his teaching to the letter. Eb's mouth finally filled with smoke and he held it for about five seconds, then coughed it out. This was not pleasant, but he knew it was a passage and Eb didn't complain.

"Pretty good, huh?" said Gaylen.

"Yeah," Eb said, pushing the words out through a throat that didn't want to work. He was dizzy, queasy and felt like he was probably cross-eyed.

"Take another puff," Gaylen urged, casting a side glance at Eb, trying not to laugh. Eb slowly turned green. He thought he might be pushing his luck with this cigar thing. Gaylen didn't know how close Eb was to dumping those three pickle and pimento loaf sandwiches and that that glass of Kool Aid on the floorboard of Gaylen's father's beloved tank.

"Better not yet," Eb said, barely getting it out, hoping to god the cigar would go out by itself and let him off the hook. A minute later, there was no smoke coming from Eb's cigar. "Thank you, Jesus," he said to himself.

The two boys quietly passed a couple of small towns before it occurred to Eb to ask about Kay. "Where'd you find your girlfriend?" he said. "An hour's a long way to drive for a date."

"Wait 'till you see her," Gaylen said. "I met her at a church camp down at Montreat—outside Asheville—a couple of years ago. We wrote each other for a while and I went down to see her a couple of times. One thing led to another and, you know …"

About forty minutes later the pair pulled into the compacted dirt driveway of a tiny, neat gray board and batten house off the main street in Old Fort, North Carolina, foothills of the Blue Ridge Mountains. "Home of Gov. Milton Snider," the sign said, "and UNC All-American Basketball Player Harold 'Neptune' Conner."

Before Gaylen stopped the Dodge, the screen door flew open, its hinges screaming, and the most beautiful girl Eb had ever seen ran through it, yelling, "Gaylen!" He hit the brake hard, turned off the engine and threw open the door in one movement. Gaylen jumped out of the car in time to catch a leaping Kay Silver Feather, who landed on his chest with a kiss that covered his entire face. They held the kiss. And held it. Eb sat uncomfortably and cleared his throat.

They broke the kiss and Kay slid down Gaylen—he was six-feet, she five-foot-two—holding tightly to him. "Hello," she said with a lovely and appealingly warm voice. "You must be Elbert."

"Eb," said Eb. "And you must be Kay. Gaylen didn't tell me you were a movie star."

Kay Silver Feather was nearly perfect, Eb thought as his eyes covered her. Huge brown eyes, cheek and jaw lines that were the personification of definition. Tiny waist that sloped into a rounded bottom, dancer's legs, well-defined breasts, long shimmering black hair and a grace of movement that was distracting.

There was a genuine curiosity about her that led to question after question about Eb—a writer, she'd heard—about Toe River High School, about the football and square dance teams. How was Gaylen doing in football? she wanted to know. Were all the girls in love with him?

Kay told Eb—Gaylen passively listening, his arm around her, occasionally kissing her on the cheek or nuzzling her neck as she talked—that her dad, Junior, drove up to Old Fort about 15 years ago from the Cherokee reservation, where they lived, for a plumbing job and he liked it so much that he started a business here and moved the family up. There was a sister, Arlene, who went off to New York and become a dancer, and a brother, Talking Pony (his real name was Phil, but he liked the Indian name), who was an Air Force motor pool mechanic in Germany. Phil sent most of his paycheck home to his dad every month and Junior put it in the bank so Phil could open a garage when he got out of the Air Force. Kay's mother wasn't mentioned. Gaylen said later that she left with a man about ten years her junior and they didn't speak her name any more in this house.

They talked—rambling all over the landscape for a good while, time slipping away—and it finally occurred to Eb that he was a third wheel and that Kay and Gaylen had to want some time alone. "Is there a place to get a pack of cigarettes?" Eb asked.

"You don't smo…" Gaylen almost said, catching himself.

"Yes," said Kay, knowing exactly what Eb was doing and playing along. It was a charade they were all in on, but they went through with it. "In the middle of town there's a drug store, People's. About five blocks from here. They have great cherry milkshakes, too. You ought to try one. I think Julia's working. Tell her who you are and that you and Gaylen came to see me. She'll probably spot you the milkshake. Gaylen and I will stay here and catch up if you don't mind."

Eb didn't tell her that at that moment and for the next hour he'd like to be Gaylen, but said, "Oh, I understand. I'll be back in an hour or so." She smiled and squeezed his shoulder, shooting a bolt of electricity through him.

The pretty strawberry blonde at the soda fountain at People's Drug Store said she was Julia Garrity as she mixed Eb's cherry milkshake. On the house. "Is Eb short for Elbert?" she asked.

"No," he said with more authority than he meant to.

Eb told her that he and Gaylen came down from Avery County to see Kay and she'd said, "Oh, Gaylen. I love Gaylen. He and Kay are so sweet together. We ought to double date. She's my best friend."

Eb sat looking at this pretty, peach-cheeked, rounded-in-the-right-places sixteen-year-old in the pink shirt-waist dress asking him for a date and couldn't speak. He had to be back at 8 and it was already 5:30. She got off at 6, but that only gave them an hour at the far outside. Eb explained the situation.

"We can get to know each other for an hour and next time you come down, we can go out. How's that?" She was cheerful, positive, thoroughly without inhibition.

Eb blurted out, "It's a date," and he reached across the counter and kissed her on the lips, a complete and utter act of spontaneity for which he took no responsibility. It was pure reflex. She looked at him, smiled and said, "We have the same color eyes. I love green eyes."

"So do I," Eb said, staring into hers.

In their hour together, spent in the front seat of Gaylen's Dodge in the driveway of Kay Silver Feather's gray house in Old Fort, North Carolina, Home of Neptune Conner, Eb got to know Julia Garrity's soft lips, her soft cheeks, her soft neck and he came close to getting to know her soft breasts. But that'd have to wait until the return trip, he discovered, as Gaylen came out of the house, looked inside the car and said, "Unlock your lips and pull up your duds. We got a deadline." Julia giggled. Eb blushed. Rosebud red. Glowing.

Eb didn't get out of the car because if he had, he would have embarrassed all four of them with the stout protrusion and stain on the front of his pants, but he looked at those pretty green eyes and whispered, "We'll be back soon and we'll pick up where we left off."

Julia nodded, smiled and whispered back, "You're so sweet, Elbert."

"Eb," he said. "Please. Just Eb."

Fifteen quiet minutes later, Eb blurted out, "Oh *shit!* I didn't get her phone number or her address!"

"I got it," Gaylen said.

"You're a god," Eb said. "I can't remember a girl saying 'yes' to me. I mean, hell, I was saying yes *to her.* I wonder sometimes if I'm ever going to figure this stuff out."

Gaylen chuckled.

It was quiet for a while, each boy in his own thoughts. "Gaylen," Eb finally said, "you think I got a chance with Joyce?"

"Joyce?! You mean Joyce Watkins who's been teaching you to dance?" he said, almost startled. "You'd better not even think 'Joyce.' Two real good reasons. She's Harold's girl and

Harold's one of those crazy-assed Elk River boys." Gaylen slowed down and pulled to the side of the road for a prayer meeting. "They're from another time and they don't take to people messing with things they think's theirs—and that includes people. We already got that basket case Mickey Buchanan to worry about. Let's not rile up Harold, too. You got to take this serious. It's not something to play with."

Eb got quiet again, thinking about how sweet and soft Julia was, how beautiful Kay was and how neither of them was Joyce. He was developing a hefty case of it for Joyce, but Gaylen was right. Joyce Watkins was danger to him, to both his teams, to the life he was trying to put together.

The baby blue tank roared up U.S. Highway 321 into the night, away from the closest Eb had been to real romance for a while and back to the reality of Joyce Watkins, the girl he couldn't have.

Life was getting more complicated for Eb McCourry.

Monday, September 9, 12:07 p.m.
Eb spotted Hap Hilton across the basement lunchroom at Toe River High School and hurried over to take the seat across from him before another student could slide into it. Hap was a magnet for students who needed to talk about something important because he listened, wasn't judgmental and always gave solid advice.

"Mind if I sit down?" Eb said, easing into the seat.

"Park it," Hap said, moving his lunch tray away from the spot Eb was taking. "You got enough to eat there, son?" Eb's plate was piled with one or two of everything on the menu. He was not yet accustomed to the fact that he wasn't at home where money and food were in short supply, and that he could have as much as he wanted to eat when he had the fifty cents for lunch, which wasn't often.

"I get hungry," Eb said, taking a large bite out of a hamburger that looked five inches thick. "Mfffl ommf loffl mummnd."

Hap laughed out loud. "Slow down, boy. And don't talk with your mouth full. What you got on? Your mind." Hap laughed at his own joke, an old Brother Dave Gardner line he uttered over and over. "What you got on …" never got old to him. He loved those Southern comedians and popped corny one-liners all day.

"Hap, something's bothering me and maybe it shouldn't be, but I can't help it." Eb stuffed another pound of burger into his face and chewed fast and hard, like it would disappear if he didn't.

"Eb, dammit, slow down with the food. You're going to wind up bringing it right back up. Now, what's the problem?"

"Aw, shoot, Hap, I learned to eat like this at home. If you don't eat fast, you don't eat. Eating is competition at my house and it's hard to change that." He pulled back the sleeve on his right forearm, showing bruises and scars up and down it.

"Mama occasionally whacks us with something when we show bad manners, like reaching across the table. I once showed a big bruise I got when Mama whacked me with a heavy serving spoon to my third grade teacher and she called the police. Mama wasn't happy with me about that, but I didn't know anything about 'child abuse,' which is what one of them was calling it. I got pretty pissed, too.

"Anyhow, today's problem's this: people won't call me by my name." Eb put down the bite of burger that remained and ran his palm over his face. Then he picked up a handful of fries and stuffed them in, all at once.

"Elbert?"

"No. Eb. That's my name. Elbert's what it came from. It sounds like a name you'd give a fat kid with big cheeks. Elbert, Egbert, Norbert …"

"Whoa, a minute here, young man. You're taking a King's name, and you're besmirching it."

"What's 'besmirching'?"

Hap kept his rhythm. "Elbert is Anglo-Saxon and it means 'noble and brilliant.' Came from Aethel-berht. Man named

60

Aethelbert, which was spelled different, was the King of Kent in the mid-ninth century, and he was a direct descendent of the Saxon invaders of the fourth century. The Elbert family has a pretty crest with armor and a big griffin. It's a bright, pretty piece." Hap looked self-satisfied as he spoke.

Eb sat quietly listening and thinking. "Hap," he said, finally, "how do you know so much about so much that doesn't make much difference?"

"I read," Hap said, "and I keep what I read. World's an interesting place if you take time to know about it."

"Elbert's still ugly," Eb said, "and I still want to be called Eb. People don't know about Saxon kings. They know Elbert is goofy."

"I've known several Ebs and all of them was Elberts," said Hap. "One of them was your uncle, Nell's husband, who had your name."

"Yeah, I was named for him," Eb said. "I didn't know him. Died a good while back."

"Eb McCourry was one of the finest men I've ever known," said Hap. "Kind and gentle soul, but a man who'd stand up for his family and who worked hard all his life. I played football against his boy Sonny in college and he'd knock you on your butt, pick you up and dust you off. Real sportsman."

"Aunt Nell speaks well about Uncle Eb," Eb said. "I know everybody called him 'Eb,' not 'Elbert.'"

"Give 'em time to know you," said Hap. "School's only been open a few days. You're new and they're still trying to figure if you're one of them or an outsider who'll stay an outsider. Be yourself and don't talk about how great it was at your old school. Appreciate Toe River and our students and teachers for what we are and we'll do the same for you."

Eb threw in the last of the burger and chased it with a handful of fries. He nodded. "I like it here," he said, "and I guess I want people to like me. I want to fit." Eb had his answer. That's why he went to Hap and would continue to. Hap knew things.

"You want to tell me about your daddy?" said Hap. "You mentioned he died when you were thirteen or fourteen I think. What happened?"

"He drank himself to death," Eb said, matter-of-factly. "He'd been sober a good while—Mama said seven years—but he got on a toot, wound up in Johnson City drinking bad moonshine and it poisoned him. Last time I saw him, in the hospital, he was in an iron lung and Mama said he weighed eighty pounds. He was a big man, six feet, two hundred and ten pounds, maybe two-twenty. That stuff wasted him."

"Did they ever find who gave him the moonshine?" Hap asked, crossing one big leg over another.

"Aw, I don't think they even looked. Dad was going to die anyway. He had diabetes, kidney and liver trouble, high blood pressure, bad heart, all kinds of things that can kill you. He smoked all the time, too. Unfiltered Chesterfields. Smelled like a burning rope when he lit one up."

"How old was he?"

"About to turn fifty."

"That's young. Awfully young."

"I guess. Mama didn't seem to be all broken up when he died. Maybe she was relieved. It was hard for her ever since they got married. He was gone a lot during the war—over on the west coast running a munitions depot, an officer. After the war he worked all the time when he wasn't drinking. She had all those kids to take care of and it weighed on her.

"You know, the odd thing and the one that always makes me mad is that Dad's family never took to Mama. Thought because she was from the country and didn't have a lot of education, she was beneath him. That made Dad madder than a swatted bee, too, but he'd never talk back to his own mother. Mama called her 'imperious' and when I looked that up, I saw what she was up against.

"Dad was Grandma's golden boy, her favorite. He was a college graduate, a sports hero, a smart, soft-spoken man. My grandma, I think, hoped Dad would take over the family business, general contracting in Johnson City, but he never had the least interest. He was a drunk and my grandmother never recognized or admitted that. I think it helped him keep drinking. Sure didn't make it any harder."

Hap sat for a long moment, digesting more than lunch. He'd heard enough from this boy who was opening up a vein and bleeding for him. Life had been difficult for Eb, but there was an acceptance in his explanations, one that said Eb was ready to move on.

"How you liking this single wing offense?" Hap said, changing the subject to something more in line with easy digestion. "You came from a T-formation, didn't you? You know, we never thought of this as a passing offense until you got here ..."

Monday, September 9, 12:30 p.m.
Smoky watched Harold Wiseman pull himself up for the tenth time on the V-shaped hydraulic door hinge on the front door of the science building, his chin touching the metal rod with each pull-up. Harold lowered himself and as he prepared to pull up for number eleven—trying to surpass Smoky's twenty-six pull-ups—J.D. Banner walked out the side door of the administration building, heading straight toward them.

Banner was sixty-four years old and finally won the principal's job he so desperately wanted for two decades when Bill Mulligan died in his office chair one morning. That was the early fall of 1960. Mulligan keeled over with a heart attack and never knew it. J.D. Banner was named interim, then permanent principal because he'd been at Toe River High School ten years longer than anybody else, not because he was the best person for the job. The feeling among the teachers was that half a dozen people on the tiny staff were better suited to lead the school.

Banner was a large, sloppy, plodding man in a rumpled and worn brown wool suit who lacked imagination, held strong John Birch political views, and was not well liked among his peers. He tended to be a pious bully. Banner padded through the halls of the school, making his rounds, as he called it, several times a day, looking for some wayward kid to make an example. He was in luck today.

The old man opened the door to the science building as Harold pulled himself up for the thirteenth time, and as the door opened and the V-shaped hydraulic rod moved outward, Harold, not expecting the sudden movement, fell. "What's goin' on here, boys?" Banner said in his slow drawl, dragging out the "o" in "boys."

Smoky thought fast. "We was checking out this door," he said. "It's been hard to open."

"Swain, I can see and what I saw was Wiseman doing pull-ups on the door. That ain't what that door was made for. Down to the office."

Banner saw them separately, got admissions of wrongdoing from each and gave them a choice of punishment. First, ten swats with the big board hanging on the wall that he called "the board of education." He thought that was funny. The board had holes drilled into it to make it sting more than it would normally, and this was a substantial piece of wood. Banner had a boy he was punishing for some minor offense take the board to shop class and bore the holes before the principal used it on him.

The second choice sounded innocuous enough. Learn Chapter 8 of Ecclesiastes in the Bible, the one about obeying authority and repeat it back to Banner without missing a word.

Harold took the paddle, Smoky Chapter Eight.

Smoky saw Harold that afternoon before football practice, as they were dressing and Harold showed him a backside that was battered and bruised far beyond any school whipping Smoky'd ever seen. Harold was cut and some of the bruises looked as mean as anything you'd get in football practice. "I never been hit so hard by anybody," said Harold. "I had to stand up through my last two classes. I swear to god, I almost cried. That man's crazy."

Harold got off easy, Smoky was to learn.

Smoky was not a good student. He was not even a marginal student. He was a year behind his class and barely kept up. Teachers passed him mostly because they liked him and knew he'd never even dream of going to college. Memorizing an entire chapter of the Bible, especially one as difficult as Ecclesiastes, would take everything he had and it would require time. When his dad, a lay preacher, found out he was being punished, he'd almost certainly add to the penalty, as well.

Smoky was to report to Banner's office every Monday morning before school and recite what he knew of the chapter. When he recited perfectly, his time would be served.

It took six weeks of some of the most intense work he'd ever done for Smoky to recite the chapter without flaw.

The Elk River Boy in Harold understood that this punishment—far out of proportion to the crime—was not something he could let go if he were to retain his dignity and the dignity of the designation, "Elk River Boy." It had meaning and part of that meaning was that one did not do injustice to those from the River.

Harold would get even. He invited Smoky to join him, explaining that his participation wasn't a requirement, though it was certainly an honor.

J.D. Banner was a man with a surprise awaiting him at some point in the near future when he least expected it.

Monday, September 9, 5:45 p.m.

Miss Lilly sat in her office off the auditorium, grading the first pop quiz of the year. She was waiting to talk to Ellen Hughes and Homer Vance, a couple of square dancers who should know better.

Among the first rules Miss Lilly established in 1949 for her inaugural team at Toe River High School was that square dancers should not date each other. It was a rule that was consistently broken, but she had to ride herd on it every chance she got because it could cause enormous discipline, unity and chemistry problems if these hormone-controlled young people ran into any of the inevitable conflicts. Miss Lilly heard rumors about Homer and Ellen spending intensive amounts of time together since the spring and it was time to confront the two of them.

Miss Lilly could only grimace when recalling some of the lengths square dancers went to hide their amorous activities. A few years ago, a senior named Bon Heath dressed up as a girl so he could sit with Bonnie Presnell (yes, Bon and Bonnie, whose favorite singing duo was Paul and Paula) in the back of the activities bus for a trip to Charlotte and Columbia where exhibitions were scheduled over two days. That incident became legendary because Bonnie wound up pregnant and her parents blamed Miss Lilly. Not Bonnie. Not Bon. Miss Lilly.

It was the year Toe River failed to win Old Smoky. Bonnie announced she had to leave the team a week before the Mountain Youth Jamboree and when she told Miss Lilly why, there was no choice but to toss Bon, as well. They were the caller couple. Toe River nearly won the trophy anyway—in fact there was still a lot of argument and bitterness about the decision to give it to Sky High—in one of Miss Lilly's near-miracle finishes.

Boys and girls sat apart on the bus on longer trips and they were always on opposite ends of the motels they stayed in when that was possible. Distance did not slow down some of these late-night lovers. Spot bed-checks resulted in too many people to a bed on rare occasions and expulsions of important dancers resulted.

Romance was as natural for dance couples as it might have been for movie leads. Dancers spent a lot of time together, physically close, working out problems and finding solutions together, sharing space and time for hours on end. Most of the pairs liked each other, respected each other and dated other people. But not all, and the younger they were, the more likely they were to try to fudge the rule.

Homer and Ellen were juniors in their first season as

starters. They were the first alternate couple last year and actually danced a lot because of sickness and accidents. It had been a year of broken toes and ankles and the flu epidemic that nearly laid out the entire team at one time or another.

Homer was a linebacker on the football team, a starter, and Ellen was Toe River's finest basketball player of either gender, an all-region guard who ran Miss Lilly's team with unquestioned authority. She would be captain of the next team as a junior and an all-state candidate.

They were good looking kids. He was stocky, bow-legged and stoop-shouldered, dark hair and eyes with a brooding aura. She was small and delicate, but unusually limber and lithe with huge, sparkling blue eyes and complexion other girls tried to find in bottles.

They arrived at Miss Lilly's office precisely on time, as was their habit, took their seats and their medicine, which they knew was coming. They denied nothing, but they didn't offer anything either. Finally, Miss Lilly put it bluntly. "Are you two sexually involved?" she asked, a direct question they had not anticipated from a teacher.

They looked at each other, then at her, then back at each other. Homer started to speak and Ellen squeezed his arm. "Miss Lilly," she said, in a measured, controlled voice that belied the herd of butterflies panicking in her stomach, "that is an *awfully* personal and inappropriate question. Homer and I dance for you and for the school and we give you our best every day. We have never once embarrassed the school. We are good students who work in the community, are involved in our churches and we are honest people.

"I don't think it is fair for you to assume we are involved in something that is forbidden just because we enjoy each other's company and because we study together. Homer is important to me and I think I am to him, too, and I will not have somebody coming between us, based on rumors and assumptions."

Miss Lilly pushed her chair away from her desk and put her hands on the edge of the desktop, her arms at full length. She knew Ellen Hughes to be smart and confident, but this answer from a sixteen-year-old was far more than she anticipated. She was taken aback and scurried to gather herself for a response.

Ellen's mother and father were college professors, he at Appalachian State in philosophy, she an English teacher at Lees-McRae Junior College up the road in Banner Elk.

"Ellen," Miss Lilly said slowly, looking straight into the young woman's piercing, but soft eyes, "I am not trying to invade your privacy and I don't want to discourage friendships. But this team and you kids are my responsibility when you are on square dance time. That makes me a surrogate parent to you, in addition to being your coach. We don't allow dancers to date each other because the risk to the team—and frankly, the risk to you students—is too great. I can't supervise you all the time and I have to trust you to do what is right.

"I'm going to ask you this one time and I want an honest answer, a direct answer and I will accept it unless and until I learn that it is not the truth. Are you doing anything that would hurt or embarrass this square dance team?"

"No, ma'am," said Ellen, forcefully and directly. Homer shook his head.

"I'll see you at practice," Miss Lilly said, hoping she had not made a mistake.

Tuesday, September 10, 3:30 p.m.
An angry Coach Buster Woodson called Monday's practice "the sorriest exhibition of uninspired, lazy gold-bricking I've seen in twenty years at this school" and he promised Tuesday would be different. He scheduled a scrimmage. This would be war, first offense against first defense with game conditions and none of those colored "no hit" T-shirts quarterbacks got to wear under these circumstances. Everybody was a target because everybody sandbagged Monday's practice, he yelled.

Mickey Buchanan's face was alight before practice. This was a scenario built for him. He had a license to pull every dirty, cheap trick he knew and maybe even take out a leg or two with a chop block.

Smoky stopped by Eb's locker as Eb was pulling his practice jersey over his head. "Don't worry chief," he said. "That red-haired bastard's gotta get by me before he gets to you."

"Thanks," Eb said absently. He hadn't even considered Mickey Buchanan until Smoky mentioned him. Eb reckoned that he probably ought to watch out, since he'd have the ball and Mickey would be trying to beat Carl Blackthorn to him. That was a fearsome pair for any offensive player to face.

Since several players were on both the starting offense and the starting defense, Woodson assigned them to the side of the line he thought they played best, which is why Smoky and Harold, who played both ways, would be blocking. That helped Eb's situation, if only marginally.

For a good hour, the intense grunting, groaning and cracking of pads broke the hot afternoon air. It was hard, clean football, until Eb heard a loud *CRACK!* and saw Ben Little lying on the ground holding his right knee. Mickey got up off the ground near him, that awful, mean grin.

Ben was a sophomore halfback trying to block Mickey on a sweep. Smoky had the defensive tackle on that play and Ben was to block the end—Mickey—while Eb darted between them. Eb was through opening as he heard that nauseating sound and reflexively looked back just as Carl Blackthorn hit him like a swinging wrecking ball. Eb went down hard, the air coming out. Carl heard Eb wheezing, gasping for the breath he'd had knocked out. He reached down, grabbed Eb's pants by the belt front and pulled up, arching his back and re-filling Eb with air. Carl lifted Eb off the ground by the shoulder pads and said, "You alive, man?" Eb nodded absently and walked back to Ben, who was crying as he was attended by the coaches.

Eb knew Ben as a quiet kid who did what he was supposed to, worked harder than most and had a good future. Mickey had no business cheaping his knee, thought Eb, anger flaring in his eyes.

In the huddle minutes later Eb called "trap right, sweep on two" as Ben was helped to the sideline. That meant Smoky would let Mickey run untouched into the backfield. The blocking back was to take a short snap from center and hand it to the wingback running toward the spot Mickey vacated. Normally, a guard would run in front of Phillip Branscon, the blocking back, but Eb told Smoky to block straight ahead. Eb would take on Mickey.

Eb wanted this one and Smoky, the usual blocker, could smell his anger, so he didn't argue. Eb had never wanted to hurt anybody on a football field before, but he was so mad that his offensive teammates thought Mickey would be lucky if he got out of this one with all his parts.

Eb set up in his stance and barked, "Down. Ready-set. Hut-one, hut-two…" and the ball went to Phillip, who spun and handed it to Perry Lafferty, streaking in front of him. Eb saw Mickey charge into the backfield, snarling and all but foaming at the mouth, before Eb unloaded everything he had in the middle of Mickey's chest.

The sharp crack of Eb's shoulder pad on Mickey's sternum almost stopped the play. Mickey went up in the air and sailed backward to the ground, hitting with a sickening thud, like a dropped watermelon. Eb landed hard on top of him, driving him further into an unconscious state. Eb resisted the urge to get up and kick Mickey.

Mickey lay there not moving for minutes, coaches working over him, players slapping Eb on the shoulder pads and the butt, whispering, "Good hit, man. That sonofabitch deserves every breath he can't take."

Eb looked over at the sideline where three people knelt over Ben, who was still crying. It was bad and they'd find out later Ben was gone for the year, a torn ligament. He never came back. Eb's vicious hit wouldn't atone for Mickey's savagery, but he felt better anyway.

After a few long minutes, Mickey was up, groggy and steaming. "Awright, bring it in," said Buster Woodson. He addressed the team as it circled him, sweating and breathing hard, some players kneeling, others sitting, a few lying down. "That is football as I remember it," he said. "Hard-nosed, clean and with purpose. This is not the same team I saw yesterday, but I hope it's the team I see tomorrow and for the rest of the season. You deserve an early day. Take it and get some rest." Eb looked at Smoky standing beside him, leaned in and whispered, "Early day? We've been scrimmaging for an hour and a half."

"Let me say one more thing," said Woodson. "Mickey Buchanan, next time you take a cheap shot at one of our players, or anybody else's players, I'm personally going to kick your sorry ass so high, you'll wear it as a pink collar. You got that?"

Mickey smirked. Hap walked over quickly, slapped a hand hard on Mickey's shoulder pad and Mickey's face went blank. He knew trouble when he felt it.

Hap Hilton walked with Eb toward the locker room minutes later. "Got your dander up a little, huh? Kid, I didn't think you had that kind of emotion in you. You always seem so dang rational and controlled. That was some hit. You made a lot of allies out there today." He trotted on off ahead of Eb, looking for Smoky.

Eb wondered if he had enough left in his gas tank for square dance practice.

Wednesday, September 11, 3:10 p.m.

Out of mild curiosity, Eb stopped by Buster Woodson's cage in the football locker room and said, "Coach, we got our first road game Friday, but we don't have our road uniforms. When do you give them out? I wanna see if those green jerseys bring out the green of my eyes." Eb smiled at his joke. Woodson missed it. "Me 'n Smoky's the only ones hadn't seen 'em and he's got green eyes, too."

Woodson paused for a moment from drawing up a play, looked at Eb and chuckled. "You got all the uniform you're

gonna get, El-bert," he said. "We only have the whites. I don't
know what you were used to before you got here, but this ain't
your fancy big-school program with a shirt for every occasion.
We don't have formal, informal, gray flannel and business
casual uniforms. We have what Bob Neyland over at the
University of Tennessee called 'work clothes,' white shirts
with numbers, white pants, white hat and black shoes. We
could pull out the green baseball socks and fancy it up, but we
don't need to do that. We play football at Toe River. We ain't
goin' to no fashion show."

That was more answer than Eb was looking for, but
everybody seemed to want to increase their word count when
he was around.

"Bet you think our school colors are green and white," said
Woodson, continuing his dissertation. "Ain't done it. They're
green and gold. Always have been, but a two-color jersey costs
two dollars more than a one-color jersey. Gold helmet costs
more than a white helmet 'cause you got to paint it. We're
'bout the only school I know of that can't afford but one school
color. Couple of years ago Lees-McRae Junior College gave us
some of their old helmets and they were gold. More yellow, to
tell the truth. Trouble was, our other helmets were white. So we
sprayed 'em with cans of paint. By the end of the first quarter
of the first game, half the paint had come off and we looked
like a bunch of mis-matched ragamuffins.

"One of our former players, who has a car dealership over
in Spruce Pine, took up the Lees-McRae hats and painted them
white in his body shop, so everything matched. That was the
last time we had more than one color and until this county gets
some money, it ain't likely to change. Hell, we don't even pay
half our coaches."

"Thanks, coach," Eb said, backing out of the cage, escaping
the lecture. This was his introduction to football's poverty level
and he'd see a good bit more of it in the days and weeks ahead.

Friday, September 13, 7 p.m.

Game time was thirty minutes away and the Toe River football team was only now getting off the bus, not even dressed for its first road game. Game time was being delayed to 8 p.m., Woodson told the team. The lead bus had a flat tire before it drove ten miles and the tire took an hour to replace. The team walked around restlessly during that hour with butterflies taking over.

The week before, Hap scouted Bakersville, a school thirty miles southwest of Toe River at the foot of Roan Mountain over narrow and winding roads. He said this was a game the Red Tail Hawks ought to win, but there were some areas where Bakersville could give Toe River trouble. From Eb's point of view, the defensive backs would be a problem. Two of the three were all-conference and the other was a senior, two-year starter. The defense had a couple of quick linebackers and a lineman, Leland McKendree, who was a good enough prospect that you could recognize the scouts in the press box by the color of their jackets. It was easy to pick out both Carolinas, Georgia, Tennessee, Maryland, West Virginia. Games at this level rarely attracted big-time scouts. The smaller schools were there, too, spread through the crowd in their easy-to-see school jackets. McKendree was out of their league, but several other players, including Eb, would love to be offered a scholarship by a small school.

Because of Bakersville's veteran defensive backs, Eb McCourry wouldn't be able to loft the ball to Terry the way he had last week. Barry Bates would need to start earning his keep as a hammering, meat-and-potatoes runner and the team's linemen were going to have to deal with McKendree.

When Eb stepped off the bus onto the gravel parking lot at Bakersville High School, he looked over to where a group of Toe River people were gathering and saw Joyce and Janice Watkins getting out of a green 1960 Pontiac Bonneville. Their dad let them have the car for the evening for the drive to the back-side of Roan Mountain. Joyce was glowing in a green outfit with a green ribbon in her hair.

He hoisted his equipment bag over his left shoulder and walked toward the locker room to get dressed. "Rack 'em up, Mr. All-American," Joyce said, smiling and looking at Eb. Harold was behind Eb and Eb didn't want to see his face. Harold would have to block that forty-pounds-heavier bull elephant tonight and it wouldn't be good to piss Harold off by getting too involved with his girlfriend tonight. Eb smiled and nodded politely at Joyce and kept walking.

***

In the middle of the second quarter, Toe River sat on a shaky six to nothing lead. Carl Blackthorn intercepted a pitchout, something only Carl Blackthorn, who played with the quickness of a chipmunk, could have done. He scored with it after running forty yards. You could hear his jubilant, celebratory scream as he crossed the goal line. This full-blooded Cherokee was joy on the football field. The center snap for the extra point kick sailed over Eb's head and Barry Bates, the kicker, tried to pick it up and run with it, but McKendree the hot prospect knocked him flat with a swing of a huge arm.

This guy was fearsome and he was devastating Toe River's offense, which had not gained a yard on four possessions. The Hawks punted three times and fumbled a third-down handoff. Harold was out of his league trying to block Leland McKendree by himself.

After the fumble Eb stood sweating and helmetless beside Coach Buster Woodson. He leaned in and said in a low voice, "We gotta get Harold some help. He can't handle the big boy."

Woodson looked at Eb and said, "What do you suggest? Our plays are set and the blocking assignments aren't all that easy to play around with during a game."

"We need to trap him," Eb said. "We need to throw some screen passes and run some draw plays. On every one of those plays, we gotta get a back or a second lineman to at least chip McKendree on a shoulder after blocking his own man. We have boys who've been playing this offense a while and they know what to do, coach. I think some general instruction will get it done. Trust the team."

Woodson responded curtly: "Get them together and tell them that. It's your offense."

Bakersville was driving on Toe River with a minute and a half to go in the second quarter when Carl slapped down another pitchout and fell on it at the Hawks' thirty-yard line. Eb, who had pulled the offense together on the sideline and told the players of the new blocking plan, looked across his choir huddle and said, "Remember to help on the big boy. Left end across, wingback curl on one." It was a quick pass to the flat that Perry Lafferty could easily break for a long gain if he caught it. The defensive back on that side knew the play, though, and he'd be ready to jump it.

As Perry broke the huddle, Eb said, "Stop and go, banana." That meant Perry would run the curl pattern and stop it where he would normally catch the pass, but when the defensive back broke on Eb's passing motion, Perry'd take off for the opposite corner of the end zone and Eb would throw the ball there. It would take time to develop and the big boy would be bearing down relentlessly.

Eb took the snap, looked left and faked the throw as the defensive back jumped. If Eb had thrown, the ball would have been intercepted for a touchdown. But now Lafferty was heading wide open for the end zone and that monster defensive tackle was bearing down on Eb. McKendree ran over Harold and let loose a scary scream. Eb had to ignore him and throw the ball. He knew he was going to get murdered, but the ball had to be gone. At the instant Eb drew back to pass, Barry Bates crossed in front of Eb and hit the big boy hard enough to slow him a step, but not enough to stop him.

As Eb was going down under the full weight of giant Leland McKendree, he heard cheering from Toe River's section of the stands. He didn't see the play and he lay on the ground struggling for air as Lafferty crossed the goal line. Eb didn't mind. Toe River was up thirteen to nothing after the extra point kick.

The help blocking Leland McKendree was what the offense needed. Toe River moved the ball nicely in the second half and scored twice more. Barry broke a fifty-three-yard touchdown run on a powerful burst up the middle. He got a block on McKendree from Eb, who did not like to block, but was bound to do his part.

Joyce met Eb in the middle of the field afterwards as he was shaking Leland McKendree's hand, telling him what a handful he was. "You look good even when you look bad," she said, taking note of a big bruise on Eb's cheek where Leland had laid him out. Joyce looked at Leland directly, put her hand on his big bicep and said, "Big 'un, you almost had me to deal with after you clocked my quarterback."

Leland, towering over Eb, grinned, threw his head back and laughed heartily.

"Yes, ma'am, I reckon I did," he said.

Joyce smiled at both boys and ran to catch up with Harold. She slid her hand through his arm and quietly walked off the field with him. Eb wistfully watched her round bottom swing.

"Pretty girl," said Leland McKendree.

"She's that," Eb said. "She is surely that. Where you think you might go to school next year? Looks like you got choices."

"I'd say you got a few, too," said Leland McKendree. "That was some offense you engineered tonight. I watched you lead your team like I haven't seen a high school quarterback do before. You need to transfer over here to Bakersville and play for us." They both laughed.

***

On the way back to the school, Woodson went back to where Eb was sitting with Gaylen, about the middle of the bus, and asked Gaylen if he could have the seat for a bit. Woodson got right to the point. "You took over this team tonight," he said after sliding into the stiff bench seat.

"I'm not trying to interfere with your job," Eb said, almost apologetically, wondering if Woodson was going to bench him.

Woodson smiled. "That's not what I mean, Elbert." Eb let the "Elbert" go. Hap was right, it wasn't important.

"This is your team now," said Woodson. "You became a leader tonight, late in the second quarter, and the others will be looking to you from now on. What you did was damn presumptuous and bordered on insubordination, but you were right and that's the kind of leadership that separates a team from the pack."

Eb had to let Woodson's words sink in. Nobody'd ever left him in charge of anything before. *So this is leadership*, Eb thought. All he did was tell Coach to trust the team. It was a good team, an experienced team. The players had to adjust to the unexpected—and you can hear about a player like Leland McKendree until your ears ring, but it's not like trying to block him or getting knocked cold by him.

"A coach from Western Carolina came over and said 'hello' after the game," Eb said. "Said he came to see McKendree, but he liked the way I played tonight."

"Keep playing like that and you'll get more attention," said Woodson.

The team was quiet the next thirty minutes, rolling into a late summer night with the first hint of fall in the evening chill.

Eb had a lot to think about with this new responsibility, with some attractive girls confusing, tempting and exciting him, and with an early trip to Asheville Saturday for a square dance exhibition at something called the Grove Park Inn. His first dance trip.

If the cup of his life filled up any more, he'd need a mop.

Saturday, September 14, 7:45 a.m.
The bus was to leave from the school at nine o'clock for the run south to Asheville. There was a convention at this fancy hotel there and a big group of teachers wanted to see some authentic mountain culture. The Toe River High School Square

Dance team was part of it, the entertainment for a luncheon in a dining room that Miss Lilly told the team was bigger than Poland. "The fireplaces in the Grove Park Inn take whole tree trunks," she said. Eb and the square dance team would see she was not exaggerating. He lived in Asheville, but had never been to the Grove Park Inn, nor had he visited the Biltmore House or half a dozen other famous tourist sites he couldn't afford. He'd been to the graves of Thomas Wolfe and O Henry at Riverside Cemetery, but that was free.

After a quick breakfast, Eb hurried back over to Little Boys Cottage to take a shower and change clothes. Miss Lilly wanted the team clean and neat, "spit-shined," she called it, even on the bus. Maryellen Streit, Judi Aldridge and Eb were to meet one of the house parents, Bill Geiger from over at Big Boys, on the quad at eight-thirty for the ride down to the school.

Eb heard Maryellen's best cheerleader's voice behind him, "El-BERT! Wait up. One of your public needs a word with you." Maryellen was nothing if not a smartass, thought Eb.

"Smartass," he said. "What do you want? I got things to do that don't include cheerleaders who don't know my name."

Maryellen had just fed Eb one of those oversized cowboy breakfasts in celebration of the twenty-seven to zip win over the Bakersville Bull Mastiffs, but her levity disappeared as soon as she dropped into step with him. "You got it bad for Joyce Watkins, don't you?"

"I wouldn't say that," Eb said. "She's got a boyfriend and he don't look a hell of a lot like me."

"I'm sure you've heard this, but you really don't want to mess with the girlfriend of one of those nutcases from down on Elk River, and that would be her. Harold is probably the nicest and closest to sane of all of them, but that's relative. He's still not somebody to trifle with. I think every one of those boys will wind up in prison some day and I don't want it to be because of what they did to you."

"Thank you for your concern, Mother Maryellen," Eb said. "I'm not sure what I feel about Joyce and I sure as hell don't know what she feels for me. Things with girls have always been pretty clear for me. 'No' is what it usually comes down to. Maybe this is another 'no,' but Joyce sure makes me feel better than anybody has and that's hard not to think about."

"Just be careful, buddy," said Maryellen, putting the palm of her hand in the middle of his back and rubbing lightly. "You're a good guy and I don't want anything bad happening to you."

"You'd better go get dressed," Eb said, turning toward his dorm.

"Don't worry about Maryellen," she said. "The world's most beautiful women have their secrets. I'll be ready." With that, she smacked his butt, picked up the tempo and broke off toward Big Girls Cottage to get pretty.

Saturday, September 14, 11:30 a.m.

Miss Lilly stood at the front of the bus looking out over the team, like she had something to say. The bus was behind schedule, passing Burnsville, rolling down U.S. Nineteen-and-Twenty-Three, about thirty-five miles north of Asheville. "Let me tell you about where you're going and who you're going to dance for," she said. "You should enjoy this." She didn't sound convinced about the last part.

Eb studied the back of Joyce's head. She was in the front of the bus, sitting with Buster—the caller couple and captains.

Miss Lilly looked at the small white pad in her hand. "The Grove Park Inn," she said, "is a big, impressive, prestigious hotel in the north end of Asheville. It was built in nineteen-thirteen of stones mined from Sunset Mountain, which stands behind it. William Jennings Bryan spoke at the dedication.

"People like Thomas Edison, Rockefeller, Harvey Firestone, Houdini, Will Rogers, Henry Ford, Scott and Zelda Fitzgerald and a number of presidents stayed there. Elbert Hubbard stayed there." Miss Lilly winked at Eb.

Joyce turned her face to him and grinned. Eb discovered later that his namesake was a writer, publisher, artist and

79

philosopher—all of which he intended to become.

"The lobby is nearly half a football field long," said Miss Lilly, putting the size into a perspective the dancers and football players would immediately understand. "Fireplaces hold twelve-foot logs and have elevators in them to take bags to the upper floors. I'll say that again: the fireplaces have elevators in them." She paused to let that fact sink in, but nobody even nodded.

"Scott Fitzgerald, who wrote *The Great Gatsby,* which some of you've studied, stayed in two suites in nineteen-thirty-five and thirty-six and wrote *Taps at Reveille,* one of his lesser-known books, and some short stories there. The room is pretty much as it was when he stayed in it, including the inkwell, which splattered some ink on the desk."

In the back of the bus, Mickey Buchanan yawned a little louder than necessary, folded his arms and closed his eyes.

"Off to the side of the Inn is Biltmore Homespun where some of the best wool in the world is spun and made into clothes," Miss Lilly continued, watching Mickey drift off. "There's an antique car collection on the grounds of the Homespun shops." Eb thought of all this opulence and knew it had nothing to do with his ragamuffin dance group.

Miss Lilly paused and surveyed her troops. "You're going to dance for nearly one thousand teachers from all over North Carolina," she said, watching several of her dancers perk up. "They are social studies and history teachers and some of them teach courses in North Carolina heritage and culture. One of the speakers is the head of Appalachian Studies at Appalachian State Teachers College. She can tell you a whole lot about yourselves and your families. I hope we have time to listen to her address."

Mickey yawned forcefully again and Joyce reached across the bus aisle and punched him, frowning when he opened his eyes. He ignored her.

Miss Lilly paused to see if any of this was sinking in. It was having some impact with the students she'd expect to be interested, but rolled off the others, some of whom had to be thinking, "Oh, no! Not a lecture!" Mickey wasn't thinking anything. He was open-mouth sleeping, ever-so-close to snoring.

"The Sky High team will be there," said Miss Lilly. That got the attention of the entire team, even Mickey, who jolted awake. "It'll either go on before us or after us. I'm not sure of the schedule, but either way we get a chance to see the team that desperately wants to replace us as the premier square dance program in the region."

"Ain't happenin'," said Mickey. "Damn bunch of queer city ballet dancers is all they got. We'll kick their teeth in."

"Mickey, shut up!" said Miss Lilly. "I will not tolerate that kind of talk." Smoky, who had been at the back of the bus, moved to the empty seat beside Mickey, the seat nobody wanted, just in case. Mickey closed his eyes again.

Miss Lilly continued, a seriousness in her voice that turned the color of new asphalt: "This is a homemade team—some say a 'bought' team—of dancers from the North Carolina School of Modern Dance and another elite ballet and modern dance school in Asheville. I think most of you already know that. It has a coach from the upper reaches of the dance world in New York City and more money than some small mountain schools we know and love have in their entire school budget. Sky High represents a bazooka pointing at us and we will get an idea what we're up against in about an hour."

Eb's pulse was running full throttle with the announcement even though there was almost no chance he would dance at this event. He only imagined what the starters felt.

There was a hush in the bus and it didn't break before the bus reached Asheville. Within the hour the driver pulled into the parking lot of a magnificent stone building and the team self-consciously got off the bus, staring at porters and people in suits. A polished, youngish woman in a slim gray suit, pink blouse and pearls greeted Miss Lilly, shook hands and spoke pleasantly. The woman led the team inside the lobby with the fireplaces.

Miss Lilly called the team over to a corner of the lobby. "We're going on in fifteen minutes," she said.

Boy! They don't waste any time, Eb thought.

"We have a room set aside so we can go through our routine, but we don't have much time."

Square dancers walked down a long hallway lined with photographs of famous former guests. Eb stopped for a moment at the portrait of Elbert Hubbard as the team walked into a large meeting room with chairs and tables pulled away from the center of the room. Hubbard's black and white photo was of a wide-faced man with sharp, dark eyes, a wide-brimmed hat and a look of intense intelligence. Eb liked the look.

"Buster, gather up your dancers," said Miss Lilly, full-throated and in control.

***

The Toe River team stood to the side of the packed ballroom, rimmed with twelve-foot windows, trimmed in heavy, ornate curtains. The dancers watched the Land of the Sky High School Constellation square dancers mount a temporary stage, put together for this exhibition. The word "pretty" came to mind as Eb examined this team of near professionals. Pretty costumes, pretty kids, pretty coach, pretty imposing.

Smoky leaned over to Eb and whispered, "See their coach, the dark woman with the long black hair?"

"Yeah. Beautiful. Doesn't look like a coach."

"That's Gaylen's girlfriend's sister," Smoky said. "I went down to Old Fort with him and she was home for the weekend."

"Oh shit," Eb whispered. "She's the New York dancer?"

"That's her. She's stiff and formal, but I liked her."

Toe River's team watched the Land of the Sky High School dancers glide through a flawless routine to a standing ovation. The Asheville team looked polished and deeply experienced.

Eb noted the dancers didn't smile, even when they took what he considered a grand bow. No emotion at all. Mannequins, Eb thought.

But they could dance.

Sky High hurriedly left the stage and Buster and Joyce led sixteen dancers to the center, shoes sliding, smiling warmly, engagingly. They looked approachable, easy to like, Eb thought.

The routine was an old one that everybody had danced a thousand times—except Eb, maybe, but he wasn't dancing. Still, the performance was ragged and the team looked nervous. Twice, dancers bumped into each other and several of them were out of step at various junctures. Buster looked furious through that big painted-on smile and Joyce seemed uneasy. Eb didn't want to look at Miss Lilly's face.

The ovation was enthusiastic, almost joyful. But this audience didn't know good square dancing from Russian folk dancing and it wasn't judging anything. These teachers were being entertained and the smiling Toe River dancers were entertaining even when they weren't fully competent.

Miss Lilly was not entertained or amused. And she certainly was not satisfied.

The team gathered in the hall, embarrassed and fidgeting, knowing something unpleasant was coming. "We're going back to the school to do some work," Miss Lilly said abruptly. "This won't do. You are better than I saw out there. You will have to be better than this or you will be *former* champions."

As the dancers boarded the bus, Miss Lilly walked toward Arlene Shining Feather on the other side of the room, to introduce herself. Arlene was talking warmly to Smoky. They hugged briefly and Smoky passed Miss Lilly on his way to the bus. He looked at the ground, not wanting eye contact with her in this mood.

Part III

Sunday, September 15, 12:05 p.m.

Eb heard Maryellen Streit yelling after him, splitting the stillness of a bright, warm Sunday afternoon. He slipped out of the Beech Mountain Children's Home campus church as the choir sang "Holy, Holy, Holy," eager to get out of his dress clothes and over to the lunchroom before all the kids got there. The younger boys wanted to sit where Eb sat because of his football success, and he wasn't up for it today. The football game Friday, the trip Saturday, the extra square dance practice into the evening and some creeping loneliness left him without much in the tank. He wanted to eat and sneak up to his room for a nap.

That would be about as close to heaven as he could imagine getting—and about as realistic a goal as getting to heaven, if Maryellen Streit had her way, which she usually did.

"Will you wait for me, El-BERT!?!" she yelped, running up behind him.

"Maryellen, I'm not up for anything this afternoon. Nothing. No English homework, no chopping wood, no dance practice, no fishing, no nothing. I'm beat."

"I got a girl for you."

"Maryellen, dammit! I don't want a girl. I told you about me and girls."

"You and a girl who has a boyfriend is what you told me about. I have a friend, a good friend, who wants to meet you and she's coming by after lunch so we can go for a walk up to the lake."

The eighteen-acre, man-made lake was a quarter of a mile from campus and was quiet, lovely and a hotbed for romantics most evenings. There were four canoes available and plenty of spots for solitude.

"Maryellen, does it hurt you to check with me before mapping out my life? I don't want a girl."

"It's Lizetta."

"Oh."

Those disciplined souls who could resist a twin assault from Audrey Hepburn and Natalie Wood had no chance against Lizetta McEntire, the best looking 17-year-old girl in five counties, as Eb had already heard.

They still told the story of the day Lizetta was late for school last year and rushed off without her bra. Boys hovered around every corner in school, waiting to get a glimpse of "them." It caused a sensation that was now legend.

Lizetta was Miss Avery County and Miss Rhododendron Festival. She won both tiaras at fifteen, the youngest contestant ever to do that. Lizetta hadn't looked fifteen since she was ten. She looked twenty-two now. She was bright, funny and talented in a number of ways that wouldn't show in a beauty pageant. She was sophisticated in ways that most boys at Toe River High School would never understand.

"Not interested," Eb said, surprising both Maryellen and himself.

"You're not interested in Lizetta McENTIRE!" Maryellen all but yelled.

"Maryellen, look at me," Eb said, staring hard into her eyes. "Where do I live? How much money do you think I have on me right now? How much do you think I might have in my room? Where is my car parked?" He paused to let the questions sink in.

"These are not unimportant questions. How in the hell am I going to date Lizetta McEntire, or anybody else—and that includes Joyce Watkins—without any means at all? I don't have a telephone. I'm a damn 'orphan.' What are we going to do, walk up to the lake four times a week?"

Eb was tired, snippy, angry and right on the edge of hurt. He was feeling sorry for himself, something that didn't usually happen.

"Settle down, big shot," said Maryellen, standing directly in front of Eb, her tiny shoes touching his, her head tilted back, looking straight up into his eyes. "Lizetta is not interested in going out with you because of what you have. It's about what and who you are."

"I don't know what I am. How would she know?" Eb's eyes were wet and he didn't want to show that to Maryellen or anybody else, but he didn't know how to turn off the powerful emotion he felt at this intense and introspective moment.

Maryellen took both his hands in hers. "Almost nobody ever dates Lizetta because she scares the hell out of them with her intelligence. I think that would be the first thing you'd like about her. Lizetta's a golden girl all right, but that wears thin when people don't expect anything of you except that you smile and look pretty. There's a lot to her and you're the one boy in school who would appreciate it. She's as smart as you—probably smarter—and I don't think that would put you off. It would attract you."

Eb looked at his shoes and thought about how intelligent and how pretty Joyce was. And how thoroughly unavailable.

"I don't like watching the way boys ogle Lizetta and treat her like some porcelain doll," said Maryellen. "The fact that you're so bonkers over Joyce, who is sharp, but not the prettiest in the sense that so many guys care about, says a lot. …"

"Joyce is as pretty as anybody I know!" Eb insisted. Maryellen talked right through his outburst.

"… Lizetta has good judgment and a level head," continued Maryellen, letting go of Eb's hands. "I think you two will get along. If it's not 'Splendor in the Grass,' you still haven't lost anything. So, will you shut up and let her like you?"

"This is embarrassing and I swear to god, I'd rather let Leland McKendree tackle me unblocked than be embarrassed," Eb said. He wiped his eyes as subtly as he could.

"Who's Leland McKendree? Don't answer that," said Maryellen. "Show up out here on the quad at one-thirty. There's a group of us walking up to the lake and you're going. It's not optional."

***

Eb skipped lunch because he was more tired than hungry after another Maryellen-sponsored monster breakfast. The short nap helped. Eb put on the long sleeved, light blue button-down Gant Oxford cloth shirt his college-football-playing brother gave him before heading for UT, a pair of khaki pants and his scuffed cordovan penny loafers to face the world and Lizetta McEntire. He knew his outfit was preppy and without imagination, but it was the best he had and close to all he had.

Lizetta was in the middle of a cluster of girls in front of the Big Girls Cottage, wearing a peach sun dress and a matching ribbon in her hair that held it off her face. Her hair was auburn, shoulder-length and shimmered in the sun. Her lightly tanned complexion was soft, natural and smooth, a beauty products ad waiting to be made. The sandals were peach and her bare legs looked like they belonged to a ballerina. She was about five-feet-one, but stood straight and looked taller. Eb walked toward her, his heart racing, his eyes unfocused.

"Hello, Eb," Lizetta McEntire said, smiling broadly, her bright, even teeth gleaming. She approached him briskly, her hand extended to shake his. It was the first time anyone at Toe River High School had called him by the name he preferred upon meeting him.

This would not hurt as much as he imagined, he thought, but he'd have to cooperate and see where it went.

"Did you see the Asheville Citizen-Times this morning?" Lizetta said.

Heck of an opening, Eb thought. "I don't get the paper."

"Bob Terrell, who writes a sports column, had a piece about your square dance team."

"No kidding? They don't even cover our football team. Why are they writing about the square dance team?"

"Probably because Sky High was dancing, too, over at the Grove Park, right? He was asking if the dynasty—the Toe River square dance dynasty—was over and he said he thought it might be, judging from the performances yesterday."

"That was an exhibition," Eb said, barely knowing what he was talking about, but taking the immediate defensive position. "Nothing was at stake. We'll do better when it is."

"I'll bet Toe River is a lot better if you're dancing," she said, a flirt that could not go unrecognized, even by Eb, who blushed.

"Thank you for thinking that," he said, turning redder than he wanted, "but if I'm on the floor, something bad has already happened and something worse is getting ready to."

She laughed out loud, a big, hearty laugh that had not a whit of self-consciousness about it. She sounded like she was well practiced at laughing.

"I liked what Miss Lilly said in the article," Lizetta said. "'These are Toe River High School dancers and they will show up when the time comes. It's their heritage.' That sounds like Miss Lilly. Always so confident."

They walked slowly, talking for nearly fifteen minutes, laughing intermittently, absently bumping shoulders, she touching his hand, his arm, looking straight into his eyes. He noted every touch, every look, every word. They were coming up on the lake.

"Where does 'Lizetta' come from?" Eb asked.

"That's a good question," she chuckled. "Mom once told me she and dad conceived me in the Hotel Lisette in Paris, but Dad says they've never been to Paris. He says it's the name of a Japanese World War II spy. I usually tell people it's Cherokee, since everybody who's ever lived in these mountains says there's some Cherokee in their families. Truth is I don't know the truth. Probably just an unusual word Mom thought up. That'd be like her. She's an artist."

Eb looked into Lizetta's captivating face as she talked. There was an unmistakable glow about her. "Wherever it comes from, it's pretty," he said. "Almost pretty enough for the girl who's wearing it." He blushed as he said that, but wanted to put it into words.

"Thank you, kind sir," she said looking straight into Eb's

eyes and nearly melting him. She took his hand and his heart leapt.

Eb picked up a flat rock and skipped it seven times into the center of the lake, which was about the size of two football fields "Nice," said Lizetta. "Now let me show you how to do that."

"Oh," said Eb, his voice climbing. "You're going to show the quarterback how to throw a pass?"

"Nope," said Lizetta. "I'm going to show Eb how to throw a rock across a lake, not to the middle of the lake." She picked up a flat gray oval, about an ounce and a half, cradled it between her thumb and forefinger, then went through a sidearm motion three times. She leaned slightly to her right, bent her knees, cocked her arm and let go a mighty fling. The rock bounced high, then settled into skip, skip, skip, ship, skippity, skippty, skippity, dribble, dribble, dribble, *CLONK!* as it hit the opposite bank.

"How'd you *DO THAT!*" he said. "You're not big enough to do that."

She grinned wide and punched his shoulder. "Don't underestimate, buddy," she said. "It'll be your downfall." Eb couldn't contain his free laugh.

"Well," said Eb, "Can I teach you to spit?" He hocked up a load and let fly, about 30 feet.

"Oh, god, that's impressive," said Lizetta, screwing up her face. "I'll concede spitting to you."

"If girls keep taking away our stuff," said Eb, feigning pitiful, "we won't have anything left but bodily functions. That's only because girls won't fart and belch in public and y'all don't pee at targets. I can belch the alphabet, but I bet you don't want to hear it." Eb was feeling it.

"Let's save that for a special moment," said Lizetta, putting her fingertip into the deep dimple in her right cheek. "What's next?"

"You know you only have one dimple?"

"Really?" said Lizetta. "How can you tell?" Eb let that one

drop.

"Would you care for ride in the royal barge, Miss McEntire, champion rock thrower?" Eb said, bowing slightly and trying to keep his composure. He pointed at an old aluminum canoe with a large dent in the port side. "I shall paddle."

"How gallant," Lizetta said. She pronounced a distinctly British gah-*lant* and dipped in mock curtsey. "Yes, my lord, I shall be quite honored."

Eb grinned and reached for her hand. She gave it to him with a flourish. He liked this confident, bold young woman with the wonderful laugh and the engaging ability to talk easily.

This was not the unapproachable Lizetta McEntire he imagined. This was a real girl, an open, likeable girl who liked him. She hadn't said "no" yet, either. Maybe she wouldn't.

Sunday, September 15, 5:27 p.m.
Lizetta and Eb slowly walked back toward Beech Mountain Children's Home, hand in hand, chattering at a brisk pace, laughing, interrupting, feeling like they'd grown up together. Hers was an active mind, one full of civil rights, women's movement, a growing and nasty war in a corner of Southeast Asia Eb never heard of, the arts, sports, college, career. Dancing and football—the immediate limits of Eb's universe— barely came up.

As they passed Big Girls Cottage at the edge of the campus, the one nearest the lake, Eb heard a commotion off to the left, looked and saw Maryellen engaged in a pulling contest with a thin, wiry man wearing a full, scraggly, black and gray beard. He looked dirty, drunk and mean.

Maryellen was screaming. The man yelled in a high-pitched, angry voice, "You're coming with me, girl! You're mine! Get your ass in the car!"

"Oh, no!" said Lizetta. "It's her father, the one she's trying to stay away from." The man pulled Maryellen toward the open door of a rusting 1949 Cadillac as she struggled with all the strength she had, pulling, twisting, hitting him in the mouth with a round-house punch and intensifying his anger. "You got-damn bitch!" her snapped as he whipped the palm of his right hand across the side of her head, making it jerk back.

Eb broke into a sprint, covering the 30 yards between him and Maryellen in seconds and he hit the small man in the center of his chest with the same kind block Mickey Buchanan felt. The man went down hard, hitting his head on the concrete with a thud, but came up furiously and wildly swinging. He hit Eb between the eyes with his ring hand and knocked him to the ground. This man was an experienced brawler and Eb was a seventeen-year-old kid who hadn't hit anybody with his fist since he was seven years old. But Eb was angry and feeling protective of his friend.

Eb sprang to his feet and closed on the man, got inside his hands and raised a knee into his crotch with force. The man buckled and as Eb started to hit him with his fist, he felt hands on both his arms, pulling him away. He watched as six-foot-six, two hundred and fifty pound Bill Geiger, the Big Boys' house parent, suddenly towered over Maryellen's father and said with a deep and expansive bass-voiced force, "Mr. Streit, get your skinny ass off this campus and don't you ever come back or I'll see to it that you get smacked in jail to stay. Now git!"

Seething, Maryellen's father got to his feet, holding his crotch, moaning and cussing. He swung into the battered Cadillac and tore out of the parking lot, screaming, "Got-dam sumbitch! You ain't heared the last of me!"

Maryellen ran to Eb and threw her arms around him. She was crying and her tears smeared on Eb's cheek. Lizetta stood slightly behind Maryellen looking at Eb's face with such tenderness that it made him weak.

She walked over to the two of them, put her arms around them and her head on Eb's shoulder. They stayed there for a while.

Eb silently wondered if Maryellen's father meant what he

said about coming back. That could get ugly.

Sunday, September 15, 7:58 p.m.

There was a tiny tapping at the door and Eb looked up from the essay he was writing for Colt Hill's class—the third in a week, this one on Elbert Hubbard, philosopher and writer—and said, "It's open, Ralphie, come on in. Aren't you supposed to be getting ready for bed?"

Ralphie Allison was a seven-year-old from Johnson City who came into the home pretty close to the same day Eb did. He latched on to Eb immediately and Eb couldn't push him away, even if he'd wanted to.

Ralphie's mama, daddy and baby sister were killed in a fire over the summer, and if Eb ever saw anybody in need of a friend, it was Ralphie Allison.

Ralphie tried to pull his unconscious mother out of the burning house, Eb was told, but he wasn't strong enough and a fireman had to fight the little fella tooth and nail to get him out of the blazing house.

"I don't go to bed 'til nine," said Ralphie, all but insulted by the suggestion of an eight o'clock bedtime. "A great big man's downstairs. He wants to see you."

"Well, Ralphie, let's go see who it is." Eb put his arm on Ralphie's shoulder and they walked down the steps. Hap Hilton sat in a big chair across the living room as Eb entered. "What's up, Hap?" he said.

The big man briskly covered the distance of the room, his hand extended and Eb shook it, puzzled. "Heard you had a dust-up here earlier," Hap said, slightly above a whisper.

"Let's go outside, Hap," Eb said. "I don't want to talk about this in front of the kids."

They found a bench on the quad and Eb explained what happened. "That's pretty much what Vance Leffler told me," said Hap. "Vance is a state trooper who covers this area and he got a call on it. Robert Wayne Streit, Maryellen's dad, was a classmate of mine and Vance's at Toe River High years ago.

He was trouble then and he's never been anything but.

"He became a second-level hoodlum down in Johnson City during the war after getting a 4F deferment because he was deaf in one ear. It never kept him from being fully engaged as a criminal or from treating his family like crap." Hap twisted in his seat, facing Eb more directly.

"Maryellen's up here at the home because she finally had enough and she had the gumption to threaten him with going to the law about what Robert Wayne's been doing all those years. She made him turn over custody of her to the home in order to keep her quiet. He done things to that girl and her mother that nobody'll ever know, but let me tell you, he's mean and my guess is you ain't seen the last of him."

"So, what am I supposed to do, Hap? Hide from him?" Eb stood and began pacing the porch.

"No, you can't do that, but you need to be aware that he could show up at any time, and that he will. Man's eaten alive with hate." Hap rose from his seat, approached Eb and put a big hand on his shoulder. "Look for things that ain't normal. Be on your toes and work with the rest of the boys here at your cabin to watch the property and to watch your back. Get as many of the kids involved as you can watching for him. They'll do that for you. Pretend it's a game. Vance will be patrolling here when he can, but he's got a wide area to cover."

Eb went back to his essay with a lot more on his mind than he cared to have.

Monday, September 16, 8:27 a.m.
Eb bent over his open locker trying to find his *Modern English Literature* text, the one he'd forgotten to take home for the weekend in the rush to get over to Bakersville, and felt a *whap!* on his butt. He quickly stood upright and looked left, in time to see Joyce Watkins entering Colt Hill's English class. She looked back and winked. "Lizetta?!?" she said, as much a statement as a question.

Monday, September 16, 11:45 a.m.

Eb exited Hap's geometry class, heading for his locker to get the lunch Maryellen packed for him. Maryellen swiped food from the kitchen and made lunches for him nearly every day, but today she piled it on. The Home had an arrangement with the Avery County Schools to pay for its children's lunches, but Eb got in too late to be part of that for this year, so at lunch he was on his own. Of course, he didn't usually have money to buy lunch, so it was Maryellen's lunch or no lunch. Eb suspected that the administration at the Home knew Maryellen was packing his lunch and chose to ignore it.

On days when Eb had football and square dance practices, it could mean nothing to eat from breakfast to breakfast the next day unless she packed his lunch and Eb could get somebody to sneak out a sandwich or something after supper and put it in his room. His buddy Ralphie, colluding with Judi Aldridge, who worked in the kitchen frequently, did that on the occasions when it was needed. Judi and Ralphie rarely failed.

Eb opened his locker and felt somebody beside him. "Hello, Mr. McCourry," said Lizetta McEntire. "Buy you lunch?" He held up his bag.

"Maryellen already did that," he said, "but if you'll pick up something in the lunchroom and join me behind the stadium in the buffalo grass, I'd like that a lot."

"Sounds lovely," she said with a chirp that made Eb feel good. "I brought lunch, too, so we'll have a picnic. Let me get it out of my locker. I try to avoid the lunchroom here. Not exactly health food."

As Lizetta turned to go to her locker, Joyce entered the hall, having just left Miss Lilly's room, and walked straight toward Eb.

"Hot date, Elbert?" she said with a bit of an edge.

"Mornin', Joyce," he said. "You sure look pretty today."

"Not as pretty as Lizetta McEntire," she said, tossing her head and passing him with a swish of her short skirt. She popped him on the butt with an English book again.

He didn't know how to take Joyce Watkins.

Wednesday, September 18, 8:44 a.m.
Colt Hill met Eb at the classroom door and Eb immediately threw up his hands and blurted out, "It's still a minute to class, sir."

"I want you to see me after class, Mr. McCourry" Colt Hill said, more mysteriously than was comfortable for Eb. He squirmed the next hour and barely heard anything that was said, worrying about what he might have done. At one point, as if far off in the background somewhere, Eb heard Colt Hill say, "...Mr. McCourry's excellent essay, which pointed out correctly the relationship between..." and it drifted off again.

"You want to see me?" Eb said as he tentatively approached Colt Hill's desk, seconds after the bell rang and the room cleared.

"Yes, Mr. McCourry, I want you on the school's newspaper staff. You can be a reporter/photographer. I'd like for you to start today." He picked up a pencil and began writing, as if that was the end of the conversation.

Eb was without words. He felt he was a writer, so this was a natural fit. He had no experience with cameras, but he wanted to learn and this would be an opportunity. He didn't have time and that was the reality.

Eb stammered and stuttered.

"Would you like to say something, Mr. McCourry?" Colt Hill asked, looking up from the paper he was grading.

"Can't," Eb forced out.

"Can't what, Mr. McCourry? Spit it out."

"Mr. Hill, I can't join the newspaper staff because I'm already playing football and I'm with the square dance team. There's not enough hours. Maybe after football season and after the Mountain Youth Jamboree ..."

"You have a study hall and a lunch hour that overlap," Colt Hill said, "giving you a nice span in the middle of the day to do the work of a newspaper reporter." He'd done his homework.

"I use that time to eat and to study," Eb said.

"Mr. McCourry, this is not a request. It is not optional. This is part of your English grade for the year. You can refuse the assignment and you will be graded with a zero for the year and this assignment represents one quarter of your overall grade."

Blackmail, thought Eb. Colt Hill was sitting there in a position of power with a Nazi principal to back him up and Eb had no choice. "What do I need to do, Mr. Hill?" Eb said, wanting to hit Colt Hill with something large and hard.

"We have an orientation for our new staff members Thursday during the lunch hour in this classroom." he said. "You may bring your lunch."

Eb, the writer. Now it was real, no more pretend. But this wasn't the way he wanted it to happen. And, if he could help it, this was not the way it would happen.

He stood outside the classroom minutes later and leaned up against the wall, feeling suddenly tired. There's got to be a way out of this, he thought. There's no changing Colt Hill, but he has a supervisor and his supervisor has a whole school board of supervisors. Maybe that's where the change could be made. It'd be worth the shot.

Thursday, September 19, 8:02 a.m.

Colt Hill parked his red VW bug in front of the school and left the keys in it, as usual. He did not notice Janice Watkins standing near the front door of the school watching him.

Occasionally, over the past three weeks Colt absently exited the school building, leaving for the afternoon and his car was not where he thought he left it. He found it behind the gym, beside the agriculture building in the garden area, behind the science building near the woods and, once, in the middle of the football field.

Colt Hill, a man who could be monumentally dense, did not yet understand that a practical joke was following closely behind him. On this day, Janice would take the car to the Time Square Restaurant and Soda Shop across the highway from the school and park the VW in the lot. She would leave the keys in it. Mr. Hill would find it after school, scratch his head, put a packet of papers to grade on the passenger seat and drive home. Janice would watch him and fall over laughing.

Janice Watkins, a tall, thin young woman who danced like shimmering moonlight on a crystal lake, was spectacularly coordinated, the team's female version of Mickey Buchanan—only as a dancer, of course. She was a sophomore, so Miss Lilly didn't elevate her in the routines, fearing an inflated sense of self-importance if that happened prematurely. But she needn't have worried. Janice Watkins took things as they came, was rarely serious about any of it and she never did less than her best.

But she had a practical joker streak in her that would not disappear.

Eb watched her move Mr. Hill's car several times in recent days and it finally occurred to him that she was not supposed to be doing this. After she parked it in the Time Square lot, Eb approached her and said, "Thank you, Janice."

"What for?"

"For giving Mr. Hill a small amount of the discomfort he's giving me."

Janice smiled and said, "My pleasure, Elbert."

Thursday, September 19, Noon
Tony Parkhill walked into the room at the exact moment of the orientation, strutted to the desk where Colt Hill sat, turned to the class and said, "I'm Tony Parkhill and I'll be your journalist today."

The class looked blankly at him. These clueless kids hadn't been out in the world enough to know how waitresses introduced themselves, so his joke was lost on most of them.

Parkhill waited briefly for the laugh that didn't come, then got to mentoring. "Let me try this again without the feeble humor attempt," he said, picking up a small, spiral-bound reporter's notebook and pen. He looked like a journalist standing with those items in his hand, Eb thought.

The students looked at each other. What humor?

"Mr. Hill wants me to tell you a bit about being a journalist. I am editor of the Avery Mountain Journal and have been for five years. I've won a bunch of North Carolina Press Association Awards, so I guess I'm as good as anybody who's readily available in this small, isolated corner of the world to tell you what you want to know."

He talked enthusiastically for the best part of an hour and Eb leaned forward the whole time, hanging on his every word, his full descriptions, his advice, his stories from the field. Parkhill loved what he did and he was not shy about saying so. Journalism sounded like a profession that would interest him, Eb thought. But it was not a profession that interested him at this minute because he didn't have time to invest in it the way he knew he would want to once he got started.

Parkhill finished in an hour and Colt Hill thanked him and told the class it would gather again Friday at noon to talk about the newspaper, The Toe River Current, that would publish once a month for the school year. There were ten people in the room and from those ten, Colt Hill believed, would emerge an award-winning newspaper that could become another impressive line on his résumé, the one the school board would read when it came time to appoint a new principal.

When the class ended, Eb stood at the end of a short line waiting to talk to Tony Parkhill and when he finally got to Parkhill he asked if they could go into the hall. "Mysterious, are we?" Parkhill said.

"I want to get out of the commotion," Eb lied. In the hall, Eb got straight to the point. "I want to write a story about the women coaches here not being paid, while the men are," Eb said.

"Whooooooah!" Parkhill said. "This is your first day on the job, right?"

"Yes," Eb said sheepishly.

"And you want the Pulitzer out of the blocks?"

Eb grinned. "Why not?" he said. "Really, though, I don't think it's fair that the best coach in the school and maybe in North Carolina doesn't get paid as much as a boys basketball coach who won less than half his games last year. She coaches two sports and is a teacher and I'd bet she doesn't even make as much as the men with her teaching salary. I'd like to find that out, too."

"All of that information is available and it's actually a good story if you don't mind the guys who hate women's lib coming after you with tiki torches and pitchforks," said Tony Parkhill. He put his hand on Eb's shoulder. "You'll piss off the county administration, the school board, the principal, Mr. Hill and every male teacher in Avery County. The women will love you. A good reporter most often considers himself a success when fifty percent agree with his story and fifty percent don't. You'll be close."

"Yeah, looks like a new way to get girls," Eb said. "I can do that." Eb smiled and Parkhill returned it.

"I can help you to a point," Parkhill said, "but it's your idea and it's your story. Why don't you start with your own principal and see what he'll tell you? Probably won't be much, if I know Banner. Then you can go to the school board. All the information you want is public."

Banner will shit a brick, Eb thought. *If he doesn't bring out that big board and wrap it around my head, he'll at least tell Colt Hill to dismiss me from the newspaper staff. And that's all I want. I can do the story later.*

"I probably won't need your help in the short term," Eb said to Tony Parkhill. "But if I get in trouble, I'll call."

"You'll get in trouble if you pursue this," Parkhill said. "Count on it. But I'm glad to help a student who wants to kick the ass of authority. That's a good thing. If this doesn't work out and you get booted, give me a call. We'll put you on as a copy boy when the football season's over."

"I'll set up an interview with Banner," Eb said. "If anything happens that I can't do the story, it's yours."

"Deal," said Parkhill. "But give it all you got. I want to be a fly on the wall for this one." He stuck out his hand for Eb to shake, colleague to colleague.

Friday, September 20, 12:15 a.m.

Maryellen, Judi Aldridge and Eb got out of the car in front of Big Girls Cottage, thanked Buster Hanford, the square dance team's caller, for the ride home from the school and walked wearily toward waiting beds. They were all bushed. The first square dance competition of the season, featuring all eight Appalachian Conference Schools, went on for hours on this school night. There wasn't much dancing; time was eaten up waiting between sets at Harris High School in Spruce Pine. Coach Woodson excused the football players from the light final Thursday practice before the Crossnore High School game because of the understanding he and Miss Lilly had about sharing athletes.

Toe River danced three sets and won first place, finishing comfortably ahead of Crossnore and Newland, Avery County's other high schools. They were good teams. Both had the same backgrounds as the Toe River team, the same love of dance and they had veteran coaches, local women who grew up dancing. Neither, however, had Miss Lilly.

Miss Lilly had worked the team ragged since the Grove Park Inn embarrassment. She put in three new routines—one of which was used in the final set on this night—and the Red Tail Hawks were jelling as a team. This first competition was an indication that the team had promise. The dance meet also indicated the team needed more work on both fundamentals and routines. Asheville would have beaten Toe River at this meet, Miss Lilly said, and the older dancers agreed.

Eb watched the girls slip quietly in the front door of Big Girls Cottage and waited about a minute outside until a light came on upstairs where the bathroom would have been. Safely in, he thought as he turned to enter Little Boys.

"Psssst!" he heard, and looked to the left of the front porch.

"Psssst." He walked cautiously over as a shadow emerged from the side of the house. A crescent moon gave an outline to a man holding something. "Git over here," Streit hissed, "or I'll put a hole in your head."

Eb saw the gun, the moon reflecting off its short barrel. He'd been scared before, but terror was new. He broke into a sweat and started shaking, his heart racing and his knees rubbery. He heard Robert Wayne Streit whisper, "Don't pee your pants, boy. Die like a man, you'll feel better." Robert Wayne chuckled in a vile way. The moon glinted off the harsh angles of the man's face, making him look like a monster.

Robert Wayne Streit put the gun in Eb's ribs and pointed toward the lake. "Git," he said in a loud whisper. "Walk slow. I'm right behind you. Move wrong and I pull the trigger." Eb's steps were unsure, uneven and halting. He could hear his heart pounding. Streit pushed him with the point of the gun, then with his other hand punched him in the middle of the back, just above the kidney. It took Eb's breath for a moment.

After they passed out of the campus, the man spoke again. "Thought you was hot shit last week," he said. "Well, we'll see how hot it is tonight. When they find your dead body in the mornin' they gonna know not to fuck with Robert Wayne Streit." He slammed a fist into Eb's right kidney again and Eb plunged forward into the gravel on the road.

"Jesus!" said Eb, his hand going to his lower back, his head dizzy and the pain from the punch searing.

"Jesus ain't helpin' you," Streit sneered. "Ain't nobody helpin'."

As they reached the edge of the lake, Streit said, "On your knees, hero. You git to die now." Eb was shaking, unable to talk. His mouth was dry. But he wasn't getting on his knees for this little creep or for anybody else. Eb shook his head. Streit hit Eb in the left side of the head with the gun and Eb went down again, this time semi-conscious. He saw Streit raise the gun, his arm straight and the barrel a foot from Eb's head.

Eb closed his eyes and said a silent prayer, something he

hadn't done in a long time.

Vance Leffler boomed, "Police! Lay down the gun Streit or I swear to god in heaven I'll put a hole in you, you halfwit sonofabitch. *DO IT NOW!*"

Robert Wayne froze. He turned and saw the gun barrel pointed to a spot between his eyes. He peed in his pants, the warm liquid running down his leg and pooling at his shoe. He slowly put the gun on the ground. "Don't shoot me," a terrified Streit pleaded. "Please don't shoot me. I was just a-foolin' around with the boy. Wasn't gonna hurt him."

"Face first on the ground, Streit," bellowed Vance. "You know the deal. Hands behind your back." In seconds Robert Wayne Streit was handcuffed and sitting on a dry blanket in the back seat of a state police car, cussing without pause. Vance Leffler reached into Streit's back pocket with his gloved hand, pulled out a dirty handkerchief and stuffed it into Streit's mouth. "Shut the hell up!" Vance said.

Eb heard sirens and saw headlights coming up Route 222, rolling beside the Beech Mountain Home for Children and straight toward the lake. Three cars pulled in together, lights blazing and sirens winding down, surrounding Vance's cruiser. That was the entire state police force for Avery County.

"How did you know?" Eb said, his voice shaking as much as the rest of him.

"Maryellen Streit called," he said. "She looked out the window while she was getting ready for bed and saw Robert Wayne pushing you up the road. She had the state police phone number written on the wall next to the downstairs phone since that night when Robert Wayne tried to kidnap her. I was patrolling about a mile from here when I got the dispatch." He closed the back door to the cruiser, Streit mumbling through the nasty handkerchief in protest.

"We're going to have to get a statement from you, son. If you're too shaky to give it tonight, I can come back tomorrow. But I'll tell you one thing, you ain't havin' no more trouble with Robert Wayne Streit. Kidnapping you's the least of it and he'll get twenty years just for that by itself."

"I'll do the statement now," Eb said. "Let's get it over with. I want this gone. Hell, I got a football game in about twenty hours and I don't want this on my head.

"Officer Leffler, I'd really appreciate it if you wouldn't tell people I was scared out of my head tonight. I never faced a gun before and I'm embarrassed." Eb stared at the ground as he spoke.

Vance Leffler put his hand on Eb's head and mussed his hair. "Kid, you have absolutely nothing to be ashamed of. I've seen more than one grown man cry or poop his pants when facing a gun. You bucked the bastard. You should be proud of yourself."

Eb looked to his left and saw Maryellen running full throttle through the lights toward him. She ran straight into him, knocked him over and hugged him, lying on the ground. He laughed at the absurdity of it and said to her, "You're safe now. He's not coming back in this lifetime."

Maryellen's nightmare was over. And tonight, Eb McCourry was her hero. Her real hero, not her football hero.

Part IV

Friday, September 20, 9:30 a.m.

Eb McCourry got to bed at three o'clock after all the commotion, overslept and missed the bus to school. Grover the caretaker took him down the mountain to the school an hour late. After hearing his story, Hap Hilton gave Eb a written excuse and a lot of sympathy. "You want to take the day off?" he said.

"If I do that I can't play tonight," Eb said, noting the county school policy that Coach Woodson laid out in one of the early practices. "I'd rather be busy than sitting up there in my room thinking about all of it. It'll hit me soon enough. That old bastard was going to kill me. He really was."

At noon, Eb parked in a chair in the principal's office to wait for his appointment with J.D. Banner. Banner's part-time secretary, the mother of one of the freshmen football players, made small talk with Eb before she waved him into the office.

"Hey, Mr. Banner," he said, "I'm Eb McCourry."

"New student, huh?" Banner said, knowing exactly who Eb was. "Welcome to Toe River High School. I hope your adjustment is going well. Understand you had some trouble last night. What can I do for you?"

"Everything's fine, sir. Thank you for asking," said Eb, sensing a complete lack of interest on Banner's part. "I've been assigned to the student newspaper and I thought I'd do a story on something I've been wondering about."

Banner looked to his wall where the Board of Education hung. "Bet I know what it's about," he said, chuckling ever so slightly. "You want to know about the board, right? The newspaper always wants to know about the board."

Eb looked at the menacing piece of discolored wood hanging on the wall. He noticed it was notched on the handle and most of the way around the edges. "What are the notches?" Eb asked.

"I'll bet you can guess," Banner said, amused.

"My guess would be that represents the number of butts that thing has whupped," Eb said.

"And you'd be right. I got the Board of Education from my fraternity at Wofford College in 1923. It's the one that was used for my initiation and they gave it to me when I was elected president of the Kappa Sigmas."

"That's interesting," Eb said, "but that's not why I'm here. My question has more to do with how the schools are run. Something I think is important for everybody to know."

"Oh," Banner said, adjusting himself in his oak swivel chair, taking a more official position without the slouch he was noted for. "Well let me hear it."

"I understand that women coaches at Toe River aren't paid and that men coaches are," Eb said. "I want to know if that's true and if it is true, why it's that way. Don't seem fair to me. The women work as hard as the men."

"Son," said Banner, fully attentive, "you're getting into areas that don't concern you. You'd best leave this one alone and write about the other Board of Education, the one hanging on the wall. All you'd do with this is stir up things you don't want to stir up.

"I think we've had enough interview for today." He waved to the door.

Eb started to speak, but Banner interrupted. "Out!" he said. Eb let himself out.

He stood out in the hall, a few doors down from the office waiting to see if Banner would react the way he expected. It wasn't two minutes before J.D. Banner charged out of his office, limping more noticeably than usual, and walked quickly across the hall to Colt Hill's classroom, closing the door behind him. Colt was alone, eating one of his end-of-season, home-grown tomato sandwich lunches, juice dripping down his chin and onto his half-sleeve blue plaid shirt. Eb heard voices through the open transom. Banner was not happy. *Who the hell is this smart-ass kid* and *where'd he get a question like that* and

I want him off the paper this minute and on and on.

Eb heard Colt try to make an argument. "But Mr. Banner, we need him..."

"You don't need him! I won't have it," Banner all but yelled. "Tell him you already have too many people and that you'll get back to him at the end of the semester. This boy's trouble. I don't want him snooping around and trying to write this thing. You had that Avery Journal reporter in here and he could be asking questions, too. Shut this off now."

Eb smiled. That was what he wanted. Journalism could wait, and Eb knew that some day...

Right now, though, he needed to get to a phone and call Tony Parkhill to tell him the story was his.

Friday, September 20, 9:03 p.m.

The minute he heard the pop, Eb knew he was gone for the night, maybe more. The joint in his right knee felt like it separated momentarily until a large spring painfully brought it back together. He went down on his face, then rolled to his back, his leg curled under him. After the initial, "Oh, SHIT!" which he suspected everybody in the stadium heard, Eb didn't say another word until the team physician, Doc Felts, an orthopedic surgeon at Canon Memorial, asked how bad it hurt. Doc knew Eb's history of knee trouble and he knew this wasn't good. "Just give me a minute," said Eb.

The game stopped while Doc extended Eb's knee and felt the reaction inside. The area around the kneecap had already started to swell and burn. Eb understood that at the least, this would mean he'd be at Cannon Memorial Hospital either later tonight or first thing in the morning with a long needle injected and taped beside his kneecap, allowing a milky pink fluid to drain into something that looked like a musical squeeze box. He'd had it done before. He was not a fan of the procedure.

Eb heard Coach Woodson, not three yards from him, say, "Barry Bates, over to quarterback. Somebody get J.W. Greene out here to play fullback."

J.W. was a freshman who played several positions and was tall, thin and probably out of position at fullback, where he'd be small, but he was a truly strong boy.

J.W. lived at the Home and did sixteen hundred sit-ups one slow morning between breakfast and lunch—breaking only because it was time to eat, which he did at impressive levels. There was no doubt J.W. would hit you and he ran the ball with authority when he knew where to run. His problem was the same as Carl Blackthorn's. He didn't know the offensive plays, so Barry would have to tell him what to do on each play in the huddle. The offensive plays Barry ran were much simpler than Eb's version, so J.W. shouldn't have much trouble adjusting.

Eb didn't have a lot of confidence in this tandem running the offense, but he had other things to think about.

Smoky and Harold picked Eb up, put his arms around their shoulders and helped him off the field. When they put him down, Harold looked straight into Eb McCourry's eyes and said, "Take care of yourself, McCourry. We need you." Eb felt like a perfect heel.

Barry, who played flawlessly up to that point, scoring twice, fumbled his first snap and Crossnore recovered at Toe River's twenty-yard-line. Eb sat on the bench behind the team, not able to see anything but those garish orange and black Crossnore uniforms going in a blur, back and forth in front of him. Toe River was up twenty-one to nothing late in the third quarter when Eb went down. Carl Blackthorn and Mickey Buchanan were still healthy and still playing defense, and it was not likely Crossnore would score once, let alone four times. It didn't. Toe River won twenty-one to nothing.

Eb didn't win anything but a case of self-doubt. He was sitting on rehab—at least some. This was a knee injury, and he wasn't confident Miss Lilly would keep him on the square dance team, either. That was his primary thought. Not football, not the good position for a conference championship Toe River was in, not the scholarship that could result from an excellent season. He was focused entirely on square dancing.

He didn't want to lose that.

Saturday, September 21, 12:01 p.m.

Eb hobbled up the two flights of steps just ahead of Lizetta, who had been his ride all morning. From up in the Toe River High School auditorium on the top floor, he could hear the thumping and sliding of dancing feet from the minute he entered the school, the sound cascading down the hallways and into the classrooms. He heard Miss Lilly shouting instructions and Buster Hanford calling.

When he entered the auditorium, Miss Lilly saw him immediately, walked over to the record player, stopped the music, waved off the drill and jumped off the stage, striding straight toward him, clapping her hands. Eb stopped dead. Team members walked to the edge of the stage. One at a time, they started clapping until they all were applauding.

Eb had no idea what was going on. Miss Lilly held up her hand like a cavalry captain halting the march and the applause died.

She stopped in front of Eb McCourry, almost too close for comfort, looked straight into his eyes and said, "I'm proud of you."

Eb was confused and didn't have a response. He'd never been applauded for entering a room, whether or not on crutches. His primary goal for the day was to avoid being tossed off the team.

"By making a substantial effort to get here when you didn't have to, when you probably shouldn't, you showed your coach and your teammates that you are committed to us," said Miss Lilly, her eyes wide and intense. "What I want from this team is a commitment like yours. Get off that knee and watch practice. You'll get a lot out of it whether or not you're dancing." She turned to the dancers and said, "Back to it."

Joyce smiled at Eb and then at Lizetta as they sat in center two seats of the front row of chairs and watched practice. Lizetta slid her hand into Eb's and squeezed. He leaned to her, put his mouth near her ear and told her exactly what was going on in the routine. He spoke with assurance and conviction and Lizetta hung on every word, even though she knew far more about square dancing than he did. Eb didn't yet know she'd been on the team for two years and was a starter as a sophomore. But it didn't matter. This was now Eb's game.

***

The examination and treatment at Cannon Memorial Hospital that morning went better than Eb expected, though the part where a tall, almost skinny, young, balding physician named Dr. Mylan Walford administered the knee drain wasn't so appealing. Dr. Walford, who wore wire spectacles reminiscent of the nineteen-thirties and carried himself with a gentle dignity, had X-rays taken and poked and prodded for some time, talking all the while.

Dr. Walford told Eb he had been accepted as a missionary to Somalia by the Presbytery that ran Cannon Memorial and that he'd leave next spring with his wife. He didn't have kids, he said, but wanted to. "The Lord's work comes first," he offered solemnly.

"Where's Somalia?" asked Eb and Dr. Walford explained that it was in East Africa on the borders of Ethiopia and Kenya. It was a Moslem country that was run by warlords and didn't really have a government of any sort that you'd recognize. Eb thought a minute. "Won't that be dangerous?" he said.

"Sure," said Dr. Walford, "but so's walking across the street in New York City. You gotta figure which one will do you the most good and walking across the street just gets you to the other side. Going to Somalia could bring people to the Lord. It'll certainly give them some medical care they don't have now."

Dr. Walford said Eb's knee was sprained and that it wasn't an especially bad sprain. However, "You have some built-up damage in there and we're going to have to go in and clean it out eventually. I wouldn't be surprised if we found ligaments that look like the waist band of an old pair of underwear. The cartilage is likely torn and will have to come out. We don't have any way of knowing without going in, though." He pulled the drain from Eb's knee slowly. Eb winced, but tried to hide the sharp pain. A few drops of fluid leaked onto his knee once the probe was out. The doctor wiped it off and put on a small bandage.

"When that the swelling goes down, you can probably finish the football season. I heard you're looking for scholarship money and I know how important that is. I got an undergraduate degree by combining academic and music scholarships—clarinet—with grants and loans. But you're going to need to be careful when you go back to the team." He straightened the knee, then pressed on both sides of the patella, which was still puffy with fluid, even after the draining.

Dr. Wolford said, "I have a knee brace for you. It's a new design with steel rods in the side. It won't do much for your speed, but I understand you're a quarterback. If I remember correctly, speed is not of the essence for a quarterback."

Eb nodded. "Yeah," he said, "that and the fact that I don't want to get hit any more than I have to. Has a tendency to shorten the life of the quarterback, especially when some of those defensive players are the size and speed of a supercharged road grader."

As bad as the assessment was, it sounded like music from Dr. Walford's clarinet to Eb's ears. A few days of rehab in the whirlpool and he could dance and throw passes to Terry Gervin and Perry Lafferty again. Sounded like a good deal.

"Can I play Friday?" Eb said.

"Probably not Friday," said Dr. Walford. "That'd be pushing it. You may feel like your knee is fine later this week, but let's let it rest. You've injured it and it needs time to heal. Don't underestimate the body's power. But don't overestimate yours, either. My advice is that you not even dress for the game Friday. Too much temptation to try to play if you do."

"Well, can I at least dance with the square dance team."

"No, no, no," said Dr. Walford. "That might be more dangerous than football because of all the lateral stress. Just take it easy. They tell me you're a writer, so write. That will have a lot less impact on your knee and more on your brain."

Lizetta met Eb in the hall following the examination. "You walk well on those crutches," she said, smiling.

"I should," said Eb. "I've been on them often enough. Doc says I'll be healthy in a few days and I'll only have to miss one game." Lizetta stood on tiptoes and kissed his cheek, knowing he was going to be a nervous wreck until he could return to the stage and the field.

Sunday, September 22, 3:50 p.m.

Eb sat on his small metal-framed bed, writing a paper for Colt Hill, this one a short history of square dancing in Appalachia. He seemed to spend most of his non-football, non-dancing time writing these thousand -word exercises, but when he got to combine his avocations with what he hoped would be his vocation, his writing was better and he wrote faster. His primary source here was his conversation with Miss Lilly, but he'd spent some time in the library to back up what she said. He liked what he was writing.

Ralphie tapped on the door, stuck his head in and said, "Gaylen's here."

Gaylen hit it off well with Ralphie when they met a week ago and Ralphie frequently asked about him. Eb promised Ralphie that before the football season was over, they'd bundle Ralphie up, put him in the car and take him to a game, one way or another. Eb meant to do that even though it would make the Little Boys dorm parents, Moms and Pops, crazy if they even suspected.

"Bring him up, buddy. Uncle Eb's writing," Eb said.

Ralphie scurried downstairs and Gaylen clunked up the polished white pine steps, came into the room and sat down on Eb's small, neatly-made twin bed, looking like he'd just returned from a funeral. "This one didn't work out so well," he said.

"What are you doing back in the middle of the afternoon?" Eb said, expecting the worst. He turned his chair around to face Gaylen.

"Got canned," said Gaylen. "Kay broke up with me, said there's too many miles between us." What Eb knew of Kay and of Gaylen told him that her announcement had a double meaning.

"How do you feel about that?" said Eb.

"I'm just fine. If she hadn't done it, I wudda. She's been dang good for me, but I can see things the way they are. She'd have found a boyfriend or I'd have found a girlfriend soon enough and it could have got ugly. I don't think either of us wanted that."

"I'm sorry to hear it," Eb said, reaching over and putting a hand on Gaylen's shoulder. "It's hard as hell to understand that this might be best when it hurts like I expect it does."

Eb admired Gaylen Anderson at that instant. There was a lot to admire in his resolve, his acceptance of circumstances and his courage.

"You still mooning after Joyce Watkins?" asked Gaylen, a smile creeping into the conversation.

"I'm not really thinking about Joyce in that way any more," said Eb. "There's not much of a shot for me there and to tell you the truth and besides, there's a lot more to Lizetta McEntire than I imagined there could be. She's special."

"Special?" said Gaylen, standing up and holding his hands out wide, like a preacher calling to his congregation. "Special? That's like saying Mickey Buchanan's mean. Bit of an understatement. She's the best looking girl in this end of the state and one of the nicest, smartest people in school."

"Whole state," said Eb, correcting Gaylen's geography. "You want to stay for supper? I'll get Maryellen or Judi to fix you something good and Ralphie would love to have you throw the football with him."

"That's not a bad idea," Gaylen said. "Maybe I can interest

Maryellen in a movie."

"I'm not so sure I'd count on Maryellen wanting to get involved," Eb said. "She's not feelin' too hot about the male of the species these days, with all that business with her father. Give her a while. Ask Judi. She's said some good about you." Gaylen was going to need some healing time, too, Eb understood, but once they got their heads straight, he could see Gaylen and Maryellen or Gaylen and Judi as an appealing pair.

Monday, September 23, 6:15 a.m.

Mickey Buchanan heard stirring in the front room of the trailer, then a loud *slap!* Then another. His mother screamed, shouted "Stop!" and started crying. Mickey, wearing nothing but dingy white Fruit of the Loom briefs, jumped from his small bed, darted through the dirty, yellowing curtain separating the two rooms and saw a man standing over his mother, who sat on the edge of the worn, heavily stained, brown couch. The man was angry. Mickey's mother was wrapped in a sheet, her large, sagging right breast exposed. The man was shirtless, barefoot and his belt was unbuckled, hanging loose.

"Bitch!" Jake Carter shouted as Mickey lunged for him, hitting him from behind with all his one hundred eighty pounds. They went down in a heap in front of the ragged couch, Mickey landing on top. Jake, who was bigger than Mickey and powerful, smelled of cigarettes, booze and old sweat. He rolled over onto his back hard, tossing Mickey into the scarred and discolored linoleum floor. The man reached a kneeling position, swung at Mickey and connected with his head, dead center on his left ear. The pain was sharp, immediate and almost debilitating, but Mickey was jacked up on adrenaline and swung back, landing square on Jake's mouth. The punch brought spurting blood and the man spat out a tooth. "You sonofabitch!" the man shouted at the instant Mickey heard a loud *gong!* and watched him go down, out cold before he hit the floor.

Melva Buchanan had run to the kitchen, picked up her twelve-inch iron skillet—the one she'd cooked a ton of fried chicken and cornbread in for Mickey—and nailed her latest overnight "friend" with a swing that started at her toes. She cried in anger and pain and she kicked Jake, lying eerily still on her living room floor. He was the same man who was inside her less than an hour earlier, grunting and bucking. The same crude drunk who needed a shave and who smelled like a barn hand.

She dropped to her knees and threw her arms around her son. "My poor boy," she said, sobbing. Mickey put his arms around his mother.

"Mama, please stop bringing these men home. They only hurt you. It's all that ever happens."

"Honey, I get so lonely without a man. Since that bastard of a father of yours left, I don't have nothin'."

Jake groaned and rolled onto his back, his eyes blinking open. Mickey rushed to him, lifted him off the floor by the hair, with one hand cupped under his left armpit and dragged him to the front door. Mickey pushed the moaning man out the door and down the three unpainted wooden steps to the rain-soaked ground. Jake struggled to an upright position and growled, "Your mama's a lousy fuck." He slipped in the mud and fell backwards. "Shit!" he screamed as he tried to get up.

Mickey leaped from the doorway, over the steps to the ground, bent and pummeled Jake until he finally said, "Enough! Enough!" Mickey kicked the man in the face with his bare foot and felt his nose break, blood spurting all over Jake's shirt. He finally stood and made his way to his car, saying nothing more.

Mickey watched as Jake Carter left and thought of having nothing. No friends, no life, no future. Everybody hated him and the only pleasure he got was when he could dance solo or take out some of his pain on somebody else on the football field, giving himself a few minutes' relief. He was mad all the time. People called him crazy, psycho.

Maybe he was. But he didn't know any other way.

Part V

Monday, September 23, 5:32 p.m.

Kay Silver Feather bolted excitedly through the screen door toward the pearl Mercedes-Benz 230SL convertible pulling into the driveway. A raven-haired beauty with a yellow scarf tied around her hair smiled wide, flung open the door and met Kay halfway, hugging her fully. "My gorgeous little sister," said Arlene Silver Feather. "I've missed you, kid-o. Is Daddy home?"

"He's working a job over in Rutherfordton," said Kay, "but he'll be home for supper. I'm cooking and we're having your favorite: grilled rainbow trout, stuffed with rice and wild mushrooms. I caught the trout and picked the mushrooms."

Arlene pulled her sister close again. "You're something," she said. "A cook now, huh? And a wild Indian hunter-gatherer!"

"Daddy started teaching me cooking last spring," said Kay. "I'm pretty good at it and some of his old family recipes are wonderful. He hasn't had much time to cook since mom..." Her voice trailed off.

"Have you heard anything at all from Mom?" Arlene's eyes crinkled and she reached for Kay's hand as she spoke.

"We don't talk about her," said Kay, casting her eyes down. "Just not a good thing. Daddy's still pretty mad and hurt and I don't understand what happened. I thought they were..." Her voice dropped again. She had difficulty speaking of her mother, whom she adored and who, suddenly one day a year ago, wasn't there.

"How's your square dance team?" said Kay, changing the subject as quickly as she could.

"Team's good," said Arlene. "But what would you expect? These are some of the best young dancers in North Carolina, every bit as good as most of the kids we have in New York. It's like asking a concert violinist to pick out 'Wildwood Flower' on a fiddle. They're dancing so far below their capability that I think they're getting bored. They look like machines going through their routines, Stravinsky playing scales. I try to keep them motivated, but this level of dance is…well…you know what it is."

"It's folk," said Kay. "It's heritage for the people here and it's important to them. I hate to hear you talk about it that way. People love this dance and this music. I love it. It's part of who we are."

"Honey, I don't intend to disparage heritage or culture," said Arlene. "I understand both. I'm a Cherokee, for chrissakes, and I know about culture being attacked. It's just that these kids have a different calling and after they've worked for years to achieve a level of excellence, they're asked to crank it back for the sake of whatever is at the heart of this. I think they are feeling used. Frankly, they are being used. So am I. Willingly. This is about my ballet school not only surviving, but thriving and becoming one of the best in the city. It's about my future and their future."

Arlene put a hand on Kay's shoulder and squeezed, then wrapped her arm around her sister.

"We have a fifteen-year-old dancer named Cynthia Frazier who's from Asheville and she's one of the most promising young dancers of any kind I've ever seen. She's been at it hard every day since she was three. She's had the best schools, best teachers, best everything because of her talent alone. Her father's a *truck driver*, if you can imagine. I think she'll be on stage in New York as a headline performer within the next ten years.

"She's half of our lead couple and it embarrasses me to watch this girl square dance. Such a waste of time and effort for her and it all has to do with a trophy for a spoiled rich kid." Arlene gave Kay the background on Joss-Lynn Ledbetter and self-described "filthy rich" Bobby Lee.

"I'm not being critical," said Kay. "I just wish there was another way to do it. I guess that car's part of the package?"

Arlene nodded, embarrassed.

"Y'all danced on a program with Toe River recently didn't you?" said Kay.

"Yes, at the Grove Park Inn for the teachers' conference a few days ago. Toe River danced right behind us."

"Gaylen says they've had a lot of problems with mono, inexperience, depth and some other stuff. Gaylen's friend Smoky—you met him here back a few weeks ago—is kind of a team bouncer who has to look after a loose cannon who dances for them." She couldn't help smiling. "Dance team bouncer" had such an absurd ring that they both laughed. "Toe River has this nutcase Smoky has been brought in to control." said Kay. "Guy's apparently a great dancer, but a head case. Gaylen told me that most people think he's the best clogger Toe River ever produced and you know what that means."

"Yes," said Arlene. "That would be a good clogger. The team looked ragged at the Grove Park. They weren't together. I've heard of Lilly Wilkerson's legendary discipline and of her creative routines, but the team looked distracted, out of step and the routine was pedestrian. This didn't look like a championship caliber team."

"Gaylen says they plugged in their backup dancers and went into the student body to fill out the roster," said Kay. "They only came up with two new dancers and one of them, the quarterback on the football team, has never square danced before. Gaylen brought him down for a visit. He and Julia Garrity spent some time together and seemed to like each other. At least Julia did. She can't talk about anything else. 'My quarterback,' she calls him."

"He's wearing pants, so Julia's going to like him. You know that. How are you and Gaylen doing?" said Arlene.

"He's an hour away and it's been a strain," said Kay. "He can only come down every couple of weeks or so and only for a couple of hours. I miss him but I told him we can't go on like this. So we broke up."

"It's tough, hon. I had a boyfriend in the Army in Germany

a couple of years ago."

"I didn't know that."

"There's a lot you don't know. Tell me about school, college. You making any progress?" Arlene walked over to the aging swing and sat in the center of the tire, lifting her feet and leaning back, smiling broadly.

"Oh, I forgot. Wake Forest has offered me a full scholarship and Winthrop is talking about a scholarship. Hollins, a girls' school up in Roanoke, has asked me to come and visit. That'll likely be an offer. I'm not sure what this means, but I bet it has something to do with integration. I'm a dark-skinned minority, but I'm not a Negro, and I suppose that looks good to them."

"Cynical, are we?" said Arlene. "Little sister, don't underestimate yourself. You're sharp and you're going to make whichever college you go to look good."

"The one I want," said Kay, "is William & Mary, but that's a long shot. You know they have the highest suicide rate among undergraduates in the country?"

"That's a recommendation?" said Arlene, her eyes widening, the swing climbing higher.

"It says they're demanding," said Kay. "I want somebody who's demanding. And the law school there is top level."

"You still set on being a civil rights lawyer?"

"Oh, yes. That's where the action is going to be for years. All this legislation that's coming is going to create a whole lot of lawsuits and I want to be part of changing our history."

"So, Gaylen doesn't fit with that?" said Arlene, pumping still higher in the swing.

"He's a good guy, Arlene," said Kay. "He's kind and sweet and thoughtful and good looking and about everything most girls would want. But he's going to get out of school and go to work in a factory or go in the Army and be perfectly happy with that. I'd die."

"Let's go cook some supper," said Arlene, leaping from the swing and landing like a gymnast, arms wide and bowing.

"There's a wrinkle I can add to that stuffed rainbow that you might like. Learned it at one of the finest restaurants in New York."

"They cook like Indians in New York?"

"Actually, yes," said Arlene. "We'll need curry, tarragon and rosemary. You have those?"

"What kind of Indian are you, Arlene?" Kay said.

They laughed out loud. Each threw an arm around the other and pranced through the screen door, which slammed behind them.

"Don't slam that damn door!" bellowed Arlene, mocking her dad's deep voice. They broke down laughing again, both with the same deep boisterousness.

Arlene felt safe and uninhibited for the first time in a while. It was a good feeling.

Monday, September 23, 5:45 p.m.

The Toe River High School football team finished its easiest practice yet. Certainly the easiest for Eb McCourry, since he stood on the sideline, holding crutches he wasn't using. Coach Woodson took note of the walking wounded and the fact that the team had gone at it hard—and well—for nearly six weeks. Players were tired. They were hurt. They were undefeated. He gave them a break.

The football team went out in shorts, ran some sprints and a few plays, mostly pass plays for the benefit of Barry, who needed the work with the receivers for timing purposes.

Square dance practice might not be so easy, Eb thought, as he arrived at the auditorium. Miss Lilly still wasn't happy with the performance of the team. The youngest dancers weren't up to the level she expected and she talked of moving people to different partners.

Joyce was sitting in a chair at the corner of the stage, strapping on her dance shoes. The "straps" were actually shoe laces Miss Lilly bought for each of the girls for the look of expensive strapped pumps without the cost. Joyce had to wrap the lace around and around her ankle and calf, finishing about halfway up before tying it. The laces never looked comfortable to Eb, but the girls didn't complain. They'd all be wearing high heels soon enough, so they might as well get used to awkward discomfort.

Eb slid into the seat next to Joyce and said, "How you doin'?"

"I'm pretty good, buddy," she said, emphasizing "buddy."

"How's the knee?"

"It's fine. You mad at me about something?" Eb said, sounding more hurt than he intended.

"No, sir," she said, "I'm not mad at you, but if I didn't have a boyfriend, I probably would be. You and Lizetta look cute together and I'm jealous."

There was so much in that sentence that Eb didn't know where to begin dissecting it. "If I didn't have a boyfriend," "cute together," "jealous." Where was she going with this?

Confused beyond response, he changed the subject. "Miss Lilly said she might move some people around," he said. "Can I dance with you? My knee's a lot better. The swelling's gone down. I don't feel comfortable with Becky and I know she'd rather have somebody who's got some experience and some talent." Eb had laid out his best case.

"Eb," said Joyce, using his preferred name, "I'm a starter and I have to dance with a starter whether or not it's as part of the caller couple. Buster and I have been dancing together for nearly four years and we know each other better than a married couple … at least as dancers. Miss Lilly may switch you and Becky off some, but I don't think she'll put you and me together."

Fifteen minutes later Miss Lilly said, "Buster and Joyce, I going to want you two to dance with Elbert and Becky later this week when Elbert's knee is better." Eb caught Joyce's eye and grinned. She wiped her nose with the back of her right hand, lowering her head and smiling ever so slightly. She did not seem displeased, even though some would take this as a demotion for her.

"You might wonder at some of what we're going to have to do in the next few practices," Miss Lilly said, "but we are thin, inexperienced and sitting on the edge of being non-competitive if we get an injury or a sickness in the right spot. There are seven football players on this team, so injury is always a possibility, as we are staring in the face right now with Elbert's injury. We have to build some depth and we have to reach a comfort level where any of you can dance with anybody else without losing our edge ... an edge we don't have yet, by the way."

Miss Lilly's best tactic in having this strategy accepted readily was to pair up her two lead dancers with her two weakest. Eb didn't mind at all. From what he could tell, Joyce didn't either.

Eb danced recently with confidence. He was not good, was not going to be good, he thought, but he could learn the routines and work at it. Joyce gave him the best shot to do that because he "felt her," as she once suggestively termed it. "When you 'feel' your partner, anticipate the next move and do it in unison," she said, "then you're a team." Eb knew the concept. Same as with the football team. If the guard doesn't know the play, the quarterback goes down.

Eb walked over to Miss Lilly, limping only slightly. "I can dance today," he said. "Swelling's down and I feel good."

"Eb, you have a great attitude and I appreciate your eagerness, but let's give it a couple of days. Just be patient." She looked at the pad in her hand and made a notation. "Alright, back to practice," she said in a firm, loud voice.

It was nearly nine o'clock when Eb hobbled up the steps to his room and he was hungry, tired and had a paper to write—another thousand-word tome for guess who?

He hoped Maryellen remembered to steal something from the kitchen.

Friday, September 27, 9:22 p.m.

Eb walked toward the mob of football players at the middle of the worn field as the game ended, knowing this could be an uncomfortable few minutes coming up. Toe River's football team took the hour's drive down to Old Fort to play Gaylen's old school, knowing they'd likely see Gaylen's now former girlfriend and Eb's almost … whatever Julia was. Both girls were at the game.

Eb, who was not in his uniform, but was still on the sideline with the team, saw Kay at halftime when she ran over with the Old Fort cheerleaders to give their welcome to the visiting crowd. Eb exited of the locker room earlier than the rest of the team because he didn't want to get caught in the stampede.

"Gaylen tell you what happened?" Kay asked.

Eb nodded and Kay asked if Gaylen was all right. She seemed genuinely pleased when Eb said he was fine and was getting on with things. He played a good first half and Kay noticed. Eb was not surprised she knew football. "He's hell on that weak side blitz," she said, a smile creeping in.

She scrambled away just as the team came back out to the field and Eb became distracted by a girl in a yellow dress on the other side of the stadium, standing behind the Old Fort bench and waving both arms. It was Julia. "Oh, shit," he thought. "This ain't gonna to be pretty."

Not much was pretty about the game, except the play of Carl Blackthorn, who had twenty-two tackles, two knocked-down laterals that went for safeties, a tackle for a safety, a blocked/intercepted pass and a fumble recovery. Three safeties in one game from one player. It was a remarkable performance and without it, the Toe River High School Red Tail Hawks might still be undefeated, but they would not have had a perfect record because their offense couldn't score on this night with Eb out of the lineup. The final score was six to nothing and Toe River's offense "couldn't piss a drop," as Woodson so delicately put it later in the locker room.

The offense was out of sync, playing like people who didn't

know each other's names. Blockers ran into each other, runners went to the wrong place and when Barry Bates tried to throw the ball—something he did not do well under the best of circumstances—the receivers fell down, ran the wrong route, something every play. Barry finished the game without a completed pass. Toe River's total offense was twenty-two yards. But the Hawks won against an average team and were still in the hunt for the Appalachian Conference championship.

As Eb neared the middle of the field, he saw Julia Garrity sprinting toward him, squealing and he braced for her last-second leap into his arms. "Why ain't you in uniform?" she said, and when Eb explained, she pleaded, "Oh, you should have written. I hadn't heard a word…" At that instant, Lizetta appeared, sliding her arm around Eb, a little tighter than he was used to. He hadn't seen Lizetta at the game before this moment.

Eb thought about going somewhere and killing himself, but knew he had to face this and he did the simple thing. "Lizetta, this is, uh, Julia. I know her through Gaylen. Julia, Lizetta's…my ride…and my girlfriend." He finished the sentence barely audibly, but, there, he'd said it. He put his arm around Lizetta. He wanted to say "sorry" or something consoling, but he wasn't about to apologize for the best thing that'd ever happened to his love life.

Julia smiled and said, "Oh, you're cute together. So good to see you again, Eb." Now Eb felt like a heel. Such class from this pretty young girl, who was obviously embarrassed and disappointed. Under different circumstances … thought Eb.

"Nice to meet you Julia," said Lizetta. "We'd better be getting back," and she spun both herself and Eb around and headed toward the car. Just in time for Eb to see Kay walking straight for Gaylen, who was talking intensely to one of Old Fort's players.

"Call me," shouted Julia in a voice that sounded almost pitiful. Eb didn't look back and he didn't feel good about it.

Eb hadn't bothered to check with Coach Woodson to see if he could ride back with Lizetta and not the team. Better to ask forgiveness than permission, he once heard somebody say. He'd deal with it later.

As Eb turned, Joyce popped him on the butt, passing behind Lizetta and him and didn't say a word. Lizetta didn't see it and Harold didn't see it and Eb didn't know who else didn't see it, but he felt it.

Eb didn't know much about what anything meant, but he knew that he and the boys were going out soon—no girls—and he'd get a break if not any more clarity. This relationship business made football and square dancing seem breezy by comparison and he was beginning to wonder how many screw-ups he was allowed before it all started to cost more than it returned. With Lizetta as his prize, he didn't want to take any more chances.

Saturday, September 28, 6:35 p.m.

Harold Wiseman and his uncle, Harold Greene, shared more than a first name. They both loved football. The younger Harold's mama gave him his Christian name in honor of her older brother, Harold Greene.

Harold Greene was an all-Appalachian Conference tackle at Toe River High School in nineteen forty-two and his nephew was making noises like he'd do the same in nineteen-sixty-three.

Harold Greene graduated from high school in forty-three and went almost straight to the Battle of the Bulge, where he won a Purple Heart and a Bronze Star as a sniper for the 106th Fighting Lions Division. Using the brand new Remington Model 1903A4 with a pistol grip and a five-round magazine, he nailed a general and fourteen other officers of various ranks, each with a single thirty-ought-six caliber round to the head. Clean shots, all. The officers were issuing orders one second, had wings the next.

Harold Greene spent fifteen months in a German prison camp under what he often understated as "Spartan conditions" after his regiment ran out of ammunition and was captured. He was one of a handful of survivors among nearly fifteen thousand POW members of his 422nd Brigade.

Harold Greene was an overalls-wearing, heavily-muscled man with a bushy dark brown beard, hefty beer belly and laugh that could be heard for miles from his trailer up on the Elk River. He was not to be trifled with. But he had a deep appreciation for a good practical joke and when Harold Wiseman told him what he was up to, Harold Greene's ice blue eyes lit up and that tree-rattling, deep bellow of a laugh traveled down the valley.

"I swear to god, boy, you shudda been mine," he howled.

Harold and Smoky formulated a get-even plan for J.D. Banner that involved a good bit of risk and required a silent partner in Harold Greene, the man who had the means to accomplish what they had in mind.

Harold Greene owned a business called Scent of Rose Elimination. He emptied septic tanks. Harold told people he was "in the turd-haulin' bid-ness" when asked, and let loose that big laugh. His wife, Elma, insisted on Scent of Rose and even designed a logo that looked more like a perfume bottle than a turd-haulin' bid-ness because "I don't want no husband of mine bein' thought of as a toilet cleaner." Which is exactly what Harold Greene was. It never bothered him one whit.

All those tons of turds gave Elma that fancy double-wide and twenty-one-inch Magnavox color TV set for her soap operas—especially "General Hospital" with the gorgeous Dr. Steve Hardy—and that Pacific Blue 1962 VW Beetle 1200 convertible she liked so much.

At forty-two, Elma was still "a pretty little thing," as Harold deemed her. She was blonde, big-eyed and big-chested with curvy dancer's legs. She had the nicest ass Harold Greene ever laid his hands on. Elma got his juices going about once a day, sometimes more.

As Harold Wiseman explained the caper to his uncle, the goal was to unload the day's take of septic filling into the sunroof of that precious red 1958 Alpha Romeo of J.D.

Banner's, the only indulgence the old bachelor ever had.

Harold Greene's truck was a beauty, a big light blue Ford cab—Elma's color choice—and a two-thousand-gallon tank perched on the back, above double wheels. Harold Greene intentionally had it equipped with the biggest engine he could find and because of that, the truck was far more efficient than an underpowered version. More important for this mission: it was much quieter than similar trucks. It wasn't much louder than Harold's Ford pickup.

***

The Alpha Romeo was a beautiful car, one J.D. Banner couldn't help but polish with a sleeve or a handkerchief every time he passed it. Each morning, as he walked to his office, he looked back at the car after parking it between those two towering maples fronting the admin building at Toe River High. You could almost see him smile. An imagined smile was the best you'd get from J.D. Banner.

"What else you boys need?" said Harold Greene, handing the keys to his favorite nephew.

"Just some luck," said Smoky. "A little luck would be good."

Saturday, September 28, 8:35 p.m.

Gaylen Anderson picked Eb up in front of Little Boys Cottage at the Home in his green 1956 Simca Aronde, which might have been pretty at some time in its life, but was past that now. Two other football players were with them, passing around a quart of beer.

They were heading for a dance at the school gym. Lizetta was in Raleigh with her dad for the weekend. Some kind of high-level government function for him and visiting the state art museum, combined with shopping for Lizetta and her mother, she said. Eb and Lizetta had a movie date Sunday, but he was on his own tonight.

Terry Gervin, the lanky end who caught everything Eb

threw these days, was in the front seat with Gaylen and the undersized, but effective blocking back Phillip Branscon, was in the back. Eb slid into the other back seat, dodging a tiny sharp metal piece on the door frame that was once covered by rubber insulation. It sat there like a solemn shark's tooth and god knows how many pairs of pants had been torn on it. Eb didn't have enough clothes to risk tearing a pair of pants, so he took pains to avoid it.

"When are you getting that thing fixed, Gaylen?" Eb said.

"Ain't botherin' me none," he said. "You fix it if you want it fixed. I'm a busy man." Eb stepped out of the car, picked up a large rock and hit the spur twice, flattening it.

"What the hell are you doing?" said Gaylen. "That's my car you're bangin' on."

"I fixed it," said Eb. "Now, tell me about the dance." Eb adjusted his butt to fit the tiny back seat. "This something new?"

"Naw," said Terry. "Home ec department puts on these every fall and spring to show off some of the cooking and organizing skills the girls are learning. Always good food and there's music on a record player. About half the girls are shopping their skills for a husband or a boyfriend. Some people dance, some go outside and drink liquor, then come in and dance." He guffawed. "Lots of needy women there."

Eb didn't know Terry well, but he knew Terry drank, that he was a dependable receiver, and that he spit tobacco juice down six-foot-four-inch center David Hanner's jersey when they were in the huddle in practice. David never did figure out where it came from. The offensive team lined up in what was called a "choir huddle," with the quarterback in front, giving the play to two lines of players, one directly behind the other. David stood in front of Terry, to his shirt's everlasting sorrow. Terry never got tired of spitting on David and David never figured out where the stain came from. He was not the sharpest pencil in the box.

Eb entered the Toe River High Coliseum and saw Joyce on

the other side of the gym. He walked over to her, leaving his traveling pals to search among the sophomores for an easy catch.

Joyce was talking to her sister, Janice, and two other girls and smiled when she saw Eb coming, stepped away from the others and walked toward him. "Hello, handsome. How are you and how is Lizetta?" she said.

"I'm fine and Lizetta's in Raleigh. Where's Harold?" Eb said, wary.

"He's not here," she said. "I think him and Smoky are coming by for while, but he said he had something important to do. He sounded secretive, so I didn't press him. I came with Janice and a couple of other girlfriends. We don't get a lot of dances and I thought you might be here—my favorite dance partner—and we could get in a waltz or a foxtrot."

"Or maybe a frug or a swim or a twist or a Watusi," Eb said, squeezing her hand. "Waltzes and me never got acquainted and I'm not sure how you're gonna waltz to 'Louie, Louie' or 'He's So Fine' anyway. Wanna dance to the one playin'?" A new California band called the Beach Boys sang "In My Room," a slow song. Joyce nodded, took his hand and moved melodically to the middle of the floor.

When the dance ended, Gaylen rushed over to Eb and said, "Harold Wiseman just walked in. You might want to break up this love fest."

"I was just dancing with her," Eb protested. "There's nothing going on with us. Wish you'd get that out of your head." Joyce joined Harold in the middle of the room. Eb didn't know if Harold had seen them dancing, and he didn't care. No harm, no foul, he thought.

***

It was getting near the end of the night when Smoky saw Eb standing alone near the door of the gym and ambled over. "Who's that girl over yonder," he said, nodding toward the opposite wall of the gym.

"The one with the rack?" Eb said.

"Now quit that. Be respectful."

"Smoky, for god's sake, what do you want me to say, 'the one with the brown hair,' or, 'the one with the short skirt'? She has a distinct physical attribute, given to her by the Good Lord. I'm just using it as a visual guide. A prominent one."

"Oh, you always have something to say." Smoky sounded impatient. "Tell me about her."

"I don't know who she is, if we're talking about The Rack," Eb said. "I can ask Joyce. You want to meet her?" Smoky didn't say anything. Eb took that as a formal request for an introduction.

Joyce said the girl was Sharon Vance, daughter of the preacher at Cranberry Primitive Baptist, a junior who had been held back a grade with some mysterious sickness a few years ago. She'd apparently fully recovered and was active in 4H and she was a good student. Joyce said people liked her, that she was a touch shy and Janice said Sharon was dying to meet Smoky. So there it was.

Joyce almost force-fed an introduction and everybody else scattered, leaving Sharon and Smoky to talk, which they did until Harold tapped Smoky on the shoulder and said, "It's time." Sharon handed Smoky a piece of paper and he left. With great reluctance. Eb took that to be Sharon's phone number and found out later it was.

Eb was beginning to miss Lizetta. When he thought of her, he felt warm. What he felt for Joyce was becoming much clearer, less confusing and more comfortable. He was relieved when seeing Harold didn't make his stomach go into a knot.

Harold and Smoky walked briskly and purposefully through the gym door, as if something vital lay ahead. Eb wondered what it might be.

Sunday, September 29, 1:22 p.m.

Nearly exhausted, Eb slept through church and lunch and almost forgot that Lizetta and he planned to see "The Great

Escape" at the Center Theater in Banner Elk. It was the first new movie the theater'd had in a good while, she said. The Center dealt in an odd mixture of movies that nobody could explain, some good, some bad, some old, some new, some just weird.

Any of the Hercules movies with musclemen like Steve Reeves, Gordon Scott, Reg Park, Mark Forest and Alan Steel got a long run. They were awful, but young boys went to see them the way they would flock to some of those B-horror atrocities. Some of the boys from Lees-McRae College that one of the ushers called "light in the loafers" hung out at the Hercules movies, as well. Eb didn't quite catch the connection.

"The Great Escape" wasn't in that lower category. It had big stars, big budget, big director, big expectations and starred Steve McQueen. He was the guy Eb wanted to play him in the movie version of Eb's autobiography when he finished writing it, Eb told Lizetta, only half in jest. Eb got one of those up-from-the-toes laughs from her.

As she drove the silver 1963 Buick Riviera—an astonishingly pretty, sleek and futuristic-looking car with exotic front-wheel drive and a flat floorboard—to the Center Theater, she was quiet until they pulled into the parking lot for the one-thirty movie.

"I may be moving," she said, abruptly.

"Oh, no," Eb said, turning to face her with a sunken look.

She looked straight ahead, over the steering wheel, a tear in the corner of her eye, trying to get out. "Daddy may have to take a job in Raleigh. Governor Sanford wants him to head up a thing called the Governor's Commission on the Status of Women."

Terry Sanford, who ran for governor when John Kennedy was elected president and who benefited from Kennedy's popularity, was a markedly progressive force in an often nineteenth-century state. Sanford renewed the fight for integration in a region that dragged its feet since Brown vs. Board of Education in 1954. He sent his children to one of the few integrated public schools in North Carolina. He saw to the creation of the state's Governor's School for the Gifted and the North Carolina School of Modern Dance. He raised teachers' salaries (except for Miss Lilly's compensation for coaching, apparently) and helped increase the general fund for schools. Sanford put a tax on food while raising welfare payments, so the tax wouldn't hurt the poor.

None of this was popular with North Carolina's traditionally conservative Southern Democrats and the Republicans were apoplectic, calling him a "tax-and-spend liberal." He most certainly was that, to the great delight of those who believed spending on anti-poverty programs and education to be the right thing to do in North Carolina.

Tobacco farmers became suspicious of Sanford when he didn't oppose the Surgeon General's recommendation of a warning on a pack of cigarettes saying, "Cigarette smoking could be hazardous to your health." Tobacco was the state's Number One product and the source of most of North Carolina's wealth. Big Tobacco had never lost a lawsuit and it owned nearly every Southern legislator.

Sanford faced Goliath with a BB gun.

Lizetta's dad, Jim McEntire ("Big Jim McEntire" to an inner circle) was a long-time Sanford supporter and friend. The family ate with the governor at the mansion in Raleigh on occasion and Big Jim was in Sanford's tight personal and political orbit.

Eb was taking Big Jim's daughter to the movies on this last day of summer. Maybe "going to the movies with her" was more accurate, since she was both paying and driving.

Eb would grow to admire Terry Sanford greatly over the coming years, but at this moment in Eb's life, he could have done without Sanford stirring that young life with a spiked spoon.

"When will you know something?" Eb said weakly. His knees and voice were about equal in this struggle and he hoped Lizetta didn't get out of the car soon. He would likely fall trying to follow her.

Lizetta turned and faced Eb. "It'll be this week and it's not certain we're moving. Daddy said he might be able to run his law practice and the commission from Newland. A lot of it depends on who's on the commission and what it'd take to get them together."

Lizetta was obviously upset, but like everything else she did, she had control and class. She was not going to cry and she was not going to complain. Eb put his hand on her cheek and kissed her lightly, feeling a warm swelling between his legs. He was embarrassed, knowing the erection couldn't come at a worse time.

"You know I don't want you to go, Lizetta," Eb said as forcefully as he could, which was a stretch at the moment. "And I know there's not much I can do about what's ahead except to enjoy your company while I can. So let's do that." He didn't feel any of that, but saying it was right. The tear fell from her eye and she put her hand on his thigh, an inch form his erect penis. She leaned forward and kissed him lightly on the lips. He felt wetness in his eyes, as well. This wouldn't do.

"Let's go watch Steve McQueen ride his damn motorcycle," Eb said. "We'll see this through and it will be all right." Now, he had to figure out how to get out of the car and walk across the street without standing out, so to speak.

Sunday, September 29, 6:07 p.m.
Eb sat his tray on the table, slipped in beside Maryellen in the dining hall, leaned over and said, "Lizetta may be moving. I'm not so sure it was a good idea to hook us up. I really like her, but Jesus! I'm wondering how much more can go wrong this weekend."

"Oh, lord," said Maryellen, putting down her fork. "I was afraid something like this might happen. Her dad's such a political big-shot and we're about as far away from the action as you can get and still be in North Carolina."

Maryellen looked at him full-faced. "Have you thought

about Joyce at all?"

"What's that got to do with it?" Eb said.

"I want you to be over her," Maryellen said. "Nothing good can happen to you in that relationship."

"Don't misjudge Joyce," Eb said. "She's special. She has a boyfriend. I know that. I don't mind. I accept it. Can I say anything else that will get you off Joyce?" Eb was annoyed, frustrated, anxious.

Maryellen placed her hand on his bicep. "I'll lay off. You deserve that." She kissed his cheek and said, "Eat your meatloaf. I made it."

Part VI

Tuesday, October 1, 7:45 p.m.

Eb was still hobbling—without the crutches—when Pops entered his room early in the morning and asked if he'd take care of the kids for the rest of the day and get them ready for school tomorrow. He and Moms had a relative die and needed to run over to Kingsport for a funeral. They'd be home before the close of school Wednesday.

"Happy to do it," Eb said, "but I'm really sorry for your loss." Pops said the "loss" was a ninety-six-year-old cousin of some distance they hardly knew, but the family was gathering, getting old and there might not be many more opportunities to see some of them.

Pops and Moms—Eb never knew their real names because they never offered them—were the house parents at Little Boys. They'd been there since Jesus was a boy, Maryellen told Eb, and they loved the Home. They were about what you'd expect from people called "Pops" and "Moms." They were gray, slightly bent, kindly, patient, attentive and good at what they were paid to do. Eb suspected they'd have done it for three squares and a bed.

Eb asked Zarelda and Margo, two teen-age sisters from Big Girls, to be there when the kids got home from school and they happily agreed. Anything for the football hero. He showed up at five-thirty after a brisk, but brief football practice to get them ready for dinner at six. Miss Lilly gave the team Tuesday off.

There was a lot of rushing around because these younger kids—most of them between five and ten—had to be herded into the house from the intense games they found themselves involved in, cleaned up and pointed toward the cafeteria. It was time consuming but Eb liked the boys and they did what he asked of them quickly and without argument, so it wasn't a lot of trouble.

There was one older kid among the residents of Little Boys

named Haywood Frakis, "Woody," whom Eb didn't like or trust. He'd showed up at the same time Ralphie and Eb got to the Home.

Woody was a big kid who probably would have done well on the Toe River football team if he'd been at Toe River High. He recently turned sixteen but was in the seventh grade.

The youngest boys seemed to shy away from him. They'd get up or fidget when he entered the room. None of the other kids on campus seemed to want to have anything to do with him, either. Eb figured it was none of his business, so he didn't go nosing around about it.

Woody was about two inches taller and twenty pounds heavier than Eb and his muscles were pronounced. He had a wide, flat head, a prominent jaw and bad teeth that were green at the gum line. His hair was not combed and his clothes were often disheveled and dirty.

The boys were back from dinner and it was time to start getting them ready for bed, so Eb called his shadow, Ralphie Allison, out of one of the two sleeping quarters—a big dorm room where eight boys slept—and gave him the roundup assignment. Ralphie was delighted, but he leaned over to Eb and whispered, "Can I tell you something?" They were alone in the room.

"What's up, buddy?" Eb said, leading down to Ralphie.

"Woody's been making some of the little boys put his thing in their mouth and I think he wants me to do it. I don't have to, do I?"

Eb put his hands on Ralphie's shoulders, squared him, looked straight into his eyes and said, as unemotionally as he could, "Are you sure that what you just told me is true, Ralph?" Eb used Ralphie's formal name on purpose. "This could get Woody in a lot of trouble."

"I saw him twice," said Ralphie. "It was dark in the room and he didn't know I was there. I was real quiet."

"Ralphie, I want you go over to the Big Boys house and tell J.W. to come over here with two or three of the older boys.

136

Then go tell Miss Lincoln I need to see her and I'll be right over. Tell her it's important. You stay at her office or room or wherever you find her. Got that?"

"Yes, sir," Ralphie said and bolted out the door.

Miss Lincoln was Dorothy Lincoln, the tall, elegant, white-haired friend Eb's Aunt Nell who ran Beech Mountain Home for Children with discipline, order and purpose. She did not suffer fools and detested disruptions in routine. Bad behavior was not tolerated. Second chances were rare. There were no third chances. She dismissed those who didn't adjust with what many thought was a quick trigger, but her rationale—she told Eb on his first day—was that "there are three children out there wanting to be here for every one of you who is here." That was part of the explanation why Eb was at the home. It indicated how much she liked, admired and respected Aunt Nell. Without his aunt, there was not even the most remote chance Eb would be in Beech Mountain Home for Children. "This is a privilege," she emphasized, "not a right."

Eb took a deep breath and went to find Woody, somewhere back near where he slept, Eb guessed. Woody wasn't given a single room, as Eb had been, sleeping, instead, among the kids. Eb thought Woody might resent the sleeping assignment, but he never said a word. Now Eb was beginning to understand why. People who prey on children need to be near them.

Eb found Woody sitting at a desk flipping through a comic book. "I need to talk to you," he said coldly.

"What about?" Woody said, "I gotta get ready for supper and I'm hungry."

"I've just learned what you're doing with the boys and I need for you to come with me to Miss Lincoln's office to talk about it," Eb said as evenly and as devoid of the strong and heated emotion he was feeling as he could. "This can't happen and you are damn lucky it didn't happen to Ralphie."

Woody didn't flinch. Eb was on the floor before he knew Woody had swung. Eb had never before seen or felt such quick reflexes. The punch to his left jaw spun him around and he went down face first. Woody leaped on top of Eb and pounded the back of his head and neck with blows that were jackhammer fast and explosive. Eb was nearly unconscious, his vision blurry and dark and his ears ringing. Eb's adrenaline kicked in. He spun over on his back, freeing his arms enough to cover his face as Woody rained more blows toward Eb's head. Eb bucked his whole body a twice and threw Woody slightly off his rhythm, just enough for Eb to cover his face better with his left arm and throw a punch with his right fist. Eb hit Woody's chest, but Woody wasn't fazed. Eb swung again and clipped the bottom of his jaw, grazed it. The punch only made Woody madder.

Woody was growling with every punch and Eb could smell him, his pores giving off some kind of animal musk. Eb thought Woody was going to kill him when Eb felt Woody's weight lifted completely and suddenly. Eb let down the arm across his face and saw that J.W and two others had taken Woody by the arms and lifted him off the floor. They were plowing him into the wall. J.W. reached back with his right hand as far as he could go and unloaded a powerful punch to the crotch and Woody hit the floor groaning and powerless.

J.W. hurried over to Eb, picked him up and said, "You're a mess." Eb was bleeding in more places than he could count and it looked like Woody had dented his head in a dozen spots.

Eb felt a presence in the room and looked at the door. Miss Lincoln filled the entryway, towering there, glaring at Woody and seeing the mayhem that came to her dominion.

"This won't do," she said firmly. "Bring that boy—that Haywood—to my office if you have to carry him. Police and social services are on the way."

Ralphie told Miss Lincoln about a problem he was far from understanding. She understood. It was one of those nasty crimes, the mere suggestion of which demanded swift and decisive action and she took that action without even talking to anybody first. On one level—this one, at this moment—Eb had to respect the unwavering certainty of her position.

In less than an hour, Woody Frakis was a bad, fading memory. The school's residents never knew what happened to him after that night and never asked. Ralphie and the other kids were safe again and that was good enough.

Wednesday, October 2, 7:15 a.m.

"But Daddy, nobody on that team will even speak to me. I'm not imaginin' nothin'. They just don't like me and I don't know why. They're a bunch of cob-up-the-ass ballet snobs, if you ask me..."

"Joss-Lynn Lee Ledbetter, we will not have cussing in this house."

"...and I think we ought to replace ever one of 'em. It'd serve 'em right. I don't think they dance that good, either."

Joss-Lynn and Bobby Lee Ledbetter sat at the massive oak dining room table at the Ledbetter's *nouveau riche* estate in Biltmore Forest, Asheville's most exclusive neighborhood. Most of The Forest, as residents called it, had a gated, old money feel and simply oozed taste. The Ledbetters' oversized splancher didn't fit.

Marian Ledbetter skittered around the table, filling coffee cups and juice glasses and placing food in front of her sullen daughter. Bobby Lee was a biscuits-and-gravy man and Marian kept that Southern delicacy piled high.

"Gimme some more of them link sausages, Honey Lamb," said Bobby Lee without even looking up at Marian. "Now Joss-Lynn, we've got a fortune in that square dance team of yours, all to get that trophy—what's it called?—at the Youth Jamboree and if I'm hearin' correct, this team not only ain't been beat, it ain't been challenged."

Joss-Lynn was near tears, or at least she wanted Bobby Lee to think she was. "Yeah, but they hate me, Daddy! What good is that? These dancers ain't even from here, most of them, and the ones that are, like that Cynthia Frazier, think they're just better'n everybody else. Her daddy's a dad-blame truck driver. A truck driver! How's she better'n anybody?"

"Now, precious baby, it don't make no difference at all what her daddy does, long as it's legal. Truck drivin's honorable work. You judge this girl on who she is. I taught you better'n that."

"Well, she's just a witch! Yesterday, she told me I was out of step with my partner! HE WAS OUT OF STEP WITH ME!! He can't dance a lick. Got that fairy ballet butt and he prances and prisses around and it just makes me ill." Joss-Lynn stood up abruptly and slammed her hand on the table.

"And that Indian coach sides with her ballet pets. She's all the time bawling me out over the littlest things. I was five minutes late for practice yesterday—I had to go to Connie's Fashions right after school to pick up that new dress that come in from New York and I hurried as fast as I could. She said a dress wasn't no excuse for being late and that just made me so mad." She balled her fists and shook her head wildly. "Daddy, I'm ready to quit."

"I'll have a talk with Miss Silver Feather," said Bobby Lee gravely.

"You do that, Daddy! And you tell her this is my team. My team! And she better show me some respect." Joss-Lynn stalked out of the room.

Thursday, October 3, noon

Lizetta was waiting for Eb outside the cafeteria and already had her lunch in hand. She'd brought some kind of Mediterranean dish she called tabouleh. Eb had never seen anything like it. Lizetta said it had something called bulgur, a mixture of several kinds of durum wheat, as a base. Eb didn't know what that was and didn't want to show his ignorance by asking, but his expression gave him away.

"It's really good," she said. "We did a tour of the Holy Land last year and I loved the food. We brought a bunch of it back and learned how to make it. Mama mixes up tabouleh every other week or so. It has things like olive oil and garlic, onion tops, mint, lemon juice and parsley and it's not just good, it's really healthy."

"Sounds delightful," Eb said, crinkling his nose. "Want a bite of my bologna and peanut-butter sandwich?" Maryellen fed him, but she didn't always feed him well.

Lizetta grinned. "I'm a vegetarian. If I weren't, I'd become one if I had to eat bologna. You know what's in that stuff? And you're eating it with peanut butter? Oh, Lord."

"Pig, Baby," Eb said. "Lots of yummy pig. Pig face. Pig butt. Pig guts. Pig eyeballs. Mmmmm."

She put her arm through his and said, "Where to, my medieval lord? Shall we sup on the grounds, perhaps near the amphitheater, perchance a shaded venue where you can wipe your hands on the dogs?" He felt her round hip on his and her breast brushed against him. Neither went unnoticed as the front of his pants testified.

"Yeah, behind the stadium will work," he said, grinning at her quick wit. Eb was smitten with her playfulness and her intellect. She was a good date, even if it was only for school lunch. It was fortunate for both that he had study hall and she home ec after lunch break because they couldn't hear the bell and even if they could, they were often so deep in conversation and other delightful activities that they missed it.

About midway through the hour Eb, lying on his back, his hand resting on Lizetta's upper thigh, made a proposal. "You going to the game here next week against Marshall?"

"I hadn't thought that far ahead," she said. "Will you be back on the field by then?"

"I think so," Eb said. "I feel like I could play tomorrow, but the doc won't hear of it."

"You know I'll be there if you want me to. Maybe we could go get a sandwich afterward." Eb raised up to his elbows.

"What I'd like is a favor," he said, looking sheepish.

"It's yours."

"There's this kid in the dorm where I live, Ralphie, and he…well…he kind of thinks I'm his big brother. He's seven and he's never been to a football game. Gaylen and I promised we'd try to get him to a game before the end of the season. Gaylen's like his other big brother. Ralphie's been asking 'when' every week and I think he's getting discouraged."

"Lucky boy," said Lizetta, leaning in and kissing Eb's nose. "Two handsome big brothers."

"Anyhow, would you…well, would you let him ride to the game with you and sit with you while you're there? Gaylen and me have to be with the team before and during the game, but we can get together and do something afterwards. Ralphie'll probably be asleep anyway."

"Oh, I'd love to," said Lizetta, more excited than Eb had expected.

"There's one more thing," Eb said, his eyes looking at the ground.

"Elbert McCourry, what are you getting me into?"

"Uh." He paused. "Ralphie isn't supposed to go out at night without an adult from the home with him. We'd have to sneak him out. I know how we can do it if you're up to it."

"Up to it! What do you mean up to it? Are you suggesting, Mr. Football Hero, that Lizetta McEntire doesn't have the proper body parts to get this done? No *cojones*? Let us not underestimate the distaff equation, sir. Of course, I'll do it! It'll be a hoot."

Let us not underestimate…Eb thought. He continued to underestimate Lizetta. There was a lot to this girl and Eb liked all of it he knew. The bulge in his pants said he'd like to know more.

Friday, October 4, 9:22 p.m.
Ralphie hadn't stopped smiling all night, sitting close as he could to Lizetta, touching her, chattering non-stop. Every time Eb looked over at them, they were intensely involved in some conversation about something that seemed to be about as important as it could possibly be.

The Red Tail Hawks were up 49-0 on a weak Marshall team and Eb had played well enough to impress Ralphie, but

Ralphie was mostly otherwise engaged. Eb was sure this good little boy was having the time of his life and if there was a bill to pay at the Home later for fracturing the rules, they'd face that. Better to beg forgiveness than ask permission, he thought. Eb had a rich, warm feeling for Lizetta. She did this deed because she was good and her goodness touched him.

Lizetta, Ralphie and Eb met at the middle of the field at the end of the game and enjoyed a group hug. Gaylen rushed over, picked up Ralphie and said, "How'd you like the game, Scout?"

"Me 'n' Lizetta loved it," he said. "Remember when you knocked that big boy down ..." and Ralphie was off to the conversational races, nonstop for the rest of the evening.

Eb kissed Lizetta full on the lips and Ralphie was impressed. "She's pretty," he said, clinging tightly to her arm. Gaylen joined them and he lofted Ralphie onto his padded shoulders.

"You got good taste, short round," Eb said. "She sure is pretty."

Eb latched onto Ralphie's hand as Gaylen put him down and trotted off to exchange pleasantries with Marshall players. The three of them walked off the field like a family, Ralphie chattering full bore.

Saturday, October 5, 9:34 p.m.
This was going to be the long-anticipated boys' night out. Gaylen, Smoky Elliot McCurry and Eb ate at Ruby's Drive Inn in Banner Elk, a diner that sat splam in a hairpin curve about half a mile from Cannon Memorial Hospital, which was fortunate. A lot of people over the years went straight from the curve to the emergency room.

Gaylen suggested the boys get away from girls, football, dancing and everything else that made life more complex than it should be for seventeen- and eighteen-year-olds and do something truly productive. They were going out to get drunk.

Eb had no experience with this. His dad died an alcoholic

and that gave him pause to try, but Gaylen made it sound so appealing that Eb wasn't about to pass up the opportunity. Eb's mother included a ten dollar bill in a letter to him early in the week and he was about as flush as he was to get during this year abroad. Ten dollars was a considerable amount of money to Eb's mother—and to Eb. He was so touched that he sat down and wrote a thank-you note tinged with homesickness. He even asked about the kids, his younger brother and sister. If she had known what he was going to do with the ten dollars, she'd want it back.

Gaylen, smoking one of his smelly cigars, had the battle plan, but hadn't let everybody in on it yet.

Eb hadn't been around Elliot much, except in practice, where Elliott played against the first offense with the second team defense. He was a decent football player, nothing spectacular and was trying to find where he fit. Tonight he'd find out. He'd already torn his pants on that metal bur that was once again sticking up from Gaylen's car despite Eb's rock-flattening efforts, and that was a start.

Elliot and Eb shared the same last name—spelled differently—and there was a good chance they were related, but neither knew for sure. Macquarie, Hap assured Eb, was spun off into a number of different spellings, but the holders of the various iterations of the name were all from the Isle of Mull and the same original seed. He guaranteed it.

Gaylen laid out the evening. The boys would go by Ruby's, load up on burgers and fries to "line our stomachs," he said, so they could drink more. Then they'd head out to this bootlegger's place on the side of the hill about two miles down Rt. 184.

Avery was a dry county, giving Velma and Luke Belton a fat niche market and a virtual monopoly on liquor sales in the Banner Elk area, Gaylen explained. They sold no moonshine. It was strictly the safe booze: bonded liquor, cheap wine and off-brand beer they'd hauled in from North Wilkesboro in a big yellow Checker. The Checker was a cab in New York years earlier and it was the dangedest bootlegger's car anybody ever saw, though hardly low profile. The constabulary of the entire county knew about the Beltons' business and accepted small payoffs to let the Checker pass.

The Beltons had a makeshift bar in the basement of their small frame house at the end of a poplar-lined dirt road, half a mile off Highway 184. They called it a bar, but they didn't let anybody drink in the house because the Bible said drinking was sinful. They didn't drink and they didn't want to watch anybody drink. But commerce was commerce and they tithed their profits at the Bee Log Primitive Baptist Church, which was glad to have the money.

Luke and Velma had lived in their house for years, selling illegal booze and fighting like they hated each other. Everybody knew about Velma and Luke's business and nobody paid much attention. The authorities understood that vice was going to happen and it might as well be run by good church-going, God-fearing Christian people like the Beltons, who gave ten percent off the top to Jesus and five percent to them.

A couple of years ago, Gaylen told Eb, Velma caught Luke in a morally compromised moment with her cousin Luella, the home-wrecking whore, and Velma stabbed him eleven times. *Eleven* times. Luke lived because those boys at Cannon Memorial Hospital did good work. He asked forgiveness, begged Velma to take him back and she took him. Rumor was he slept with one eye open.

Gaylen figured that a six-pack of sixteen-ounce Falstaff, a pint of Cobbs Creek and another pint of King Kong—cheap whisky brands that bootleggers sold for three dollars, double what it cost them—would put the whole gang at the desired level of physical and mental instability. That was nine dollars worth of booze, split among four of boys, a fair deal. Smoky and Eb put in three dollars each, Elliot two dollars because that's what he had and Gaylen a dollar because it was his Simca they were riding in. Elliot wanted to reverse his and Gaylen's contributions because of the torn pants, but Gaylen wouldn't have it. "I didn't tear your damn pants," he growled. "You did."

Gaylen and Eb went into the house to get the booze because Gaylen was the driver and knew the bootleggers and because Eb was the oldest, five weeks older than Smoky.

Velma met them at the door. She was an ample woman in tight pink pedal-pushers left over from about 1956, a sweater that looked like paint, emphasizing breasts that were sturdy, well supported and pointed like bombs. Velma had a tiny waist that served to frame a bottom that resembled two basketballs pressed together. Hers was a cartoon figure. She obviously had somewhere to go because her faux-blonde hair was in toilet-paper-roll-sized curlers and she held a bottle of fingernail polish.

"Can I help you boys?" she said, her eyes adjusting to the outside darkness. She leaned in toward them. "Oh, hi, Gaylen. I didn't recognize you in the shadow. How's your daddy and who's this good looking young man with you?"

"Daddy's not feeling so well and this is Elbert McCourry, our new quarterback," said Gaylen with a hint of impatience. He put his hand on the door and opened it wider.

"Luke said you'uns was a-doin' real well with the football team and said that new quarterback was awful good," Velma said, winking knowingly at Eb and causing a level of discomfort he hadn't felt for a while. She smiled and Commie-red lipstick smudged her teeth. She pushed the door open wide and ushered them in.

"What can I get for you'uns, honey?"

Gaylen gave Velma the order. "Must be a bunch of you," she said. "That's a lot of spirits for boys your age."

They didn't answer and she went down the steps toward the goodies. Gaylen and Eb heard her open and close the big cooler where the beer was kept. Velma and Luke didn't do the sophisticated forty-three-degree beer. When you went to their place for a cold beer, you got a cold beer, one that was almost frozen.

The Falstaff came in the new pop-top cans, invented in 1959 by a guy named Emal Fraze in Dayton, Ohio, after Emal spent a hot Sunday afternoon at a church picnic with a lot of cold beer and no church key. They drank cold beer in Ohio at church picnics, something that would have been unthinkable in Avery County, North Carolina. Emal opened beer on car bumpers and that didn't work to suit him, so he invented something that did.

Alcoa bought Emal's idea and Iron City Beer tested pop tops in Virginia in 1962. Now Falstaff had them. They couldn't get Iron City Beer in Banner Elk, but Falstaff, which tasted like piss from a tall horse, was readily available. In the commotion about this new convenience and about what the hell to do with the pull tab, everybody forgot about Emal, who should be a prominent name in the beer history and lore, but isn't.

Eb and Gaylen walked back to the car, where Eb pulled the bottle of Cobb's Creek out of the bag and looked at it closely. Gaylen told Eb that a few years ago Velma and Luke—and the Avery County Sheriff—got caught up in a stink because of a scam they were involved in. Seems the Sheriff was catching people pretty close to the bootleggers' house in Banner Elk on a regular basis. He was confiscating their booze and letting them go with a warning. A suspicious and enterprising customer thought he'd test a theory because he'd been caught several times. He marked the bottles of whisky he bought on this particular night and was stopped by the Sheriff shortly afterwards. The next night, he was back buying again—same brands—and as he walked out the door, he checked the bottles and, sure enough, two of them had his ballpoint pen mark in a corner of the label. He called the Avery Journal and told them what happened. The Journal followed up with a call to the Sheriff—though its reporter never wrote anything—and the scam stopped. Eb didn't find any writing on the labels he looked at.

Soon as Eb and Gaylen got back to the car, Smoky popped one of the Falstaffs, threw the tab on the floorboard, drunk half of it in one long sip and passed it to Eb. Smoky was already high. He either didn't have much tolerance for alcohol, or the power of suggestion was such that he willed himself snockered on about eight ounces of beer. Cheap that way, Eb thought.

It was at this point in the evening that Gaylen looked down and realized he was close to running out of gas.

"Gotta gas up," he said.

Smoky and Eb reached into their pockets to see if they had any money left.

"Keep your money," said Gaylen. "I got a siphon hose."

***

It took an hour, a goodly consumption of their booze stash and a couple of driver changes to get enough gas to leave Banner Elk. Eb wound up behind the wheel, reluctantly, since he didn't have a driver's permit, and his driving was uneasy at best.

After a few false starts, they headed down Rt. 194 toward Time Square Restaurant six miles away in Elk Park where some of their buddies—and maybe even a few girls—would be hanging out in the parking lot, listening to music and drinking illegal booze. There might even be a good fight if the Elk River Boys were there looking for trouble, as was their custom.

Sunday, October 6, 10:30 a.m.

The day following the August football practice in which team members had first hit each other at Toe River High, Eb was so battered he didn't want to go back. His first drunk was similar. When he finally poured himself onto the floor and crawled down the wooden steps to the bathroom the morning after the booze, he was ready to pledge his soul to the porcelain throne for a minute of relief. He hurt everywhere. He was nauseated, depressed, dehydrated and so sick that death would have been a blessed relief. Never again, he promised himself, in the grand tradition of lying drunks.

He didn't remember much beyond driving toward Time

Square and had no idea how he got home, how he got in the dorm, how he got to bed, how he stayed in the bed. Now he had to bathe, brush his teeth, catch a ride to school and be energetic and smiley-faced. The team had a square dance exhibition at Appalachian State and Miss Lilly told Eb he was dancing. The opportunity couldn't have come at a worse time.

The team rode thirty miles north to Boone in a caravan of five cars because the activity bus—which wasn't all that active most of the time—was broken down again. It was the distributor this go-round. Carburetor a couple of weeks ago and a fuel line several days before that. Eb rode with Smoky, Joyce and Janice. Nice quartet, they were. Joyce and Eb were dancing as a pair at Appalachian and he wasn't just sick. He was nervous—scared, really. He was the weakest, least experienced, least knowledgeable dancer on a team that was a competitive juggernaut and growing stronger. He had no business being on the floor with these talented people, he told himself, but he had to give it all he had. That was the only way he could save any face at all.

Miss Lilly promised to keep the routines basic and told Eb she wouldn't throw anything new in at the last minute, as she often did. He pulled her aside after the team's practice Wednesday to beg off the debut "until I'm more ready."

She didn't take that kindly. "Elbert McCourry, I'll decide when you're ready unless you're prepared to take on the coaching of this team," she said. "If you're not satisfied that you know the steps and the routines, put in some extra work. Learn it until it's like walking. If it's harder than that, you need to work some more. You will not let this team down."

Eb asked Joyce to dance with him twice during the week and Maryellen worked some with Eb after supper for about two hours one night at the Home. But it wasn't like walking. It never would be.

The team's performance was to be before a group from the Appalachian Studies program. Its students and teachers seemed to have an interest in Toe River High's square dance team in the same way an anthropologist would study a pygmy tribe. The auditorium was large, heavily draped and impressive to these kids from a tiny, poor high school. As the dancers walked in through the front door, Eb pointed to the stage and said to Joyce, "That's our specimen cage."

"Will you quit that?" said Joyce. "Those students are trying to help us maintain at least some of our heritage before the developers and land speculators get all of it and put high-rises and ski slopes on it."

Word leaked out that week that somebody was buying up Beech Mountain, which towered over the children's home in Banner Elk, in order to build a ski slope and ten-story hotel. Smoky cracked, "Yeah, just high enough for an airplane to run into once they get the airport built." All that was coming and everybody knew it. It was a matter of time. But would continuing to square dance make a difference? Joyce thought so.

Eb hadn't actually walked to the top of Beech Mountain yet and wanted to before it was paved, so he and Smoky planned to ask Sharon and Lizetta to hike up there with a picnic lunch on a Sunday soon. But this Sunday, they were dancing their native dance and being studied at Appalachian State Teachers College.

Eb was smack in the middle of the culture specimens.

The team went through its routines twice before the burgundy velvet curtain was pulled. The dancers looked out on an audience of about seventy-five people in an auditorium that held fifteen hundred. Not impressive, he thought, but how big could the Appalachian Studies program be?

If Eb was nervous and self-conscious—and hung over—he could take some comfort that Joyce was his partner. Dancing with her was natural for him. She was in enough control that he didn't feel threatened by the intricacies of some of the steps and moves and she seemed to have confidence in him.

Appalachian State furnished a four-piece old-time band that was smooth and tight. Toe River High blistered its performance, looking better, Miss Lilly said, than it had in some time. Eb was pleased, really pleased, because he'd held his own and that was all that Miss Lilly expected of him. Truth be told, it was all he had.

The applause from the students died and the team turned to exit the stage, when Joyce leaned over and kissed Eb on the lips. It was open-mouthed, firm, warm, wet with a hint of tongue. The kiss was so sudden that Eb didn't close his eyes and as Joyce kissed him, he saw Smoky just offstage chuckle, and Miss Lilly, beside him, smile, cover her mouth and turn away quickly. She couldn't watch a major team felony taking place, Eb guessed.

"What's that for?" Eb said, embarrassed, surprised and knowing his face was glowing red.

"'Cause you deserve it, El-bert," she said. "You worked that fine butt off and I'm proud of you."

Dancing had rewards football could only dream about.

Monday, October 7, 12:07 p.m.

Maryellen packed two bacon-lettuce-tomato sandwiches and an apple for Eb's lunch, but she didn't pack Lizetta, so Eb was on his own. Lizetta had a dentist's appointment and Eb was on the prowl for some company. He went into the lunchroom to see who wasn't occupied and over in the corner sat Janice Watkins, whom Eb would not have imagined being alone for more than five minutes during any break in the school day. She was pretty, smart, funny, talented and everybody liked her.

Eb plunked down across from her and put his sandwiches and the big green apple on the Formica tabletop. "Mind if I join you?" he said.

"What have I done to deserve this blessing?" she said, a slight twinkle in her eye.

"You're available. Nobody else seems to be." Janice smirked.

Eb slid into his seat and said, "Actually, I've been wanting to talk to you. Joyce tells me you didn't make the square dance team right off, that you came in as an alternate and worked your way to starter. Now you're a star."

"I *am not* a star!" she protested.

"Are too!"

"Am not am not am not," she said, catching the tenor of banter quickly.

"Tell me what happened with you," Eb said, leaning toward her and taking a huge bite out of a BLT, dripping juice from one of the prized heirloom tomatoes that Grover the caretaker grew at the Home. Pink juice splattered on the yellowed Formica table top. Eb wiped the juice up with the heel of his hand and licked it off.

"Nice move," said Janice, suppressing an outright laugh.

She thought about Eb's question for a second, then launched into a monologue. "The day of the tryout I went to school with a knot in my stomach and my heart pounding. My best friend and I were trying out together—in front of the whole student body. Her sister and brother danced with the team in previous years and she was more comfortable than me. After weeks of practicing in front of a mirror it was down to this." She leaned forward, elbows on the battle, hands folded in front of her. Eb took another bite, spilled more juice, wiped it up, licked it off. Janice shook her head.

"I had to learn to paste a smile on my face while keeping the beat with my left foot and to remember the steps for the clog—*a-slap-ball-change*—and the buck—*a-slap-brush-heel-brush-heel-brush-heel-a slap*. Those steps should have come natural, but I was on the verge of total nervous breakdown. I knew if I failed to get on that stage there was no chance of getting on the team. So, there I stood with the others calming myself by listening to the music and keeping beat in my head and with my left foot. I don't know how many people went before me, but I finally heard my name called." She ran the fingers of both hands through her hair, then rested her chin on the back of her hand and continued. She looked pretty, thought

Eb.

"The audience was terrifying. I remembered Miss Lilly said, 'Don't make eye contact with the audience, look over their heads. Smile.' I tapped my foot to get in time to the music. Left, left, left, then went up the middle of the stage with a clog, stopped to go into a buck, fake-smiling all the time, my lips jerking with every step. I didn't trip and I kept time. As I left the stage I did this big inner celebration that nobody outside saw." She spread her hands wide, as if taking a bow.

"Then I had to wait for the names of the winners to be posted on a bulletin board in the hall. I was so nervous when the list went up, that I couldn't look. Then a big group formed a mob in front looking for our names. Girls squealed and boys smiled and whooped it up. A couple of girls walked away crying and two boys cussed. I couldn't find my name and it just broke my heart. It was one of the longest days I'll ever spend here and I was certain I'd collapse and cry, but I didn't. My friend made the cut and I was happy for her, but I didn't want to go to school the next day." She sighed deeply.

"Several days later Miss Lilly asked me if I would attend practices and I was reluctant because I didn't want people looking at me like I was some kind of loser. But I did and darned if the first night I was there, one of the girls was out and I was called to the stage. I was shaking all over when I fell into line with the team, but it felt natural from the start and I haven't been out of the lineup since."

"That's a good story," Eb said, still leaning in toward Janice. "Nothing like that will happen to me because I'm not in your league as a dancer, but it's encouraging to hear it."

"Eb, from what I've seen, you're a pretty good dancer. Joyce says you're a natural and I haven't seen you do anything but get better." She touched his hand lightly, reassuring.

"Thank you for saying that, but y'all been square dancing forever and I'm still learning steps you knew in first grade. I don't have any illusions about being good, about starting or anything like that. I just want to contribute what I can."

"Don't underestimate yourself, buddy," said Janice, sounding a lot like her sister. "The rest of us don't."

"Buddy" didn't sound so bad coming from Janice.

Wednesday, October 9, 6 p.m.

The dance team was gathered in a tight group on stage in the third floor auditorium at Toe River High School. The curtains on the high auditorium windows were open and the fading afternoon sun lit the space with an almost eerie glow, early-fall yellow and beautiful. Miss Lilly stood directly in front of the dancers, three feet lower on the auditorium floor, her bent shadow stretching to their feet. She was in near silhouette against the floor-to-ceiling windows at the back of the auditorium when she spoke.

"You young people have done a lot of difficult work and have overcome some real challenges this year," she said, "but we are not where we need to be and we are going to have to find a way to get there."

She stepped closer to the stage and several dancers fidgeted. "Our competition is better than it ever has been and when we get to the Mountain Youth Jamboree in about five weeks we will be facing dancers on this Asheville team that are all but professional in their talent level.

"So what does that leave us? First, we have to be the best we can. That is the one goal we can achieve immediately and without question. I will expect no less of you and you will give no less to this team."

Eb looked to his left and saw Joyce and Maryellen standing beside each other, listening intently. Mickey Buchanan was behind them, ogling their bottoms, his hands reaching out as if to squeeze them.

"Beyond that, though, we will need something because we are dealing with a level of technical perfection we've not seen before. That means we're going to have to push innovation to the limits and that we'll have to take some chances with who we are and what smooth square dancing is."

154

Eb knew that in general Miss Lilly was talking about changing and adapting, the way the football team had been forced to do, but he had no clue what that could mean. On the field, he could call for an extra blocker or quickly draw up a pass route to exploit a weakness, but what could Miss Lilly do to bring out the best in this team and take it to another level of creativity? He had no idea.

"We have generally known this form of dance to be tame, predictable and without a lot of drama," said Miss Lilly, no emotion in her voice. "It's time to change that. Two years ago, we added taps and people objected, protested and finally we put them away. We've been slowly emphasizing clogging and buck dancing, though not during competition." She turned and began walking from one side of the dance line to the other, looking each dancer in the eyes as she slowly walked.

"Clog is the most dramatic form of this dance and when we incorporate it in the right places and with the proper emphasis, we will not only bring the house down, we will impress the judges with who we are and what we know about our own culture." She stopped, turned and faced the team, full-faced, direct and with an implied challenge.

"We are going to be taking a chance with this when we use it and it could blow up in our faces with a disqualification." She paused to let the thought sink.

"But I think it is where we need to go at this time, with this team and against this competition, so line up and let's get started. Mickey Buchanan and Janice Watkins, I want you front and center. We're going to put you in the spotlight."

Mickey smiled broadly, the first time Eb had seen that delighted expression from him. Usually anything resembling a smile from Mickey was quickly read as a smirk. Janice did not smile. She looked terrified. Not only was her role being upgraded, but she'd be dancing with Mickey Buchanan, the team's—and maybe the state's—best dancer and the meanest creep she knew.

So began Miss Lilly's grand experiment, one that would

either give Toe River a chance to retain Old Smoky or would launch a new square dance dynasty in Asheville.

***

Because the team had just eighteen of the usual complement of twenty dancers, and sixteen were on the stage at any given time, there was little room for sickness, injury or other commitments from a group that had a lot of involvements to consider. Almost everybody on the team was an athlete in a varsity sport and at this point in the year, the dance team had not only football and cheerleading to consider, but boys' and girls' basketball were on the verge of starting pre-season workouts. Two of the dancers took musical instrument lessons. Zillia Stuart was a virtuoso autoharp player and won "most talented" at the Mountain Youth Jamboree the year before. She sang and played "Just One More Day" in a near operatic mezzo-soprano clear as a mountain spring. Another dancer, Bill Langford, took an evening credit class at Lees-McRae College in physics, something Toe River didn't offer, getting ready for college engineering. Several had young siblings at home and were occasionally needed to babysit. Square dancing, sometimes, was necessarily a secondary consideration for team members.

Miss Lilly didn't like the conflicts, but there wasn't much she could do about them. Square dancing was a sport without a season and it had to be practiced when time and dancers were available. The team generally got three practices and either a competition or an exhibition each week. A couple of times there were multiple competitions in a short span, but that was rare.

Given all the disruptions and the fact that Eb was there at every practice—he simply moved up to the auditorium from the football field after practice and a shower—he got a lot of work. It was with a variety of dance partners, but he often wound up with Joyce, more a follower than a leader, learning far more from her than from anybody else. He watched Mickey

Buchanan clog and buck dance with deep admiration, though that admiration did not spread to Mickey personally. This guy was a jerk, but his talent was on another level from the one Eb understood.

Tonight, everybody was at practice and Eb's time on the floor would likely be limited, he thought, so when Miss Lilly told the team to pull it in, Eb moved over to the side with his natural partner, Becky Blake, and they followed as they could beside the action. During breaks, Eb practiced clogging— closely watching and emulating Mickey. Say what you would about Mickey Buchanan, but he worked at both square dancing and football, Eb thought. Nobody ever saw him sandbag or take a shortcut or fail to do anything he was supposed to do in order to improve. He would have been a model athlete had he been anybody else. As it was, he required a bouncer just to keep him in line.

Miss Lilly took note of the work going on during the break, but didn't say anything. "Back at it," she said after a few minutes. "I want you clogging the entire dance this time. No sliding." The dancers looked at Miss Lilly and smiled. The game was really on now.

It was exhausting. This routine was a hard dance to do in short form, but for twelve minutes at a stretch, it was draining everybody. Eb boxed Golden Gloves the year before and he found boxing, one of the most exhausting sports he was aware of, wasn't nearly as tiring and intricate as clogging. Boxing rounds were three minutes long and there were only three of them with a sit-down rest period between rounds. Clogging didn't stop for the equivalent of four continuous boxing rounds, which would have dropped a boxer like a right cross to the jaw.

When Miss Lilly called "Break!" again, Eb looked around at a room full of people panting and sweating, bent over with hands on knees. They looked like overworked horses. Becky and Eb went through the entire routine clogging alongside the team and Eb wanted to lie down somewhere, but dared not even suggest it. He put the record back on and kept dancing while others rested.

"I can see right now," said Miss Lilly over the music, "that we're going to have to spend some time on conditioning. You are not in shape for this. We will not appear before five-thousand people expecting a classy, good-looking team and getting one that comes out soaked in sweat and gasping for breath. This will have to look easy, like we could do it while writing a speech. And you know what that means."

As the music ended, Eb bent over, hands on his knees, suppressing a heave, sweat pooling at his feet like it was coming from a dripping faucet. He rose and saw a shadow at the doorway. It was Lizetta. She stood just outside the auditorium watching practice intently. When their eyes linked, she winked and smiled. She mouthed, "You look great." Eb, soaked with sweat, shook his head, embarrassed, and wiggled the pinky on his right hand, a sign of intimate recognition they'd developed for moments like this. She wiggled hers back.

The dancers went through one more full routine without the clogging and Miss Lilly said, "That's it for tonight. I liked the way you went after that clogging routine," she said. "I saw some enthusiasm."

Miss Lilly didn't know the half of it. The dancers loved clogging because of the drama, the noise, the idea that they were doing something on the edge, something that might even be illegal. Miss Lilly grew a foot taller to each of the dancers on this night.

Eb walked down the steps at the side of the stage and Lizetta came over and put a hand on his sweat-soaked back. "I need to talk to you, Eb," she said.

Oh, shit, he thought. *Here it comes.*

Wednesday, October 9, 8:33 p.m.
"Can I get a quick shower?" Eb said to Lizetta. "It won't take ten minutes. I'll run up to the gym, shower and dress and we can meet at your car if that works. Can I get a ride to the Home?"

"That sounds perfect," she said.

"Hope this is not serious," Eb said. "Been a long day and I still got some homework to do."

"I'll see you in ten," she said.

***

Lizetta leaned against the driver's side rear fender of the Riviera as Eb ran over to her, hair still soaked and smelling of Ivory soap following his shower. She looked radiant, standing under the parking lot's lone light in a lime shirt-waist dress, pumps and a tiny silver necklace, dangling a pendant she once told Eb came from Italy. A lime ribbon held her hair off her face.

Lizetta wasted no time. "It'll be spring before we know if Daddy's going to Raleigh," she said, "so we get the rest of the school year, at least." She smiled, spread her arms to hug Eb and moved to meet him. He kissed her long and soft, sighing. "I'm happy," he said as simply as he could when they finally broke the embrace. Her body stayed close and he felt her warmth.

"You don't know happy," she said. "I've been giddy since Daddy told me this afternoon after school and I couldn't wait to tell you." She moved closer to him and wrapped her arms slightly tighter. Eb felt all of her and began to stir in sensitive places. He kissed her again and held it, moving against her. She placed her left hand squarely on his bottom and squeezed.

They broke, both breathing deeply. She pushed him back gently, looked into his eyes and said, "We'd better get moving before we get in trouble. You have homework and I do, too. We'll pick this up another time."

"Promise?" he said, almost pleading. He was erect again and there was a small wet spot on his pants. He slid his hand over her round behind and he pulled her close.

"Oh, you bet," she said and she kissed him, pressing herself into him and feeling his swelling.

Part VII

Thursday, October 10, 8:10 a.m.

Eb rushed straight off the bus and up the two steep flights of steps to Miss Lilly's room just off the auditorium. He stopped at the door, lightly knocked as he barged in and breathlessly said, "Can I talk to you a minute, ma'am?"

"What's so urgent that it can't wait until your sociology class, Elbert?"

"I wanted to know if I can get a key to the building from you so I can come in and work on clogging and buck dancing on the nights we don't have practice." His tone was breathless, hurried, almost urgent, partly from the sprint up the steps, mostly from his excitement.

"Elbert, I really appreciate your enthusiasm for the square dance team, but I can't have you rattling around in this building after hours by yourself, regardless of your motives." She stood, turned toward the blackboard, picked up an eraser and began erasing the most recent class assignment.

"Oh, I won't be by myself, Miss Lilly," Eb said, thinking quickly. "I'm going to have other members of the team with me."

"Who?"

"Uh. Joyce. And maybe some of the others. I ain't had time to ask yet, but I wanted to see if I could get the key before asking. We need the work, especially the conditioning."

She tapped the eraser on the blackboard, creating a chalk cloud and looked intently at Eb for a long moment. "Why does somebody as intelligent as you use the word 'ain't'? Can you explain that?"

"No, ma'am," he said. "Habit, I guess. Laziness, maybe." He grinned sheepishly.

"Tell you what," she said, "if you can get at least ten others to join you two, a total of twelve, then I'll see to it that the auditorium is open for an hour in the evening after football

160

practice on the days we don't have a scheduled practice or meet. Let me know by class time today if you get the ten and I'll get you in tonight.

"One more thing: If I hear you use the word 'ain't' again, the deal's off."

Eb's face turned red. "Yes, ma'am," he said. "I'll remember that. And thank you. I think this will make a difference. A big difference."

Thursday, October 10, 3:17 p.m.

Coach Woodson yelled at Eb to double-time it over to where he stood with a tall, blond, heavily-muscled man of about thirty-five near the football field's grandstands. Eb threw another pass Terry in the waning minutes of warm-ups before the week's light final practice.

"Elbert McCourry this is Coach Lesley Sand from Western Carolina," said Woodson. "I think you may remember him from the Bakersville game. He coaches quarterbacks."

"Good to see you again, sir," Eb said, extending his hand and looking into a pair of intense blue eyes. "Call me Eb." Woodson walked away toward the center of the field where practice had begun.

"You throw a good ball, Eb," Sand said. "Tight spiral, nice velocity, excellent accuracy. As you may know, our coach retires at the end of this year and we have a new head man coming in, Billy Edmondson, the quarterback of the San Francisco 49ers, who's retiring from pro football at the end of this season. Western will be his first coaching job and he wants to run the shotgun formation they've been so successful with in San Francisco the past few years. It looks like the single wing, but like your version, it's a passing offense. His will be quite a bit more sophisticated, as you might imagine. We're looking for somebody who can run that offense and what you're doing here is not far off what we have in mind."

"You have a running offense now, don't you?" Eb asked, excited about the prospect of helping take a college football team into what could be its next big phase, breaking from the boring T-formation which was predominant. "You're ditching that to throw the ball all over the field?"

"That's what we plan," Sand said. Eb took his helmet off and held it by the facemask at his side. His imagination was going at light speed, considering the prospects of operating a college offense with good receivers and instructions to play in high gear.

The offense at Toe River—the single wing—was actually an unimaginative holdover from the nineteen-thirties and forties, except when the team was passing. That happened when Eb was on the field and the offense became wide open and occasionally wild, but never undisciplined. Some of the offense was improvised in the huddle because much of the passing game hadn't been anticipated until Eb arrived.

"I've seen what you've done on the fly with this team," said Sand, "and I like the way you take over. That requires a level of confidence most high school seniors don't have."

"Thank you," Eb said, "but we have some good athletes and I can promise you that it's not just me. There's a bunch of them better'n me."

"Regardless of who you think the heroes are here, Eb," said Sand, "you're the one we're interested in. How are your grades?"

"Pretty good. I want to be a writer, so I'm strong in subjects that would support that. Not much of a math and science guy, though."

"Can we look at your transcripts?"

"Sure."

"How's your knee, the one you hurt against Crossnore?"

"You know about that?" said Eb, looking at his shoes, embarrassed.

"Son, it's my business to know everything I can about you because we're interested in you. A scholarship is worth a lot of money and we only have a certain number. We won't give more than one to a quarterback this year and if you get it, you'd be the only freshman quarterback we have next year. That's a risk for us."

"The knee's fine," Eb said. "It was a sprain. I could have played the next week, but the doc told Coach Woodson to hold me out. I kept on square dancing, though."

"Square dancing?"

"The team," Eb said. "Square dancing's big here, like wrestling at some schools or lacrosse or soccer at others. We've got a couple of national championships and a bunch of state championships. We're on the verge of retiring Old Smoky."

"Old Smoky?" Sand said, puzzled.

"It's a big deal trophy, but I doubt you want to talk about square dancing. Anyhow, I didn't stop dancing and I stayed in shape because I didn't."

"National champion is pretty impressive, even if it's tiddly-winks," Sand said. "Takes special people to win it all and it's great training for everything else you'll ever do." Sand extended his right hand and Eb shook it. "I just wanted to come by and tell you to keep it up. You're playing well and we think you could have a future in football. It might be as a Catamount. I'll be in touch."

"Thank you for your interest," Eb said, as he turned on his heel and ran back to the passing line, a huge smile on his face, his heart pounding. He felt a fluffy, supporting cloud beneath him.

Thursday, October 10, 5:32 p.m.

Winston Craighill, the custodian at Toe River High School and the only black person Eb had seen since arriving in Avery County months ago, met him at the side door of the school with a hefty ring of keys. "Miz Lilly told me to let you in for an hour if you have eleven other people with you," Winston said. "I don't see nobody else."

"Give them a few minutes," Eb said. "Some of them's football players finishing showering and there's a couple of girls basketball players coming after practice. Some of them's driving back to school from home. They'll be here."

By five forty-five Eb proved correct and Winston opened the main door and said, "You got a hour. Miz Lilly said to hold you to it strict."

Winston was a favorite of just about everybody in school. He was a bulky, gentle, almost sweet man, whose primary goal in life seemed to make Toe River High School the best place possible for the three-hundred-eighty-odd students who had to spend seven hours a day there.

The yearbook staff tried to dedicate the annual to him last year, Joyce told Eb, but J. D. Banner vetoed the idea, saying the seniors couldn't it to "a custodian" when they meant "a nigger." It was disheartening and several yearbook staffers quit in protest.

Eb put out the word about the impromptu practice and recruited twelve dancers by the sociology period, but he hadn't counted on getting sixteen together, which is what happened. Even Mickey Buchanan was there. Mickey worked hard, but Eb didn't figure him for something like this, which some of the team members thought of as more a social gathering than a practice. They were in for a surprise. Miss Lilly told Eb it was his responsibility to run the practices and he meant to make the workouts rigorous and valuable.

"Everybody line up," said Eb. "Miss Lilly said we could do this as long as we were working. This is going to be a conditioning session. We're going to clog until we can't clog any more."

There was no resistance to Eb as the session's leader. He had earned his wings with the football team and coming back from his knee injury to be at square dance practice.

Eb waved to Joyce, who put the record player arm down on the small vinyl disk, hurried over to him, joined hands and, when the music started, the dancing began. Full-on clogging.

The clattering shoes weren't anywhere near in synch, but after a few adjustments, the rhythm of the clogging was clear—

and quite beautiful, Eb thought. It was noisy, melodic, exciting and invigorating. After a while, it was exhausting, but nobody slowed down. An hour passed quickly and Winston appeared at the door, waved at Eb and ran his hand across his throat. *Cut!*

Eb grinned at him, waved his hand and bellowed, "That's it for tonight. Y'all worked your butts off and I'm proud of all of us. Old Smoky's staying home!" That brought a rousing cheer. Joyce threw up one hand and the team formed on it. The dancers touched in a peak—everybody but Mickey—and sharply yelped, "CLOG!"

Eb was soaked and tired, but wore a thorough sense of something accomplished on his face and in the way he stood. There was the hint of a strut as he walked toward the door.

He felt even better when he looked into the shadows behind Winston and saw Lizetta waiting for him.

Thursday, October 10, 6:52 p.m.

Eb slid onto the luxurious leather front seat of the Riviera as Lizetta almost leapt across the seat to him, her lips meeting his before he was settled, her kiss deep and passionate. Her hand was on the back of his head, pulling him urgently to her as her tongue darted in and out of his mouth. He was all but breathless when she finally pulled back and said, "Hello, handsome. I've been waiting for you."

"I can see that. Nice greeting." He softly kissed her cheek, her nose, her ear, her lips. A familiar stirring began again in his nethers. Lizetta put a hand on his chest and rubbed in a circular motion.

"There's more where that came from. Wanna go see the Brown Mountain Lights?"

That was Avery County teen code for a love session in the car. The Brown Mountain Lights, Eb learned, were some kind of natural phenomenon in Burke County, twenty miles away down near the Morganton foothills. People had studied the lights for years. Scientists couldn't figure out what they were but kids knew all about them and how they affected the moods in the front and back seats of cars at night.

"Are you kidding?" Eb said, looking back over a day of school, football and some of the most intense square dancing anybody could remember. He was nearly exhausted. "Of course, I want to see the lights." He pulled her close, put his right hand on her breast and lightly stroked.

"I want to make love with you, Eb," said Lizetta, dropping all pretense.

His mouth went stone dry and he couldn't speak for nearly ten seconds.

"Was it alright for me to say that?" she said, her brow suddenly wrinkled and her eyes intense. "I don't want you to think I do this all the time, but you're so important to me…"

"No, Lizetta. I don't think that. It's just … I want this to be right. I've thought about it a lot and I don't want to just screw in the car. It's not what I want for us. You've been on my mind almost constantly, making love to you in my head over and over, but I'd rather wait until we can make it something we can remember with a good feeling for a long time. I love you."

Eb was talking himself and Lizetta out of what he wanted most in the world and his penis was telling him he was crazy. It was hard and throbbing and the feeling was urgent. Lizetta saw what was happening and lightly stroked him on the outside of his jeans. "Ooooh, god," he said. He put his hand on hers and moved it to his chest. "This is crazy, but I want it to be right"

Lizetta looked deep into his eyes and smiled softly. "My dad has a small cabin on Squirrel Creek," she said. "It's cozy and private, a fishing and hunting getaway for him. He's spending so much time on this new job both in Raleigh and at home that we can probably go up there any time we want. He's on the Outer Banks this weekend at some kind of conference, so…"

"Yes," Eb interrupted. "That sounds perfect. How about Sunday afternoon? I have a good sized square dance meet Saturday, but Sunday works."

"I'll pick you up at one o'clock and we'll have all

afternoon. I think it's supposed to rain. That and a fire would be so nice."

Eb pulled her close, looked into her eyes and kissed her tenderly. He put his hand on her right breast and squeezed gently. Neither of them said another word until they got to the Home. He kissed her goodnight and floated up to his room, a large wet stain on the front of his pants.

Friday, October 11, 9:23 p.m.

A deeply tanned older man walked briskly toward Eb, extended his hand and said, "Nice game, son. You seem to be growing by the week out there." The man wore a black ASU baseball cap tilted back on a large head that rested on shoulders with no apparent neck. "I'm Roger Walker of Appalachian State and we're keeping an eye on you," he said. "What was that tonight, five touchdown passes?"

"Something like that," said Eb, sliding his helmet off a soaked head. "Hope you noticed our defense. It hasn't been scored on." Eb talked easily, less embarrassed than he was with the recruiter from Western. He enjoyed this new wrinkle.

Toe River embarrassed a good Marion team thirty-five to nothing, its fourth straight shutout. The only touchdown the Hawks had given up all year came on the first series of plays in their first game against Cloudland and that was on a fumble by the offense. The Marion win was especially significant because previously unbeaten Marion was a larger school than Toe River was accustomed to playing, AA to the Hawks' Class A. With the loss Marion was four and one, so it wasn't a weak AA school.

"The defense is stellar," said Roger Walker, "but you're the one we're interested in." They chatted briefly and casually, essentially the same conversation Eb had with other recruiters: they liked the way he led the team, passed the ball, used his head.

Lizetta latched on to Eb just as Walker turned and walked toward Coach Woodson to make a courtesy call. "Another college coach?" she said, knowing the answer and taking a degree of pride in her guy. "What's on your dance card for the rest of the evening?"

"You." Eb put his arm around her and squeezed, then kissed her cheek.

"Want to run down to Elizabethton for a burger?" she said.

"How 'bout we see if Smoky and Sharon want to go. That'd be fun."

"I'd rather have you to myself for a while," she said, patting his bottom. "A little slap and tickle."

"Yes," said Eb, "and maybe we can figure out what to do with this bulge."

"That could take teamwork," said Lizetta, hugging his upper arm with both hands as they walked toward the locker room.

Saturday, October 12, 3:34 p.m.

As the Toe River dance team climbed down from the activity bus and began walking toward the large high school gymnasium just outside Charlotte, North Carolina, Eb pulled up alongside Miss Lilly and put the question to her that everybody was whispering. "Are we doing the new routine today?"

"Let's see which teams are here and how it goes," she said. "We don't want word of this getting out before we want it out. I'm not sure we're ready anyway. We have some serious training to do before we can do twelve minutes of clogging without looking ragged eight minutes into it."

"Could we just finish with the clog?" Eb said, almost pleading and with no expectation that he'd be on the dance floor anyway. "We've been working our butts off for this."

"Elbert, be patient. The time will come. And young man, I want you to be ready when it does. You never know what might happen. You need to be as good as anybody you might replace. We can't lose a step."

"I'll be ready and so will everybody else," he said with a

level of confidence and assertion that Miss Lilly liked, but that he hardly felt.

An hour later, the team was through two rounds of competition and it was all smooth dancing. There were five teams taking part, none of them familiar to Eb and none at the competitive level Toe River was accustomed to.

Finally, as the teams prepared for the final round, Miss Lilly pulled everybody aside and put her hand on Buster's shoulder. "You're going to finish with a clog," she said. "The last four minutes of the routine. It's going to be quick and dramatic and I want you to gather around Mickey and Janice and let them go at it for the final thirty seconds before finishing in a line at the front of the stage. We've practiced this and you know it, so do it well and we'll expand on it."

The routine was beautiful to watch, an explosion of motion and noise, flashing feet, hands slapping thighs and knees all in unison and all in time to the lively music. The large crowd was on its feet clapping and yelling as Mickey finished with a dramatic flourish, turned, bent down to Janice and faked a kiss as the rest of the dancers circled them clogging. It all stopped with a crash and the cheering and wild applause continued for minutes.

Eb wasn't on the floor but he could feel the welling emotion, the sense of accomplishment, the drama of the moment. The team clogged off the stage, smiling broadly and when the dancers were safely behind the curtain, the hugs, back pats and butt slaps began. The team members wanted to cheer, but couldn't yet.

There was no question about who the winner was on this day, one where Toe River could easily have won without the clogging.

On the bus ride home, Miss Lilly went up front, got the team's attention and spoke directly. "You did well today," she said. "I expected we'd get some resistance from the judges and we did. Two of them questioned the legality of the clogging, but they couldn't find anything in the rules against it, so it looks like we're in free for now." There was a mumble through the team.

"I want you to get plenty of work this week," said Miss Lilly. "Being in shape is going to be crucial November sixteenth in Asheville. We have to be at the top of our form. If we're not, Old Smoky's going to live in Asheville for a while."

Sunday, October 13, 2 p.m.

It was a slow drive from the Home over curvy mountain roads in a heavy rain, so when Lizetta and Eb pulled the Riviera up to the front of the picturesque cabin on Squirrel Creek, he was ready to release pent-up stress, emotion and desire.

The rain was steady and had been since early Saturday morning. Squirrel Creek running high with the rain. Normally a babbling, gentle creek, it roared over its banks and looked threatening. The bridge across the creek to the cabin was concrete, so there was no worry about a washout. The cabin was a good 30 feet higher than the creek, and flooding wasn't a consideration. They'd be safe.

The cabin was built of hand-hewn poplar logs, cut from the property by her dad, Lizetta said. He used wood that he shaved and dried and, with the help of two hired men, notched and stacked, packing in mud from the creek bank mixed with straw, the way a settler might have done it two centuries before. There was some sort of preservative on the wood, but Lizetta didn't know what it was. The smell was distinct, though light.

The doors were made of the same poplar, milled nearby, and the windows were formed to fit by Jim McEntire's friend, who owned a furniture company in Hickory, Lizetta said. The chimney was built of rocks from Squirrel Creek.

It was a beautiful, rustic cabin about eight hundred square feet with a living room/kitchen, two small bedrooms and a bathroom. The kitchen took up a fourth of the primary living area and a bar that served as a dining room table separated the kitchen from the living room.

The interior walls were the same as the cabin's exterior, unfinished and rough. It was darker inside than Eb liked because the windows were small, but it was cozy and intimate, especially on a day like this when the rain was steady.

"Got any firewood?" Eb said, noticing the fireplace as they entered the lightly furnished cabin.

"It's on the back porch," said Lizetta. "If you'll start a fire I'll put on some hot chocolate." He stepped to the porch and loaded up eight bulky pieces of wood, a "lazy man's load," his mother would have commented had she seen it.

"May I have a small kiss?" said Eb as he dropped the wood beside the fireplace.

"How 'bout a big one?" Lizetta said, wrapping her arms around Eb. He put both hands on her cheeks and held her face close to his, a gesture Maryellen said was just about the most tender a man could make to a woman. Lizetta cooed.

***

Lizetta pulled her dad's worn army blanket off the back of the sofa, spread it on the floor, tossed some pillows and lay back in front of the fire, looking up at Eb through her thick lashes. She held his gaze with her special blend of hard and soft, and slowly slid her tongue across her bottom lip, her mouth softly open, inviting. Eb smiled and handed her the cup of hot chocolate, two large marshmallows floating on top. Lizetta picked out one of the marshmallows and slowly sucked, eyes flirty, dimples growing deeper.

Eb pulled in a shaky, deep breath. "Sweet girl, you are one delicious, naughty thing." His voice was raspy with sudden heat. He felt the bulge in his pants and Lizetta's eyes locked onto it.

Lizetta carefully sat the cup of chocolate down on the hearth, conscious of Eb's eyes watching her every move. Her auburn hair fell like a silken curtain against her cheek. She slowly unbuttoned the top three pearl buttons of her white blouse and pulled the fabric aside to expose her soft, full cleavage, golden in the glow of the fire. Her chest was rising and falling more quickly, her pearly skin glowing, and when she looked up at him, she looked vulnerable. Open. Fragile. For just an instant. Then she smiled and held out her arms. "You sound like Tab Hunter when he's close to getting his girl." Her tease had returned with the sassy edge Eb loved.

"You mean Steve McQueen," he said. "Tab Hunter's too pretty."

He chuckled and, in one clean move, sat down next to Lizetta, pulled her deep into his arms, and firmly rolled her on to her back. She was open, warm, inviting, pliable … and his.

"Why am I so lucky?" Eb, said, brushing Lizetta's hair off her forehead and slowly tracing her perfect eyebrow with his long fingers. When Lizetta didn't answer right away, he bent down close to her ear, so close that when his lips moved, it tickled her lobe. "You're my girl, aren't you?" She giggled on cue and when her shoulders scrunched up, he nuzzled her neck and kissed her delicate collarbones and the rise of her breasts. He pulled back her blouse and slipped her thin bra strap off her well-defined shoulder. The ticking of the antique mantle clock slowed time and Eb pulled back, suddenly serious, looking for permission. He didn't want to mess this up or confuse serious flirting with something that meant a whole lot more to him.

"Come here." Lizetta pulled him close and put her tongue between his lips, licking the moisture, her hands working up under his shirt, running over his smooth teen-ager's chest, her body opening to him.

Their breath was becoming ragged and the heat off their bodies rivaled the embers in the fireplace. They were shedding their last layers of clothing when headlights flooded through the rain-spattered front window and moved across the wall like a searchlight in the dim evening atmosphere. "Who the hell is that?" said Eb as he urgently jumped up and pulled Lizetta with him. They scrambled for clothing.

"It must be Daddy." She quickly pulled on her underwear and red slacks, then pulled back the curtain to see. "It's him.

And he's got someone with him."

The gold Mercedes 230SL Roadster pulled in behind Lizetta's Riviera in the narrow curved driveway.

Eb zipped his pants and Lizetta laughed at his erection straining at the zipper. "You have no idea how lucky you are not to have to go through this," Eb said, cringing as he pulled his penis loose from the zipper, which was threatening to pinch it off. She pushed him down on the sofa and threw a pillow in his lap and set a cup of chocolate in his hand.

"Relax, Eb. It's just my dad."

"That's what I'm afraid of," said Eb.

Lizetta was collected, cool even. She folded the blanket, clicked on a table lamp, throwing a fresh log on the fire as she moved quickly about the room and buttoned her white blouse. They heard a key in the lock.

The door opened briskly and Jim McEntire entered with a large gray-haired man, each carrying a suitcase, briefcase and long fly rods. "Well hello there, young lady," said her dad, as delighted as he was surprised. "And this must be Eb. How are you, son? We didn't imagine you two'd be up here on such a nasty afternoon."

"We were riding around," said Lizetta, "and I thought I'd show Eb the cabin." It was true enough to avoid being a lie and Jim McEntire didn't seem to notice.

"Lizetta says you built this cabin," said Eb, directing the conversation away from him and Lizetta, hoping his voice sounded normal, knowing he felt anything but. He could hear his heart beat and he felt the strain in his crotch quickly recede. Nothing like a daddy's arrival to douse the fire in his personal furnace. "It sure is impressive. She said you cut and prepared the logs. Must have been a lot of work." Eb's voice was hurried, nervous.

"Yes," said her dad, setting down the cases and propping his hand-tooled bamboo fly rod in the corner, "it was. Satisfying work. Kids, this is Senator Terrell Aiken of Hickory."

Eb stood cautiously, holding the pillow in front of him with his left hand while he faced the two men and stuck out his right hand. "Terrell, this is my daughter, Lizetta, and her friend Eb McCourry." Eb shook hands firmly. "Terrell's the chairman of the Ways and Means Committee and we are working on legislation that will set up the cabinet department for the women's program I told you about. We needed to get away from that mob at the beach in order to get some work done and we thought we might catch a few trout, too, if the rain ever stops."

"We were just getting ready to take off," said Lizetta, "so we'll leave you the fire and the rest of our hot chocolate."

If Big Jim McEntire was suspicious, he held it well. Eb studied his eyes and the set of his mouth, but they stayed friendly and open. "Tell your mother I'll be here until Tuesday. There's no phone, so we're as isolated as we're likely to get, Terrell. Perfect to get a lot of work done."

"And maybe a little fishing," the Senator added.

Yep, and the perfect place to make sweet love with your daughter, Eb thought dismally as he and Lizetta slipped on their raincoats, pulled up their hoods and ran out into the rain hand in hand.

Part VIII

Tuesday, October 15, 3:45 p.m.

Once again Arlene Silver Feather stewed in the waiting
area of Bobby Lee Ledbetter's large office on the fourteenth
floor of the First and Merchants Bank Building in downtown
Asheville, a strange place, she thought, for a used car
dealership to be housed. But Bobby Lee was nothing if not
ostentatious and this was the tallest building west of Charlotte,
so it was here—on the top floor—he wanted to be.

Finally, fifteen minutes after the appointed time, Lottie,
Bobby Lee's secretary, waved Arlene in with a friendly gesture
that went unnoticed.

"Mornin', Miz Silver Feather," said Bobby Lee, reaching
his hand out pleasantly to greet her. "You're lookin' good.
Hope the job's suitin' you."

"We're doing fine," she said. "I think we've met
expectations thus far."

"You've hit all the goals but one," said Bobby Lee, getting
to the point.

"What would that be, Mr. Ledbetter?" Arlene looked
surprised and crinkled her eyebrows.

"Joss-Lynn is not happy," said Bobby Lee without pause.
"In fact, she's right miserable. Says the other dancers are
arrogant and they dismiss her both as a dancer and personally.
She says they won't have nothin' to do with her. We can't have
that, can we?"

"Mr. Ledbetter, I was hired as a dance coach and instructor,
not as a social director for teenagers. I will mention that your
daughter is not always the easiest person to get along with."
She paused for effect, half-expecting Bobby Lee to interrupt
with defensive vigor. He didn't. "I have heard her say some
pretty…well…abrupt things to the other dancers. She has
questioned their sexual orientation, their social standing in the
community, their heritage, among other things."

175

"Give me some examples." Bobby Lee sounded concerned.

"She has called the male dancers 'queers.' All of them. She suggested our best dancer is somehow less worthy because her father drives a truck. She called one dancer 'Jewboy,' another one 'Wop,' one and another 'Wetback.' She's called several of them 'dirty Yankees.' Do I need to go on?"

Bobby Lee didn't reply. He walked toward the large window at the back of his office, then slowly turned back toward Arlene and leaned against his desk, arms folded.

"I'm not sure what to think about this," he said. "Joss-Lynn is a good girl, slightly spoiled maybe, but that's my fault. She's lashing out at these kids 'cause of something that's goin' on that you're not seein'. I think if you'll pay more attention, you'll see this different. I want you to do that. I don't want my daughter bein' unhappy. This whole effort is for her. It don't mean dip shit to me, so I can drop support for it in the time it'd take you to pirouette and I will if she ain't happy."

"I hope you understand that."

Arlene looked at Bobby Lee, attempting to hide her disbelief. "I understand," she said with tight lips.

"And I hope you'll do somethin' about it, startin' today."

"Is that all?" she said, her fists clinched so tightly that her knuckles were white. This was no time to lose her temper over these temporary indignities. Saving her school was more important.

"That's all for now. But I want to see Joss-Lynn smilin' when she talks about that got-damn square dance team."

Thursday, October 17, 8:10 a.m.

Eb wanted to catch Hap Hilton before the day got started. Toe River High School, which didn't pay its women's coaches, had just one school color because it couldn't afford two, and rarely had an activities bus that worked, certainly would not consider hiring somebody to help students get into college. So, academic advising fell to Hap, as far as Eb was concerned.

Sunday's interrupted intimacy with Lizetta forced them to

think about the future more intensely than they already had, especially Lizetta, who had not figured on a relationship with a boy being part of her plan. Eb, too, was bent on taking the possibility of a football scholarship more to heart, getting information, talking to the right people, filling out the forms, taking the tests. College would be his press pass to a future as a writer, a career choice that was important to him and one Lizetta smiled about every time it was brought up.

Hap attended school on a football scholarship for two years at a small college, Lenoir Rhyne in Hickory, so he should know how to play in those waters, Eb reasoned. Eb hadn't made plans yet and discovered just this week that he needed a foreign language to qualify for most colleges. The only foreign language Toe River offered was French. Eb was too late for that class, but he believed he could work it out. The French teacher said she could tutor him after hours next semester and give him a grade for the year, if it came to that. Other issues were more urgent.

"What's cooking?" Hap asked as Eb walked in, a sense of urgency in his stride.

"I need some guidance and you're my guidance counselor," said Eb, plopping into a front-row seat and resting his books on the desktop.

"Glad to help if I can." Hap was unloading his briefcase, getting ready for the day.

"I've had two college coaches talk to me about going to their schools just this week and in the past few days, I got letters from coaches at Mars Hill College, East Carolina, Newberry, Catawba, Presbyterian, Wofford and Lenoir Rhyne, your school. I don't know what they know or how they know it, but I'm starting to think I'd better do something before opportunity runs by me like that all-state Mars Hill High back is supposed to November first." Eb was referring to a runner named Chuck Tolley who'd already signed with Clemson and was setting North Carolina high school yardage and scoring records.

"You taken the SAT?" said Hap.

"I take it Saturday in Johnson City. Riding down with Lizetta and a couple of others."

"She already took it," said Hap. "Banner was saying something about her making a fifteen eighty on it, highest in school history and nearly a perfect sixteen hundred. What's she want to take it again for?"

"Oh, she's not taking it," Eb said. "She's just driving me down."

"You dating her?" Hap asked, grinning.

Eb squirmed uncomfortably. "Just don't say nothin' about that, Hap. You know Lizetta and I have been seeing each other and you know any guy'd be nuts not to consider that important, but I really need some help here."

"Do you know anything about any of these schools, or do you have a preference at all? Do you have any idea what you want to study?"

"I am going to be a writer," Eb said with certainty. "I want to go where they teach writers to write."

"Well, Eb, there's a lot of ways to go about being a writer and there's a lot of different kinds of writing. There's books, newspapers, plays, movies and TV, commercials, corporate annual reports. Anything you see that is in writing, some writer worked on. You can also teach writing, which gives you a job while you write your books or plays or whatever else you want to write."

"I want to write books some day, but first I'd like to be a journalist and learn on the front lines. Maybe even a sports writer. I'm not sure, but writing's what I want to do."

"'Course you're looking for scholarship money, right?"

"I won't be goin' anywhere without it, but if I can latch onto a football scholarship, that could do it. These are all small schools and I don't know much about their programs. Do you?"

Though Hap had attended Lenoir Rhyne for two years, World War II interrupted his schooling and he wound up on a submarine, where he learned enough geometry to become a teacher in this rural school, which couldn't be inflexible about requiring degrees of its teachers.

"Western Carolina might be the best place for you because it has a good writing program and a respected history curriculum. I think pairing English and history or something like political science is smart for somebody wanting to write, especially a journalist. A few of the other schools do well in those areas, but I think at this point, Western might be a good fit for you. That was one of Western's coaches up here last week, wasn't it?"

"He seemed interested," Eb said. "And they were the first school I heard from. They're putting in an offense like the 49ers run and I'd sure like to play in that."

"If you want to go down and take a look at the campus, I can take you one Saturday. Providing you can get time off from square dancing. I'm sure one of Western's coaches would be happy to give us the grand tour, since you're such a hot property."

"Oh, hush, Hap. I'm no hot property. The hot property is that dang defense of yours, the one everybody's ignoring. I sure wouldn't want to play against it. Except in practice and I'm not even sure about that. I think it makes our offense better."

"You get your SATs out of the way and when we get your scores and know where you qualify, we can start looking at where you want to go and who wants you. You should have scores by Christmas if you take the test this weekend. All that has to fit together, but I don't think it will be much of a problem if you keep playing football the way you're playing. Some college will make sure you get in."

"So I can count on you?"

"Son, you can always count on me. I'll be here."

"Hap, could we go off the record for a minute? I think I need to talk to you about something else that's on my mind a lot, too."

"This would be about Lizetta, right?"

"Yes, this would be about Lizetta."

Thursday, October 17, Noon

Eb sat in the grass behind the football stadium, studying the 50-foot-tall maple that was a rich, deep red and cast a glow on all sides. He looked toward the school and saw Lizetta running down the hill toward him. He jumped up in time to catch her, almost out of control. "Easy, girl," he said, wrapping her up and kissing her before she could say a word.

"Mumfl-mfl," she said through the kiss. Eb broke off laughing.

"What's so important?"

"I'm in!" she said. "Wake Forest accepted me. It's the one I wanted."

"That's just great," Eb said, "but was there ever any doubt? Who on god's earth would turn you down? Beauty, brains, wit. The package, baby. Shoot, you even have me. They're showing good sense."

She hugged him again quickly, let go, pushed him slightly back and said, "It's where Mom and Daddy went and I've always had a soft spot for Wake. It's a gorgeous campus and I'll get the education I want. Wish you could go with me, but Winston-Salem won't be that far from wherever you are."

"I hope I can go somewhere, anywhere. I really want to write and writing's probably gonna take college or maybe four years of Colt Hill's essays." Lizetta chuckled, plopped down in the deep, soft grass and he joined her.

"Have you heard any more?"

"I got some more letters, but you know I'm not anywhere near in yet. I'm going to have to have some good games against the best teams on our schedule. Except for Marion, we haven't really played anybody above average and I don't have an idea how good I am or whether I can play at the level of a Western Carolina or an Appalachian State. I'm just five-foot-nine-and a half, a hundred-sixty pounds and they're going to want a quarterback closer to six feet, a hundred and eighty or more. I don't run especially well with these knees and that'll only get worse. What I can do is throw the ball. Western says that's what it's looking for. Maybe so. We'll see."

"You going down to Winston to look over the campus any time soon?" Eb said, changing the subject back to Lizetta.

"Oh, I've already done that," she said. "I even know which dorm I'm in. It's nice. And the International Relations program is as good as those at the D.C. schools. I'm excited."

Eb was happy for her, but felt a small twinge of the beginnings of loss, looking ahead. He pulled her to him and held her tighter than he meant to. A tear formed at the edge of his left eye. He blotted it on her blouse.

"Are you alright, hon?" she said.

"Fine," he lied. "I'm fine. I'm really happy for you." They sat quietly for a moment.

"We're going to have a good time driving to Johnson City for the SATs Saturday," he said. "I'm hoping we can slip over to the cabin again Sunday if your dad's going to be away. You up for that?"

"Mmmmm," she purred. "But we have tonight first."

"Yeh," Eb said. "My grand audition with your parents."

"You ready to take the SAT?" she said.

"Sure," Eb said. "It's just a test and I do well on these kinds of tests usually. The test with your parents might be an exception."

Thursday, October 17, 6:43 p.m.

Lizetta eased the silver Riviera into the circular drive at her family's contemporary stone and glass home on a windblown hill overlooking Lees-McRae College and downtown Banner Elk.

Eb swallowed hard. "Impressive," he said.

"It's just a house," said Lizetta.

"To you, maybe. Lot more than that to somebody who lives in the attic of an orphanage."

"Elbert McCourry," Lizetta said sharply, "I don't want to hear that self-pitying crap from a boy I'm pretty sure I love. It's

181

unbecoming and not like you."

That stopped him. "Love," she'd said. Maybe that's what he was feeling, too.

"I'm sorry," Eb said. "It's still hard for me to picture me with you and when I see this side of it, it gets even harder."

"Well, close your eyes to the trappings and remember Sunday. That's closer to reality for both of us. And we'll finish what we started this weekend." Eb looked at her softly, scarcely believing what was ahead, what she said and that she said it.

"Deal," he said. "I guess I get to face the music now. By the way, what do you mean by 'pretty sure'?" She punched his shoulder.

"Mom and Daddy are not what you expect. You'll see."

Jim and Collette McEntire were handsome, trim and outgoing. He towered over Eb at six-feet-two, nearly two hundred pounds and he looked like a linebacker, though he'd never played football. Lizetta told Eb Jim was an athlete from the time he was a boy, but never in team sports and his size was natural, not something he worked on. He kept trim, said Lizetta, "because he thinks people respect big men more than small men or fat men. He swears by that and says, 'Just look around at who's powerful.'" He had a point. The curly blond hair, chiseled facial features and fluid baritone only added to his personae.

Collette was the perfect match: barely five-feet tall with boyish-short, deep red hair, she looked French and carried herself like a ballerina. Her face was open and expressive and her hands moved instinctively when she talked. Her natural enthusiasm supplemented a deep set of values that she easily discussed, rarely imposing her beliefs, but never holding them back, even in company where they might not be appreciated. Lizetta told Eb of the loud verbal battles Collette often engaged in with Congressmen, battles legislators' wives whispered about at cocktail parties. The wives steered clear of her, intimidated.

Jim met Collette when they were sophomores at Wake Forest and—Lizetta told Eb "off the record"—when Collette found herself pregnant, they quickly eloped and gave the news to two sets of disapproving parents afterwards.

Lizetta gave Eb the deep background earlier in the day: Jim just missed being drafted for the final stages of World War II and managed to finish at Wake Forest before earning a law degree from Washington & Lee College in Virginia. Collette's college days were over with the pregnancy, but she continued to take art courses as she could and became an accomplished water-colorist and the founder of the North Carolina Watercolor Society. Her paintings, especially of the diminishing wildness on the Outer Banks, which was being developed at breakneck speed, were highly sought.

"Dad, you remember Eb from the cabin," said Lizetta. "Mom, this is Eb." Collette looked puzzled. "You two have met?" she asked Jim.

"Oh, I forgot to tell you," he said. "It was just briefly."

Lizetta finished the introductions and Jim quickly told Eb to call him and Collette by their first names and that "we can't get Lizetta to do that. She's old-fashioned."

"So you're the quarterback everybody's talking about?" said Jim.

"I hope not," Eb said. "Couldn't be anything good coming out of that conversation."

Jim laughed and Eb saw where Lizetta's came from. Eb scored right off and relaxed.

"You heard, I guess, that Lizetta got into Wake," he said. "What's your plan?"

"I'm trying to find one," Eb said, sliding into a chair Collette directed him to. "Lizetta probably told you I live at Beech Mountain Home for Children and that my family doesn't have any money. Dad died three years ago and college means 'scholarship' if I'm to go at all. That's why the football is so important right now. My brother's in school on a football scholarship."

"Does that mean you wouldn't play football without the possibility of a scholarship?"

"No, sir. I enjoy it, but it's time-consuming and you get pretty banged up when you're my size. I like the square dancing. Guess I took to it immediately. I got introduced to it this year when the team was short-handed and pretty desperate. It's just the best thing. I never even heard of competitive dancing before, but I'll tell you it's just as competitive as anything I've ever done, and I've played several sports and even boxed."

"He's a good dancer, too, Daddy. He'll tell you he's not, but I've seen him and he picked it up so fast."

Eb smiled at Lizetta and winked.

"So have you looked into any schools at all?" said Jim.

"They seem to be doing the looking," Eb said, grinning again. "I've heard from several about playing for them and I'm interested in both Western Carolina and maybe Elon, which is supposed to have a good journalism program."

"The University of South Carolina has the best journalism program around," said Collette. "Have you considered it?"

"That's out of my league in a lot of ways," Eb said. "The level of football is a long looping pass over my head. If I play at all—and I don't know if I'm big enough, good enough or healthy enough with my bad knee—it'll be for one of the NAIA schools, the small schools. And I'll be happy about it. I just want a chance to get an education so I can be a writer."

Eb was comfortable enough by now to take on the role of interrogator. "Tell me about the governor's appointment ..." Eb paused, uncertain about whether to call Jim McEntire by his first name. "... Uh, Jim, if you don't mind. Lizetta mentioned it, but I'm not quite sure what it means."

"It's a commission that I'm heading looking into the idea that women have been systematically denied full citizenship and trying to determine what we need to do to change that."

"Kinda like civil rights?" Eb said.

"Exactly." Jim leaned forward in his chair, his forearms

resting on his knees. Collette slid in beside Lizetta on the couch and slipped her arm around her daughter, who snuggled closer. Eb liked that. "There are a lot of legal barriers against women that haven't been erased over the years and we want to dispose of them. One of the tools is to pass the Equal Rights Amendment to the Constitution, a simple statement that says women and men have the same rights. North Carolina hasn't passed it yet. There's nothing fancy about it at all, but it means turning the cart upside down for a lot of people with ingrained notions of women's roles and there is some fierce opposition, some of it from a variety of church groups."

"What are you planning to do?"

"That's what the commission's about. We're going to figure it out."

"Let me ask you one more question and I don't mean to be disrespectful, but why, if it's the Governor's Commission on the Status of Women, is a man heading it?"

"Oh, my goodness, Eb," said Collette, grinning broadly, "what a wonderfully prescient question. I'd love to hear your explanation, Mr. Commission Chairman."

"Pretty simple," said Jim, "and at the heart of what we're getting at here. Women don't have an Old Girls Network. It's time they get one. We hope to help with that and a lot of other issues."

"Pretty good response, Jim," said Collette. "I can see why the governor is taken with you. I didn't even have to put in a good word for you. Yet."

"What would you like to drink?" Collette asked, looking at Eb.

"Nothing now, thanks," Eb said, "but would you show me some of your paintings? I guess the ones on the wall here are yours, judging from Lizetta's descriptions." He pointed toward a spot with six views of the beach. Eb looked closely at Collette's face and studied her mannerisms. She was Lizetta through and through.

"Well, thank you for asking," Collette said. "I'd love to

show you." She talked with increasing passion about both the artwork and the diminishing wild sections of the Outer Banks, describing the paintings and pointing out that much of what was pictured was on the verge of being lost to development. She said "developers" as if she were spitting.

"They have no idea what they're doing to the delicate ecological balance out there," she said. "All of that building is going to wind up in the sea and the developers don't seem to be able to visualize anything but the dollars they're making today. It just fries me. The stupidity, the arrogance."

"What I see, ma'am, is a passionate painter who loves what she does. I like your work and this is a good way to make your point. 'Here's what we're losing. Let's save it!' You don't need me to tell you that, but I like it, anyway."

"Thank you, Eb," she said. "You're not exactly a bashful teenager, are you?"

"My mama said when I came up here to school that if I'd just be myself, say what I needed to say and be polite, people would talk to me and they'd listen to me. She's usually right about things. Adjusting's hard enough without having to pretend things about yourself."

"Smart mama," said Jim.

Lizetta sat quietly taking all this in, looking back and forth among Eb and her parents. Finally, she moved over beside Eb, to the arm of his chair, tousled his hair, looked at her parents and said, "Told you." Eb turned bright red and smiled, embarrassed.

Lizetta's parents nodded, and Collette said, "Let's eat. Eb, I hope you like salmon."

"Not sure whether I do or not," he said, "but it smells good, like it was cooked on a grill."

"It was," said Collette as she put her hand through Eb's arm and nodded toward the dining room.

As soon as everyone was seated, Jim started the food around and got back to the topic of college. He handed Eb a bowl of what looked like large grain grits. "Cous-cous," said

Lizetta, a wide smile spreading. "You'll like it. Got it in Raleigh."

"I guess Lizetta told you she's interested in international relations," Jim said. "She went to American University's summer seminar series last year and got truly immersed in it. American's near Embassy Row, where all the diplomats live in D.C., and they are generally available to the students to answer questions and to teach a few classes. Some of them even offer internships."

"It's just fascinating," said Lizetta. "I got to learn so much about so many cultures and countries. It makes me want to see everything, go everywhere. I love the different people."

"You would," Eb said, putting his hand on hers and imagining Lizetta kissing him goodbye at the airport as she left for Morocco or somewhere equally exotic on a diplomatic mission.

Eb was seeing clearly who Lizetta was, why she was and that there was nothing false about her in any way. He liked all that and he liked her life. He was captivated by her parents. Eb didn't know how long he'd be in this spot, but he was happy to be sitting here with these people on this night. They were enriching him.

And his mama was right, he thought. *They like me for who I am.* Good thing, because it'd have to do.

Friday, October 18, 8:30 p.m.
Harris High School in Spruce Pine, a gem mining village about twenty miles south of Toe River High on U.S. Twenty-Five South, was one of the Red Tail Hawks' oldest and most intense rivals, and the games were always brutal. It was no different on this night at Toe River's home field. In a steady rain, Harris put up a blitzing, harassing defense that shut Toe River out in the first half and left Eb battered and limping. He'd been hit hard from the blind side twice by linebackers running past Harold. The tackle on the right side got to Eb twice as Smoky's blocking broke down while Eb tried to pass a

slippery ball. One of those hurried passes was batted in the air at the line of scrimmage and intercepted by a lineman, the first interception Eb had thrown all year.

The Blue Devils couldn't generate any offense against the Hawks' league-leading defense and a wet field, but Coach Buster Woodson was mightily unhappy as the players clomped into the dressing room for a halftime break in a scoreless game. He did some stomping and yelling, which almost everybody ignored as they clustered in small groups of offensive and defensive players and looked for some answers. "Bunch of sissies," Woodson screamed. "Yellow-bellies. This ain't the team I've been coaching all year," and on and on he went, his face red, veins popped, arms waving.

Hap was talking to linemen in the corner as Woodson continued his rant, talking about blocking schemes, defensive rush patterns, Harris' tricky series of plays that had three options for the quarterback. The defense had read them all well, but the blocking by the offensive line was ineffective and Hap knew he and Eb had to make some changes in assignments.

"We're going to have to run some plays that develop quickly," Eb told the backs and ends at the other end of the locker room, "and get some of the pressure off our line. I think a couple of draws and screens will slow them down and we can get a passing game going, rain or no rain. Every one of us is going to have to pick up our game a notch and that especially means the quarterback, who hasn't played for shit." Woodson had virtually turned over the coaching and adjustments of the offense to Eb and the young quarterback took the responsibility with relish, pacing in front of the sitting players, stopping to address each one individually.

Toe River was to kick off to start the second half and the Bulldogs' return man was dangerous, a senior named Corwin Alberts, who'd transferred in from out west where his dad was a mine supervisor. Toe River got the game-opening kickoff and there hadn't been another, so the Hawks would have to find out for sure if Alberts was as good as people said.

He was.

Smoky's kickoff was a low line-drive, a perfect return ball, and Alberts caught it on his ten and ran it back seventy-five-yards to the Toe River fifteen before Carl ran him down from the other side of the field. Harris couldn't gain a yard from there, but it kicked a field goal and held a three-nothing lead. Those were the first points scored against the Hawk defense all year and the defensive team was suddenly in a foul mood.

J.W. took the ensuing kickoff back to the thirty-five and when the team broke the huddle, Eb looked at the linebackers and saw they were getting ready to blitz from both sides. They seemed to be daring the Hawks. Eb called a sweep to the right for Barry, but he checked it off at the line, changing the play to a screen pass to Barry, instead. Eb took the snap, backed up quickly as the tackles intentionally let the linebackers run past them—out of the play—and Eb flipped a short pass over the head of the backer on the left. Barry took it twenty-five yards before one of the defensive backs caught him and they all slid and created a wake in the mud and water. Barry got up smiling, covered in mud and soaked. "I love this shit," he said when he got back to the huddle.

Toe River mixed two screens, a draw, a slant off the right side and a quick pattern to the left sideline before Eb found Terry Gervin slanting over the middle of the field for a fifteen-yard touchdown. It was almost too easy, but Toe River had its rhythm and didn't let up the rest of the night, laying it on in the third quarter with four touchdowns and a twenty-eight to three lead as the rain pounded. The Hawks got two more scores in the fourth, the second by the backup players and won forty-two to three in a game that was dead even at the half. The only part of its game Harris had left after the half was its kickoff receiving game. Alberts compiled five impressive returns, but the offense couldn't penetrate Toe River's defense, so the returns were wasted.

Toe River's players felt good about themselves because their last two wins—by a combined score of seventy-seven to three—which came against teams that were impressive before playing the Hawks. They celebrated exuberantly as they left the field, carrying Carl part of the way after another all-state-level game where he dominated the opposing offense by disrupting its rhythm, making nearly twenty tackles and knocking down laterals and passes.

Two more college assistant coaches—these from Elon and Catawba—introduced themselves to a wet and muddy Eb as he walked off the field, and Eb said, "You two should be talking to Carl Blackthorn. He's the best player on this end of the state." But Eb knew Carl's grades and his lack of size would never allow him to play college football.

He looked for Lizetta, whom he had not seen. At one point he stood at midfield and turned a complete circle. He asked one of the cheerleaders if she'd seen Lizetta, but she hadn't.

Joyce ran across the field straight to Eb, looking pale and troubled. "I just heard," she said, "Lizetta's had an accident and is at Cannon Memorial. Do you want me to take you over?"

Eb stood paralyzed and terrified for a minute as players walked by and slapped him on the shoulder pads or the bottom, saying something like, "Good game," which he did not hear. He looked at Joyce, still disbelieving. "How bad is she hurt?"

"I don't know. I heard about it a few minutes ago from one of the teachers. Lizetta was on the way down off the mountain, coming to the game in the rain, I guess, and a truck went into a curve on the wrong side of the road, heading straight for her. She went down the bank and into the creek. There was apparently a car behind her and the driver saw it, stopped and flagged down another car to go get help while he climbed down to Lizetta."

"Let me get out of this uniform," Eb said, his voice shaking, tears running down his face. "I'll be right back."

Part IX

Friday, October 18, 10:07 p.m.

Lizetta's parents paced the waiting room at Cannon Memorial Hospital in Banner Elk when Eb—who knew the hospital well from his frequent visits there to treat his knee—stormed in, still soaked and dirty. He hadn't stopped to shower and told Buster Woodson he had to go immediately with Joyce. Woodson, who knew about the accident, nodded, feeling the urgency. As they parked in front of the hospital, Eb left Joyce, bounding out of the car and running by the elevator to the steps. He ran up the two flights to the floor where the information nurse said Lizetta was being treated.

"Is she all right?" he blurted to her parents. Jim and Collette held hands tightly as if they might float away, reassuring each other as they could. Jim towered over Collette and she looked like a child beside him, vulnerable and frightened. She had been crying, her mascara smeared, her cheeks red, but she regained that McEntire composure and smiled when she saw Eb.

"It's tricky right now," said Jim McEntire. "The doctor says she has broken her neck. That's damn serious, but there are internal injuries they're just not sure about yet. We'll have to wait and see." Jim's hand was shaking and he looked pale as he struggled to pull his words together.

"Have you seen her? Can I see her?" Eb said, running the sentences together.

"No," said Jim. "We haven't and you can't. We just have to be patient. She's in good hands." That sounded more like hope than certainty and Jim's voice was beginning to break.

Joyce quietly entered the room and Eb introduced her to the McEntires. They smiled politely, but didn't fully absorb who Joyce was. Eb explained the situation, just above a whisper to her.

"There's not anything you can do here, Eb," said Collette

McEntire, taking his hand. "Why don't you go on home and we'll let you know if there's any change. We appreciate you being here and I know Lizetta would like that, but it's out of our hands now."

"If you don't mind, ma'am, I'll stay," Eb said, as firmly as a seventeen-year-old in the face of a parent could speak. He pulled Joyce to the side.

"Would you go by the Home and tell Moms and Pops at Little Boys dorm that I'm at the hospital and I don't know when I'll be home? There's no phone in the cottage and I don't want to have to send somebody over from administration this time of night. I'm staying until I know Lizetta's getting better. You know which one Little Boys is, don't you?" She nodded.

Joyce looked at Eb like she wanted to say something. She put a hand around his bicep, squeezed and said, "I'll let them know." She took out a pen and piece of paper and wrote on it. "This is my phone number. Call me the minute you know something or the minute you need something. Is there anything you want me to bring you from the Home, maybe your books or some clean clothes or something?"

"I'm fine, but I'll probably need my writing notebook. I have a couple of essays I need to complete. Pops will show you my room and the notebook and pencils are on the little desk. One of the interns showed me a shower here that they use on those long shifts and I'll take one in a few minutes. My clothes are clean. Thank you for understanding. I don't know what I'm going to do about the SATs in Johnson City tomorrow. I may have to re-schedule. Lizetta was going to drive me."

Eb sat on the uncomfortable vinyl-covered sofa, put his head in his hands and murmured to himself, "I just don't know what else bad can happen."

Saturday, October 19, 7:10 a.m.

Eb heard whispers through a haze of consciousness. He was stiff, sore and uncomfortable. He didn't know where he was as his eyes opened to a strange, stark room with too much light.

Seconds later, he remembered and he saw Miss Lilly talking to Collette McEntire on the other side of the waiting room.

"Heard anything?" he said in a voice as normal as he could manage. They both looked at Eb, and then walked over to the couch where he slept.

"Lizetta's pretty banged up," said Collette, smiling wanly with that mother's reassurance. "She was lucky that Colt Hill decided not to go to the football game and was behind her on the road. He may have saved her life."

"Mr. Hill pulled her out?" Eb said, a look of surprise on his face.

"Yes," said Collette. "Police are still looking for the truck driver. They're not even sure he knew he ran Lizetta off the road. It was so dark and wet. Mr. Hill said it happened so fast that he didn't get a look at the truck, except to see it was a truck, a farm truck."

"What are you doing here, Miss Lilly?" Eb said, turning from Collette.

"Lizetta is one of my students," she said, "and you are one of my dancers. I wanted to see how Lizetta is and I need for you to come with me. Mrs. McEntire said Lizetta will probably be unconscious all day and that the doctors are not going to let anybody see her until they are sure she's safe.

"I am going to take you to Johnson City for your SATs and we have that dance meet tonight at the school. We need you because we are short-handed. Bon Heath has some kind of stomach virus and you and Becky will dance for him and Bonnie Presnell." She put her hands on her shoulders and looked directly into his full face.

"You need to be occupied, Eb. You can't sit around here all day worrying about Lizetta. That won't do anybody any good. I know her well enough to know that she'd tell you just exactly that."

"Miss Lilly!" Eb said, too intensely. "You can't expect me to *square dance* when Lizetta is in the other room with god knows what wrong with her!"

"This is a grown-up moment, son," said Miss Lilly. "You have to make an important decision here about your college future and square dancing and your school and your teammates. I would not ask this of you if Bon was healthy or if there was something you could contribute to Lizetta healing. But you have to make a hard decision and you need to make it now."

Jim McEntire heard the conversation, waking and stretching from his own fitful sleep in a nondescript red vinyl hospital chair. He walked over to Eb and Miss Lilly, put his hand on Eb's back and steered him away from the women. "Go with Miss Lilly," he said softly, but with a stern conviction. "There is every reason to do that and no reason to stay here. I know it will be hard to concentrate on the SATs and a dance meet while Lizetta's in trouble, but you'll be here with us in spirit and Lizetta will know that."

Eb liked Jim McEntire and in one meal he had learned to trust him. "Alright," Eb said. "But please…"

"We'll keep you up to the minute," Jim interrupted.

At that moment Dr. William Grigsby, the McEntire family physician, entered the room in full hospital garb and took Jim and Collette McEntire to one side. Eb could hear his voice, though it was just above a whisper. "We are not equipped here to deal the kinds of injuries Lizetta has suffered," he said, "and we want to move her to the Duke Medical Center in Durham. There's a world-renowned neuro-medicine team there— including surgeons—and I think we would all feel better if she were in their hands. We will, of course, need your permission to do that." The McEntires looked shaken and listened closely. Collette hung on Jim's large bicep.

"Of course, Bill," said Jim to his long-time handball buddy. "What have you found? Be as clear as you can because we won't know the medicine."

"She has fractures in the second and third cervical vertebrae and the fractures could be a threat to her spinal nerves and cord," Dr. Grigsby said. "It is extremely delicate and there is danger here. We simply don't have the expertise to deal with it.

She has also suffered a head injury and she will need to be observed closely for several days or even weeks.

"There's the possibility of a subdural hematoma from the breaking of blood vessels, and the pressure on her brain from the blood collecting between the brain and the skull would need to be relieved, if that's the case. We're watching her closely for symptoms. Meanwhile, we have given Lizetta something to reduce swelling and an anti-convulsion medication." Dr. Grigsby paused, took a deep breath and continued.

"On top of it all, she has a number of internal injuries. I think you can surmise that she is going to need some intensive treatment over a period of time. The truth is that Lizetta is extremely fortunate to still be with us. The man who found her so quickly likely saved her life."

Jim put his arm around Collette, both fighting back tears and breathing unevenly. Dr. Grigsby said, "We'll go ahead with the helicopter transfer right now. Will you be meeting us in Durham?"

The McEntires nodded and Dr. Grigsby said, "We'll get the neuro-medical team to do a complete workup on Lizetta immediately after she gets to Duke. She will not be available to you before tomorrow at the earliest if you want to wait until then to go down."

"No," said Collette. "We'll be there with her through all of this. The least we can do is to be there for our little girl. Is there room in the helicopter for me?" Dr. Grigsby could see the deepening pain in Collette McEntire's face. She looked drawn, pale and near exhaustion. "No," he said. "Lizetta and the medical team will be all the helicopter can carry."

Eb stood helpless beside Miss Lilly, who put a hand on his shoulder, the first sign of real warmth and intimacy he'd ever experienced from her.

"It's going to work out, Eb," she said. "Just have faith. Let's get this long day started."

Saturday, October 19, 9:12 p.m.

The auditorium at Toe River High School, which held about two hundred fifty people if you used a large trash compactor to get them in, was hot, crowded and noisy. There was a capacity crowd of spectators for this rare home square dance meet, pushing the five competing teams into the halls and onto the lower floors of the school.

The visiting teams were from Boone and North Wilkesboro, just up the road, and from Jonesborough and Unicoi County, Tennessee, less than 40 miles away. Bootleggers went to North Wilkesboro to haul booze back into dry Avery County. Wilkes was the closest wet county. Unicoi County High was a tiny school over the line which won the overall state Tennessee basketball championship back in the 1950s, a feat still talked about in reverent whispers. Jonesborough earned an international reputation as the home of a huge annual storytelling festival, something these old mountaineers excelled in. They were country schools, steeped in tradition, proud of their dance teams.

They would each push Toe River High under normal circumstances. Now, with all those starting dancers out with mono and stomach flu, the Hawks looked to some more like a junior varsity than a dynasty.

Miss Lilly didn't see it that way. She gathered the team for the one twelve-minute dance it would perform for this competition—one shot to win or lose—and said, "Buster is going to call clog for the last half of the routine. That's six full minutes flat out and I don't want to see anybody panting or sweating. Everybody is smiling hard through the whole dance and all the way back off stage."

With Eb leading extra sessions, the team had been working out regularly on its own in the gym, dancing for an hour at a time with almost no letup and the conditioning was showing in the routines.

Toe River waited through the visiting teams' routines, seeing two of them and spending the other two downstairs, listening through the floor to the shuffling, thumping and the music.

As Unicoi came off stage and Toe River prepared to take it, Miss Lilly quickly walked over to Eb, leaned in close and whispered, "I just got a call downstairs in the principal's office. Lizetta's awake and talking. The first thing she said was, 'Does Eb know?'"

Eb's heart soared. There was a swelling in his chest, a tear in his eye, and he shook ever so slightly. Joyce, who was his partner for this dance, put her arm around his waist and squeezed. She wiped his tear and kissed his cheek, but didn't need to say anything. They'd do their celebrating on the dance floor.

Sunday, October 20, 1:15 p.m.
Joyce drove her dad's big car up in front of Little Boys Cottage as Eb was on his way back from lunch, tooted her horn, got out and walked toward him. "Heard anything?" she said.

"The Duke medical staff is testing her today," Eb said. "Lizetta's dad called this morning and left me a message. It'll be a day or two before there's any certainty. I wish to god I was down there. I feel like I'm deserting her when she needs me."

"Eb, be real," said Joyce, her palm on Eb's back moving in a soothing circle. "There's not a thing in the world you can do but pray and live your life the best you can. Make Lizetta proud of you. By the way, I forgot to ask how the SATs went yesterday."

"Oh, it was fine," said Eb. "I don't know why, but I do well on tests. Always have. Strange thing. Miss Lilly was awful nice the entire time. I felt good about having her there. We didn't say anything much, but she felt like family."

Eb and Joyce were walking aimlessly, quietly toward the lake when Eb saw Gaylen's Simca pull into the campus, followed by three other cars. Football players piled out of all four cars and the boys walked toward Joyce and Eb. One of the football players was complaining loudly to Gaylen about his torn pants.

Three more cars came in at the other end of campus, parked in front of Little Boys. Most of the square dance team got out, saw the two of them and walked toward them.

They were there to comfort Eb and he was touched. "They love you," said Joyce. "They really do. I do, too."

Eb's tears, held back for a day, finally boiled over as the waves of fear and grief washed over him. Joyce put her arms around him and held him. The teams gathered close, quietly there with Eb, sharing, encouraging, supporting.

His new family.

***

They all walked to the lake—where Lizetta and Eb first spent some time—and while most sat on the beach, threw a football or took boats out, Joyce stayed with Eb, sitting quietly on the bank. It was overcast, the sun breaking free occasionally. Eb didn't much feel like playing, but he stood, picked up a flat silver-dollar-sized rock and skipped it across the lake. It skipped 14 times. Eb smiled, thinking of Lizetta with that rifle arm shooting rocks across the lake.

After more than an hour, they all went back toward the Home, most of the dancers and football players needing to get back to chores and families. As they approached Little Boys, Eb saw Hap Hilton sitting in the big rocker on the front porch, reading an Asheville Citizen newspaper, which he put down when he saw Eb coming.

Joyce stopped and said, "I'd better be going. Harold will be looking for me."

"Thank you for coming, Joyce," Eb said, "but don't worry about me. I'll be fine. This whole thing is new to me. I'll figure it out."

She kissed him on the cheek and left.

Eb waved to a couple of the football cars as they passed and said, "See you guys at practice tomorrow. Thank you for being here."

Hap patted the seat of the rocker next to him and Eb took it. "You doin' awright, boy?" he said. "This is a tough hand to be dealt."

"She's going to be fine, Hap. I know it. She's tough as a longshoreman and she's healthy. I just don't see anything that can defeat her." Eb looked down at his hands, which wouldn't stop shaking.

"Long time ago," said Hap, "I heard somethin' that helps me when things don't go right. It's called the Serenity Prayer and it says, 'God, grant me the serenity to accept the things I cannot change, the courage to change the things I can and the wisdom to know the difference.' It's that last bit that causes most of the trouble." Hap folded the newspaper and put it on the porch floor.

"A lot of us seem to think we can change anything if we fight it hard enough, but sometimes just sittin' back and waitin' for nature to take its course is the best action. Don't seem like much of an action, but what it does is it sets our mind free to know what to do when the time comes that we can do something worthwhile." Hap paused and let that sink in. The sun broke from behind a cloud just as Hap finished his sentence, as if to put an exclamation point on the thought.

"You ain't goin' help Lizetta by worryin' yourself to death ever' minute you're awake," Hap continued. "Do the things you're good at, the things that need to be done. Make sure your effort is being put in the right place and you'll see some results soon enough. You gotta be prepared to accept what those results are, son, even if they ain't the ones you laid out ahead of time. Sometimes God don't do it our way. But you'll find out sooner or later that it's the right way, the way it's supposed to be."

Eb wasn't sure what he thought about God, and Hap had given him a lot to chew on. Hap's absolute certainty in what he was saying made Eb feel confident that, yes, this was going to be what it was supposed to be and Eb would have to make sure it was all right with him. Whatever the result.

Thursday, October 24, 3:30 p.m.

Eb was distracted to the level of uselessness all week. He didn't pay attention in class, didn't have his homework ready, practiced football half-heartedly, and missed steps at square dance practice.

The football team was to play Cane River Friday night and the Red Raiders (whom a couple of the smarter Toe River players called the Red Baiters) weren't an opponent that would strike fear into most, and certainly not the Hawks. This was a game Toe River was heavily favored to win. The Hawks were undefeated and led the Appalachian Conference in both offense and defense. They were facing a two-win, five-loss team with the worst defense in the league. But Toe River would have to show up. Eb would have to be there, too.

Eb threw pass routes in a light, steady rain to backs and ends in the team's weekly light practice and Hap left his linemen alone so he could trot over and talk to Eb. "What do you hear from Durham?" Hap said, slapping Eb on the bottom.

"Not much change. She's awake and talking some, but she still doesn't remember what happened and her dad says there's a lot of pain all over, especially in her neck." Eb snapped off a 30-yard pass, a frozen rope that hit the receiver in the hands at full speed. "She broke—smashed, really—two vertebrae and got beat up inside pretty good. They're thinking the head injury was just a concussion, not something more serious. She's still not out of bed." Eb waved Terry deeper into his route, then threw a long arching pass to the end zone.

"You're missin' her, aren't you?" said Hap, picking up a ball and squeezing it with both hands.

"Am I that obvious?" Hap flipped the ball to Eb, who quickly launched another crisp pass.

"Might as well be wearin' a neon sign."

"Hap, I told you that I feel useless, helpless, and I don't know what to do. I don't even have a phone to call her and if I did, I don't have the money for long distance. What kind of goddamn boyfriend is that?"

"Don't take the Lord's name in vain 'cause you're feelin' sorry for yourself, son. You're sellin' Lizetta short. I keep seein' you do that. She's smarter than most of us—includin' you—and she's one of the good ones. She understands the deal and I'm sure she's not even thinkin' about why you ain't called. She knows. Ease off." Hap tossed another ball to Eb who threw it hard to Perry in a short route.

"Hey, man!" yelled Perry. "Ease off. You'll break my fingers."

Eb nodded toward his receiver. "Sorry," he said.

"You know," said Hap, "if you're distracted tomorrow night, you may not be worth a warm pile of cat poop to us. If you want to do somethin' for that pretty girl of yours, send her a passel of touchdown passes, the kind that help kids like you get into college. She wants that for you much as she wants anything and you're the only one who can do it."

Eb looked at his shoes, embarrassed. Hap had a way of reading the situation, making sense of it and boiling it down. Perry tossed a ball back to Eb, who wasn't looking. It bounced off his helmet and they all laughed.

"I'll do my best," Eb said. "Promise." With that, he waved for Terry to run a long pass pattern, picked up another football and threw a tight spiraling bullet sixty yards. The ball landed on the tips of Terry's fingers as he crossed the goal line.

"Like that?" Eb said, as Hap grinned, smacked Eb's helmet and went back to his linemen.

Friday, October 25, 7:45 p.m.

Coach Buster Woodson reminded the team in his pregame preparations that Cane River's defense had its problems, but emphasized that none of those problems was because of a six-foot-two, two-hundred-forty-five-pound linebacker named Jackie Lee Sturgis. He was as fast as a receiver, a two-time all-state defender on a bad team who had a mean streak that made Mickey Buchanan look like Howdy Doody.

He was responsible for ending the football year for two opposing quarterbacks already this season and he put two others out of games with vicious hits. He didn't do it with cheap shots like Mickey, either. He simply bowled over anybody in his way and went growling into a collision. He was one of the biggest players in the conference—huge even for a tackle at this level—and he was a force.

Toe River's offensive line would have to deal with him or he'd send Eb down to Duke with Lizetta. He certainly intended to try.

Eb pulled Woodson over to the side just before game time and made a radical proposal. "Can we put Carl in at center and have him key on Sturgis?" Eb said, with a level of assertion he hadn't expected.

"Carl don't know the plays," said Woodson, taking off his baseball cap and slicking back his dark Brylcreemed hair. "You know that. He's never snapped a ball, either, that I know of."

"Carl doesn't have to know the plays and he has snapped to me in pre-game warm-ups and in practice a number of times. He's a great athlete and he's just fine with centering. Carl has to block Sturgis. From center he can watch Sturgis at middle linebacker and get to him. Cane River has one player and I think Carl can neutralize him. We can take care of the rest of them with normal blocking. How 'bout we try it on our first series? If it fails, we'll figure it out another way."

Woodson shrugged. "You know it's your ass that's in a sling if Carl can't block him and Carl's giving away eighty pounds. That boy's got eighty-five pounds on you, too, and he can outrun you." Woodson's face was uncomfortably close to Eb's facemask, but Eb didn't back up, even though the coach's breath would wilt a flower.

"Carl Blackthorn is not giving away anything," Eb said sternly. "He never has and he never will. Sturgis will just be a bigger guy than usual for him to knock down. You know his energy level and if Sturgis can stay with him even for a little while, I'll stand naked in the middle of the field for our whole practice Monday."

"We won't need to go that far," said Woodson, backing away, not recognizing the joke. "You got one series to see how it works." Woodson turned, took a few steps toward the sideline and placed his attention elsewhere.

Eb stayed with Carl after practice Thursday to work on the center snap, which Carl did with ease. His snap was accurate and brisk. Simple fact that Eb knew well: Carl was the best natural athlete around. He could play any position, and in this game he wouldn't even need to know the plays. He simply had to block Sturgis. Hunt him down and neutralize every play. The rest of the line could take care of the others.

Carl was to serve the same purpose as a boxer's jab. He represented annoyance, distraction and occasional pain. He didn't have to manhandle Sturgis. Eb's guess was that he would not be able to block Sturgis in a conventional way, but Carl was not a conventional player and he'd find a way. He had the Biblical task for an offensive lineman: protect his quarterback. Eb was, indeed, *his* quarterback. It would be personal from the first contact between the two. Carl would make certain everybody in the stadium knew his assignment with his piercing yell cracking the night air during and after every play. Eb couldn't wait to watch.

He didn't have to wait long. Cane River took the opening kickoff and because Carl made three straight tackles for loss on the first series, the Raiders had to punt from their own thirty-two-yard-line. J.W. called for a fair catch on Toe River's thirty after a solid kick.

Carl looked lost in the huddle. Eb called an off-tackle play to the left with Barry Bates running. This was about Carl teeing off on Sturgis, not about Barry Bates running the ball. As the huddle broke, Eb grabbed Carl's jersey at the neck. "Just block number fifty-five," he said. "Don't worry about anything else. Nothing else."

"Okay, boss," Carl said, his searchlight smile illuminating the stadium.

The first collision was huge and you could hear the crack all the way to Spruce Pine, Eb guessed. Sturgis made the tackle, but Barry ran ten yards and had a first down. Sturgis got up shaking his head, obviously annoyed and stunned at the contact with Carl.

Toe River ran the same play to the other side with the same result. Sturgis saw what the Hawks were doing and he looked intent when they came up to the line again, standing feet from Eb and looking straight into his face.

"You're dead," he said. Carl grinned at him. Sturgis' brow crinkled and he showed his teeth. Eb thought he heard a growl.

Eb faked an off-tackle play to Barry, took two steps back and dropped a thirty-five-yard pass into Terry's hands. He went the rest of the way for a touchdown. As Terry caught the ball, Eb's lights went out. He didn't see the touchdown or anything else for about five minutes.

A frustrated Sturgis, blitzing on the play, hoping to jam up the middle before Carl could hit him, broke free just behind Eb's sightline to the left and hit him in the middle of the back—leading with his helmet—after Eb had let the ball go. It was an illegal hit and Cane River was penalized on the kickoff. But that didn't do Eb much good.

Eb woke up looking into Woodson's out-of-focus face.

"What planet's this?" Woodson said, straining at a joke.

"What happened?"

"How many fingers do you see?"

"Oh, quit that," Eb said, getting to his feet and shaking his head briskly. "Did that damn Sturgis get to me?"

Carl was in front of Eb now. "Sorry, man," he said. "Won't happen again. He nearly ripped my jersey off getting by me, but the ref didn't see it. Didn't see much else, either. The hit was after the play."

"If it happens again, I hope you can figure out how to pay for my funeral," Eb said. "That guy's an animal." He put an arm around Carl's shoulder pads.

"Tell me about it," said Carl, who went at Sturgis for

another series while Eb sat on the bench, retrieving his breath.

"I'm ready," Eb said to Woodson, pulling on his helmet and heading out onto the field.

"Whoa," Woodson yelled. "Let's wait until we're on offense. You're a quarterback. Remember?"

***

Once again, Carl played at all-state levels, this time on both offense and defense. He was responsible for another safety and picked up a fumble he caused and ran it thirty-three yards for a touchdown. For the most part, he kept Sturgis off Eb—and Barry—while they took advantage of Cane River's ineptitude elsewhere and won this one fifty-one to nothing. Eb had five touchdown passes to send to Durham with his love.

***

Eb pulled on his pants in the locker room as Hap came over with an urgent look on his face. "You got a call upstairs in the principal's office," he said. "Sounds important. Better get on up there."

"Who is…"

"Just go. Hurry."

Eb's heart was rushing. He assumed his mother must have had something bad happen in Asheville. Who else would call and who'd know where to call at this time of night on a Friday?

Eb picked up the phone as if it might break. "H'lo," he said tentatively.

"Hi, sweetie," said a chirpy Lizetta. "Heard you sent me some touchdowns."

Eb sat down hard in Banner's chair, grinning as wide as ever he had. "Oh, Jeeeeeesus," he said. "Is it really you? How are you? You walking? I miss you. I've wanted to call. It's so frustrating. I love you. Are you getting good treatment? When are you coming home…"

"Hey, hotshot, can I get a word in? I miss you too and I love you, too. I didn't know how much until I got down here

205

and you weren't with me. I'll be home soon. You just keep being good at everything you do so we can both go to college and do wonderful things.

"I gotta go 'cause there's a big Nazi nurse standing here wanting the phone. I'll be thinking of you. I hope, Steinbeck, that you'll pick up a pen and paper this week and write something sweet to me. I want that."

"It's yours," Eb said, relieved, happy and feeling about as good as a human being could feel. Tonight, he would write her a thousand words and they would all be good. John Steinbeck-good.

Part X

Saturday, October 26, noon

Miss Lilly paced in front of the team, standing on stage, awaiting practice. The dancers were soaked in sweat, several bending over, hands on knees and breathing hard. Joyce had her left shoe off, rubbing her sore toes. Janice sat on the stage, her arms extended behind her, hands on the floor. Eb paced nervously, breathing hard and dripping sweat as he walked.

"You have three weeks to get ready for Sky High," said Miss Lilly, by way of reminder and warning. "Twenty one days from now, you'll be going into the quarterfinal round of the Mountain Youth Jamboree and you'll be facing one of the most formidable opponents we've ever seen here. It is an opponent that doesn't respect you, that believes Old Smoky is its for the taking."

A loud clap of thunder dramatically interrupted her. She turned and looked out the big windows, watching sheets of rain fall, pounding hard against the big windows of the auditorium.

"I hope you understand that we can't sit back and defend that trophy," said Miss Lilly, ignoring the hard rain and the lightning that flashed like somebody was playing with a light switch. "Right now, we have to take the trophy from a team that has been better than us, more consistent than us, deeper and, frankly, more talented than we are. We have to be perfect in everything we do and our game plan has to be more creative, more aggressive, riskier, and more in tune with who we are than theirs does."

Miss Lilly paused and surveyed the faces. Everybody was listening closely but Mickey. "Mickey Buchanan, will you give me your attention!" Miss Lilly snapped. "This is about all of us." Mickey reluctantly turned to face her. She continued.

"For the Asheville dancers, this is a lark, something they won't even remember Sunday morning, unless we make it a bad memory. For Toe River High School, this is our heritage, our identity and we can't allow somebody to come in here and take it from us." She scanned the eyes of her team.

"Are you ready to work like you've never worked before?" The gauntlet was on the floor in front of the square dance team.

"Yes!" the dancers shouted in unison, searching for enthusiasm through the near-exhaustion. This felt like being at Marine at boot camp. Eb's guess was that Miss Lilly would intensify that feeling soon, as the dancers went into a six-team meet at East Tennessee State Teachers College in Johnson City, where he'd just taken his SATs.

Eb was still shaky and sore from the Cane River football game. The toll Sturgis took on him with the few clean hits and a couple that were penalized left Eb battered, bruised and wondering how many more guys like Sturgis he could take. In college, Sturgis would be the norm, not the exception and Eb doubted his ability to absorb that kind of battering on a daily basis. He would not likely dance at ETSTC unless an emergency arose. It didn't look like any surprises were hanging around corners. A huge crack of thunder rang through the auditorium and the lights flickered off, then on again. The dancers stood transfixed, looking at the pouring rain.

Eb remembered what Hap said in one of Eb's frequent confused moments. "Just do what's next the best thing you can and don't worry about what comes after that. It's all you can do, anyway."

"Let's get back to it," said Eb. "We got a trophy to win."

Sunday, October 27, 3:30 p.m.

"Miz Silver Feather, I wanted to thank you for putting me with Billy Staples," said Joss-Lynn Ledbetter. Arlene looked up from her front seat on the bus and saw the soft, pretty face, blue eyes and large smile. "He's the nicest boy on the team and he dances like a dream. He's not one of those ballet boys, either. He's a real boy."

Arlene Silver Feather didn't know how to answer the resident brat's fumbling attempt at gratitude, a concept she was obviously unfamiliar with, but Arlene nodded and said, "Just keep dancing well."

"Oh, we will," Joss-Lynn said, shaking her head, blonde hair flying. "I think we'll be the stars." Joss-Lynn flounced down the steps of the bus, her pink shirt-waist dress flashing stepped onto the parking lot at Emory & Henry College in Virginia.

Billy Staples had the reputation of make-out artist—among both the boys and the girls at the School for the Arts, where he was a prized ballet student—and when Arlene asked him if he would mind dancing with the petulant blonde, he saw something besides a dance partner. An "opportunity," he would likely have called it. Nice buns. Better ta-tas. A girl hungry for attention.

He was a handsome boy, Mediterranean dark, chiseled features, graceful, easy with conversation, one who appeared worldly and experienced. He had been to school in France and Italy and picked up a slight accent, which the girls adored.

Arlene reasoned that this arrangement did not have to work over the long haul. It didn't even have to last beyond mid-November and the Jamboree. After that the kids could do what they would. No shine off Arlene Silver Feather's dancing shoes.

The bonus here was that Billy was such a good dancer that Joss-Lynn improved just to keep up. Her dancing was far better and as a dance couple, they were quite good.

Billy Staples was the only opening she could find in the narrow definition Bobby Lee Ledbetter gave her. Joss-Lynn seemed not only happy with it, but ecstatic and—perhaps most important—she was under the control of somebody Joss-Lynn appreciated, for whatever reason. Billy could work with her on the dance floor, teach her, keep her happy.

It was one more annoyance out of Arlene's way, clearing a path toward the goal. There were three weeks remaining to hold together this delicate coalition of rednecks and artists, money and creativity, greed and desperation.

Minutes later, Arlene called the team together in the lobby of the auditorium at Emory & Henry, about fifty miles north of Bristol. This was another of those multi-state meets at a college where Appalachian culture was important. The ten teams in the meet represented Virginia, North Carolina, West Virginia and Tennessee and it would be good for Sky High to see dancers from other regions and for Arlene Silver Feather to study routines that would be different from what she was accustomed to.

"I don't need to tell you to pay strict attention to what you're doing," Arlene told the twenty dancers, lined in an almost military formation, all fully attentive. "Watch the other teams and learn what you can from them." She saw some of the dancers' eyes roll.

She left it at that. "Get to it," she said, not recognizing the growing boredom of her team. "Go dance."

Monday, October 28, 8:15 a.m.

Harold Wiseman stood in front of Eb as he turned from his locker, headed for Hap Heaton's homeroom. "Gotta talk to you a minute," he said in a low voice, slightly above a whisper.

That was the longest sentence Harold had ever spoken to Eb. Mostly what Eb got from him was grunts and nods in football practice, not much else. There was that one time when he and Smoky carried Eb off the field and Harold said he hoped Eb got better, but Eb didn't count it as a conversation, since he was essentially in another world.

"What's the deal?" Eb said, shifting his English book to his left hand. "Can I help with something?"

"Yeah, you can," Harold said, rubbing his face nervously. "Sheriff Richard Lee Birchfield's coming by the school today to interview people about what they was doin' the night of the school dance and to see if they know anything about Old Man Banner's car getting trashed."

"You mean the shitmobile?" Eb said, chuckling.

"Yeah, that. You don't know nothin' 'bout that, right?"

Harold almost grinned at "shitmobile," but he didn't get that far.

"Right. I don't. I've heard things and I suspect what I heard's true, but I don't know anything. Even if I did know anything, I don't think I'd say it because the old bastard got what he deserved. Ain't Birchfield some kind of cousin of yours, or something?"

"Or something," Harold said. "He's from over on Elk River."

That meant if he wasn't part of the family officially, he was certainly part of the family, extended, and that river was just as thick as blood to the people who lived along it. Banner didn't live along it. Harold did and Richard Lee Birchfield did.

"Harold, if there's anything I can do here, I'll do it. I'm not an Elk River boy, but by god you're my left tackle."

"Uh, fine," Harold said, looking slightly embarrassed. He paused and shuffled his feet, as if trying to find a sentence he knew was out there somewhere. Finally, it came: "I 'preciate you not tryin' to make a run at Joyce."

"What do you mean?"

"Oh, hell, you know what I mean. Everybody in school can see it, that you got a thing for her. But I 'preciate you not actin' on it. She means a lot to me."

"She means a lot to me, too, Harold, and I want her to be happy. She seems to be happy with you and that's good enough for me."

Harold cautiously and slowly extended his hand. Eb shook it. "Let's kick some Mars Hill ass this Friday," Eb said.

Harold smiled this time for certain and went about his shit detail.

***

Sheriff Richard Lee Birchfield's "investigation" was the talk of school all day. More like the joke of the day, as it turned out. Seems everybody in Avery County, save J.D. Banner, knew how things worked. Even Eb knew and he'd only been

211

here a few months.

Banner was not going to find the culprits, even though he knew who they were, and he was not going to punish anybody for the crime, either. That would not sit well with the sheriff, following his "complete investigation" and the exoneration of the obvious suspects.

Eb couldn't help but feel sorry for Banner and his illusions. And his shitmobile. Eb couldn't spend a lot of time worrying about a car and its jerk owner when Mars Hill, maybe the best team on Toe River's schedule, stood just a few days away. But he could laugh every time he thought of Banner opening the door and all that crap falling out. It was much, much more a metaphor than Banner would ever understand.

Monday, October 28, 3:30 p.m.

This was Mars Hill week for the football team and everybody was keenly aware that the next two games—ending with East Yancey—could lead to the playoffs and an undefeated season.

East Yancey and Toe River were undefeated and Mars Hill—playing without its all-state runner Chuck Tolley, whose grandfather died the day of the game—had lost only to East Yancey. There was a good possibility a three-way tie could result at the end of the two weeks. Tolley would be in the lineup against Toe River Friday and he was the difference between Mars Hill being an average team and a title contender.

He was big—six-foot-two, two hundred fifteen pounds— and fast and he had already signed with Clemson, one of the few Appalachian Conference players ever to get a football scholarship from a major university. He was leading the state in scoring, averaging more than four touchdown runs a game.

Coach Woodson told the team the details, as the players knelt in front of him prior to practice, but he didn't need to. It was all they talked about for days among themselves and even the Asheville newspaper, which generally didn't know the Appalachian Conference existed, was taking special notice because its teams were good and they were interesting. Toe River was one of the top scoring teams and had the stingiest defense in the region. Mars Hill featured a dynamic back. East Yancey was a solid, veteran team with good size and speed. Each of the schools had easily beaten a respected squad in a higher classification.

The consensus was that this was likely the best Class A conference in North Carolina and that its top three teams could compete for the championship in most AA conferences. It was a rare case of overachievement among small schools.

Notice was spreading. WLOS-TV in Asheville televised a story on Tolley and there was talk that the Asheville Citizen would have a reporter at Mars Hill College Friday for Toe River's game there. Mars Hill was only twenty miles from Asheville, but the Appalachian Conference might as well have been on another planet from the coverage standpoint in most years. Many of the stadiums in the conference, including the one at Toe River, didn't even have press boxes. No need for them. No press.

Toe River would be playing at Mars Hill College's stadium with its seventy-five hundred concrete seats and Eb was interested to see how many people showed up for the game. Appalachian Conference teams were accustomed to playing before a few hundred fans in their tiny stadiums, which often had stands on only one side and whose lights were sometimes supplemented by lights from cars parked around the edges of the field. Bakersville's and Spruce Pine's fields didn't have enough scraggly Bermuda grass on them to require more than occasional mowing. Cane River's field had a creek running along the back of the end zone that you needed to be aware of it you were running a pass pattern there. Cloudland High's field was on top of the school, which was cut out of a mountain. Crossnore's gridiron had such a slope that rain was never a problem, though standing up could be. Water quickly ran off and into a creek behind the stands.

Mars Hill College was one of the schools that showed some

interest in Eb, so this would be something of an audition. Eb hadn't seen the school, but he'd be playing the most important game of the year—to this point—on its first-class small college football field. So would Chuck Tolley.

Wednesday, October 30, 6:10 p.m.

Practice was barely forty minutes old and Miss Lilly was increasingly frustrated, especially with the football players who'd been distracted for days.

"Gentlemen of the football team," she finally said, stopping the dancing in mid step and using her voice as a weapon. "You are obviously somewhere else tonight and I need you here." She stomped her left foot as an exclamation point. "I understand you have important considerations in your near future, but tonight your presence at this practice required. We have an important event ourselves less than three weeks away and I don't want you to lose sight of that because of distractions that you can control if you will."

She walked to the stage and stood at the feet of Mickey Buchanan, looking up directly into his intense blue, heavy-lidded eyes.

"We are going to set a new standard for square dancing November sixteenth in Asheville and we are going to do it without flaw, without looking like we're making it up as we go, and without obvious effort. You have to look like this comes naturally. That takes work and concentration.

"So get your head out of your butt and get back into this room *RIGHT NOW!*"

That last sentence was not exactly vintage Lillian Bales Wilkerson and maybe that's why the team became fully attentive, looking at her, then at each other, wondering if they'd all heard the same thing. Eb tried without success to suppress a smile, but Joyce caught him and smiled back.

They got down to work and by eight p.m., Lilly Wilkerson had a room full of exhausted, sweat-soaked, sore-footed dancers who were getting better by the minute. The question remained, though: Were they improving enough to beat Sky High?

Friday, November 1, 8:37 a.m.

The entire student body of Toe River High School, all three hundred and eighty, showed up on what was being called Mars Hill Day. They were jammed into the tiny top-floor auditorium for the first pep rally anybody could remember. Some of those memories were long, too.

The air was festive as Toe River's tiny band—fifteen members, including six-foot-four-inch football player David Farris, the tallest member of the team—played tune after tune surprisingly well. The cheerleaders were on stage dancing, as everybody took seats and the football team, in white and green game jerseys, stood behind them. Bigger schools did this every week, regardless of the record, and it was noisy, but rarely like this. The Toe River students were excited, the faculty was excited, the cheerleaders were about to explode and the team members were grinning, ear-to-ear.

J.D. Banner introduced Coach Woodson, who introduced each member of the team, telling the students to hold their applause until the end. The students systematically ignored the directive, cheering their favorites as their names were called. Those responsible for touchdowns got a lot of cheers, but the unbridled roar was reserved for Carl Blackthorn. His was a long, raucous standing ovation. Eb was tickled to death with Carl's recognition because Carl was his favorite of all the boys on the team and there was little chance to win against good competition without him. Carl stepped to the front of the stage, threw up both hands and shined that beam of a smile, lighting the room by double.

After introductions, an obviously uncomfortable Woodson, who did not like speaking in front of groups, said he appreciated all the yelling and that the school had a pretty good team that deserved support. "These boys has worked their butts off for you," he said, turning his best phrase yet. Then he looked at Eb, waved him over and handed him the microphone, knowing the senior quarterback with the talented pen would not be at a loss for words.

"What do you want me to say?" Eb said, holding the mic at arm's length and surprised at the gesture. "Shouldn't one of the captains be talking?"

"You are the captain, Elbert. Captain of the offense, as of today. Carl's captain of the defense, but you know about Carl and talking. Say something."

Woodson turned to the students and said, "Here's a few words from your football team's brand new offensive captain." Eb gestured for Carl to join him.

Again a big ovation. Carl walked over and put his arm around Eb and waved his other arm in a circle, keeping the noise coming.

Eb turned to the students, held up his hand to calm down the crowd and said, "Toe River High School puts eleven boys out there at a time, but if we can field twelve at Mars Hill tonight, we'll roll them up and send them home. The twelfth player will be you and the noise you make in that big stadium, the enthusiasm you show for your team. We are countin' on you not only to be there, but to out-yell Mars Hill *while we kick their butts!"*

The students arose in unison, screaming and yelling for a full minute. Eb had never seen such electricity in a school gym of any size and every player on that country football team was feeling more energized about what they were doing than they had all year.

This was a big game and suddenly it had a big game feel.

Friday, November 1, 7:18 p.m.

The team went over and over Mars Hill's offensive and defensive schemes and tendencies for nearly an hour until it was time to go out and play football. Toe River was as ready as it was going to be. When Coach Woodson said, "Let's show 'em what a Red Tail Hawk eats for supper," the team let out one of those simultaneous primal roars, stood up and clattered out of the locker room—metal-tipped cleats on concrete, sounding almost like tap shoes, Eb thought.

As the players went through the door, the entire stadium was splendidly presented before them. It was full, noisy and anticipating a football game that had been the lead story in the Asheville Citizen sports section this morning. There were thirty nine games listed in the paper's coverage area and this one was number one. The house was packed and over on Toe River's visitors' side, the center of the section was stacked with about a thousand people wearing Kelly green and making more racket than anybody had ever heard in an Appalachian Conference game before.

The stadium was beautiful and the field deep green, soft and perfectly lined. This was no Appalachian Conference cow pasture, but a college stadium that some of the players on both sides hoped to be playing on again in a year or so when they went to one of those Carolinas Conference small colleges.

Carl and Eb, dressed in their usual dingy white uniforms, went to the center of the field for the coin toss and there met Chuck Tolley and one of the Mars Hill tackles, their captains, both of whom dwarfed the one-hundred-sixty-pounders from Toe River. It looked like the kids against the adults if that was all you had to go on. Tolley and his co-captain, dressed helmet to socks in gold with dark blue numbers, trimmed carefully in a lighter blue, were friendly and relaxed, shaking hands warmly. They seemed to mean it when they wished Eb and Carl good luck and no injuries. Carl grinned and Eb smacked both opponents on the butt as they turned to re-join their teammates. Mars Hill won the toss and elected to go on defense. Eb guessed the Golden Tornadoes wanted their defense to show Toe River who was boss right away.

J.W. took the kickoff at the five and returned it to midfield, tripping over the kicker, the last man he had to beat to go all the way. It was a masterful run, one where J.W. broke and eluded tackle attempts from most of the Mars Hill players.

Good start. But that was where Toe River's offense ended for the entire half.

Mars Hill and its vaunted rushing attack—which hadn't played against Carl and Mickey and Gaylen and J.W. and Harold and Smoky—hit a wall, too. Nothing to nothing at the half in a game everybody thought might generate a hundred points.

Eb watched Mars Hill's offense throughout the half and picked up a few tendencies, but the most significant "steal" was that its right tackle was giving away the plays almost on cue. If his right foot was back when in his stance, it was a running play to his side. If his feet were even and he seemed to be leaning back slightly, it would be a pass. Toe River's defense jammed up Mars Hill's running lanes well, but Tolley came nerve-wrackingly close several times to breaking away. Gang tackling and good backup prevented that. Still, it would be a huge advantage if Toe River's defense knew where the plays were going.

Eb talked to Carl about what he saw and Carl passed it along…after smacking Eb on the helmet and saying, "Good catch, Cap'n."

Now the Hawks had to figure out what the hell they were going to do on offense. They came this close several times, but Terry—always so sure-handed—dropped three passes and Perry dropped one. Perry fell down on a route, which nearly resulted in an interception that would have been an easy touchdown. Barry ran the ball well, but Toe River's players were committing stupid penalties at important times or simply making the kinds of timing mistakes they almost never made. The Hawks were on the edge of a breakout, but they had to determine how to accomplish it, while holding the Tornadoes at bay.

Toe River's players learned early in the season that Coach Buster Woodson, who was in charge of the offense, was not exactly a Rhodes Scholar in these matters and, frankly, Eb called the plays and even arranged special blocking assignments on occasion. The offense was full of veteran players who knew what was going on, what they did well and what the defense was executing that they might exploit. Every time the offensive players went to the sideline, they sat together and talked strategy.

Eb called Terry over to see what was wrong. "Sorry about the drops," Terry said. "I can't explain it. Perfect passes. I just dropped 'em. But I can get open about any time. Both defensive backs are looking for interceptions and they're taking chances. Any of those drops would have been touchdowns for us because the backs made their moves too early and I was open. We just need to keep doing that. You know, if you'll run a couple of out patterns—one to each sideline—in the first series and pump fake the pass, the backs will break and I can turn and go up field. Should be an easy touchdown. Those Mars Hill backs are their own worst enemies and I think we can burn them."

And so it was.

After halftime, the defense held Mars Hill to fifteen yards on its first possession and Toe River got the punt at its own thirty-five. Eb passed left to Terry for twenty yards, then did the pump fake and let fly for a fifty-five-yard touchdown on the second play of the series.

Once again, it was almost too easy, but a seven-point lead was not safe with a back like Tolley probing Toe River's defense with his power and speed. He showed his all-state credentials on their first play after the kickoff, tearing up the middle and breaking a Carl Blackthorn tackle—which Eb had never seen anybody do before—then running 80 yards about as quickly as it can be done. The score was seven to seven just three offensive series and three minutes into the second half. So much for Eb catching Mars Hill's tackle in a tip-off.

This was going to be a fight, Eb thought, as he watched the impressive Tolley, with an intense sense of purpose, run through a defense he would have bet on against God and the Archangels.

Through the third quarter, as the chill night air became cooler, both teams slugged and feinted, moving the ball well but getting stopped with a mistake, a penalty, a good defensive play. The crowd on both sides was growing restless, groaning at the mistakes, looking for something to cheer.

When a pass slipped out of Eb's hand, one of the Mars Hill defensive backs picked it off and Eb was forced to make the tackle. Eb was the only player with a shot at him. He didn't like tackling. It's why he played quarterback and not linebacker. Eb grumbled all the way back to the bench.

Mars Hill scored a short field goal to start the fourth quarter. Later, the Tornadoes looked like they'd score a touchdown after reaching the one-yard-line at the end of a long drive. Carl, however, turned on his motor and threw, first Tolley, then the quarterback for losses back to the twenty-yard line. The kicker missed the field goal attempt.

On the following series, Terry and Perry each dropped a pass and Eb threw one into the ground to keep from being tackled behind the line. A bad kick by Barry put Mars Hill in good enough position to come up with another field goal. Suddenly, it was thirteen to seven, Tornadoes, with three minutes left.

Toe River was up against it here and this offensive juggernaut was looking more like a train with a broken wheel.

The Hawks huddled at their own thirty after J.W.'s short kickoff return and Eb could see the determination on the faces of the Mars Hill defenders. Its middle linebacker—who played magnificently—was walking up and down the line chattering, encouraging the linemen.

"Gentlemen, it's time for the Red Tail Hawk to assert itself," Eb said. "We're scoring here. I mean it. Thirty-one draw on two." Eb leaned over to Terry and said, "Hold your block for one count, then do a banana to the right corner."

Eb got the snap, ran behind Barry and pretended to slip the ball into his hands for the draw. Eb yelled, "Fumble!" and Barry turned around looking for the ball. Eb moved three steps to the side, hiding the ball on his hip, as Mars Hill's defense ran toward Barry, looking for the ball on the ground. Eb stared up-field and saw Terry sprinting alone.

He threw what may have been the best pass of the evening, a tight bullet on a straight line, hitting Terry in dead stride, wide open at the fifty. Terry dropped it. He fell to the ground screaming and pounding the grass.

"What the hell was that?" said Barry on the way back to the huddle.

"Not much," Eb said. "But we got to find something." Eb intentionally left the team out of the real play so he could sell the fake fumble. That part worked to perfection. His receivers were struggling.

Eb stood in front of the choir huddle, looked directly at Terry and said, "Sport, you're going to get it again and this time you're going to catch it. Let's do that hitch-and-go we did earlier. Perry, hang in the backfield for a count then drift to the left just in case Terry's covered."

Terry was, indeed, covered. Mars Hill knew what was coming and put two backs on him. Perry was open, but the Hawks only gained fifteen yards, enough for a first down. There were less than two minutes left in the game.

"Sprint right, double-down on one," Eb said in the huddle, sending two receivers toward the right, one at twenty yards, one at ten and Eb sprinting parallel to the line of scrimmage with them. Both were covered and there was no outlet. The linebacker was on Eb, but Smoky cut him down, creating a lane Eb had to take. He hated to run because his knees were suspect, but there was no choice here. He cut behind Smoky's block and followed Harold as Harold leveled both a lineman and a defensive back before Eb was caught from behind and rolled out of bounds, stopping the clock. Another fifteen yards, but time was ticking away. The Hawks were at the Mars Hill forty-five, a minute and a half left and options dwindling.

Eb called time out and ran over to talk to Woodson. "I need J.W. in the game," he said.

"What the hell for? He's a dang freshman, Elbert!"

"Because he can catch a pass and Barry's hands are made out of wood tonight. Nobody's catching the ball."

"Who's going to be back there blocking?"

"Coach, if we don't score here, it won't matter who's blocking or who's not. What I need right now is another receiver and J.W.'s it."

"Greene, get your ass out there," gruffed Woodson.

Eb trotted out behind J.W., trying to figure out how to do this. The Hawks rarely used three regular receivers and one more out of the backfield because Woodson always wanted maximum protection for his passer. But Mars Hill played the last few downs with five defensive backs and it was a loose defense, not the swarming, aggressive one the Tornadoes had used all night. There'd be a hole somewhere. Eb just had to find it.

"Terry and Perry, do the double banana route, crossing about twenty yards down the field and pulling everybody with you. Linemen, hold your block for two counts, then let your guy go and stay in place while J.W. goes just beyond you. We're going to throw a middle screen and I don't want any of you down field and getting a penalty. Got that?" They nodded. "The play doesn't have a name, but you know what to do. On three."

The play looked like the same one Toe River had been running throughout the night, and Mars Hill was all over Terry and Perry, two backs on each of them, but the middle of the field was wide open. The linemen held their blocks— one…two…let go—and J.W. slipped by, ran eight yards and turned toward Eb. Eb dropped back nearly fifteen yards and the Mars Hill linemen were running hard at him. He flipped a basketball pass over their heads to J.W. and the freshman took off toward the right corner of the end zone, down to the thirty…twenty…ten…and that big linebacker lunged and caught J.W.'s shoe, tripping him at the eight, the shoe going its own way.

When Toe River lined up quickly, there were twenty-eight seconds left as the second hand on the new scoreboard clock swept toward ending the game and sending the Hawks home a loser. *What haven't we done?* Eb thought as quickly as he could.

"Spike," Eb yelled and called signals, the ball coming to him almost instantly. He threw the football into the ground at his feet to kill the clock, officially an incomplete pass. That gave the Eb some time.

In the huddle, he drew up another play, one that had been rattling around in his head since the middle of the season. "Perry, you and Terry line up on the right side *on the line.* Make sure you're both on the line. Terry you're outside and I want you in the corner of the end zone. Perry, you're not eligible for a pass, stay in and block, but make it look like you might go out. That'll hold the linebacker and keep him out of the play.

"J.W., line up a yard behind the line on the left side. Run to the back of the end zone and take the defensive back with you across to the right. Harold, you're going to be an end on this play, so hold your block two counts and then run just past the goal line, just left of the goal post, and turn and look at me. The ball's coming to you and you're damn well gonna catch it."

It was a tackle-eligible pass and Eb's guess was that nobody on the field in an old gold Mars Hill jersey had ever seen it before. Because the end on Harold's side lined up in the backfield, leaving Harold on the end of the line, Harold was eligible to catch a pass, where normally, he wasn't. The play was rarely used, so seldom, in fact that it had to be reported to the official, which Eb did, subtly as he could, as he broke the huddle, but it was legal. He leaned to the official as the huddle broke and said, just above a whisper, "Tackle eligible." The official nodded slightly.

On the snap, Terry sprinted for the corner, double-covered again and J.W. headed for the back of the end zone, then cut right toward the same corner Terry was in. The linebacker waited for Perry, who never showed. There was nobody on the left but Harold, looking confused and terrified standing between the goal posts, on the goal line.

Eb turned quickly to him and tossed the ball like he was throwing it to little Ralphie and the ball hit Harold square in the middle of his chest. Harold grabbed it like he was hugging Joyce and fell flat down on his back, holding the ball up and letting go a sound like nobody'd ever heard from Harold Wiseman. He was mobbed as the zebra-striped official signaled touchdown.

Tie game, thirteen-thirteen, with Barry coming on to kick the extra point and five seconds left. Mars Hill stacked everybody it could in the box for the block, but Barry wouldn't have dared go back to Avery County if he'd missed, and he didn't. Straight line down the middle.

Those thousand Toe River fans filled that big stadium with their noise as the team celebrated in the middle of the field.

But the Hawks still had to kick off and Mars Hill still had Chuck Tolley.

Barry's kick—his best of the season, coming off that adrenaline—sailed to the five and Tolley caught it, looked intently to the right and left, then took off up the middle where a wedge was forming.

He shrugged off two tackles at the twenty, broke another at the thirty and looked like he was on his way. But out of nowhere came Carl Blackthorn hitting Chuck Tolley with such force that Tolley went up in the air like a rope jerked him and the ball went the other way, straight up. J.W. slapped it, tapped it again, caught it on the dead run and sprinted into the end zone for a touchdown after time expired. The Hawks didn't even need to kick the extra point.

The final score was Toe River twenty, Mars Hill thirteen in what the Asheville Citizen would call "an Appalachian Conference classic" the next morning.

As J.W. crossed the goal line, Eb fell to his knees, exhausted and relieved. He watched the players mob J.W., pick him up and carry him twenty yards before picking up Harold and carrying him a while. Eb went back and sat on the bench and soaked it all in. He'd never felt such unbridled joy before. Tears streamed down his face and his hands shook.

God, how he wanted Lizetta to be running toward him, arms wide.

Friday, November 1, 11:15 p.m.

The bus ride back to the high school was rowdy and festive, songs every foot of the way, piercing yells, constant chatter about this play or that, a great hit, the big crowd, the entire medieval festival of football that these players saw and felt.

They'd ridden the hour home in their uniforms without shoulder pads and helmets, sweaty, smelly, happy. They clattered into the Toe River locker room, which looked so much more humble than usual after the Mars Hill facilities, tired, happy and ready to get home to a warm bed. As Eb approached his locker, he noted an envelope taped to it. He pulled it down, opened it and read, "I called Lizetta and told her about the win and about how great you played. She said to tell you she loves you. Joyce."

Happy as Eb was already, this completed one of the best days he'd spent in seventeen years on earth.

Part XI

Saturday, November 2, 1:27 p.m.

The activities bus broke down as it drove through Hickory on the way to a dance meet just south of Charlotte in Rock Hill, S.C., home of Winthrop College. Winthrop was an all-women's college that produced a lot of teachers for the South Carolina educational system.

As annoying as the breakdown was, costing the team two hours and lunch, most of the football players were still high from the win over Mars Hill. They were looking forward to what Miss Lilly said would be a full-blown rehearsal for the Mountain Youth Jamboree clog-fest in this out-of-the-way place where square dancing was hardly noticed.

Miss Kay told the dancers that the three South Carolina teams—and two over from Georgia—were capable, but not on the level Toe River saw almost every time out in North Carolina and Tennessee. They were relatively new to smooth-style square dancing as a competitive sport and Toe River's clog shocker would give them ample food for thought.

Eb stood with the Toe River dancers as they watched the other teams fumbling and bumbling through basic routines, obviously needing a lot more experience before they would be competitive outside their own areas. "How'd we get matched up with these guys?" Eb said to Joyce, leaning over to whisper. "I could be a caller for half of them." Joyce grinned and punched him in the shoulder.

When it came Toe River's time to dance, the team was waiting backstage in the lovely old auditorium with a Saturday night crowd of several hundred, Eb estimated. The coach of the Rock Hill team told Miss Lilly, as Eb eavesdropped, that the people came to see Toe River because of an article in the Rock Hill paper that morning. She said nobody ever showed up for a local square dancing meet. The tiny North Carolina mountain school was making papers all over the place these days and its athletes took notice of the notice.

As the music started, Buster tapped three times and the rest of the team—Eb dancing with Joyce—quite literally kicked in, creating a ruckus that perked up the audience and had its members sitting on the edge of their seats as the dancers burst from backstage with a fast, lively and vibrant brand of square dancing these new enthusiasts had never seen before. Not many people anywhere had, in fact. By the second minute of the twelve-minute routine, the crowd was on its feet and by the tenth minute people were clapping with the music and mimicking the clogging. As Toe River hit the finale, the audience was heavily involved, clapping and cheering and when Buster slammed down the final tap and started offstage, the building shook from the cheering.

They'd done it. Just the way Miss Lilly wanted. The dancers weren't sweating obviously and nobody was panting from the exertion. The dancers shook hands and hugged backstage, their pasted-on smiles wider and more real, their eyes alight.

While the crowd was still applauding, Miss Lilly walked over to the team, circled it around her and said, "That's what we want." Not a word more. She turned and walked back out on the stage toward the judges.

A few minutes later, a note came from below that Toe River was disqualified for not dancing the way it was supposed to. Miss Lilly stormed down to the judges' table and involved herself in an animated discussion, picking up a small book, turning to a page and pointing to it. She talked for five minutes, then returned to the team as the crowd booed.

"They took it from us," she said, "but listen to that crowd. This is a second-level competition with judges who are learning and who are trying—at least tonight with us in the field—to exert themselves. We'll ignore it. I like what we did."

The eighteen Toe River High School square dancers saw a new day dawning for their sport.

They also saw risk ahead.

***

On the way home, driving uncertainly through the North Carolina mountains on a bus that was a direct reflection of the poverty of Avery County, Miss Lilly took a minute to issue a reminder.

She stepped out in the aisle at the front of the bus, beside her seat and faced the team. "I think you all know that today was the last competition we'll have before the Jamboree and it's going to be up to us to remain sharp for two weeks without being pushed by outsiders. We're going to have to rely on ourselves to be the best we can be and to peak at just the right time."

Joyce, sitting next to Eb about halfway back, reached across the aisle and poked Mickey, who was sleeping. He awoke with a start and cast a threatening glare at Joyce. She ignored him.

"You football players have a special challenge that is going to be difficult to meet because of what you're facing on two fronts—three if you count your grades, and I do." Janice slapped a textbook resting open on her lap, and nodded toward Eb, a grin on her face. "But you have all shown great character and determination and I expect that continue."

Miss Lilly continued without interruption. "As a team, you danced well tonight. It will take that and more against Sky High, but I think we have a shot at it if we dance the way I know we can.

"Relax now and get some rest. We'll be back at the school in about two hours. We're going to run through routine a couple more times before you go home."

Monday, November 4, 3:30 p.m.

Buster Woodson had the team kneel in a circle again before football practice began, this time, he said, for a few announcements.

"We had our annual coaches meeting at Cane River High School yesterday and picked the All-Appalachian Conference football team," he said, looking around at different faces. "I'll tell you that the coaches like this team."

"But we ain't played East Yancey yet," snarled Mickey Buchanan. "How can you pick an all-conference team before the last game, the biggest game of the year?"

"We gotta pick the all-conference before we pick the all-regional and all-state," said Woodson. "We want the all-state team to be announced the day of the championship game, so this is the way it's done." Mickey whispered "Bullshit!" under his breath and Woodson looked down at a sheet of paper.

"As I said, they liked you. We placed four offensive and four defensive first team players, the defensive player of the year and the offensive player of the year runner-up. The defensive player, of course, was Carl Blackthorn, who was also picked as the overall player of the year unanimously. That's a first for Toe River High School and a pretty good indication that we might get our first all-state player, too, since this is probably the toughest Class A conference in the state."

The team leaped to its feet, yelled in unison and mobbed Carl, who stayed on his knee, lowered his head and looked sheepish as everybody pounded his shoulders, back and head.

"Mickey Buchanan, Smoky Swain and Gaylen Anderson were on the defensive first team and J.W. Greene was on second team, the only freshman on the offensive or defensive first team.

"On offense, we had Terry Gervin, Barry Bates, Harold Wiseman and Elbert McCourry, who finished second—by one vote—to Chuck Tolley of Mars Hill as offensive player of the year. Elbert was a unanimous all-conference pick at quarterback, which means he has a good shot at all-region and maybe all-state. Perry Lafferty and J.W. Greene were second team. J.W. was the Newcomer of the Year. That's a pretty big vote of confidence in our passing game. Our quarterback and three receivers on the first and second team."

Woodson did not mention that he was not nominated for the Coach of the Year award, which went to East Yancey's coach with Mars Hill's head man finishing second. Toe River had not expected to challenge for the league title, but nobody even remotely suggested Woodson was responsible for the success. Hap Hilton was nominated as Coach of the Year on one ballot, but he couldn't accept the nomination because he was an assistant coach. It was a slap in the face of Woodson by his colleague.

Woodson paused after his announcements and looked up the hill toward the school where a truck with a huge TV camera on the back pulled into the parking lot.

"That up there on the hill is WLOS-TV in Asheville come to talk about the East Yancey game," he said. "We ain't ever had any kind of publicity like this and it's good for the school and the conference, so I want you boys to behave yourselves. They asked to talk to Carl and Elbert and I want to make sure it's all right with you Carl."

Carl looked embarrassed. "You know I don't talk so good," he said, looking at his shoes.

Eb put his hand on Carl's head and mussed his wavy black hair.

"You don't talk so good," Eb said, "but you knock the snot out of the whole conference and we all know what you're saying. I think you need that good looking face in front of the camera. Just say, 'Yes, sir' and 'No sir.' That's all they want anyway."

The team murmured its agreement.

"Two more things before Elbert and Carl go off to become TV stars," said Woodson, as Eb blanched at Woodson still calling him "Elbert." "We're playing Friday's game at Lees-McRae College because we expect a good-sized crowd and we want everybody to see us in the best possible situation. Several newspapers—we ain't sure how many—will be covering the game and there's a press box at the stadium. The game's being carried on WZJS radio in Banner Elk and WTOE in Spruce Pine, which they pick up next door in Yancey County." The level of pressure on this game increased on every word from

Woodson.

"If we beat East Yancey, we'll be playing Andrews, which already won the Smokys Conference championship and looks like they'll finish undefeated for the second straight year. The game's in Asheville's Municipal Stadium Saturday, November 15, at noon. Stadium's about the same size as the one at Mars Hill, but it's older and shabbier." Woodson looked around at the faces again, this time noting the surprise the dancers showed.

"Before you square dancers start getting your jocks in a twist," said Woodson, "the date and time were decided last year at the conference meeting and we didn't even think about what impact it would have on the Mountain Youth Jamboree, which has always been a week later. My guess is that nobody was thinking about square dancing, anyway." All the coaches knew full well, thought Eb, that they had dancers on their teams and they'd be going to the Jamboree.

"You'uns who dance will just have to buck up and remember you ain't gettin' a chance like this more'n once in your life, if you get it this time," said Woodson. "So just play ball and dance the best you can. You got your whole life after Saturday to rest."

That was easy for pot-bellied, soft Buster Woodson to say, but it might not be so easy for those playing ball against a tough, veteran, defending state champion football team and dancing against that Sky High juggernaut.

They'd have to do it, though, if Toe River beat East Yancey, which was far from a certainty.

Carl and Eb bounded up the hill toward that bulky-looking camera and a young crew-cut man plugging in a microphone. "Do your Richard Burton imitation for the TV guys, Carl," said Eb, running hard to stay even with his Cherokee friend.

Tuesday, November 5, 7 p.m.
Miss Dorothy, the Beech Mountain Home for Children director, called Eb to the administration building after supper

and when he got there, Maryellen Streit met him at the door, smiling broadly.

"We have a goodie for our all-conference quarterback," she said, ushering Eb into what Miss Dorothy still called the "parlor." It was a large formal room with, floral wallpaper, Georgian furniture, and a full-sized grand piano. The entire campus gathered in the well-lit, elegant room for Sunday evening vespers and a sing-along, following a light supper, usually cold sandwiches.

Miss Dorothy rose from the huge piano with the open lid, where she had been playing for a few of the older girls, and said, "Elbert, we wanted to do something for you because of all the good publicity you've brought us here at the Home." Her voice was higher, more chipper than usual, almost friendly.

"Miss Dorothy, I haven't done a thing that even comes close to what you did by taking me in," said Eb, embarrassed. "You don't have any idea what the Home, you and everybody here means to me. I am thankful for all of you."

Maryellen leaned over and whispered, "Stick that nose up her butt as far as you can, Elbert. It just keeps getting browner." Eb bumped her with his shoulder and suppressed a grin.

"Judi, hand Elbert the phone and we will all leave him alone for a short while."

Eb looked at the phone like it was a foreign object, put it to his ear and said, "This is Eb," and Lizetta came back with, "So now that you're all-conference, does that mean all the girls are falling at your feet?" She laughed that big, hearty laugh and Eb melted. He joined her laugh out of nervousness, joy and relief.

"Tell me how you're doing," he said. "Are you getting better?"

"This isn't about me," she said. "This is about all-everything quarterback who is on TV. Mom said she saw you and you were so polished that she fell in love with you herself. She said Carl looked and sounded good, too. I'm proud of both of you. Unanimous all-conference. My goodness."

"Are you getting out of bed and walking?" Eb said.

"I'm wheeling around, racing a little," she said. He could see the twinkle in her eyes. "I'm good with that wheel chair. The neck brace makes me look like a bleached–out African princess, but I'm getting better every day. The doctor—the famous one that Daddy says is known all over the place—said I should be good as new in a few months. He said it in German. Doesn't speak a word of English. *Sprechen sie Deutsch?*"

Eb laughed nervously and said, "How about school work?"

"Oh, I was so far ahead that I won't lose anything," said Lizetta. "My average and class standing will be fine and I heard from admissions at Wake and they told me not to worry about anything. Have you heard from any more colleges?"

Eb looked at the door to the parlor where several of the children were gathered, eavesdropping. He winked at them.

"I get letters almost every day and coaches show up at practice and games, but Lizetta, I don't know how serious any of this is. I don't know if it's just that we're winning games and getting a lot of attention from TV and the newspaper or does it mean they really think I can play? Am I big enough? Am I fast enough? Can I take the punishment? Hell, can I pass class at that level? There's so many more questions than answers right now. But I'm loving every minute of the attention. I'd swap it all for a hug and kiss from the prettiest girl in seven states."

"Which states?" she demanded. Eb could see her smile through the phone.

"Baby," she cooed, "It's going to work out and you're going to be great. Just keep doing what you're doing. So much has come to that poor, isolated county since you got there and I know you're going to say you didn't have anything to do with it, but you did. You're leading in a lot of ways that nobody has had the courage to do before and I'm proud of you, just as proud as I can possibly be. And I want to suck your face."

Eb stood silent for a moment. "I miss you," he said weakly.

At that moment, Miss Dorothy re-entered the room and announced firmly, "Elbert, sorry, but it's long distance and you'll have to stop you for now. Say your goodbyes."

"I love you, Lizetta," he said. "Hurry back to me."

"I will," she said, her voice breaking ever so slightly, and they hung up.

"Thank you, Miss Dorothy," Eb said, handing her the phone. "That was awful thoughtful of you. I guess you know I've been worried sick about Lizetta."

"Yes, son, I do. I talked to her mother and she said it looks like Lizetta will be home in a week or so, maybe in time for the Jamboree. She's going to be in a wheel chair for a while, but Miz McEntire said that a complete recovery is highly likely. She said the doctors at Duke have done a magnificent job."

"Yeah," said Eb, "and Lizetta McEntire is as tough as any football player in the Appalachian Conference."

Part XII

Friday, November 8, 6:12 p.m.

It went down on the calendar as The Week the Press Came to the Sticks. The newspapers—most of which Toe River football team members had never heard of—and TV stations from Asheville and even Johnson City, Tennessee, were at practice nearly every day, watching, evaluating, questioning, pumping up what they considered a big story with a great hook.

The players were flattered, but wary. The journalists could go away as quickly as they came. All it took was a loss. Mars Hill likely knew just how quickly they could disappear. It had a team every bit as good as Toe River's or East Yancey's, but it lost to both in games Mars Hill could have won. Now the team was part of history.

Toe River High School was still the mystery, a tiny, backwater school that ran an outdated, but often radically modified, single wing offensive formation. It came out of nowhere to challenge the defending league champion. The Hawks beat Mars Hill with Chuck Tolley playing, which East Yancey did not. Toe River held him and his team to a single score. The Hawks had gaudy offensive and defensive statistics. They were Cinderella.

East Yancey was a senior team that had won the title as a junior team. It was bigger, smarter, stronger and older. It pounded nine opponents as impressively as Toe River had.

The Panthers ran a conservative offense and a simple, attacking defense that swarmed to the ball and overwhelmed with speed and size.

No wonder the press was so interested. The match was dramatic and there was something intensely cultural about these two mountain schools—which weren't yet consolidated into big county high school—playing at a level nobody dreamed they could.

In the spare, old sweat-smell of the Toe River locker room,

the Hawks were getting their ankles taped and slipping on their gear for the seven-mile, winding trip over to Banner Elk, where Lees-McRae's two thousand-seat stadium was the biggest venue in the county. It was a remote junior college stadium that only recently added lights and had never been filled to capacity. The stadium would be full on this night. Once again, the stadium was better than what the Hawk players were accustomed to, perhaps a symbol of their new-found fame.

Coach Woodson and Hap Hilton walked into the noisy locker room together carrying two large cardboard boxes. They sat them down in the center of the room and Hap bellowed above the din, "Bring it in." The team gathered in a circle around the mysterious boxes.

"This county's proud of you boys," Woodson said. "The Avery County Board of Supervisors and some of the businessmen in the county pooled resources after you'uns beat Mars Hill Friday and put in a rush order for what we're gettin' ready to pass out." Hap pulled out an aging Buck knife, opened the blade and split open the top of the boxes.

Woodson went on: "I want you all to understand the impact your play has had on the way this county is feelin' about itself these days and on the way people who don't know us are thinkin' about us. You've all become good will ambassadors, whether it's appearin' on TV or just being good sports on the football field."

"Here's one small token of the county's gratitude," said Hap. He pulled out a kelly green football jersey with white numbers sewn on front and back—not the plastic numbers that were becoming so common. The sleeves were old gold three-quarter length with green numbers on the top of the shoulder pads and "Hawks" written just under the collar in old gold. There was a loud "Ooooooo," and then a louder cheer from a bunch of kids who'd been wearing nearly worn out football jerseys most teams would have been embarrassed to pull on for practice.

"Elbert McCourry, come up here and get number eleven,"

236

Hap Hilton said, holding up the jersey.

Eb rushed to the front as if the shirt would disappear, pulling off his white jersey as he hurried forward. He slipped the new jersey over his shoulder pads, jumped up on a bench and said, "Let's go Hawks!" Not original, but he couldn't think of what else to say.

The thirty-eight other football players repeated the line and moved forward to get their new look, one East Yancey High School would get to know up close before the night was over.

Now, if they could play to the level of the new look.

Friday, November 8, 7:08 p.m.
At the golden twilight of peak leaf season in the mountains, the Red Tail Hawk football team ambled off the bus, which parked at the door of its locker room, blocking the view of the disembarking team from the stands. The fans would not see the new jerseys until the team ran out to warm up. A few fans stood nearby and saw the jerseys. They applauded and shouted their approval.

Minutes later, the Hawks exited the locker room and sprinted onto the field in front of stands that were already full. The tiny school band played "Toe River Forever Home" only slightly off-key and the rowdy cheers echoed off the mountains surrounding the stadium as the fans noted the team and its surprising new look.

The coaches broke the players up into linemen and backs and they went through warm-up paces. Minutes later, East Yancey stormed noisily through a cloud of white smoke out of the locker room at the other end of the stadium. The smoke machine was a glamorous touch, but the all-black uniform trimmed in gold was a menace. It was an imposing look. The Bad Guys, Eb thought.

East Yancey's players were noticeably larger than Toe River's and quite a bit noisier as they went through their drills sounding like a para-military outfit getting ready for battle.

Carl and Eb met the East Yancey captains at the fifty-yard-line for the coin toss. "If we win the toss, we want to kick off," Hap had instructed. "Let's give 'em a good taste of what our defense can do before we light into their defense with the ball."

That's exactly what happened. Toe River opened the game on defense and East Yancey's Panthers looked straight into the blinding smile of Appalachian Conference Player of the Year Carl Blackthorn.

Friday, November 8, 7:30 p.m.

East Yancey's offense was led by six-foot-two, two-hundred-pound Felton Tolliver, the starting quarterback since he was a freshman and the all-conference first-teamer as a sophomore and junior. He couldn't be happy that Eb beat him for that honor this year—with a unanimous vote. He already signed to play with East Tennessee State next year and Eb's guess was he wanted to show the Bucs what a good deal they made. He strutted to the line, head high in the air, barking commands.

Carl was going to have something to say about Toliver and his offense and on the first play, crouching at middle guard, Carl shot under the center—*under* him—as the center snapped the ball and wrapped Tolliver's ankles before he could move away to hand the ball off. It was a stunner for East Yancey. The Panthers' players went back to the huddle mumbling to each other.

On the second play, Carl was standing up in the middle like a linebacker, walking back and forth and smiling, pointing to the center, then the guard. On the snap of the ball, he rushed forward, jumped over the right guard and center and landed a full load on Tolliver again.

It was third down and fourteen yards to go and Carl Blackthorn was causing the Panthers to wonder what manner of plague had befallen them. This was beginning to feel Biblical. It was going to get worse.

Carl was back in his three-point stance in front of the center when the ball was snapped for the third time. He slipped almost sideways between the guard and center and was on Tolliver before the big senior could get rid of the ball. It was fourth and eighteen when East Yancey lined up to punt. Tolliver was gesturing, shaking his fist and complaining loudly as he left the field. The players were already angry, dispirited and confused. This was the reigning champion looking like a team full of freshmen.

On the snap to the punter, Carl, who moved to the left end of the line, shot through the gap, stormed into the middle, leaped high into the air and blocked the kick with his chest, knocking the ball back to the East Yancey twenty-four-yard-line before Smoky fell on it.

The Toe River Fans were ecstatic and the offensive team charged onto the field with a mission.

"Left end down, wingback across, on two," said a full-throated, confident Eb in the huddle. "Keep it simple, Terry. The ball will be there."

It was. The Red Tail Hawks weren't breathing hard and they had a seven to nothing lead.

***

Carl continued unabated and nearly unblocked for the half, playing like he was possessed, but smiling, laughing and joyously celebrating on every play. East Yancey looked terrible and its fans began to grumble. Eb saw a bottle fly out onto the field as he went on offense halfway through the second period with a twenty-one to nothing lead.

It was more of the same in the second half as the night grew darker and the stadium louder. The Panthers couldn't figure out Carl when they were on offense and couldn't slow Toe River to a sprint with their defense. By the middle of the fourth quarter it was forty-nine to nothing and Woodson took out the starters.

He told Carl he could play one more series, but that he'd have to come out, too. "Awwwww, Coach," said Carl, running out to the field, smiling broadly and speaking in his broken English. "I make one more good hit."

He didn't get the chance. Carl broke through the offensive line on the next play, but East Yancey's solid, stocky fullback, Elswick Rominger, who hadn't blocked him all night, got up a head of steam, anticipating Carl's arrival and hit Carl with a full load from the blind side square in the ribs. You could hear them crack as Carl screamed, quieting the entire stadium.

"Oh, shit!" Eb said to nobody in particular as he watched in horror from the sideline. The players knew exactly what happened as Carl lay there, squirming in pain, kicking his feet and rolling back and forth. The East Yancey fullback stood over Carl for a minute, terrified at what he was watching. He knelt down, took Carl's hand and said something, then moved off. Smoky later told Eb the fullback apologized. Eb had never heard of anything like that happening before in a football game. He guessed it was a sign of the respect everybody had for this joyous boy, this magnificent football player.

Carl was carried off, put into a waiting ambulance and hurried the half mile to Cannon Memorial for X-rays and a virtuoso tape job from one of the medical interns working the emergency room. He insisted on being returned to the sidelines before the game was over and he was driven back to Lees McRae by a doctor getting off duty. "Son," the doc said, "you don't have any business standing up, let alone going back to the game." Carl smiled the physician drove on.

The rest of the game was played in a mental fog, East Yancey out of gas and Toe River out of spirit. The ambulance with Carl inside arrived back at the field with 40 seconds left in the game. It ended forty-nine to nothing, a statement win if anybody ever imagined one, but part of that statement had to be a question. It appeared to be the definition of a Pyrrhic victory. Could Carl wear his sparkling new Number fifty-one jersey in the regional the next Saturday in Asheville? If he could not, what then?

Saturday, November 9, 3:27 p.m.
The talk all over Avery County was of Carl Blackthorn and

his ribs. The docs at Cannon Memorial patched him up as well as they could, then turned him back to the life of virtual homelessness he lived. Gaylen took him home after the game for the rest of the weekend. Carl would be on his own again Monday morning. He was a proud boy who would ask nothing of anyone, who would maintain his cheer in the face of obvious pain and a living situation that would push many teens over the edge. To Carl, it was just another day in the life.

The square dance team was gathering for a practice in which Miss Lilly would grant no relief to those who played football until late into the evening Friday. If she'd been asked, she would have said, "You're young, you're supposed to be in shape and we have a Mountain Youth Jamboree to win. Rest later." It was the same song Coach Woodson sang.

As the dancers stood waiting for practice to begin, Millie Turbyfill slipped in the side door to the auditorium, trying not to be obvious, since Miss Lilly was not one who handled tardiness well. Eb watched from across the room, but could see that Millie's face was red and bruised. Joyce saw Millie and hurried to her side, putting an arm around her.

She talked to Millie quietly for a moment, stepped over to Miss Lilly and said a few words, then led Millie out of the room. "Go up to the stage and work on your clogging," said Miss Lilly to the team in a forceful voice. "I'll be right back." She slipped out the door toward her office, behind Joyce and Millie.

They were all back in the auditorium in ten minutes and Millie and Joyce climbed up to the stage and paired off with their partners. The team was two dancers short, so Becky Blake and Eb took the floor together.

The practice was focused and intense for more than an hour and Miss Lilly finally called out, "That's enough for today. Nice workout everybody. Get some rest. Millie, meet me in my office, please."

As the team filed out, Eb hurried to catch up with Joyce. "Ride?"

"Sure," she said. "Let me get my purse."

They weren't in the car two seconds before Eb said, "What's the story with Millie? Is that sonofabitch Harley Burleson manhandling her?"

"Of course he is," said Joyce. "Boys like him don't change and Millie just won't hear about it. She says he's really a great guy, that he gets liquored up and jealous and starts hitting her. She's wanting to marry him and thinks that'll make him better. She won't listen to anything."

"Maybe he'll listen to a good ass-kicking," Eb said. "Me an' some of the boys can…"

"Stay out of it," Joyce said as firmly and directly as Eb had ever heard her speak. "Not only would he probably shoot you, but you wouldn't do anything but make it worse for Millie. He'd blame it on her and he'd slap her around again. I don't know what to do. Miss Lilly's talked to her over and over and she even tried to talk to her daddy, but he's a drunk, too. Thinks Harley's great because he brings her old man booze. Her mama left over the drinking."

"I don't mean to get away from what's important here," Eb said, "but is she going to be able to dance next weekend? How shaky is she emotionally?"

"Eb, I just don't know. This has been going on for a while—not so bad as tonight, but still going on. You can tell when Harley's been on one of his toots. Millie falls to pieces. She's fragile and I swear I think he loves to know he can control her like that. He might do something for spite, to make what should be one of the best nights of her life one of the worst."

"Jesus, Joyce, we're thin already. We have that playoff game at noon against a heck of a team, then we have to almost run over to the auditorium for the Jamboree. I don't know how we're going to do against everything that keeps piling up. I mean, what if we lose the football game? We're not going to be feeling too festive. What if one of us gets hurt? This is a disaster sitting there waiting on us."

"The thing you still don't understand, Elbert McCourry, because you haven't been here long enough, is that we have Miss Lillian Wilkerson and nobody else does. Whatever we're short, we're Miss Lilly long. You'll see for yourself when the time comes."

Eb shook his head, not fully comprehending.

Sunday, November 10, 8 a.m.

Eb strode into the dining hall at the Home half-starved, breathing in smells of bacon, biscuits, gravy, coffee, fried apples and eggs, anticipating one of Maryellen's breakfast specials. A stern-looking Miss Dorothy met him at the door, holding a Sunday Asheville Citizen, rolled up in her hand. She looked like a Beech Mountain Home for Children administrator with something weighing on her mind.

"I didn't know you were talking to reporters from the Asheville newspaper," she said, slapping the rolled paper in her hand. "You should have talked to me before you spoke to them." She looked unhappy and a lump appeared in Eb's throat. Before he could answer, she said, "But it turned out all right." She smiled brightly and put a hand on his shoulder, a gesture that was about as familiar as Miss Dorothy got.

Eb stammered before finding words. "He showed up at practice one day last week and started talking to me between plays," he said, sliding both hands into his khaki pants pockets. "I didn't think much about it."

A short, crew-cut reporter named Dickie Morris was at practice Wednesday and, after talking to Buster Woodson, he called Carl and Eb over separately and chatted with them. Woodson didn't normally let anything interfere with the flow of practice, but all the press attention lately had changed his attitude.

The talk seemed informal, but Eb thought it was strange that Morris, a middle-aged man with thick, metal-rimmed glasses, who spoke in a high, almost girlish voice, asked him more about his background and the children's home than he did about football. Carl said Morris asked the same kinds of questions of him: about his life off the field more than his ability as a player, but neither player was concerned. They were flattered by the attention.

Apparently, Morris did a lot of asking of a lot of people and put together a story for the front page of the Sunday paper about the two outcast football players at Toe River High School and how they helped the community, the school and the county coalesce. In a long, front-page story titled "Orphans of the Game," Morris referred to Eb and Carl as "orphans," which neither was, and he said Carl lived in a car most of the time, which he didn't. Carl stayed with people most of the time. He stayed overnight in cars sometimes, but not "most of the time."

Dickie Morris was a small, middle-aged man with a pot belly and a disarming stutter who had been writing sports in Asheville for nearly 25 years. He wrote that Eb was from a "broken home," which made Eb furious. His home wasn't broken. His father died and the family was poor. The bare facts made for a lot of drama and, by Dickie Morris' and the Asheville Citizen's standards, a pretty good story.

There was a large black and white photograph on the front of the paper of Eb and Carl standing next to each other, talking at practice. Carl was animated and Eb remembered the moment: Carl had just leveled Eb as the attempted a pass. Inside, where the story continued, there were more pictures of Hap, Miss Dorothy, Miss Lilly at square dance practice, as well as Eb and Carl in action in Friday's game. The paper ran a picture of Carl being carried off the field.

Morris found out that the daughter of the director of the Governor's Commission on the Status of Women and this young "orphan boy" were an item and that she'd been in a wreck. There was a school picture of Lizetta. The more Eb read, the redder he got.

"Miss Dorothy," Eb said, "this is not fair. Don't he have to have some kind of permission before he writes this kind of stuff?"

"No, Eb, he doesn't," she said. "But if you take the article as a whole, it reflects well on the Home, the school and the community. I think you need to put it into perspective." Her blue eyes were piercing and her brow was pinched and serious, recognizing his discomfort.

"What you said about the Home's importance in your life and in the lives of the children who live here was eloquently stated, young man, and it was perceptive of you. Most of the children here take it all for granted and you seem not to. This is, after all, a good place to be reared." She smiled at that.

Eb heard every word she said, but still didn't know what Carl's and his living status had to do with being anybody's business. "I think I ought to be able to have some privacy," Eb said, "and he had no business bringing in Lizetta and her family. That's just not right."

Monday, November 11, 8 a.m.

Eb jumped off the school bus into a puddle caused by a light morning rain and ran full bore to Hap Heaton's room, his homeroom. He knew Hap would be in there early, getting ready for the day.

Eb barged straight over to Hap's desk, pulled one of the student desks up close and sat down. "I need to ask you some stuff," he said.

"I was kind of expecting you." Hap put down the pencil he was using to grade papers, placed his hands like a steeple in front of his nose, elbows on the desk and waited for the question.

"Did you see that article in the Asheville paper yesterday, the one about me and Carl?"

"I saw it and so did everybody else in Avery County. Maybe everybody in this end of the state. Jim McEntire called me last night and said Governor Sanford called him about it. Said the governor *congratulated* Lizetta on having such good sense as to have you as a boyfriend. That, my boy, is a line for the top of your resume."

"Awwww, Hap, dang it," Eb said, running both hands through his short, red hair. "I'm embarrassed for everybody, especially the McEntire family. They've been good and generous with me. And my mama, I can only imagine what she must be thinking, her son the orphan."

"I talked to your mama late last night and she's really proud of you."

"You talked to Mama? How'd you get the number? How are the kids? How's she?"

"The school has the number and I pulled the file and called her. I wanted to make sure she was good with the story because you told me she didn't want people thinking she just pawned you off on the orphanage for no good reason."

"It's not an orphanage." Eb's face was crimson and getting redder by the moment.

"Oh, Eb, ease up. You know everybody calls it 'the orphanage' and nobody thinks that's what it is. It's shorthand. Anyhow, she is happy you've made such a good adjustment that you have become what the story called 'a leader in the community at seventeen.' That's something else to put in your resume when you get one, boy. It can go right up there next to the Governor's recommendation. Sentences like that'll get you a job."

"How'd Mr. McEntire sound about it?"

"He's just tickled. Said he really likes you, that you're what he called a 'straight shooter who doesn't seem to be afraid of anything.' He said the governor's coming over for the Andrews game and wants to meet you and Carl."

"Oh, good god, Hap! I got enough to think about without the dadgum governor coming by. The *governor*!"

"I told Jim that the governor could come to the game, but that you had to leave as soon as it was over for the square dance competition and he said he'd pass that along. Maybe the governor would want to be there, too. He is a politician, after all, and that'd be two of the biggest crowds he could find around here in one day."

"Hap," Eb said.

"Yes."

"This is getting out of hand. Don't you think?"

"Well," he said, "it sure as hell is bigger than I ever thought it would be."

Monday, November 11, Noon

The rain stopped mid-morning turning into a fresh, brisk fall day and Eb ambled down to the big maple near the stadium, the one Lizetta liked so much, to eat his Maryellen special and maybe catch a few minutes for himself. As he started down the hill, he heard a shout from about twenty-five yards behind. It was Jim McEntire.

"Glad I caught you," Jim said. "Can we talk a few minutes?" Jim was in a mid-gray flannel business suit with a crisp white shirt, red tie and black shoes that shined like patent leather. He wore aviator sunglasses and Eb saw his gold watch as Jim stuck out his hand to shake Eb's.

"Sure. I was wanting to call you yesterday and apologize anyway."

"Apologize for what?" said Jim, genuinely surprised, Eb thought.

"That story in the Asheville paper." Eb looked at the sandwich in his hand, avoiding eye contact.

"That's why I'm here," said Jim McEntire. "You have nothing to apologize for, son. It was a heck of a story and it's good for our whole county. The governor even read it and called me about it. He wants to come to the game and meet you and Carl."

"Hap told me. I don't think I'll have time to see him after the football game. I gotta dance at the Mountain Youth Jamboree across town right after the game. Sounds like I'm trying to stand him up, but I don't mean to be disrespectful. It's just that we're competing for two titles in different sports back to back and I need to put all my energy there."

"It doesn't get easy for you, does it, Eb?"

"Just a busy time, sir. I don't want to sound like I'm being arrogant, turning down the governor, but I don't have any control over the schedule." Eb looked at his scuffed shoes and dusted them on the back of his jeans one at a time.

"Reason I came by is that Lizetta called me last night and made me promise to tell you she's 'very, very proud,' unquote, of you. I think a lot of us feel that same way. What's happening in this county right now is something I've never seen before. People who haven't had a lot to feel good about the last few years are feeling good about themselves and about their home. That's not something to apologize for. You're a fine young man, Eb, and the whole McEntire family is proud to know you."

Eb didn't know what to say, so he didn't say anything. Jim McEntire tapped Eb on the shoulder, turned and left.

Eb sat down under the aging red maple and ate his sandwich. He thought softly of Lizetta. "Very, very proud," she said. He smiled.

Monday, November 11, 7:13 p.m.

That tiny, urgent tap belonging to nobody else but Ralphie interrupted yet another thousand-word essay for Colt Hill's English class, this one about the Cranberry Iron Mines that lasted a century, and Eb said, "Come on in, Ralphie."

"How'd you know it was me?" he said.

"You have a distinctive touch, buddy. What's up?"

"You have a long distance call and Miss Dorothy says come quick because it costs a bunch of money."

Eb slipped penny loafers onto his bare feet—a breach of Home dress code that Miss Dorothy emphasized at every turn—and charged out the door, mussing Ralphie's hair as he passed. "Thanks, pardner."

When Eb cleared the door at the admin building, Miss Dorothy was standing straight holding the phone, looking impatient.

"Talk quickly," she said. "Long distance is not

inexpensive."

He thought, but didn't say, "You're not paying for it, so what's your worry?"

Eb plucked the phone from Miss Dorothy, thanked her and said, "This is Eb McCourry."

"Hi, sweetie," sang Lizetta. "I'm sorry to call you at the Home, but this wouldn't wait. It's just too precious."

Eb tried to break in with a "hello" or a "how are you?", but Lizetta kept going in an unbroken string.

"I got a call today from a girl named Joss-Lynn Ledbetter— she spelled it for me, J-O-S-S L-Y-N-N." Lizetta giggled. "She's a square dancer at Sky High and she said she read the story about you and Carl and was so touched by it that she asked her daddy, who has a car dealership, if he'd send me a Riviera to replace the one I wrecked. She said 'one of our people' looked into it and found out all about me, where I live, my parents, the car, my medical condition, the whole thing. And she was just so touched. She said she decided she was going to Wake Forest because that's where I was going and would I like to be roommates? My mouth was hanging open the whole time." Eb tried to break in again, but couldn't slip through.

"I didn't know what to say. I told her I couldn't accept the car, but I appreciated the thought. This is the girl who is responsible for Asheville spending all that money to bring in a New York coach and recruit all those dancers from the School of Modern Dance. I asked her about the square dance team and she said, yes, they were good, but all the boys except one were stuck up, arrogant queers and she didn't like them and they were going to win Old Smoky and disband the team. She said she was sorry she had to take Old Smoky away from our school, but she really wanted it. She said she has a place for it on the mantle in her bedroom. Miss Lilly would kill her."

Lizetta let loose that hearty laugh that Eb so loved.

"I got a truly creepy-crawly feeling from her and I said she probably hadn't better count on taking that trophy home quite yet," said Lizetta with a good bit of force. "She'd best beware the CLOG, I told her, and she'd especially better beware Elbert McCourry, my beau. She said, yeah, that Eb McCourry sure is a good lookin' boy, but the trophy was heading to Asheville."

Eb was laughing so hard he was shaking. Several kids gathered at the door of the parlor as he laughed and they began laughing, having no idea what the joke was. As Lizetta told the story, she affected a spoiled brat with a Minnie Mouse voice.

"I thought you might appreciate that tale," said Lizetta. "I love you, bub. You'd better hang up before Miss Dottie-belle gongs you with the telephone base. I'll see you sooner than you think.

"Dance well and throw some more touchdown passes for me. I like those. They're like roses without all the thorns."

Wednesday, November 12, 5:02 p.m.

Barry was on the sideline being attended, the back of his right ankle bleeding profusely. He had just been cleated—on purpose, Eb thought—by Mickey in the middle of a pileup.

Mickey behaved well—for him—for the past few weeks, so this came as a complete surprise. Hap was in a foul mood over it .

"Who the hell are you playing for, Mickey?" Hap yelled, holding Mickey by the neck of his jersey close to Hap's face, Mickey's feet off the ground and Hap's breath hot on his face. Mickey grinned. Eb thought Hap might hit him with his full strength. His huge fist was clenched and he was fresh blood red. Mickey was asking for it and didn't seem to care if it came. Eb ran over to Hap and said, "Easy. You'll be in more trouble than he is if you hit him. Let me do it."

Hap put Mickey down, slapped Eb's helmet lightly and said, "Mickey get out of my sight before I get mad."

Carl paced the sideline as practice wound down, every so often putting a hand on his wrapped ribs, grimacing. He was obviously restless and filled to brimming with anxiety. You only had to look at him to see it written clearly on his face.

"Gather up," yelled Woodson. The team knelt in its customary circle around him and he said, "We have one more day of real practice before slowing down and concentrating hard on what's ahead.

"Andrews High School, as you know from Coach Hilton's scouting report, is closer to Mars Hill in style than to any other team we've played and you understand what that means. Mars Hill was, by far, the best team we played in the regular season and we had to reach deep to win that one. We also had Carl Blackthorn playing at his best. We won't have that Saturday and we will need to find some way to compensate." Most of the team was either kneeling or sitting, but a couple, including Eb and the hobbled Carl, stood.

"We have a lot of good football players on this team and I have no doubt at all that you can find something somewhere down deep inside you that will help you make up for Carl not being there. If each of you approaches every hour between now and the end of Saturday's game looking at what you can do to make a difference, then you will make that difference and we'll beat a good team." Woodson was on a roll, sounding like more of a coach than he was. "If you don't...if you look around for Carl to be behind you when you miss a tackle or fail to beat your man, then we lose. It is up to you as individuals to contribute to the team and to think only of what the team can accomplish."

So Carl was going to miss the game. The players sat back on that revelation. Carl had never missed a game—even a minute of a game, save for the short time Friday against East Yancey—and now he was going to be watching from the sideline in the most important game in his four years at Toe River High School, maybe even in the history of the school. Eb felt for Carl and he felt for himself and his team.

Carl Blackthorn was the heart and soul of this team and as shallow as it sounded to say it, the truth was that simple. With a healthy Carl, Toe River High School had a formidable Class A football team.

Without him…they'd have to see.

Friday, November 15, 8:45 a.m.

The pep rally was cranked wide open on what many could argue was the day before the most important pair of events in the history of Toe River High School, maybe even Avery County as a whole. The air was electric and noisy. The cramped auditorium was filled with Kelly green and a smattering of old gold and smelled of cheap aftershave, sweat, old wood and musty curtains. Players were in their new game jerseys, wearing them like tuxedos, and cheerleaders were dressed to entertain, bouncing and yelping with little girl voices.

Principal J. B. Banner introduced the All-Appalachian Conference team members and when Carl stood up, the reception from the students was ear-splitting. It was a long, loud, emotional cheer for the hero of the moment, and of the thirty-six-year history of the school. Here was this shy, grinning, happy young Cherokee boy who faced so much that was worrisome on a daily basis, playing a game to entertain and showing all that life was about living, fulfilling their dreams, the sheer joy of being. Eb cheered as loudly as anybody for Carl Blackthorn and for all the Carl Blackthorns who never had a moment like this one.

The various members of the local and regional media hovered over Toe River's football players all week, making a fuss and getting in the way with self-important intrusions of what the team was doing. Eb was tired of it and was waiting for the time when quiet returned. He tried to remain respectful, but when a photographer inserted himself into the team's choir huddle Wednesday during practice, he broke.

"Will you get your fat ass out of my huddle, you arrogant, intrusive sonofabitch?!!" he screamed. His teammates and the photographer were taken aback and the air was dead still for a long moment. The photographer backed out, his head down and both hands on his Nikon F1 as to protect it.

Hap Hilton sprinted to get between the photographer and Eb, apologized to the photographer and told Eb to go to the sideline. Hap met him there moments later.

"This ain't a good time to lose everything you've worked for because you couldn't maintain your composure," Hap said, as firmly as he could speak. "There's pressure when you get this far and what you're seein' right this minute is pressure. You're the leader of this offense—and of the whole team with Carl gone—and I expect you to act like it. Now, get your ass over there and apologize to that damn photographer. I don't care if what happened was his fault or not. Your reaction is your fault and you're responsible for it. So take the responsibility to apologize and get back to practice."

Hap had a way of making things so clear to Eb that there could be no mistake. This was, Eb knew, his fault and it was his job to clear it up. It didn't make apologizing any easier, but as Hap predicted, Eb felt better after doing it. He even threw the ball better.

***

As the pep rally proceed, Eb wished there was some way to bring in the square dance team, and just as he was thinking in those terms, Buster Woodson said, "We want to get a word from our captain now."

This was his chance and he jumped on it without hesitation. He was beginning to enjoy speaking for the team. "We have a lot to celebrate at Toe River High School this week," Eb said. "We have a conference champion football team and maybe the best square dance team in the south. We certainly have the best coach anybody anywhere has seen." He looked directly at Miss Lilly, who was on the opposite side of the room from Woodson, then at Hap, who winked and smiled. "Stand up, Miss Lilly, and let everybody appreciate you for a minute." Eb didn't make eye contact with Woodson, who might or might not have felt slighted. Eb didn't care. He was telling the truth.

Miss Lilly looked thoroughly embarrassed as the applause

for her rose to the levels of that given Carl. "Miss Lilly and her dancers face a huge challenge to their standing as the premier square dance program in the state tomorrow night in Asheville. There's a showdown at the Civic Auditorium after we play that football game we've been talking about, and I hope everybody in this room who possibly can, will be there to support a great coach, great team and a great program."

More applause, prolonged and enthusiastic. "Miss Lilly, would you come up and say something?" Eb extended his hand full length.

Gracefully and elegantly, she walked to the side of the stage, mounted the steps and stood by Eb. "Thank you, Eb, and congratulations to the football team. I want to reiterate that we would love to have you all in Asheville tomorrow so we can show those who believe they can come in and take our heritage away from us that it isn't that easy. No matter what team is representing this school, we always have to be gracious, competitive and at our best. Tomorrow, we get the opportunity to impress a couple of large crowds—and I understand the governor may be in both of them—so let's go to the city and show them that those of us from the country are quite a bit more than they might imagine us to be."

Wild applause, more enthusiasm. Miss Lilly turned to Eb, leaned in and said in a loud whisper, "Thank you, Elbert. This is just the kind of gesture I want to be the norm for our school, one with grace. I'm proud of you."

Eb took Miss Lilly's hand, stepped slightly to the side, looked at her for a moment and they bowed to each other, royal teammates. Elegant teammates.

Part XIII

Saturday, November 16, 8:45 a.m.

The two school buses carrying the football team, its gear and the fifteen-member band with its instruments pulled out of the parking lot at Toe River High School for the nearly two-hour drive to Asheville. Eb slept little, rose at 5:30 for a quick two-mile run to get his energy level up and ate a hearty breakfast with the Children's Home kids hovering over him.

Ankles, knees and wrists were already taped as the football players climbed on to the fragile old bus, so all the players would need to do when they got to the stadium was to pull on their uniforms and warm up. They secretly prayed the bus wouldn't break down. They might be uptown in everybody's minds these days, but Toe River High was still a poor country school with few resources and not much backup.

The bulk of the square dance team and cheerleaders were going to Asheville in cars and Miss Lilly had the football players' dance outfits packed in a box. If the game ran long, there was a danger the football players could be late for a preliminary round of dancing. If the seven football-playing dancers and four cheerleaders were still involved in football at the start of the dance competition, Toe River High would be unable to field a square dance team and would forfeit. Injury was another possibility. The odds didn't look good for a smooth operation. Every dancer knew that.

Saturday, November 16, Noon

All the warm-ups, pregame festivities and preparations were over as Andrews High School's kicker mashed the ends of the football with both hands and put it on the tee to kick it deep to J.W. Greene, who had become a force for Toe River.

The governor and his aides were ten rows up, fifty-yard-line, on the home side of the field—Toe River's side—in seats set off with red, white and blue bunting. Gov. Sanford waved at

Eb when he arrived and Eb self-consciously waved back. The governor made his way to the field to shake hands with Eb and Carl and to have their photo taken together on the sideline by one of the newspaper photographers. Carl was dressed to play, proudly showing off his green jersey with the white three-inch "C" for "captain" on the left breast, but nobody had any notion that playing was a possibility for him. He wasn't warming up. He was there for the team, the injured warrior inspiring with his presence, dressed for the occasion.

The place was packed, all seven thousand seats taken and standing room only around the end zones. Eb's guess was that the story in the paper Sunday brought out people who didn't even care about the game. They just wanted to see the two "orphans." Eb was still annoyed, but he wouldn't take that to the field.

The opening kickoff was high and deep from a kickoff specialist who had been named all-state the year before as a junior. J.W. fielded it at the five yard line and ran it to the twenty-three before a slicing tackle nearly separated him from the ball.

The Toe River offensive players were a bag of nerves as Eb looked over the Andrews defense, seeing a team that, as Hap had said, looked a lot like Toe River's. It was a fast, smallish, swarming group without a weakness. It didn't have a Carl Blackthorn, but neither did Toe River today.

Eb went straight to the well and called a deep pattern with Terry and J.W. running toward the sidelines, then bending to the middle, eventually crossing if they got that far. Terry was wide open twenty yards into the pattern and Eb hit him square in the chest and he covered another thirty five yards before the off-side defensive back—the one covering J.W.—caught him at the Andrews twenty-two. It was a fifty-five-yard gain on the first play and this looked like a repeat of the East Yancey game getting ready to happen.

No need to be greedy, Eb thought. He'd probe a little. He ran Barry up the middle, then off tackle and picked up five tough yards to the seventeen. Third and five. Eb called a seven-yard hook pattern for Perry and had Terry run to the right sideline, just beyond the first down marker. Andrews' left tackle blew by Harold and before Eb could set his feet, he was sitting on his butt at the twenty-two. It was fourth down and Barry would have to attempt a field goal.

The kick was blocked by a quick left defensive end who looped around J.W. on the corner of the kick formation and got a hand on the kick at the last instant, slapping the ball back to the twenty-eight, where Andrews recovered it and took over.

The Andrews offense lined up in a tight T-formation, a set designed to run with a maximum of blocking, much like the single wing. Like the wing, it was an old formation, one out of date, but effective when run properly and especially good for undersized teams because of the maximum blocking it provided.

The Wildcats ground out two first downs and had a fourth down and three at the Toe River forty-two when their kicker dropped a punt dead at the Toe River three yard line. This was dangerous territory and Eb would have to run it out of this hole and get some room before he could pass. Passing would be dangerous this deep. For once, Eb was going to have to do his share of the running.

Eb took the first shot over left tackle between Harold and Smoky and picked up seven yards. Barry ran essentially the same hole on the next play for another seven and a first down. The Hawks were out to the seventeen and had more room now, so Eb thought he'd risk a pass, a relatively safe sideline pattern to Terry.

The Andrews defensive back looked like he'd been in the huddle with Toe River, breaking in front of Terry just as Eb released the ball, picking if off and scoring without being touched. Seven to nothing, Andrews.

This was not going to be easy.

***

There were four minutes left in the fourth quarter and Toe River trailed twenty-seven to twenty-one, a six-point difference because of a Mickey Buchanan blocked extra point.

Andrews had the ball at midfield with a third down and eight yards to go for a first down. Toe River's defense set up for a pass and got one, a bullet over the middle to Andrews' left end, who caught the ball and ran hard down to the Hawks' fourteen-yard-line, in the shadow of the goal posts. Toe River's defense stiffened there and with a fourth down from the ten and just under three minutes to go in the game, Andrews and its all-state kicker lined up to kick a field goal for what would be a ten-point lead with three minutes, thirty-two seconds remaining. This short kick was almost automatic for Andrews' kicker and Toe River didn't have Carl to challenge that.

Coach Buster Woodson screamed for Gaylen to call time out. As Gaylen ran over to talk, Woodson called Carl over and said, "Can you go?"

Carl grinned and said, "Yeah, coach. I can play. I'm fine."

"Go in and block the kick," said Woodson, slapping Carl on the butt.

Eb was standing next to Woodson when he gave the order and yelled, "Coach, dammit, you can't do that! He has three broken ribs."

"Shut up, McCourry! The game's on the line and Carl's tougher than anybody around. He can do this."

Eb looked around for Hap and saw him back at the bench, facing four players and talking intensely. He ran back to tell Hap what was happening.

"Woodson just put Carl in to block a kick," Eb said in a voice that carried considerable urgency.

"He *what?*" said Hap, who immediately stood and made his way through the team to Woodson. He talked furiously to the head coach for a few seconds, but the ball was snapped and Carl charged forward through all the obstacles Andrews set for him, knowing who he was and what he could do.

The picture of Carl suspended in the air, spread flat out and taking the ball off the toe of Andrews' star kicker—square in the ribs—stopped time for those in the stadium. Everybody there heard his scream when the ball hit him in the chest and gasped as he collided with the ground in pain, the ball bounding hard toward Toe River's end of the field.

Long-legged J.W. Greene was on it quickly, picking the ball up in full stride and loping seventy yards to the Andrews five yard line at the other end of the field, slightly more than three minutes left and Carl lying helpless.

Eb was so upset he refused to take the field as Carl was carried off in a stretcher, his left hand aloft with his index finger lofted skyward and that bright smile gleaming through his grimace. "Woodson, you're a sonofabitch," Eb barked, livid. "Football is not more important than Carl."

Hap rushed over, grabbed Eb by the shoulders and pulled him away from Woodson, who looked devastated. Eb went to the bench, his head buried in his hands, embarrassed beyond speech at what had just happened to this Cinderella season. Suddenly, it was a nightmare.

Woodson had Barry, substituting for Eb, run the ball into the middle three times and he gained nothing. Barry kicked a short field goal and Toe River remained behind twenty-seven to twenty-four. The clock showed two minutes, thirty four seconds left. If Toe River could hold Andrews to three downs, it could get the ball back, Woodson reasoned in kicking the field goal. Another field goal could tie and a touchdown would win it.

Carl had been taken off the field on a stretcher for the second straight week. He wouldn't let the medics put him in the ambulance until the game was over. Normally the medical team would ignore a player's request, but this was Carl Blackthorn. The big crowd watched as he protested.

The following kickoff was deep and Toe River had to stop a return, contain Andrews, force a punt and score a touchdown in order to earn a berth in the state championship game. All Andrews needed to do was run out the clock. One first down and that would be a cinch.

Smoky's kick went to the fifteen where Andrews' quick offensive end Steve Little Pony, a Cherokee, caught it, cut to the right, found an opening. He sprinted seventy-one yards to the fourteen of Toe River, giving the Wildcats safe field position and an opportunity to run out the clock.

Andrews lined up to run the ball, the clock running and the offense in no hurry. The team formed its tight T and handed off safely to a left halfback who cradled the ball with both hands. Mickey Buchanan watched all this with great interest. As the ball carrier, behind two blockers, ran into the line, Mickey rushed up from behind and rammed his fist through the runner's arm and into the ball, punching it straight into the hands of Smoky who fell with it, holding it tight.

Toe River had the ball at the twelve, eighty-eight yards from a touchdown. The clock read one minute, forty-three seconds remaining.

"Offense, get out there," said Woodson. Eb didn't budge. "All right, McCourry, move it."

Eb sat unresponsive, head down, tears streaming.

Hap knelt before the bench where Eb was sitting, put a hand on his shoulder aid said, "Son, you're right to be mad, but you have a team to think about, a team that needs you. This is your family. Now's the time for you to be a man.

"It's your team and it's your community. You've defined what we're doing here and you've told the coach he was wrong for his action. It's time to go do what you can to salvage this for the right reasons."

Eb lifted his head, reached for his helmet, got up and ran onto the field as the offensive players lined up in the choir huddle, waiting for him. He wiped his eyes and dripping nose and stood before a stunned group.

"This game's still ours to win," he said, his confidence obvious. "Let's go win it. We'll deal with Woodson later."

Something like a unified growl went up. Eb saw resolve.

"Double hitch, wingback across on two," Eb said, pulling

Terry close and saying, "Hitch, then break back to the sideline. That'll be open."

He hit Terry in the chest at the thirty-seven-yard-line and Terry stepped out of bounds, stopping the clock with one minute, thirty-eight seconds showing.

Another deep route, this one to Perry, run quickly and efficiently, got the Hawks to the Andrews twenty-five, but Perry didn't get out of bounds before he was tackled and the clock continued to run. Toe River had covered sixty-three yards in two plays. The clock was the enemy.

"Terry, I want you in the right corner of the end zone. I'm going to put the ball on the end line over your right shoulder so only you can catch it. Watch where your feet are. You gotta have one in bounds. J.W. and Perry, clear out the middle by crossing at about the five. That'll keep Terry one-on-one and he can handle that."

The play developed perfectly and Eb lobbed the ball high and to the corner so Terry could simply leap at the last instant and catch it. The defensive back, beaten, reached out and wrapped his left arm around Terry's waist just as Terry was about to leap, but the defender's body blocked the referee's view of the foul. The ball dropped untouched. It was clearly pass interference to everybody in the stadium except the back judge, who had responsibility for the call. It was no TD and no call. Second and ten at the twenty-seven.

"Forget it," Eb said. "Ref missed that one. We have time and downs. Let's get ten here. Terry, run the same route. J.W., spread wide and sprint across the middle. Perry, go down eleven yards and loop to the inside."

Perry caught the ball in his stomach, turned to run and was belted down hard. He lay on the field gasping for breath and Harold ran over to him—one of his Elk River Boys—rolled him onto his back and lifted Perry by the waist of his pants. The officials stopped the clock because of the injury. Perry's breath returned shortly and he was up and ready.

The clock had run all the way down to twenty-two seconds

before the officials stopped it as Perry lay there. There would be time for two more plays if everything worked as it should. A field goal would tie and put the game into overtime, but Eb wanted a win now. There was a square dance competition waiting. Eb told all three receivers to run to the end zone, Terry to the corner, Perry to the middle on the goal line, just under the goal post and J.W. to the left.

"Barry, hold your block and count to two, then run just to the left of the middle. That'll be open."

Barry was open long enough to catch the ball and carry it to the two yard line. Eb called timeout. Ten seconds left. Pass or run or kick? Too close to pass, too far to run if Andrews bunched up and no thought of a tie. Woodson signaled kick from the sideline. Eb ignored him.

"Let's spread it out," Eb said. "Line, split a yard further apart from each other than usual. Terry and J.W., move out another seven yards to each side. Perry, get in the gap on the right side. Sell the pass. Sixty-two draw on set. Let's get this win and go do some dancing."

Eb looked at Barry's right foot as he set up. His sock was soaked with blood from the deep cut Mickey gave him Wednesday. "Your ankle good enough for this?" Eb asked at the last instant.

"I'm fine. I'll get it." Barry's jaw was set, his dark eyes intense.

Eb took the direct snap, backed up slightly standing up as if he were looking for a receiver, then slipped the ball from behind into Barry's stomach. He bolted straight ahead as middle opened wide. Barry hit the hole at the instant an Andrews linebacker showed up with all his force within inches of the goal, creating a huge collision. It was an instant mob scene of Andrews' players pushing back and Toe River linemen trying to help push Barry over the line.

They all went down and the whistle blew. The game was over, but there was not yet a conclusion. The concrete stadium, full of noise an instant before, was quiet as a library at midnight.

The officials would decide the winner in a few seconds after they un-piled the players and found out where the ball was. There was considerable noise and movement coming from the bottom of the pile and the referees pulled players off the pile one at a time, looking intently for the ball.

At the bottom Barry had a loose, one-handed grip on the football, pushing it firmly to the ground just over the goal line near his face. He saw the chalk line and the ball, though bodies pressed every inch of him. A hand slapped through the muddle, jamming Barry's middle finger painfully. As his hand clinched, he saw another hand push the ball backward to the other side of the goal line and press down, holding it firmly in that spot. Barry was pinned from every direction, but moved his strong arm backward, cupped the ball and pushed hard against resistance. Just then, light shone into the mob of players and another hand came in, laying directly on top of his painful hand, the other player's palm, and the ball.

"Got it!" yelled the linesman. "Short!"

Finally, after nearly half a minute of pulling at a mound of players, the referee stood straight up and waved his arms across each other. *"No touchdown! Game over! Andrews wins!"* A cheer went up from the side with all the blue and yellow and a groan from the green and gold side.

Eb, tears streaming down his face, put out a hand and pulled Barry to his feet.

"Good effort, buddy. Good effort."

"I was in!" shouted Barry. "It was a touchdown! They stole it from us!"

Barry turned toward the head official and started to yell, but Eb pulled him away. "It's over," he said. "It's over. Let it go. They won't change it now."

Barry put his arm around his quarterback and they trudged off the field as the other Toe River players gathered near them, many of them crying, all knowing they'd been robbed. The excited Andrews players walked in among them, congratulating the effort. It was no comfort.

Buster Woodson shook the Andrews coach's hand and yelled for everybody to meet at mid-field. The team shuffled on toward the locker room, ignoring him. His sin was too great at this moment for forgiveness. They wanted to be away from him.

Toe River still had a trophy to win in another venue, a trophy that had just grown geometrically in value.

Could it be stolen, too?

Part XIV

Saturday, November 16, 4:02 p.m.

Terry, Mickey, Barry, Smoky, Buster Hanford, Homer Vance and Eb were shuttled by car from the stadium after they showered and dressed, all still in a state of disbelief following the loss. There was no team meeting, even though Buster Woodson tried to have one. The distressed and discouraged players simply weren't interested in what he had to say and Hap finally convinced Woodson that saying nothing was the right thing to do at this point. Woodson had lost this team.

The four cheerleaders who square danced left immediately, using the stadium's bathroom to slip quickly into the brand new outfits Miss Lilly designed for the Jamboree. They were brown and yellow with big flowers on the brown top and one large cutout flower just above the hem of the mid-calf-length skirt. The flower was from the same material the home ec girls used to make the blouses. The girls wore a yellow scarf and their normal black shoes with the high laces. Miss Lilly did not go to the expense of buying brown shoes for the outfits because the shoes would have been paid for by her.

When Maryellen Streit first saw the costumes, she laughed out loud and said, "We've gone from spacemen to Brownie Scouts. This is ridiculous." But the outfit grew on her.

At the dark, cavernous, nineteen-twenties-era Asheville Civic Auditorium, the boys hurried into their outfits, brown, except for yellow suspenders and string ties. They, too, wore black shoes.

The team went through its routine several times and took the stage midway through the first round, shuffling through a basic routine that would give away nothing, but would place Toe River high enough to advance. The early rounds were about moving forward. There was no statement to make, no point to prove. Those rounds eliminated teams that were marginal.

Saturday, November 16, 7:22 p.m.

The team broke from the competition after two rounds and dancers walked two blocks to the elegant—and inexpensive—S&S Cafeteria on Prichard Park in the center of town. It was a Depression-era marble art deco building with a looping, brushed stainless steel rail staircase and some of the best food smells any of the dancers had been exposed to in a long time. When he was at home, Eb's mom occasionally took him and his brothers and sisters to the S&S when she had some extra money.

Eb loaded up with fried chicken, macaroni and cheese, green beans, one of those big homemade chef's hat rolls that were buttery and yeasty, and strawberry shortcake. Miss Lilly stopped by Eb's table and said, "Are you going to be able to dance after eating all that? Are you going to be able to walk?" She laughed. Eb had never seen her laugh before. It was a good sign, meaning she was loose. That could only mean she was confident.

Eb nodded, his cheeks fully inflated. He couldn't speak.

Eb's mother moved in beside Miss Lilly and said, "Looks like you've been taking good care of, my boy."

Eb stood quickly and hugged his mother quickly, not lingering. The McCourrys were not a huggy bunch with each other. "How did you know we'd be here?" he said, excited to see her. It had been months.

"I didn't. I brought your little brother and sister here tonight to eat." She leaned in to Eb and said, "Fewer hungry mouths to feed. More food for those left at home." Eb laughed.

"Where are the kids? Did you see the game today?" Eb said.

"Didn't have a ticket," she said, the signal that she didn't have the money to buy one. "The kids are over there." She pointed across the room to two small children shoveling down strawberry shortcake.

"You want to come to the dance final tonight?" Eb said,

excited by the prospect.

She leaned close to Eb, looking embarrassed. "No money for that, either," she whispered.

Eb looked at Miss Lilly, introduced her to his mother and said, "Can we get her and the kids in with us?"

Miss Lilly knew the situation. "Yes," she said. "That won't be a problem. We'll be delighted to have you, Mrs. McCourry. Your boy has meant a lot to our school."

"Eb has written a lot about you, and dancing and the school" said Eb's mother. "I feel good that he has you to take care of him."

"Sometimes," said Miss Lilly, "it feels the other way around. He's quite a young man."

Mrs. McCourry smiled broadly.

Eb went to his mother's table to say hello to Harry and Dane, who had heard about the close football loss, but were too young to care. He told them they'd be at the dance competition. They grinned and continued eating, Dane sitting in his lap and spilling shortcake on him.

After about thirty minutes of visiting, Eb went back to his table, where Miss Lilly was waiting. She was at the football game and watched the scene between Woodson and Eb. She was close enough to the field to hear Eb call Woodson a "sonofabitch." She pulled him aside.

"You know what you did was wrong, don't you?" she said.

"What he did was more wrong," Eb said. "He put Carl's life in jeopardy. One of those ribs could have punctured his lung. Victory in a game is not worth that."

"No, it isn't," she said, "but all you can be responsible for is how you react and you did not react responsibly or maturely. I would have expected more from you."

"Miss Lilly, have you ever been in a situation like that where what was happening right in front of you was just so wrong? I think the school should fire Woodson over that. There was no way I could be passive in the face of that kind of irresponsibility from somebody who was supposed to be in

267

charge."

"Elbert, none of that is your decision. If something needs to be done about Coach Woodson's handling of the game, it will be, I assure you. We all make mistakes. And we all need to learn to forgive and go on.

"We need your head in *our* game tonight, not thinking about what somebody else either did or didn't do, something you can't influence at all tonight. I need your word your mind is going to be where it is supposed to be."

"It will, Miss Lilly. I promise."

***

The dancers got back to the auditorium at seven forty-five and Miss Lilly instructed them to take bathroom breaks if they needed them because they'd have to be ready to dance when called for the semifinals.

Eb was in the men's room standing at one of the urinals next to Mickey when an Asheville dancer walked up, unzipped and started using the urinal beside Mickey.

"You one of them Asheville queer ballet boys?" said Mickey, turning toward the dancer and peeing on the Asheville boy's shoes.

The dancer turned to Mickey and before Mickey could even see what was happening, the boy had hit him in the throat with a karate chop and laid him out on the floor with a sharp and sudden blow to the solar plexus. As Mickey lay on the tile floor gasping for breath, the dancer shook his penis, splattering pee over Mickey's face and shirt.

"Yes," said the boy. "I'm one of those queer ballet boys, who can kick your country ass. Name's Billy Staples. Remember it. I'm taking your trophy." He zipped up and, with a flourish, spun and walked out the door, hands unwashed, his arm bent at the elbow, his wrist dangling and him walking with an exaggerated swish.

At that moment, Smoky crashed through the men's room door and asked in an urgent voice, "Anybody seen that damn

Mic… "

He stopped and looked at Mickey lying on the floor, out cold.

"What the hell happened here?"

Eb explained and as Smoky recovered from his uncontrollable laugh, he said, "I'm supposed to be protecting you all from Mickey and nobody's protecting Mickey from the ballet boys!" They all erupted as Mickey groaned and rolled over.

Smoky picked Mickey up and said, "Let's get you washed off and back in one piece."

Mickey was groggy. "What the hell happened," he said. Then he remembered and he bolted for the door, looking for trouble.

Smoky tackled him, put him in an arm lock and said, "You're my responsibility and you're dancin', not fightin'."

If the roughed-up teammate had been anybody but Mickey, the Toe River dancers would have been all over that Asheville dancer. But, Eb thought, Mickey got exactly what he deserved and Mickey's teammates were a lot closer to applauding Billy Staples than attacking him.

But now they needed him in the most urgent way.

Saturday, November 16, 8 p.m.

Miss Lilly instructed the team to finish the semifinal round with three minutes of clogging to wind up the set. That would introduce intent and it should soften the judges and wind up the crowd. Nothing livened a crowd like clogging and buck dancing.

Mickey would have to forget the ass-kicking he just took and dance. Fact was, he was tough enough to do it. Janice would not be told that those wet spots on Mickey's shirt were pee until after the competition. She would die if she knew, Eb thought.

Saturday, November 16, 8:18 p.m.

269

Barry Bates peeled the bulky white football sock down his ankle, watching the thin scab of dried blood pull away from his skin. As it tore loose, rivulets of fresh crimson blood bubbled up. He grimaced. He kept the sock on after the game because he was afraid just this would happen.

If Miss Lilly saw the jagged rip running down his Achilles, she'd pull him out immediately, and the team would be in trouble as it entered the climactic moment of the season.

Barry Bates' stumble in the quarterfinal nearly cost the team a spot in the semis. He was shaky. He ran into his partner once. His limp was impossible to hide. Miss Lilly would be by shortly, checking on him and he'd better have an answer and a clean sock if he wanted a prayer of dancing again tonight. Even at that, he knew his chances of dancing were slim.

As Barry left the floor at the end of the performance minutes ago, Miss Lilly leaned in to him when he passed and asked, "You hurting?" It wasn't a question. It was Miss Lilly's knowing, almost accusing tone. She sensed everything about every move, every call, every piece of clothing, every dancer, every opponent. Nothing got by, so how could he hide a deep, bleeding cut?

Mickey stood over Barry, that mean grin glaring and said, "Bet that hurts."

"If you say another word, you inbred bag of dog vomit, I'll…"

Mickey's face crinkled, the mass of freckles closing on each other. "You and what other homo?" Mickey said sharply, just above a snake's whisper.

Barry jumped up, drew back a fist and Smoky—always watching—leaped between them and said, "Mickey, haven't you learned nothing'? We got work to do and not much time to do it. Let me get some gauze and tape and we'll put you back together, Barry. Mickey, get the hell out of here or Barry won't need to kill you. I will."

At the other end of the room, Eb stood by his locker silently watching, listening and waiting, not knowing what to do. He tried to make himself small so nobody would see him. If Barry couldn't dance, this team's season and the school's reputation as a square dance Mecca would fall on him, a rookie who'd never square danced until a few weeks ago. He would need to dance better than he knew how.

***

Three Toe River dancers hovered over a sobbing Millie Turbyfill, sitting and shaking on a hard pine bench in the corner of the girls' locker room of the Asheville Civic Auditorium.

"He said he'd be here," she rasped. "He promised. He's such a *liar*."

"It's early, give it a while," assured Joyce Watkins, not convinced of her point. "Be patient, hon. Let's concentrate on what we're doing here. We need you to be focused. That Asheville team's good and we could lose this thing."

Janice sat down with them and put an arm around Millie.

Joyce knew Harley Burleson was probably off drinking somewhere with his Elk River pals and had no thought of Millie. Why she stayed with that sorry drunk-without-prospects Joyce would never figure. He was an unemployed twenty-year-old dropout with a mean streak and Millie was a pretty, smart, talented girl that any boy in school would love to date. But they dared not ask her out with Harley hovering menacingly.

Miss Lilly's voice boomed from the door of the locker room, "All right girls, get it together. We have changes to make. Asheville's dancing our routine out there right now."

Miss Lilly warned this might happen. Somebody from Asheville—who looked an awful lot like the new Asheville coach—used one of those new video tape machines—the same type used in the 1960 Olympics—at an exhibition Toe River danced in Marion in July. When Miss Lilly went over to ask about it, she was told they wanted to study some good dancing. Study they had. It was now their routine.

Joyce put her arm around Millie's shoulder. "Come on, baby. We're getting ready to go do something with your life that's going to last a hell of a lot longer than Harley Burleson."

Saturday, November 16, 8:22 p.m.

Miss Lilly called the team into one of the five locker rooms in the Civic Auditorium, which was also used for basketball occasionally. She closed the door and locked it.

Miss Lilly studied the team members closely in the past hour and she knew everything she needed to know. Pressing her were Barry's cut and Millie's fragility.

"Barry, you and Millie are going to have to sit this one out," she said directly. "We have to be in top form and neither of you is right now. Buster, you're dancing with Becky and Joyce, you're getting Elbert."

Eb sat down hard on the bench in front of a bank of lockers, his stomach in his mouth, his heart sounding like a kettle drum.

Barry pulled off his shoe and threw it across the room directly toward Mickey's head, the shoe clanging off an open locker door. Millie broke down again, sobbing loudly. Mickey smirked, but didn't say anything.

"This is for the team," scolded Miss Lilly, taking it easy on both of them because she knew how much the final meant to each. "You helped put us here, now it's up to your teammates to get us through."

Miss Lilly was quiet for a minute, letting everything sink in. Eb was stunned and trying to find Joyce with his eyes. Finally, he made contact and she winked. That was enough. He stood up, ready, and walked over to her side, squeezing Barry's shoulder on the way, his recognition of Barry's disappointment. Joyce slid her hand into Eb's and squeezed.

"Asheville must think it's pulling one over on us," Miss Lilly said, smiling. "That routine they've just done is one we did earlier in the year and one we did last year and the year before. They did it well, but it's already out of date. People who know our sport will see that."

Miss Lilly pulled a large box to the middle of the floor. "I have a surprise for you," she said as she pulled out a pair of brown tap shoes from the box. "We're going to do this routine right. We're using taps."

The excitement was palpable as the team erupted with approval. "The shoes have your names in them," she said. "Put them on, walk around and make sure they fit.

"We're taking a big chance here with these new tap shoes because they will be slick and we won't have enough time to work out with them or to even test them on that old oak floor of the stage.

"The clogging and the drumming these shoes will make can be the difference in winning and losing tonight," she emphasized. "Be careful not to fall, but don't be so careful that your dancing looks altered."

The shoes had large taps covering the heel and half of the front of the soles. They were new, shiny, slick and noisy.

Miss Lilly continued as the dancers pulled the shoes on and wiggled and bent their feet, testing flexibility. "You may get a blister before this night is over, so put some of this Vaseline between your foot and your sock before you put the shoes on for good. And remember, you just have to put twelve good minutes on these shoes and then you can take them off. We need those twelve good minutes."

As dancers walked and clogged, the clattering in the locker room over the next few minutes was such that one of the guards knocked on the door and yelled, "Everything all right in there?" He was assured it was and the team filed out, as quietly as taps would allow, toward the stage area.

Asheville was dancing for the last time, giving its best in a final effort to reach the goal of putting Old Smoky on Joss-Lynn Ledbetter's bedroom mantle. Toe River gathered at the edge of the stage to watch. The team didn't need to. It was the same Sky High the dancers had seen several times: perfect pitch, a clinic in technique, not a hair or a step out of place. Not a smile on any face.

In twelve minutes to the instant, the team shuffled off the floor to applause that was more appreciative than enthusiastic.

In the audience, Bobby Lee Ledbetter looked satisfied, as if he wanted to light up a cigar.

The performance was flawless and without a single shred of the soul of mountain heritage. It was more mechanical than creative, but impossible to criticize if you were sitting in a judge's seat. On paper, it couldn't be beaten.

Toe River wasn't dancing on paper, and it wasn't dancing with soft soles, as the packed house began to hear. There was an audible stir beneath the house lights.

Eb looked across the stage and saw Arlene Silver Feather staring at the Toe River team, a worried look on her face. Her team stood behind her, bored.

Miss Lilly lined up her troops, pointed to Buster as the music started and he tapped the floor four times with his front toe. That was the signal.

Buster's four taps were answered by four from the team. Four more and four more, then a shuffle forward, brushing the taps, toe-heel, toe-heel in a rhythmic procession to the center of the auditorium floor and the full attention of five thousand people sitting on the front edge of their seats.

Buster tapped four times again and said "Hit it!" and the thunder of the taps exploded in the auditorium as the crowd leaped to its feet and roared. Buster led the dancers precisely through the determined steps and moves, clogging every step of the way, thumping noisily up and down the stage, front to back, circling and spinning, squaring up, ducking under arms, sitting on knees, faking kisses with a *do-se-do!*

The big crowd was in a frenzy when Buster yelled *"CLOG!"* and the dancers moved into a semi-circle with Janice and Mickey at the middle, the long-legged, pretty, fresh-faced young sophomore dancing with the wild abandon of a Paris floor show and driving the crowd to new heights with her freedom and sexuality.

When Buster shouted "Buck!" Mickey erupted like he was escaping a cage and became Ray Bolger, the Tin Man, all elbows, knees and taps, slapping his thighs and the bottom of his shoes, throwing his head back and roaring with the crowd, wild in his abandon.

Mickey felt the floor give twice, but compensated quickly. His right foot was sliding uncontrollably from under him, and he was heading for the deck and disaster. But Mickey was nothing if not graceful. He threw his whole body backwards, his hands downward to the stage and turned a perfect, fluid back flip, not missing a step. The crowd was delirious, believing this part of the routine.

Finally, he eased back to the middle of the circle, joining Janice step for step and melding into the line of dancers as they vigorously danced to the front edge of the stage. They stared straight into the faces of the crowd, always smiling, beginning the finale that looked like the end of a Broadway chorus Big Number. Taps crashing in rhythm, energy rising and noise at an ear-splitting level.

People yelled, pounded their hands together, clogged in front of their seats and it was pandemonium as the dancers, slowing progressively began to exit the stage. When Buster yelled, "Hit it!" one more time, they all stomped in unison and it was over.

The cheering continued at an explosive level for nearly two minutes. The Toe River dancers rushed back on stage for a bow, unprecedented at the Jamboree. Eb saw the governor in the front row and, beside him, his dear, sweet Lizetta, crying and cheering from her wheelchair. Down the front row his mother hugged Harry and Dane, who had no clue what was going on, but loved it anyway. Dane blew a kiss at her big brother and he caught it in his right hand and kissed it back.

At the other side of the stage stood the Asheville team, stunned, defeated, humiliated, blank faced. One young blonde was screaming, crying and yelling at her teammates and they were ignoring her. Slowly, one by one, led by karate chopping Billy Staples, they began to applaud Toe River's remarkable performance.

Their coach, the elegant New York star Arlene Shining

Feather, who received her final paycheck from Bobby Lee Ledbetter three hours earlier, briskly walked to the Toe River side of the stage and stood in front of Miss Kay. Eb was on the end of the line and heard her say, "You remain the standard. Oh, how I admire your work. This was simply magnificent. I hope you'll consider coming to New York and seeing where we work and maybe teaching a master class." Miss Lilly smiled and they hugged.

Eb turned back to the still cheering audience, his arm comfortably tight around Joyce, his touchstone these few months, and saw a tall man in a brown suit,

his face contorted, shaking a finger at the young man next to him. He was obviously furious.

The crowd began to quiet and the dancers left the stage to await the voting. Eb hugged Joyce when they got off stage and she said, "All that work paid off, kiddo. I'm really proud of you." He hugged her again.

The team waited anxiously, despite the crowd's obvious approval. It could go either way, crowd or no crowd. Would the judges accept the taps or rule Toe River ineligible and in violation of the rules? Eb saw the man in the brown suit go to the judges' table and talk with considerable animation. Two ushers rushed over and led him away.

They watched as the judges talked back and forth, sometimes briskly until finally, after five full minutes, the lead judge held up a hand, meaning there was a decision.

Eb thought back to the pileup at the goal line several hours earlier when everything hung on an official's call.

Saturday, November 16, 8:58 p.m.
The master of ceremonies, a local television weather girl, walked toward the table from center stage, leaned down and took a folded piece of paper from the chief judge.

"We have a decision," said the MC. She paused and looked at the audience, then smiled.

"Second runner-up is Dobbyns-Bennett High School of

Kingsport, Tennessee." There was brisk applause. Then another deathly quiet pause.

"First runner-up," she said, dragging it out for dramatic effect, "is ... Land of the Sky High School of Asheville, North Carolina, *and the winner and still champion is Toe River High School of Avery County, North Carolina!"*

The overflow crowd at the Asheville Civic Auditorium erupted again.

Eb jumped off the stage and landed directly in front of Lizetta, bent down and kissed her without even adjusting to balance himself. He couldn't hug her because of her casts and braces, but he knelt beside her and said, "I didn't know you were coming! This is unbelievable!"

Gov. Terry Sanford looked over and stuck out his hand. "What a great victory for you and your team, Eb. Congratulations, son."

Eb nodded, still looking at Lizetta, whom he had not seen in weeks and who looked like a goddess to him. Lizetta laughed out loud and said, "Elbert, the governor is talking to you."

Eb stood quickly, shot out his hand to shake and said, "Good to meet you sir, it's just that ..."

"Oh, I know, son. Get back to Lizetta. She's a hell of a lot prettier than me. But I'd sure like to have my picture made with you and that crackerjack square dance team before tonight's over."

"I think we can do that, sir," Eb said. "I think we can do just about anything we want to. Hap taught me that."

He knelt and kissed Lizetta the way he wanted to. The governor smiled.

ABOUT THE AUTHOR

Dan Smith is a 2010 inductee into the Virginia Communications Hall of Fame and founding editor of FRONT Magazine. A journalist since 1964, he has won awards in every significant journalistic discipline and was Virginia Business Journalist of the Year 2005. Other awards are for business ethics, environmental education, environmental journalism, support of the arts and the first (2009) Perry F. Kendig Literary Award, given by the Arts Council of the Blue Ridge. He is an active community volunteer and member of a number of boards of directors. He is an is award-winning public radio essayist, a freelance writer/photographer and the founder of the Roanoke Regional Writers Conference. This is his fifth book, and his first novel. He has two children and two grandchildren and lives in Roanoke, VA. E-mail: pampadansmith@gmail.com. (Photo by Liv Kiser.)

Made in the USA
Las Vegas, NV
26 August 2021